Australian
NIGHTS
WAVES OF DESIRE

CAROL
MARINELLI

NIKKI
LOGAN

HELEN
LACEY

MILLS & BOON

AUSTRALIAN NIGHTS: WAVES OF DESIRE © 2022 by Harlequin Books S.A.

DR DARK AND FAR TOO DELICIOUS
© 2013 by Carol Marinelli
Australian Copyright 2013
New Zealand Copyright 2013

First Published 2013
Third Australian Paperback Edition 2022
ISBN 978 1 867 25393 8

THE BILLIONAIRE OF CORAL BAY
© 2017 by Nikki Logan
Australian Copyright 2017
New Zealand Copyright 2017

First Published 2017
Second Australian Paperback Edition 2022
ISBN 978 1 867 25393 8

THE CEO'S BABY SURPRISE
© 2015 by Helen Lacey
Australian Copyright 2015
New Zealand Copyright 2015

First Published 2015
Second Australian Paperback Edition 2022
ISBN 978 1 867 25393 8

This is a work of fiction. Names, characters, places, and incidents are either the product of the author's imagination or are used fictitiously, and any resemblance to actual persons, living or dead, business establishments, events, or locales is entirely coincidental.

Published by
Mills & Boon
An imprint of Harlequin Enterprises (Australia) Pty Limited
(ABN 47 001 180 918), a subsidiary of HarperCollins
Publishers Australia Pty Limited (ABN 36 009 913 517)
Level 13, 201 Elizabeth Street
SYDNEY NSW 2000
AUSTRALIA

MIX
Paper from
responsible sources
FSC
www.fsc.org   FSC® C001695

Printed and bound in Australia by McPherson's Printing Group

CONTENTS

Dr Dark And Far Too Delicious

Carol Marinelli

Dear Reader,

I really enjoyed writing Penny and Jasmine's stories, which make up my *Secrets on the Emergency Wing* duet. Even though they are sisters they are very different, and that is what makes them so real to me. I love that even though they have the same parents and share the same past, because of their unique personalities they look at things differently.

Penny and Jasmine don't look alike; they don't even get on. No one could even guess that they are sisters—they really are two different sides of the same coin. Yet for all their differences there are similarities, and I had a lot of fun with a little secret of Penny's that you shan't find out till near the end of the second book.

I really would love to know which sister ends up being your favorite. Except, as my mother tells me, you're not allowed to have favorites....

You may yet be surprised!

Happy reading!

Carol

x

SECRETS ON THE EMERGENCY WING

Life and love—behind the doors of an Australian E.R.

Book 2 in Carol Marinelli's Secrets on the Emergency Wing duet, *Secrets of a Career Girl,* is also available this month.

The *Secrets on the Emergency Wing* duet is also available in ebook format from www.millsandboon.com.au.

CHAPTER ONE

JUST CONCENTRATE ON WORK.

Jed said it over and over as he ran along the damp beach.

He ran daily, or tried to, depending on work commitments, but as much as he could Jed factored running into his day—it served as both his exercise and his relaxation, helped him to focus and to clear his head.

Just concentrate on work, he repeated, because after the last two hellish years he really did need to do just that.

Jed looked along the bay. The morning was a hazy one and he couldn't make out the Melbourne skyline in the distance. Not for the first time he questioned whether he had been right to take the position at the Peninsula Hospital or if he should have gone for a more prestigious city one.

Jed loved nothing more than a big city hospital—he had worked and trained at a large teaching hospital in Sydney and had assumed, when he had applied for jobs in Melbourne, that the city was where he would end up, yet the interview at Peninsula Hospital that he had thought would be a more a cursory one had seen him change his mind.

It wasn't a teaching hospital but it was certainly a busy one—it served as a major trauma centre and had an NICU and ICU and Jed had liked the atmosphere at Peninsula, as well as the proximity to the beach. Perhaps the deciding factor, though, had been that he had also been told, confidentially, that one of the consultants was retiring and a position would be opening up in the not-too-distant future. His career had been building up to an emergency consultant position and, his disaster of a personal life aside, it was where he was ready to be. When Jed had handed in his notice six months ago an offer had been made and he'd been asked to reconsider leaving, but Jed had known then that he had to get away, that he had to start again.

But with new rules in place this time.

Jed missed not just Sydney and the hospital he had trained and worked at but his family and friends—it had been the first birthday of Luke, his newest nephew, yesterday, another thing he hadn't been able to get to, another family gathering he had missed, when before, even if he hadn't been able to get there on the day, he'd have dropped by over the weekend.

A phone call to a one-year-old wasn't exactly the same.

But the decision to move well away had surely been the right one.

Still he questioned it, still he wondered if he had overreacted and should have just stayed in Sydney and hoped it would work out, assumed it was all sorted.

What a mess.

Jed stopped for a moment and dragged in a few breaths.

Over and over he wondered if he could have handled things differently, if there was something he could have said to have changed things, or something he had done that had been mis-construed—and yet still he could not come up with an answer.

It was incredibly warm for six a.m. but it wasn't a pleasant heat—it was muggy and close and needed a good storm to clear it but, according to the weather reports, the cool change wasn't coming through till tonight.

'Morning.' He looked up and nodded to an old guy walking his dog. They shared a brief conversation about the weather and then Jed took a long drink of water before turning around to head for home and get ready for work.

He should never have got involved with Samantha in the first place.

Still, he could hardly have seen that coming, couldn't have predicted the train wreck that had been about to take place, but then he corrected himself.

He should never have got involved with someone from work.

Jed picked up the pace again, his head finally clearing. He knew what he needed to focus on.

Just concentrate on work.

CHAPTER TWO

'JASMINE?' IT WASN'T the friendliest of greetings, and Jasmine jumped as the sound of Penny's voice stopped her in her tracks.

'What are you doing here?' her sister demanded.

'I'm here for an interview.' Jasmine stated what should be the obvious. 'I've just been for a security check.'

They were standing in the hospital admin corridor. Jasmine was holding a pile of forms and, despite her best efforts to appear smart and efficient for the interview, was looking just a little hot and bothered—and all the more so for seeing Penny.

Summer had decided to give Melbourne one last sticky, humid day before it gave way to autumn and Jasmine's long dark curls had, despite an awful lot of hair serum and an awful lot of effort, frizzed during the walk from the car park to the accident and emergency department. It had continued its curly journey through her initial interview with Lisa, the nurse unit manager.

Now, as Penny ran a brief but, oh, so critical eye over her, Jasmine was acutely aware that the grey suit she reserved for interviews was, despite hundreds of sit-ups and exercising to a DVD, just a touch too tight.

Penny, of course, looked immaculate.

Her naturally straight, naturally blonde hair was tied back in an elegant chignon—she was wearing smart dark trousers and heeled shoes that accentuated her lean body. Her white blouse, despite it being afternoon, despite the fact she was a registrar in a busy accident and emergency department, was still impossibly crisp and clean.

No one could have guessed that they were sisters.

'An interview for what, exactly?' Penny's eyes narrowed.

'A nursing position,' Jasmine answered carefully. 'A clinical nurse specialist. I've just been to fill out the forms for a security check.' Jasmine was well aware her answer was vague and that she was evading the issue but of course it didn't work—Penny was as direct as ever in her response.

'Where?' Penny asked. 'Where exactly have you applied to work?'

'Accident and Emergency,' Jasmine answered, doing her best to keep her voice even. 'Given that it's my speciality.'

'Oh, no.' Penny shook her head. 'No way.' Penny made no effort to keep her voice even, and she didn't mince her words either. 'I'm not having it, Jasmine, not for a single moment. You are *not* working in my department.'

'Where do you expect me to work, then, Penny?' She had known all along that this would be Penny's reaction—it was the very reason she had put off telling her sister about the application, the very reason she hadn't mentioned the interview when they had met up at Mum's last Sunday for a celebratory dinner to toast Penny's *latest* career victory. 'I'm an emergency nurse, that's what I do.'

'Well, go and do it somewhere else. Go and work at the hospital you trained in, because there is no way on earth that I am working alongside my sister.'

'I can't commute to the city,' Jasmine said. 'Do you really expect me to drag Simon for an hour each way just so that I don't embarrass my big sister?' It was ridiculous to suggest and what was even more ridiculous was that Jasmine had actually considered it, well aware how prickly Penny could be.

Jasmine had looked into it, but with a one-year-old to consider, unless she moved nearer to the city, it would prove impossible and also, in truth, she was just too embarrassed to go
back to her old workplace.

'You know people there,' Penny insisted.

'Exactly.'

'Jasmine, if the reason you're not going back there is because of Lloyd…'

'Leave it, Penny.' Jasmine closed her eyes for a second. She
didn't want to go back to where everyone knew her past, where
her life had been the centre stage show for rather too long. 'It
has nothing to do with Lloyd. I just want to be closer to home.'

She did—with her marriage completely over and her soon-to-
be ex-husband having nothing to do with either her or her son
and her maternity leave well and truly up, Jasmine had made
the decision to move back to the beachside suburb to be close
to the family home and the smart townhouse where her sister
lived and to start over again, but with family nearby.

She wanted to be closer to her mum, to her sister and, yes,
she wanted some support, but clearly she wasn't going to get
any from Penny.

It was career first, last and always for Penny, but then again
it was the same with their mum. A real estate agent, though
now semi-retired, Louise Masters had made a name for herself in their bayside village for being tough and no-nonsense. It
was the rather more dreamy Jasmine who did stupid things like
take risks with her heart and actually switch off from work on
her days off—not that she didn't love her work, it just wasn't
all that she was.

'We'll talk about this later.' Penny's blue eyes flashed angrily—it was the only feature that they shared. 'And don't you
dare go using my name to get the job.'

'As if I'd do that,' Jasmine said. 'Anyway, we don't even share
the same surname, *Miss* Masters.'

Penny was now officially a Miss—the title given to females

once they gained their fellowship. It caused some confusion at times, but Penny had worked extremely hard to be a Miss rather than a Doctor—and she wasn't about to have anyone drag on her coat-tails as she continued to ride high.

'I mean it,' Penny flared. 'You are not to even let on that you know me. I'm really not happy about this, Jasmine.'

'Hey, Penny.' Her sister turned, and so too did Jasmine, to the sound of a deep, low voice. Had Jasmine not been so numb right now, so immune and resistant to all things male, she might have more properly noticed just how good looking this man was. He was very tall and though his dark brown hair was cut fairly short it was just a bit rumpled, as was his suit.

Yes, a couple of years ago she might have taken note, but not now.

She just wanted him gone so that she could get back to the rather important conversation she had been having with Penny.

'It's getting busy down there apparently,' he said to Penny. 'They just called and asked me to come back from lunch.'

'I know,' came Penny's clipped response. 'I've just been paged. I was supposed to be speaking with Legal.'

Perhaps he picked up on the tension because he looked from Penny to Jasmine and she noticed then that his eyes were green and that his jaw needed shaving and, yes, despite being completely not interested, some long-dormant cells demanded that she at least deign to acknowledge just how attractive he was, especially when his deep voice spoke on. 'Sorry, am I disturbing something?'

'Not at all.' Penny's response was rapid. 'This nurse was just asking for directions to get back to Emergency—she's got an interview there.'

'You can hardly miss the place.' He gave a wry smile and nodded to a huge red arrow above them. 'Follow us.'

'Mrs Phillips?' Jasmine turned as she heard her name and saw it was the receptionist from Security, where she had just come from. 'You left your driving licence.'

'Thank you.' Jasmine opened her mouth to say that she was soon to be a Ms, but it seemed churlish to correct it as technically she was still a Mrs—it was there on her driving licence after all. Still, in a few weeks' time she'd be a Ms and she'd tell everyone the same.

Jasmine couldn't wait for the glorious day.

For now, though, she followed Penny and her colleague towards Emergency.

'I didn't mean to literally follow,' Jed said, and he waited a second for her to catch up. Jasmine fell into reluctant step alongside them. 'I'm Jed… Jed Devlin—I'm a registrar in the madhouse, as is Penny.'

'Jasmine.' She duly answered. 'Jasmine Phillips.'

'So?' he asked as Penny clipped noisily alongside them. She could hear the anger in her sister's footsteps, could feel the tension that was ever present whenever the two of them were together. 'When do you start?'

'I haven't got the job yet,' Jasmine said.

'Sounds promising, though, if you've been sent up to Security.'

'They have to do a security check on everyone,' Penny said abruptly.

They all walked on in silence for a few moments.

'Here we are,' Jed said. 'See that big red sign that says "Accident and Emergency"?'

'How could I miss it?' She gave a brief smile at his teasing as they headed through the swing doors and stepped into Emergency. 'Thanks.'

'No problem.'

'Good luck,' Jed said.

Of course Penny didn't offer her best wishes. Instead, she marched off on her high heels and for a second Jasmine stood there and blew out a breath, wondering if she was mad to be doing this.

It clearly wasn't going to work.

And then she realised that Jed was still standing there.

'Do I know you?' He frowned.

'I don't think so,' Jasmine said, while reluctantly admitting to herself that they had definitely never met—his was a face she certainly wouldn't forget.

'Have you worked in Sydney?'

Jasmine shook her head.

'Where did you work before?'

She started to go red. She hated talking about her time there—she'd loved it so much and it had all ended so terribly, but she could hardly tell him that. 'Melbourne Central. I trained there and worked in Emergency there till I had my son.'

'Nice hospital,' Jed said. 'I had an interview there when I first moved to the area, but no.' He shook his head. 'That's not it. You just look familiar...'

He surely hadn't picked up that she and Penny were sisters? No one ever had. She and Penny were complete opposites, not just in looks but also in personality. Penny was completely focussed and determined, whereas Jasmine was rather more impulsive, at least she had been once. She was also, as her mother had frequently pointed out throughout her childhood whenever Jasmine had burst into tears, too sensitive.

'There you are!' Jasmine turned as Lisa came over and Jed made his excuses and wandered off.

'Sorry,' Jasmine said to Lisa. 'They took ages to find all the forms I needed.'

'That's Admin for you,' Lisa said. 'Right, I'll walk you through the department and give you a feel for the place. It just got busy.'

It certainly had.

It had been almost empty when Jasmine had first arrived for her interview and the walk to Lisa's office had shown a calm, even quiet department, compared to the busy city one Jasmine was more used to. Now, though, the cubicles were all full and she could see staff rushing and hear the emergency bell trilling from Resus. Not for the first time, Jasmine wondered if she was up to the demands of going back to work in a busy emergency department.

The last two years had left her so raw and confused that all she really wanted to do was to curl up and sleep before she tackled the process of healing and resuming work, but her ex didn't want to see their son, let alone pay child support, and there was no point going through appropriate channels—she couldn't wait the time it would take to squeeze blood from a stone, but more than that Jasmine wanted to support her son herself, which meant that she needed a job.

However much it inconvenienced Penny and however daunted she was at the prospect.

'We do our best with the roster. I always try to accommodate specific requests, but as far as regular shifts go I can't make allowances for anyone,' Lisa explained—she knew about Simon and had told Jasmine that there were a couple of other single mums working there who, she was sure, would be a huge support. 'And I've rung the crèche and said that you'll be coming over to have a look around, but you know that they close at six and that on a late shift you don't generally get out till well after nine?'

Jasmine nodded. 'My mum's said that she'll help out for a little while.' Jasmine stated this far more generously than her mother had. 'At least until I sort out a babysitter.'

'What about night shifts?' Lisa checked. 'Everyone has to do them—it's only fair.'

'I know.'

'That way,' Lisa explained, 'with everyone taking turns, generally it only comes around once every three months or so.'

'That sounds fine,' Jasmine said confidently while inwardly gauging her mother's reaction.

It was a good interview, though. Really, Jasmine was confident that she'd got the job and, as she left, Lisa practically confirmed it. 'You'll be hearing from us soon.' She gave a wry smile as Jasmine shook her hand. 'Very soon. I wish you didn't have to do orientation before you start—I've just had two of my team ring in sick for the rest of the week.'

Walking towards the exit, Jasmine saw how busy yet efficient everyone looked and despite her confident words about her experience to Lisa, inside she was a squirming mess! Even though she'd worked right up to the end of her pregnancy she hadn't nursed in more than a year and, again, she considered going back to her old department. At least she'd maybe know a few people.

At least she'd know where things were kept. Yet there would still be the nudges and whispers that she'd been so relieved to leave behind and, yes, she should just walk in with her head held high and face the ugly rumours and gossip, except going back to work after all she had been through was already hard enough.

'Jasmine?' She turned as someone called her name and forced back on her smile when she saw that it was Jed. He was at the viewfinder looking at an X-ray. 'How did you get on?'

'Good,' Jasmine answered. 'Well, at least I think I did.'

'Well done.'

'I'm just going to check out the crèche.'

'Good luck again, then,' Jed said, 'because from what I've heard you'll need it to get a place there.'

'Oh, and, Jasmine,' he called as she walked off, 'I do know you.'

'You don't.' Jasmine laughed.

'But I know that I do,' he said. 'I never forget a face. I'll work it out.'

She rather hoped that he wouldn't.

CHAPTER THREE

'How did you go?' her mum asked as she let her in.

'Well,' Jasmine said. 'Sorry that it took so long.'

'That's okay. Simon's asleep.' Jasmine followed her mum through to the kitchen and Louise went to put the kettle on. 'So when do you start?'

'I don't even know if I've got the job.'

'Please,' her mum said over her shoulder. 'Everywhere's screaming for nurses, you hear it on the news all the time.'

It was a backhanded compliment—her mother was very good at them. Jasmine felt the sting of tears behind her eyes—Louise had never really approved of Jasmine going into nursing. Her mother had told her that if she worked a bit harder at school she could get the grades and study medicine, just like Penny. And though she never came right out and said it, it was clear that in both her mother's and sister's eyes Penny had a career whereas Jasmine had a job—and one that could be done by anyone—as if all that Jasmine had to do was put on her uniform and show up.

'It's a clinical nurse specialist role that I've applied for, Mum,' Jasmine said. 'There were quite a few applicants.' But her mum made no comment and not for the first time Jasmine questioned her decision to move close to home. Her mum just wasn't mumsy—she was successful in everything she did. She was funny, smart and career-minded, and she simply expected her daughters to be the same—after all, she'd juggled her career and had independently raised Jasmine and Penny when their father had walked out.

Jasmine wanted nothing more than to be independent and do the same; she just wanted a pause, a bit of a helping hand as she got through this bit—which in her own way her mother had given. After four weeks of living at home Louise had had a very nice little rental house come onto her books—it was right on the beach and the rent was incredibly low and Jasmine had jumped at it. It was in other areas that Jasmine was struggling, and nursing with all its shift work wasn't an easy career to juggle without support.

'I'm going to have to do nights.' Jasmine watched her mother's shoulders stiffen as she filled two mugs. 'A fortnight every three months.'

'I didn't raise two children just so that I could raise yours,' Louise warned. 'I'll help you as much as I can for a couple of months, but I take a lot of clients through houses in the evenings.' She was as direct as ever. 'And I've got my cruise booked for May.'

'I know,' Jasmine said. 'I'm going to start looking for a regular babysitter as soon as I get the offer.'

'And you need to give me your off duty at least a month in an advance.'

'I will.'

Jasmine took the tea from her mum. If she wanted a hug she wasn't going to get one; if she wanted a little pick me up she was in the wrong house.

'Have you thought about looking for a job that's a bit more child friendly?' Louise suggested. 'You mentioned there was one in Magnetic...' She gave an impatient shrug when she couldn't remember the terminology.

'No. I said there was a position in MRI and that even though the hours were fantastic it wasn't what I wanted to do. I like

Emergency, Mum. You wouldn't suggest Penny going for a role she had no interest in.'

'Penny doesn't have a one-year-old to think of,' Louise said, and then they sat quietly for a moment.

'You need to get your hair done,' her mum said. 'You need to smarten up a bit if you're going back to work.' And that was her mum's grudging way of accepting that, yes, this was what Jasmime was going to do. 'And you need to lose some weight.'

And because it was either that or start crying, Jasmine chose to laugh.

'What's so funny?'

'You are,' Jasmine said. 'I thought tea came with sympathy.'

'Not in this house.' Her mum smiled. 'Why don't you go home?'

'Simon's asleep.'

'I'll have him for you tonight.'

And sometimes, and always when Jasmine was least expecting it, her mum could be terribly nice. 'My evening appointment cancelled. I'm sure you could use a night to yourself.'

'I'd love that.' Jasmine hadn't had a night to herself since Simon had been born. In the weeks when she'd first come home and had stayed with her mum, the only advantage she had taken had been a long walk on the beach each morning before Simon woke up. 'Thanks, Mum.'

'No problem. I guess I'd better get familiar with his routines.'

'Can I go in and see him?'

'And wake him up probably.'

She didn't wake him up. Simon was lying on his front with his bottom in the air and his thumb in his mouth, and just the sight of him made everything worth it. He was in her old cot in her old bedroom and was absolutely the love of her life. She just didn't understand how Lloyd could want nothing to do with him.

'Do you think he's missing out?' Jasmine asked her mum. 'Not having a dad?'

'Better no dad than a useless one,' Louise said, then gave a shrug. 'I don't know the answer to that, Jasmine. I used to feel the same about you.' She gave her daughter a smile. 'Our taste in men must be hereditary. No wonder Penny's sworn off them.'

'Did she ever tell you what happened?' Jasmine asked, because one minute Penny had been engaged, the next the whole thing had been called off and she didn't want to talk about it.

'She just said they'd been having a few problems and decided that it was better to get out now than later.'

Before there were children to complicate things, Jasmine thought, but didn't say anything. It was her mum who spoke.

'I know it's tough at the moment but I'm sure it will get easier.'

'And if it doesn't?'

'Then you'd better get used to tough.' Louise shrugged. 'Have you told Penny you're applying for a job at Peninsula?'

'I saw her at my interview.'

'And?' Louise grimaced. They both knew only too well how Penny would react to the news.

'She doesn't want me there—especially not in Accident and Emergency,' Jasmine admitted. 'She wasn't best pleased.'

'Well, it's her domain,' Louise said. 'You know how territorial she is. She used to put thread up on her bedroom door so she'd know if anyone had been in there while she was out. She'll come round.'

And even though she smiled at the memory, Jasmine was worried that Penny wouldn't be coming round to the idea of her little sister working in her hospital any time soon.

Jasmine was proven right a few hours later when, back at her own small house, adding another coat of paint in an attempt to transform the lounge from dull olive green to cool crisp white, there was a loud rap at the door.

'Can you knock more quietly?' Jasmine asked as she opened it. 'If Simon was here—'

'We need to talk,' Penny said, and she brushed in and straight through to the lounge.

If Louise hadn't exactly been brimming with understanding, then Penny was a desert.

Her blouse was still crisp and white, her hair still perfect and her eyes were just as angry as they had been when she had first laid them on Jasmine in the hospital corridor earlier on that day. 'You said nothing about this when I saw you last week,' Penny said accusingly. 'Not a single word!'

'I didn't exactly get a chance.'

'Meaning?'

She heard the confrontation in her sister's voice, could almost see Pandora's box on the floor between them. She was tempted just to open it, to have this out once and for all, to say how annoyed she still felt that Penny hadn't been able to make it for Simon's first birthday a couple of months earlier. In fact, she hadn't even sent a card. Yet there had been no question that Jasmine herself would be there to join in celebrating her sister's success.

Or rather celebrating her sister's *latest* success.

But bitterness wasn't going to help things here.

'That dinner was to celebrate you getting your fellowship,' Jasmine said calmly. 'I knew you'd be upset if I told you that I had an interview coming up, and I didn't want to spoil your night.'

'You should have discussed it with me before you even applied!' Penny said. 'It's my department.'

'Hopefully it will be mine soon, too,' Jasmine attempted, but her words fell on deaf ears.

'Do you know how hard it is for me?' Penny said. 'All that nonsense about equal rights… I have to be twice as good as them, twice as tough as any of them—there's a consultancy position coming up and I have no intention of letting it slip by.'

'How could my working there possibly affect that?' Jasmine asked reasonably.

'Because I'm not supposed to have a personal life,' was Penny's swift retort. 'You just don't get it, Jasmine. I've worked hard to get where I am. The senior consultant, Mr Dean, he's old school—he made a joke the other week about how you train them up and the next thing you know they're pregnant and wanting part-time hours.' She looked at her sister. 'Yes, I could complain and make waves, but how is that going to help things? Jed is going after the same position. He's a great doctor but he's only been in the department six months and I am not going to lose it to him.' She shook her head in frustration.

'I'm not asking you to understand, you just have to believe that it is hard to get ahead sometimes, and the last thing I need right now is my personal life invading the department.'

'I'm your sister—'

'So are you going to be able to stay quiet when the nurses call me a hard witch?' Penny challenged. 'And when you are supposed to finish at four but can't get off, are you going to expect me to drop everything and run to the crèche and get Simon?'

'Of course not.'

'And when I hear the other nurses moaning that you hardly ever do a late shift and are complaining about having to do nights, am I supposed to leap to your defence and explain that you're a single mum?'

'I can keep my work and personal life separate.'

'Really!'

It was just one word, a single word, and the rise of Penny's perfect eyebrows had tears spring to Jasmine's eyes. 'That was below the belt.'

'The fact that you can't keep your work and personal life separate is the very reason you can't go back to Melbourne Central.'

'It's about the travel,' Jasmine insisted. 'And you're wrong, I can keep things separate.'

'Not if we're in the same department.'

'I can if they don't know that we're sisters,' Jasmine said, and she watched Penny's jaw tighten, realised then that this was where the conversation had been leading. Penny was always one step ahead in everything, and Penny had made very sure that it was Jasmine who suggested it.

'It might be better.' Penny made it sound as if she was conceding.

'Fine.'

'Can you keep to it?'

'Sure,' Jasmine said.

'I mean it.'

'I know you do, Penny.'

'I've got to get back to work. I'm on call tonight.' And her sister, now that she had what she came for, stood up to leave. Jasmine held in tears that threatened, even managed a smile as her sister stalked out of the door.

But it hurt.

It really hurt.

CHAPTER FOUR

IT WAS HER favourite place in the world.

But even a long stretch of sand, the sun going down over the water and a storm rolling in from the distance wasn't enough to take the harsh sting out of Penny's words.

Jasmine hated arguments, loathed them and did her very best to avoid them.

She could still remember all too well hearing the raised voices of her parents seeping up the stairs and through the bedroom floor as she had lain on her bed with her hands over her ears.

But there had been no avoiding this one—Jasmine had known when she'd applied for the role that there would be a confrontation. Still, she couldn't just bow to Penny's wishes just because it made things awkward for her.

She needed a job and, no matter what her mother and sister thought of her chosen career, nursing was what she was good at—and Emergency was her speciality.

Jasmine wasn't going to hide just because it suited Penny.

It had been cruel of Penny to bring up her relationship with Lloyd, cruel to suggest that she wasn't going back to Melbourne Central just because of what had happened.

It was also, Jasmine conceded, true.

Finding out that she was pregnant had been a big enough shock—but she'd had no idea what was to come.

That the dashing paramedic who'd been so delighted with the news of her pregnancy, who'd insisted they marry and then whisked her off on a three-month honeymoon around Australia, was in fact being investigated for patient theft.

She'd been lied to from the start and deceived till the end and nothing, it seemed, could take away her shame. And, yes, the whispers and sideways looks she had received from her colleagues at Melbourne Central as she'd worked those last weeks of her pregnancy with her marriage falling apart had been awful. The last thing she needed was Penny rubbing it in.

'I knew I recognised you from somewhere.' She looked over to the sound of a vaguely familiar voice.

'Oh!' Jasmine was startled as she realised who it was. 'Hi, Jed.' He was out of breath from running and—she definitely noticed this time—was very, very good looking.

He was wearing grey shorts and a grey T-shirt and he was toned, a fact she couldn't fail to notice when he lifted his T-shirt to wipe his face, revealing a very flat, tanned stomach. Jasmine felt herself blush as for the first time in the longest time she was shockingly drawn to rugged maleness.

But, then, how could you not be? Jasmine reasoned. Any woman hauled out of a daydream would blink a few times when confronted with him. Any woman would be a bit miffed that they hadn't bothered sorting their hair and that they were wearing very old denim shorts and a T-shirt splashed with paint.

'You walk here?' Jed checked, because now he remembered her. Dark curls bobbing, she would walk—sometimes slowly, sometimes briskly and, he had noticed she never looked up, never acknowledged anyone—she always seemed completely lost in her own world. 'I see you some mornings,' Jed said, and then seemed to think about it. 'Though not for a while.'

'I live just over there.' Jasmine pointed to her small weatherboard house. 'I walk here every chance I get—though I haven't had too many chances of late.'

'We're almost neighbours.' Jed smiled. 'I'm in the one on the end.' He nodded towards the brand-new group of town houses a short distance away that had been built a couple of years ago. Her mother had been the agent in a couple of recent sales there and Jasmine wondered if one of them might have been to him.

And just to remind her that he hadn't specifically noticed her, he nodded to another jogger who went past, and as they walked along a little way, he said hi to an elderly couple walking their dog. He clearly knew the locals.

'Taking a break from painting?' He grinned.

'How did you guess?' Jasmine sighed. 'I don't know who's madder—whoever painted the wall green, or me for thinking a couple of layers of white would fix it. I'm on my third coat.' She looked over at him and then stated the obvious. 'So you run?'

'Too much,' Jed groaned. 'It's addictive.'

'Not for me,' Jasmine admitted. 'I tried, but I don't really know where to start.'

'You just walk,' Jed said, 'and then you break into a run and then walk again—you build up your endurance. It doesn't take long.' He smiled. 'See? I'm addicted.'

'No, I get it.' Jasmine grinned back. 'I just don't do it.'

'So, how did you go with the crèche?' He walked along beside her and Jasmine realised he was probably just catching his breath, probably pacing himself rather than actually stopping for her. Still, it was nice to have a chat.

'They were really accommodating, though I think Lisa might have had something to do with that.'

'How old is your child?'

'Fourteen months,' Jasmine said. 'His name's Simon.'

'And is this your first job since he was born?' He actually did seem to want to talk her. Jasmine had expected that he'd soon jog off, but instead he walked along beside her, his breathing gradually slowing down. It was nice to have adult company, nice to walk along the beach and talk.

'It is,' Jasmine said. 'And I'm pretty nervous.'

'You worked at Melbourne Central, though,' he pointed out. 'That's one hell of a busy place. It was certainly buzzing when I went for my interview there.'

'Didn't you like it?'

'I did,' Jed said, 'but I was surprised how much I liked Peninsula Hospital. I was sort of weighing up between the two and this…' he looked out to the bay, '…was a huge draw card. The beach is practically next to the hospital and you can even see it from the canteen.'

'I'm the same,' Jasmine said, because as much as she loved being in the city she was a beach girl through and through.

'You'll be fine,' Jed said. 'It will take you ten minutes to get back into the swing of things.'

'I think it might take rather more than that.' Jasmine laughed. 'Having a baby scrambles your brains a bit. Still, it will be nice to be working again. I've just got to work out all the shifts and things.'

'What does your husband do?' Jed took a swig from his water bottle. 'Can he help?'

'We're separated,' Jasmine replied.

'Oh. I'm sorry to hear that.'

'It's fine,' Jasmine said. She was getting used to saying it and now, just as she was, it would be changing again because she'd be divorced.

It was suddenly awkward; the conversation that had flowed so easily seemed to have come to a screeching halt. 'Storm's getting close.' Jed nodded out to the distance.

Given they were now reduced to talking about the weather, Jasmine gave a tight smile. 'I'd better go in and watch my paint dry.'

'Sure,' Jed said, and gave her a smile before he jogged off.

And as she turned and headed up to her flat she wanted

to turn, wanted to call out to his rapidly departing back, *'It's okay, you don't have to run—just because I don't have a partner doesn't mean that I'm looking for another one.'*

God, talk about put the wind up him.

Still, she didn't dwell on it.

After all there were plenty of other things on her mind without having to worry about Jed Devlin.

CHAPTER FIVE

THERE WAS, JASMINE decided, one huge advantage to being related to two fabulously strong, independent women.

It sort of forced you to be fabulously strong and independent yourself, even when you didn't particularly feel it.

The hospital squeezed her in for that month's orientation day and after eight hours of fire drills, uniform fittings, occupational health and safety lectures and having her picture taken for her lanyard, she was officially on the accident and emergency roster. Lisa had, as promised, rung the crèche and told them Simon was a priority, due to the shortage of regular staff in Emergency.

So, just over a week later at seven o'clock on a Wednesday morning, two kilograms lighter thanks to a new diet, and with her hair freshly cut, Jasmine dropped her son off for his first day of crèche.

'Are you sure he's yours?' Shona, the childcare worker grinned as Jasmine handed him over. It was a reaction she got whenever anyone saw her son, even the midwives had teased her in the maternity ward. Simon was so blond and long and skinny that Jasmine felt as if she'd borrowed someone else's baby at times.

Until he started to cry, until he held out his arms to Jasmine the moment that he realised he was being left.

Yep, Jasmine thought, giving him a final cuddle, he might look exactly like Penny but, unlike his aunt, he was as soft as butter—just like his mum.

'Just go,' Shona said when she saw that Simon's mum looked as if she was about to start crying too. 'You're five minutes away and we'll call if you're needed, but he really will be fine.'

And so at seven-twenty, a bit red-nosed and glassy-eyed, Jasmine stood by the board and waited for handover to start.

She never even got to hear it.

'I've decided to pair you with Vanessa,' Lisa told her. 'For the next month you'll do the same shifts, and, as far as we can manage, you'll work alongside her. I've put the two of you in Resus this morning so don't worry about handover. It's empty for now so I'll get Vanessa to show you around properly while it's quiet—it won't stay that way for long.'

'Sure,' Jasmine said, in many ways happy to be thrown straight in at the deep end, rather than spending time worrying about it. And Lisa didn't have much choice. There wasn't much time for handholding—experienced staff were thin on the ground this morning, and even though she hadn't nursed in a year, her qualifications and experience were impressive and Lisa needed her other experienced nurses out in the cubicles to guide the agency staff they had been sent to help with the patient ratio shortfalls this morning.

Vanessa was lovely.

She had been working at the hospital for three years, she told Jasmine, and while it was empty, she gave her a more thorough tour of the resuscitation area as they checked the oxygen and suction and that everything was stocked. She also gave her a little bit of gossip along the way.

'There's Mr Dean.' Vanessa pulled a little face. 'He likes things done his way and it takes a little while to work that out, but once you do he's fine,' she explained as they checked and double-checked the equipment. 'Rex and Helena are the other consultants.' Jasmine found she was holding her breath more than a little as Vanessa worked through the list of consultants and registrars and a few nurses and gave titbits of gossip here and there.

'Penny Masters, Senior Reg.' Vanessa rolled her eyes. 'Eats lemons for breakfast, so don't take anything personally. She snaps and snarls at everyone and jumps in uninvited,' Vanessa said, 'but you have to hand it to her, she does get the job done. And then there's Jed.' Jasmine realised that she was still holding her breath, waiting to hear about him.

'He's great to work with too, a bit brusque, keeps himself to himself.' Funny, Jasmine thought, he hadn't seemed anything other than friendly when she had met him, but, still, she didn't dwell on it. They soon had their first patients coming through and were alerted to expect a patient who had fallen from scaffolding. He had arm fractures but, given the height from which he had fallen, there was the potential for some serious internal injuries, despite the patient being fully conscious. Resus was prepared and Jasmine felt her shoulders tense as Penny walked in, their eyes meeting for just a brief second as Penny tied on a large plastic apron and put on protective glasses and gloves.

'This is Jasmine,' Vanessa happily introduced her. 'The new clinical nurse specialist.'

'What do we know about the patient?' was Penny's tart response.

Which set the tone.

The patient was whizzed in. He was young, in pain and called Cory, and Penny shouted orders as he was moved carefully over onto the trolley on the spinal board. He was covered in plaster dust. It was in his hair, on his clothes and in his eyes, and it blew everywhere as they tried to cut his clothes off. Despite Cory's arms being splinted, he started to thrash about on the trolley

'Just stay nice and still, Cory.' Jasmine reassured the patient as Penny thoroughly examined him—listening to his chest and palpating his abdomen, demanding his observations even before he was fully attached to the equipment and then ordering some strong analgesia for him.

'My eyes...' Cory begged, even when the pain medication started to hit, and Penny checked them again.

'Can you lavage his eyes?' Penny said, and Jasmine warmed a litre of saline to a tepid temperature and gently washed them out as Penny spoke to the young man.

'Right,' Penny said to her young patient. 'We're going to get some X-rays and CTs, but so far it would seem you've been very lucky.'

'Lucky?' Cory checked.

'She means compared to how it might have been,' Jasmine said as she continued to lavage his eyes. 'You fell from quite a height and, judging by the fact you've got two broken wrists, well, it looks like as if you managed to turn and put out your hands to save yourself,' Jasmine explained. 'Which probably doesn't feel very lucky right now.

'How does that eye feel?' She wiped his right eye with gauze and Cory blinked a few times.

'Better.'

'How's the pain now?'

'A bit better.'

'Need any help?' Jasmine looked up at the sound of Jed's voice. He smelt of morning, all fresh and brisk and ready to help, but Penny shook her head.

'I've got this.' She glanced over to another patient being wheeled in. 'He might need your help, though.'

She'd forgotten this about Emergency—you didn't get a ten-minute break to catch your breath and tidy up, and more often than not it was straight into the next one. As Vanessa, along with Penny, dealt with X-rays and getting Cory ready for CT, Jasmine found herself working alone with Jed on his patient, with Lisa popping in and out.

'It's her first day!' Lisa warned Jed as she opened some

equipment while Jasmine connected the patient to the monitors as the paramedics gave the handover.

'No problem,' Jed said, introducing himself to the elderly man and listening to his chest as Jasmine attached him to monitors and ran off a twelve-lead ECG. The man was in acute LVF, meaning his heart was beating ineffectively, which meant that there was a build-up of fluid in his lungs that was literally drowning him. Jim's skin was dark blue and felt cold and clammy and he was blowing white frothy bubbles out through his lips with every laboured breath.

'You're going to feel much better soon, sir,' Jed said. The paramedics had already inserted an IV and as Jed ordered morphine and diuretics, Jasmine was already pulling up the drugs, but when she got a little lost on the trolley he pointed them out without the tutting and eye-rolls Penny had administered.

'Can you ring for a portable chest X-ray?' Jed asked. The radiographer would have just got back to her department as Jasmine went to summon her again.

'What's the number?' Jasmine asked, but then found it for herself on the phone pad.

Jed worked in a completely different manner from Penny. He was much calmer and far more polite with his requests and was patient when Jasmine couldn't find the catheter pack he asked for—he simply went and got one for himself. He apologised too when he asked the weary night radiographer to hold on for just a moment as he inserted a catheter. But, yes, Jasmine noticed, Vanessa was right—he was detached with the staff and nothing like the man she had mildly joked with at her interview or walked alongside on the beach.

But, like Penny, he got the job done.

Jasmine spoke reassuringly to Jim all the time and with oxygen on, a massive dose of diuretics and the calming effect of the morphine their patient's oxygen sats were slowly climbing and his skin was becoming pink. The terrified grip on Jasmine's hand loosened.

Lisa was as good as her word and popped in and out. Insisting she was done with her ovaries, she put on a lead gown and shooed them out for a moment and they stepped outside for the X-ray.

Strained was the silence and reluctantly almost, as if he was forcing himself to be polite, Jed turned his face towards her as they waited for the all-clear to go back inside. 'Enjoying your first day?'

'Actually, yes!' She was surprised at the enthusiasm in her answer as she'd been dreading starting work and leaving Simon, and worried that her scrambled brain wasn't up to a demanding job. Yet, less than an hour into her first shift, Jasmine was realising how much she'd missed it, how much she had actually loved her work.

'Told you it wouldn't take long.'

'Yes, well, I'm only two patients in.' She frowned as he looked up, not into her eyes but at her hair. 'The hairdresser cut too much off.'

'No, no.' He shook his head. 'It's white.'

'Oh.' She shook it and a little puff of plaster dust blew into the air. 'Plaster dust.' She shook it some more, moaning at how she always ended up messy, and he sort of changed his smile to a stern nod as the red light flashed and then the radiographer called that they could go back inside.

'You're looking better.' Jasmine smiled at her patient because now the emergency was over, she could make him a touch more comfortable. The morphine had kicked in and his catheter bag was full as the fluid that had been suffocating him was starting to move from his chest. 'How are you feeling?'

'Like I can breathe,' Jim said, and grabbed her hand, still worried. 'Can my wife come in? She must've been terrified.'

'I'm going to go and speak to her now,' Jed said, 'and then I'll ring the medics to come and take over your care. You're doing well.' He looked at Jasmine. 'Can you stay with him while I go and speak to his wife?'

'Sure.'

'I thought that was it,' Jim admitted as Jasmine placed some pillows behind him and put a blanket over the sheet that covered him. After checking his obs, she sat herself down on the hard flat resus bed beside him. 'Libby thought so too.'

'Your wife?' Jasmine checked, and he nodded.

'She couldn't remember the number for the ambulance.'

'It must have been very scary for her,' Jasmine said, because though it must be terrifying to not be able to breathe, to watch someone you love suffer must have been hell. 'She'll be so pleased to see that you're talking and looking so much better than when you came in.'

Libby was pleased, even though she promptly burst into tears when she saw him, and it was Jim who had to reassure her, rather than the other way around.

They were the most gorgeous couple—Libby chatted enough for both of them and told Jasmine that they were about to celebrate their golden wedding anniversary, which was certainly an achievement when she herself hadn't even managed to make it to one year.

'I was just telling Jasmine,' Libby said when Jed came in to check on Jim's progress, 'that it's our golden wedding anniversary in a fortnight.'

'Congratulations.' Jed smiled.

'The children are throwing us a surprise party,' Libby said. 'Well, they're hardly children...'

'And it's hardly a surprise.' Jed smiled again. 'Are you not supposed to know about it?'

'No,' Libby admitted. 'Do you think that Jim will be okay?'

'He should be,' Jed said. 'For now I'm going to ring the medics and have them take over his care, but if he continues improving I would expect him to be home by the end of the week—and ready to *gently* celebrate by the next.'

They were such a lovely couple and Jasmine adored seeing their closeness, but more than that she really was enjoying being back at work and having her world made bigger instead of fretting about her own problems. She just loved the whole buzz of the place, in fact.

It was a nice morning, a busy morning, but the staff were really friendly and helpful—well, most of them. Penny was Penny and especially caustic when Jasmine missed a vein when she tried to insert an IV.

'I'll do it!' She snapped, 'the patient doesn't have time for you to practise on him.'

'Why don't you two go to lunch?' Lisa suggested as Jasmine bit down on her lip.

'She has such a lovely nature!' Vanessa nudged Jasmine as they walked round to the staffroom. 'Honestly, pay no attention to Penny. She's got the patience of a two-year-old and, believe me, I speak from experience when I say that they have none. How old is your son?' She must have the seen that Jasmine was a bit taken aback by her question, as she hadn't had time to mention Simon to Vanessa yet. 'I saw you dropping him off at crèche this morning when I was bringing in Liam.'

'Your two-year-old?'

'My terrible two-year-old,' Vanessa corrected as they went to the fridge and took out their lunches and Vanessa told her all about the behavioural problems she was having with Liam.

'He's completely adorable,' Vanessa said as they walked through to the staffroom, 'but, God, he's hard work.'

Jed was in the staffroom and it annoyed Jasmine that she even noticed—after all, there were about ten people in there, but it was him that she noticed and he was also the reason she blushed as Vanessa's questions became a bit more personal.

'No.' Jasmine answered when Vanessa none-too-subtly asked about Simon's father—but that was nursing, especially in Emergency. Everyone knew everything about everyone's life and not for the first time Jasmine wondered how she was supposed to keep the fact she was Penny's sister a secret.

'We broke up before he was born.'

'You poor thing,' Vanessa said, but Jasmine shook her head.

'Best thing,' she corrected.

'And does he help?' Vanessa pushed, 'with the childcare? Now that you're working...'

She could feel Jed was listening and she felt embarrassed. Embarrassed at the disaster her life was, but she tried not to let it show in her voice, especially as Penny had now walked in and was sitting in a chair on the other side of the room.

'No, he lives on the other side of the city. I just moved back here a few weeks ago.'

'Your family is here?' Vanessa checked.

'Yes.' Jasmine gave a tight smile and concentrated on her cheese sandwich, deciding that in future she would have lunch in the canteen.

'Well, it's good that you've got them to support you,' Vanessa rattled on, and Jasmine didn't even need to look at Penny to see that she wasn't paying any attention. Her sister was busy catching up on notes during her break. Penny simply didn't stop working, wherever she was. Penny had always been driven, though there had been one brief period where she'd softened a touch. She'd dated for a couple of years and had been engaged, but that had ended abruptly and since then all it had been was work, work, work.

Which was why Penny had got as far as she had, Jasmine knew, but sometimes, more than sometimes, she wished her sister would just slow down.

Thankfully the conversation shifted back to Vanessa's son, Liam—and she told Jasmine that she was on her own, too. Jasmine would have quite enjoyed learning all about her colleagues under normal circumstances but for some reason she was finding it hard to relax today.

And she knew it was because of Jed.

God, she so did not want to notice him, didn't want to be aware of him in any way other than as a colleague. She had enough going on in her life right now, but when Jed stood and stretched and yawned, she knew what that stomach looked like beneath the less than well-ironed shirt, knew just how nice he could be, even if he was ignoring her now. He opened his eyes and caught her looking at him and he almost frowned at her. As he looked away Jasmine found that her cheeks were on fire, but thankfully Vanessa broke the uncomfortable moment.

'Did you get called in last night?' Vanessa asked him.

'Nope,' Jed answered. 'Didn't sleep.'

Jed headed back out to the department and carried on. As a doctor he was more than used to working while he was tired but it was still an effort and at three-thirty Jed made a cup of strong coffee and took it back to the department with him, wishing he could just go home and crash, annoyed with himself over his sleepless night.

He'd had a phone call at eleven-thirty the previous night and, assuming it was work, had answered it without thinking.

Only to be met by silence.

He'd hung up and checked the number and had seen that it was *private*.

And then the phone had rung again.

'Jed Devlin.' He had listened to the silence and then hung up again and stared at the phone for a full ten minutes, waiting for it to ring again.

It had.

'Jed!' He heard the sound of laughter and partying and then the voice of Rick, an ex-colleague he had trained with. 'Jed, is that you?'

'Speaking.'

'Sorry, I've been trying to get through.'

'Where are you?'

'Singapore… What time is it there?'

'Coming up for midnight.'

'Sorry about that. I just found out that you moved to Melbourne.'

He had laughed and chatted and caught up with an old friend and it was nice to chat and find out what was going on in his friend's life and to congratulate him on the birth of his son, but twenty minutes later his heart was still thumping.

Two hours later he still wasn't asleep.

By four a.m. Jed realised that even if the past was over with, he himself wasn't.

And most disconcerting for Jed was the new nurse that had started today.

He had found it easy to stick to his self-imposed rule. He really wasn't interested in anyone at work and just distanced himself from all the fun and conversations that were so much a part of working in an emergency department.

Except he *had* noticed Jasmine.

From the second he'd seen her standing talking to Penny, all flustered and red-cheeked, her dark curls bobbing, and her blue eyes had turned to him, he'd noticed her in a way he'd tried very hard not to. When he'd heard she was applying for a job in Emergency, his guard had shot up, but he had felt immediate relief when he'd heard someone call her Mrs Phillips.

It had sounded pretty safe to him.

There had been no harm in being friendly, no chance of anything being misconstrued, because if she was a Mrs then he definitely wasn't interested, which meant there was nothing to worry about.

But it would seem now that there was.

'Thanks, Jed.' He turned to the sound of Jasmine's voice as she walked past him with Vanessa.

'For?'

'Your help today, especially with Jim. I had no idea where the catheter packs were. It's good to get through that first shift back.'

'Well, you survived it.' He gave a very brief nod and turned back to his work.

'More importantly, the patients did!' Jasmine called as she carried on walking with Vanessa.

They were both heading to the crèche, he guessed. He fought the urge to watch her walk away, not looking up until he heard the doors open and then finally snap closed.

Not that Jasmine noticed—she was more than used to moody doctors who changed like the wind. For now she was delighted that her first shift had ended and as she and Vanessa headed to the crèche, Jasmine realised she had made a friend.

'He's gorgeous!' Vanessa said as Jasmine scooped up Simon. 'He's so blond!'

He was—blond and gorgeous, Simon had won the staff over on *his* first day with his happy smile and his efforts to talk.

'This is Liam!' Vanessa said. He was cute too, with a mop of dark curls and a good dose of ADD in the making. Jasmine stood smiling, watching as Vanessa took about ten minutes just to get two shoes on her lively toddler.

'Thank goodness for work,' Vanessa groaned. 'It gives me a rest!'

'Don't look now,' Vanessa said as they walked out of the crèche, 'they're getting something big in.' Jed and Lisa were standing outside where police on motorbikes had gathered in the forecourt. Screens were being put up and for a moment Jasmine wondered if her first day was actually over or if they were going to be asked to put the little ones back into crèche.

'Go.' Lisa grinned as Vanessa checked what was happening. 'The screens are for the press—we have ourselves a celebrity arriving.'

'Who?' Vanessa asked.

'Watch the news.' Lisa winked. 'Go on, shoo…'

'Oh,' Jasmine grumbled, because she really wanted to know. She glanced at Jed, who looked totally bored with the proceedings, and there was really no chance of a sophisticated effort because Simon was bouncing up and down with excitement at the sight of police cars and Liam was making loud siren noises. 'I guess I'll have to tune in at six to find out.'

And that was the stupid thing about Emergency, Jasmine remembered.

You couldn't wait for the shift to finish—even today, as much as she'd enjoyed her shift, as soon as lunchtime had ended, she had been counting the minutes, desperate to get to the crèche and pick up Simon.

Except that the second she had finished her shift, she wanted to go back.

'I've missed it,' she told Vanessa as they walked to the car park. 'I was looking at a job in MRI, but I really do like working in Emergency.'

'I'm the same,' Vanessa admitted. 'I couldn't work anywhere else.'

'The late shifts are going to be the killer, though,' Jasmine groaned, 'and I don't even want to think about nights.'

'You'll work it out.' Vanessa said. 'I've got a lovely babysitter: Ruby. She's studying childcare, she goes to my church and she's always looking for work. And if she can deal with Liam she can more than handle Simon. She's got really strict parents so she loves spending evenings and sometimes nights at my place.' She gave Jasmine a nudge. 'Though I do believe her boyfriend might pop over at times. Just to study, of course...'

They both laughed.

It was nice to laugh, nice to be back at work and making friends.

Nice to sit down for dinner on the sofa, with a for-once-exhausted Simon. 'Come on,' Jasmine coaxed, but he wasn't interested in the chicken and potatoes she was feeding him and in the end Jasmine gave in and warmed up his favourite ready meal in the microwave. 'I'm not buying any more,' Jasmine warned as he happily tucked in, but Simon just grinned.

And it was nice to turn on the news and to actually feel like you had a little finger on the pulse of the world.

She listened to the solemn voice of the newsreader telling the viewers about a celebrity who was '*resting*' at the Peninsula after being found unconscious. She got a glimpse of Jed walking by the stretcher as it was wheeled in, holding a sheet over the unfortunate patient's face. Then Jasmine watched as Mr Dean spoke, saying the patient was being transferred to ICU and there would be no further comment from the hospital.

It wasn't exactly riveting, so why did she rewind the feature?

Why did she freeze the screen?

Not in the hope of a glimpse at the celebrity.

And certainly not so she could listen again to Mr Dean.

It was Jed's face she paused on and then changed her mind.

She was finished with anything remotely male, Jasmine reminded herself, and then turned as Simon, having finished his meal and bored with the news, started bobbing up and down in front of the television.

'Except you, little man.'

CHAPTER SIX

JED DID CONCENTRATE on work.

Absolutely.

He did his best to ignore Jasmine, or at least to speak to her as little as possible at work, and he even just nodded to her when they occasionally crossed paths at the local shop, or he would simply run past her and Simon the odd evening they were on the beach.

He was a funny little lad. He loved to toddle on the beach and build sandcastles, but Jed noticed that despite her best efforts, Jasmine could not get him into the water.

Even if he tried not to notice, Jed saw a lot as he ran along the stretch of sand—Jasmine would hold the little boy on her hip and walk slowly into the water, but Simon would climb like a cat higher up her hip until Jasmine would give in to his sobs and take him back to the dry sand.

'You get too tense.' He gave in after a couple of weeks of seeing this ritual repeated. He could see what Jasmine was doing wrong and even if he ignored her at work, it seemed rude just to run past and not stop and talk now and then.

'Sorry?' She'd given up trying to take Simon into the water a few moments ago and now they were patting a sandcastle into shape. She looked up when Jed stood over her and Jasmine frowned at his comment, but in a curious way rather than a cross one.

He concentrated on her frown, not because she was resting back on her heels to look up at him, not because she was wearing shorts and a bikini top, he just focused on her frown. 'When you try to get him to go into the water. I've seen you.' He grinned. 'You get tense even before you pick him up to take him in there.'

'Thanks for the tip.' Jasmine looked not at Jed but at Simon. 'I really want him to love the water. I was hoping by the end of summer he'd at least be paddling, but he starts screaming as soon as I even get close.'

'He'll soon get used to it just as soon as you relax.' And then realising he was sounding like an authority when he didn't have kids of his own, he clarified things a little. 'I used to be a lifeguard, so I've watched a lot of parents trying to get reluctant toddlers into the water.'

'A lifeguard!' Jasmine grinned. 'You're making me blush.'

She was funny. She wasn't pushy or flirty, just funny.

'That was a long time ago,' Jed said.

'A volunteer?'

'Nope, professional. I was paid—it put me through medical school.'

'So how should I be doing it?'

'I'll show you.' He offered her his hand and pulled her up and they walked towards the water's edge. 'Just sit here.'

'He won't come.'

'I bet he does if you ignore him.'

So they sat and chatted for ten minutes or so. Simon grew bored, playing with his sandcastle alone, while the grown-ups didn't care that they were sitting in the water in shorts, getting wet with each shallow wave that came in.

Jed told her about his job, the one he'd had before medical school. 'It was actually that which made me want to work in emergency medicine,' Jed explained. 'I know you shouldn't enjoy a drowning...'

She smiled because she knew what he meant. There was a high that came from emergencies, just knowing that you knew what to do in a fraught situation.

Of course not all the time; sometimes it was just miserable all around, but she could see how the thrill of a successful resuscitation could soon plant the seeds for a career in Emergency.

'So if I drown, will you rescue me?'

'Sure,' Jed said, and her blue eyes turned to his and they smiled for a very brief moment. Unthinking, absolutely not thinking, he said it. 'Why? Is that a fantasy of yours?'

And he could have kicked himself, should have kicked himself, except she was just smiling and so too was he. Thankfully, starved of attention, Simon toddled towards them and squealed with delight at the feeling of water rushing past his feet.

'Yay!' Jasmine was delighted, taking his hands and pulling him in for a hug. 'It worked.'

'Glad to have helped.' Jed stood, because *now* he was kicking himself, now he was starting to wonder what might have happened had Simon not chosen that moment to take to the water.

Actually, he wasn't wondering.

Jed knew.

'Better get on.' He gave her a thin smile, ruffled Simon's hair and off down the beach he went, leaving Jasmine sitting there.

Jed confused her.

Cold one minute and not warm but hot the next.

And, no, being rescued by a sexy lifeguard wasn't one of her fantasies, but a sexy Jed?

Well...

She blew out a breath. There was something happening between them, something like she had never known before. Except all he did was confuse her—because the next time she saw him at work he went back to ignoring her.

As well as confusing, Jed was also wrong about her getting

right back into the swing of things at work. The department was busy and even a couple weeks later she still felt like the new girl at times. Even worse, her mum was less than pleased when Lisa asked, at short notice, if Jasmine could do two weeks of nights. She had staff sick and had already moved Vanessa onto the roster to do nights. Jasmine understood the need for her to cover, but she wasn't sure her mum would be quite so understanding.

'I'm really sorry about this,' Jasmine said to her mum as she dropped Simon off.

'It's fine.' Louise had that rather pained, martyred look that tripped all of Jasmine's guilt switches. 'I've juggled a few clients' appointments to early evening for this week so I'll need you to be back here at five.'

'Sure.'

'But, Jasmine,' Louise said, 'how are you going to keep on doing this? I'm going away soon and if they can change your roster at five minutes' notice and expect you to comply, how are you going to manage?'

'I've a meeting with a babysitter at the weekend,' Jasmine told her mum. 'She's coming over and I'll see how she gets on with Simon.'

'How much is a babysitter going to cost?' Louise asked, and Jasmine chose not to answer, but really something would have to give.

Paying the crèche was bad enough, but by the time she'd paid a babysitter to pick Simon up for her late shifts and stints on nights, well, it was more complicated than Jasmine had the time to allocate it right now.

'How are things with Penny at work?' Louise asked.

'It seems okay.' Jasmine shrugged. 'She's just been on nights herself so I haven't seen much of her, and when I do she's no more horrible to me than she is to everybody else.'

'And no one's worked out that you're sisters?'

'How could they?' Jasmine said. 'Penny hasn't said anything and no one is going to hear it from me.'

'Well, make sure that they don't,' Louise warned. 'Penny doesn't need any stress right now. She's worked up enough as it is with this promotion coming up. Maybe once that's over with she'll come around to the idea a bit more.'

'I'd better get going.' Jasmine gave Simon a cuddle and held him just an extra bit tight.

'Are you okay?' Louise checked.

'I'm fine,' Jasmine said, but as she got to the car she remembered why she was feeling more than a little out of sorts. And, no, she hadn't shared it with her mum and certainly she wouldn't be ringing up Penny for a chat to sort out her feelings.

There on the driver's seat was her newly opened post and even though she'd been waiting for it, even though she wanted it, it felt strange to find out in such a banal way that she was now officially divorced.

Yes, she'd been looking forward to the glorious day, only the reality of it gave her no reason to smile.

Her marriage had been the biggest mistake of her life.

The one good thing to come out of it was Simon.

The *only* good thing, Jasmine thought, stuffing the papers into her glove box, and, not for the first time she felt angry.

She'd been duped so badly.

Completely lied to from the start.

Yes, she loved Simon with all her heart, but this was never the way she'd intended to raise a child. With a catalogue of crèches and babysitters and scraping to make ends meet and a father who, despite so many promises, when the truth had been exposed, when his smooth veneer had been cracked and the real Lloyd had surfaced, rather than facing himself had resumed the lie his life was and had turned his back and simply didn't want to know his own son.

'Are you okay?' Vanessa checked later as they headed out of the locker rooms.

'I'm fine,' Jasmine said, but hearing the tension in her own voice and realising she'd been slamming about a bit in the locker room, she conceded, 'My divorce just came through.'

'Yay!' said Vanessa, and it was a new friend she turned to rather than her family. 'You should be out celebrating instead of working.'

'I will,' Jasmine said. 'Just not yet.'

'Are you upset?'

'Not upset,' Jasmine said. 'Just angry.'

'Excuse me.' They stepped aside as a rather grumpy Dr Devlin brushed passed.

'Someone got out of the wrong side of bed,' Vanessa said.

Jasmine didn't get Jed.

She did not understand why he had changed so rapidly.

But he had.

From the nice guy she had met he was very brusque.

Very brusque.

Not just to her, but to everyone. Still, Jasmine could be brusque too when she had to be, and on a busy night in Emergency, sometimes that was exactly what you had to be.

'You've done this before!' Greg, the charge nurse, grinned as Jasmine shooed a group of inebriated teenagers down to the waiting room. They were worried about their friend who'd been stabbed but were starting to fight amongst themselves.

'I used to be a bouncer at a night club.' Jasmine winked at her patient, who was being examined by Jed.

Greg laughed and even the patient smiled.

Jed just carried right on ignoring her.

Which was understandable perhaps, given that they were incredibly busy.

But what wasn't understandable to Jasmine was that he refused a piece of the massive hazelnut chocolate bar she opened at about one a.m., when everyone else fell on it.

Who doesn't like chocolate? Jasmine thought as he drank water.

Maybe he was worried about his figure?

He stood outside the cubicle now, writing up the card. 'Check his pedal pulses every fifteen minutes.' He thrust her a card and she read his instructions.

'What about analgesia?' Jasmine checked.

'I've written him up for pethidine.'

'No.' Jasmine glanced down at the card. 'You haven't.'

Jed took the card from her and rubbed his hand over his unshaven chin, and Jasmine tried to tell herself that he had his razor set that way, that he cultivated the unshaven, up-all-night, just-got-out-of-bed look, that this man's looks were no accident.

Except he had been up all night.

Jed let out an irritated hiss as he read through the patient's treatment card, as if she were the one who had made the simple mistake, and then wrote up the prescription in his messy scrawl.

'Thank you!' Jasmine smiled sweetly—just to annoy him.

She didn't get a smile back.

Mind you, the place was too busy to worry about Jed's bad mood and brooding good looks, which seemed to get more brooding with every hour that passed.

At six a.m., just as things were starting to calm down, just as they were starting to catch up and tidy the place for the day staff, Jasmine found out just how hard this job could be at times.

Found, just as she was starting to maybe get into the swing of things, that perhaps this wasn't the place she really wanted to be after all.

They were alerted that a two-week-old paediatric arrest was on his way in but the ambulance had arrived before they had even put the emergency call out.

Jasmine took the hysterical parents into an interview room and tried to get any details as best she could as the overhead loudspeaker went off, urgently summoning the paediatric crash team to Emergency. It played loudly in the interview room also, each chime echoing the urgency, and there was the sound of footsteps running and doors slamming, adding to the parents' fear.

'The doctors are all with your baby,' Jasmine said. 'Let them do their work.' Cathy, the new mum, still looked pregnant. She kept saying she had only had him two weeks and that this couldn't be happening, that she'd taken him out of his crib and brought him back to bed, and when the alarm had gone off for her husband to go to work... And then the sobbing would start again.

She kept trying to push past Jasmine to get to her baby, but eventually she collapsed into a chair and sobbed with her husband that she just wanted to know what was going on.

'As soon as there's some news, someone will be in.' There was a knock at the door and she saw a policeman and -woman standing there. Jasmine excused herself, went outside and closed the door so she could speak to them.

'How are they?' the policewoman asked.

'Not great,' Jasmine said. 'A doctor hasn't spoken to them yet.'

'How are things looking for the baby?'

'Not great either,' Jasmine said. 'I really don't know much, though, I've just been in with the parents. I'm going to go and try to find out for them what's happening.' Though she was pretty sure she knew. One look at the tiny infant as he had arrived and her heart had sunk.

'Everything okay?' Lisa, early as always, was just coming on duty and she came straight over.

'We've got a two-week-old who's been brought in in full arrest,' Jasmine explained. 'I was just going to try and get an update for the parents.'

'Okay.' Lisa nodded. 'You do that and I'll stay with them.'

Jasmine wasn't sure what was worse, sitting in with the hysterical, terrified parents or walking into Resus and hearing the silence as they paused the resuscitation for a moment to see if there was any response.

There was none.

Jed put his two fingers back onto the baby's chest and started the massage again, but the paediatrician shook his head.

'I'm calling it.'

It was six twenty-five and the paediatrician's voice was assertive.

'We're not going to get him back.'

He was absolutely right—the parents had started the resuscitation and the paramedics had continued it for the last thirty-five futile minutes. Jasmine, who would normally have shed a tear at this point before bracing herself to face the family, just stood frozen.

Vanessa cried. Not loudly. She took some hand wipes from the dispenser and blew her nose and Jed took his fingers off the little infant and sort of held his nose between thumb and finger for a second.

It was a horrible place to be.

'Are you okay?' Greg looked over at Jasmine and she gave a short nod. She dared not cry, even a little, because if she started she thought she might not stop.

It was the first paediatric death she had dealt with since she'd had Simon and she was shocked at her own reaction. She just couldn't stop looking at the tiny scrap of a thing and comparing him to her own child, and how the parents must be feeling. She jumped when she heard the sharp trill of a pager.

'Sorry.' The paediatrician looked down at his pager. 'I'm needed urgently on NICU.'

'Jed, can you...?'

Jed nodded as he accepted the grim task. 'I'll tell the parents.'

'Thanks, and tell them that I'll come back down and talk to them at length as soon as I can.'

'Who's been dealing with the parents?' Jed asked when the paediatrician had gone.

'Me,' Jasmine said. 'Lisa's in there with them now. The police are here as well.'

'I'll speak first to the parents,' Jed said. 'Probably just keep it with Lisa. She'll be dealing with them all day.'

Jasmine nodded. 'They wanted a chaplain.' She could hear the police walkie-talkies outside and her heart ached for the parents, not just for the terrible news but having to go over and over it, not only with family but with doctors and the police, and for all that was to come.

'I'll go and ring the chaplain,' Greg said. 'And I'd better write up the drugs now.' He looked at the chaos. There were vials and wrappers everywhere, all the drawers on the trolley were open. They really had tried everything, but all to no avail.

'I'll sort out the baby,' Vanessa said, and Jasmine, who had never shied away from anything before, was relieved that she wouldn't have to deal with him.

'I'll restock,' Jasmine said.

Which was as essential as the other two things, Jasmine told herself as she started to tidy up, because you never knew what was coming through the door. The day staff were arriving and things needed to be left in order.

Except Jasmine *was* hiding and deep down she knew it, had been so relieved when Jed had suggested keeping things with Lisa. She screwed her eyes closed as screams carried through the department. Jed must have broken the news.

She just wanted to go home to her own baby, could not stand to think of their grief.

'Are you okay, Jasmine?' Vanessa asked as she stocked her trolley to take into Resus, preparing to wash and dress the baby so that his parents could hold him.

'I'll get there.' She just wanted the shift to be over, to ring her mum and check that Simon was okay, for the past hour not to have happened, because it wasn't fair, it simply was not fair. But of course patients kept coming in with headaches and chest pains and toothaches and there was still the crash trolley to re-stock and plenty of work to do.

And now here was Penny, all crisp and ready for work.

'Morning!' She smiled and no one really returned it. 'Bad night?' she asked Jed, who, having told the parents and spoken to the police, was admitting another patient.

'We just had a neonatal death,' Jed said. 'Two weeks old.'

'God.' Penny closed her eyes. 'How are the parents?'

'The paediatrician is in there with them now,' Jed said. Jasmine was restocking the trolley, trying not to listen, just trying to tick everything off her list. 'But they're beside themselves, of course,' Jed said. 'Beautiful baby,' he added.

'Any ideas as to why?' Penny asked.

'It looks, at this stage, like an accidental overlay. Mum brought baby back to bed and fell asleep feeding him, Dad woke up to go to work and found him.'

She heard them discussing what had happened and heard Lisa come in and ask Vanessa if the baby was ready, because she wanted to take him into his parents. She didn't turn around, she didn't want to risk seeing him, so instead Jasmine just kept restocking the drugs they had used and the needles and wrappers and tiny little ET tubes and trying, and failing, to find a replacement flask of paediatric sodium bicarbonate that had been used in the resuscitation. Then she heard Penny's voice...

'The guidelines now say not to co-sleep.'

And it wasn't because it was Penny that the words riled Jasmine so much, or was it?

No.

It was just the wrong words at the wrong time.

'Guidelines?' Jasmine had heard enough, could not stand to hear Penny's cool analysis, and swung around. 'Where are the guidelines at three in the morning when you haven't slept all night and your new baby's screaming? Where are the guidelines when—?'

'You need to calm down, Nurse,' Penny warned.

That just infuriated Jasmine even more. 'It's been a long night. I don't feel particularly calm,' Jasmine retorted. 'Those parents have to live with this, have to live with not adhering to the *guidelines*, when they were simply doing what parents have done for centuries.'

Jasmine marched off to the IV room and swiped her ID card to get in, anger fizzing inside her, not just towards her sister but towards the world that was now minus that beautiful baby, and for all the pain and the grief the parents would face. Would she have said that if Penny hadn't been her sister?

The fact was, she *would* have said it, and probably a whole lot more.

Yes, Penny was right.

And the guidelines were right too.

But it was just so unfair.

She still couldn't find the paediatric sodium bicarbonate solution and rummaged through the racks because it had to be there, or maybe she should ring the children's ward and ask if they had some till pharmacy was delivered.

Then she heard the door swipe and Jed came in.

He was good like that, often setting up his drips and things himself. 'Are you okay?'

'Great!' she said through gritted teeth.

'I know that Penny comes across as unfeeling,' Jed said, 'but we all deal with this sort of thing in different ways.'

'I know we do.' Jasmine climbed up onto a stool, trying to find the IV flask. She so did not need the grief speech right now, did not need the debrief that was supposed to solve everything, that made things manageable, did not really want the world to be put into perspective just yet.

'She was just going through the thought process,' Jed continued.

'I get it.'

He could hear her angrily moving things, hear the upset in her voice, and maybe he should get Lisa to speak to her, except Lisa was busy with the parents right now and Greg was checking drugs and handing over to the day staff. Still, the staff looked out for each other in cases like this, and so that was what Jed did.

Or tried to.

'Jasmine, why don't you go and get a coffee and…?' He decided against suggesting that it might calm her down.

'I'm just finishing stocking up and then I'm going home.'

'Not yet. Look—' he was very patient and practical '—you're clearly upset.'

'Please.' Jasmine put up her hand. 'I really don't need to hear it.'

'I think you do,' Jed said.

'From whom?'

'Excuse me?' He clearly had no idea what she was alluding to, but there was a bubble of anger that was dangerously close to popping now, not just for this morning's terrible events but for the weeks of confusion, for the man who could be nice one minute and cool and distant the next, and she wanted to know which one she was dealing with.

'Am I being lectured to by Dr Devlin, or am I being spoken to by Jed?'

'I have no idea what you're talking about. You're distressed.' He knew exactly what she was talking about, knew exactly what she meant, yet of course he could not tell her that. Jed also knew he was handling this terribly, that fifteen minutes sitting in the staffroom being debriefed by him wasn't going to help either of them.

'I'm not distressed.'

'Perhaps not, but I think it would be very silly to leave like this. It would be extremely irresponsible to get into a car and drive home right now, so I'm suggesting that you go to the staffroom and sit down for fifteen minutes.' She stood there furious as she was being told what to do, not asked, she knew that.

'Fine.' She gave a terse smile. 'I will have a coffee and then I'll go home, but first I have to put this back on the crash trolley and order some more from pharmacy.'

'Do that, and then I'll be around shortly to talk to you.' Jed said, 'Look, I know it's hard, especially with one so young. It affects all of us in different ways. I know that I'm upset...'

She didn't say it, but the roll of her eyes as he spoke told him he couldn't possibly know, couldn't possibly understand how she felt.

'Oh, I get it,' Jed said. 'I can't be upset, I don't really get it, do I? Because I don't have a child, I couldn't possibly be as devastated as you.' His voice was rising, his own well-restrained anger at this morning's events starting to build. 'I'm just the machine that walks in and tells the parents that their baby's dead. What the hell would I know?'

'I didn't mean that.' She knew then that she was being selfish in her upset, but grief was a selfish place and one not easy to share.

'Oh, but I think you did,' Jed said. 'I think you meant exactly that.'

And he was right, she had, except that wasn't fair on either of them, because she had cried many times over a lost baby, it just felt different somehow when you had one at home. There was a mixture of guilt and pain tempered with shameful relief that it hadn't happened to her, because, yes, she'd taken Simon into bed with her, despite what the guidelines might say, and it wasn't fair on anyone.

It simply wasn't fair.

Jasmine had no idea how the next part happened. Later she would be tempted to ring Security and ask if she could review the security footage in treatment room two between seven twenty and seven twenty-five, because she'd finally located the sodium bicarbonate and stepped down from the stool and stood facing him, ready to row, both of them ready to argue their point, and the next moment she was being kissed to within an inch of her life.

Or was it the other way around?

She had no way of knowing who had initiated it, all she was certain of was that neither tried to stop it.

It was an angry, out-of-control kiss.

His chin was rough and dragged on her skin, and his tongue was fierce and probing. He tasted of a mixture of peppermint and coffee and she probably tasted of instant tomato soup or salty tears, but it was like no other kiss she had known.

It was violent.

She heard the clatter of a trolley that moved as they did.

It was a kiss that came with no warning and rapidly escalated.

It was a kiss that was completely out of bounds and out of hand.

She was pressed into the wall and Jed was pressing into her; his hands were everywhere and so too were hers; she could feel his erection pressing into her. More than that she too was pushing herself up against him, her hands just as urgent as his, pulling his face into hers, and never had she lost control so quickly, never had she been more unaware of her surroundings because only the crackle of the intercom above reminded them of their location—only that, or shamefully she knew it could have gone further. Somehow they stopped themselves, somehow they halted it, except they were still holding each other's heads.

'And you thought driving would be careless and irresponsible,' Jasmine said.

He sort of blew out his breath. 'Jasmine…' He was right on the edge here, Jed realised, shocked at himself. 'I apologise.'

'No need to apologise,' Jasmine said. 'Or should I?'

'Of course not.' His mouth was there, right there, they were holding each other, restraining the other, and both still dangerously close to resuming what they mustn't. She could hear their breathing, fast and ragged and fighting to slow, and slowly too they let go of each other.

Her blouse was undone, just one button, and she didn't really know how, but he looked away as she did it up and moved away from him to pick up the flask she had dropped. She left him setting up his IV and went to head back out, but she could still taste him, was still not thinking straight. And then Lisa came in.

'Shouldn't you be heading home?'

'I couldn't find the paediatric sodium bicarb,' Jasmine said. 'There's only one left after this.'

'Thanks,' Lisa said. 'I'll get Joan to add it to the pharmacy order. Thanks for everything, Jasmine. I know that can't have been an easy shift.'

'How are the parents?'

'They're spending some time with him. The hospital chaplain is in with them and the police have been lovely.' Lisa looked at Jasmine. 'Maybe go and get a coffee before you go home.'

'I think I just want my bed,' Jasmine admitted. 'I just need to finish the crash trolley off and order some more of this.'

'I'll do that.' Lisa took the flask from her and they stepped aside as Jed walked past with his IV trolley. Very deliberately, neither met the other's eye.

'You go to bed and get a well-earned rest,' Lisa said.

Fat chance of that.

Jasmine did have a cup of coffee before she drove home.

Except she certainly wasn't hanging around to see Jed. Instead, she chose to head to the kiosk and get a takeaway.

And, of course, on the way to her car, she rang her mum.

'How was Simon last night?' Jasmine asked the second her mum answered.

'Fantastic. I haven't heard a peep out of him.'

'He's not up yet?'

'No, but he didn't go down to sleep till quite late.'

'You've checked him, though?' Jasmine could hear the anxiety in her voice

'I checked him before I went to bed. Jasmine, it's eight a.m. Surely it's good if he's having a little lie-in when he often has to be up at six for crèche?'

'Mum...'

She heard her mother's weary sigh as she walked through the

house and then silence for a moment. She was being ridiculous, but even so, she needed the reassurance.

'He's asleep,' her mum said, 'and, yes, he's breathing.'

'Thank you.'

'Bad night?'

'Bad morning.'

'I'm sorry.' And then Louise started to laugh. 'He's just woken up—can you hear him?'

Jasmine smiled at the lovely morning sounds Simon made, calling out to anyone who was there, but she was dangerously close to tears a second later as she realised again just how lucky she was.

'Go and have a nice sleep and I'll see you here for dinner.'

'Thanks, Mum.'

Her mum could be so nice, Jasmine mused as she drove home. When she had Simon she was wonderful with him. Jasmine completely understood that her mother didn't want to be a permanent babysitter and she decided that when she woke up she *was* going to ring Ruby, Vanessa's babysitter, and maybe get together and see if they could work something out.

All the drive home she thought very practical thoughts, aware she was a little bit more than tired.

And upset.

And confused.

She parked in the carport and looked over at the beach, wondered if a walk might be soothing, but knowing her luck Jed would be running there soon and another encounter with him was the last thing either of them needed now.

So she showered and tried to block out the day with her blinds, set her alarm and did her level best not to think of those poor parents and what they were doing right now, but even trying not to think about them made her cry.

And it made her cry too, that she had been here twelve weeks now and Simon's father hadn't even rung once to see how he was, neither had he responded to the occasional photo of his son she sent him.

And then she got to the confusing part and she wasn't crying now as she went over the latter part of her shift.

Instead she was cringing as her mind wandered to a man who at every turn bemused her, and then to the kiss that they had shared.

She hadn't been kissed like that, ever.

Their response to each other's kiss had been so immediate, so consuming that, really, had the intercom not gone off, they'd have been unstoppable, and she burnt in embarrassment at the thought of what Lisa might have come in and found.

And she burnt, too, because in truth it was a side to him she had known was there—something she had felt the second he had jogged up to her on the beach. Jed was the first man to move her in a very long time, but she had never thought her feelings might be reciprocated, had never expected the ferocity of that kiss.

And she'd do very well to forget about it!

They had both been upset, Jasmine decided.

Angry.

Over-emotional.

It had been a one-off. She turned over and very deliberately closed her eyes. Yes, it would be a bit awkward facing him tonight but, hell, she'd faced worse.

She'd just pretend it had never happened.

And no doubt so would he.

She had her whole life to sort out without confusing things further.

And a man like Jed Devlin could only do that.

CHAPTER SEVEN

'MUM!' SIMON SAID it more clearly than he ever had before, and Jasmine scooped him up and cuddled him in tight the second she got to her mum's.

'You're early,' Louise commented. 'I said you didn't need to be here till five.'

'I didn't sleep very well,' Jasmine admitted. 'I'm going to go shopping at the weekend for some decent blinds.' Not that that was the entire reason! 'How has he been?'

'Okay. He's been asking after you a lot,' Louise said, when Jasmine rather wished that she wouldn't as she already felt guilty enough. 'Right, I'd better get ready.'

Louise appeared a little while later in a smart navy suit, with heels and make-up, looking every bit the professional real estate agent. 'How did you do it Mum?' Jasmine asked. 'I mean, you had evening appointments when we were little.'

'You were older than Simon when your dad left,' Louise pointed out. 'Penny's a good bit older than you and she was born sensible—I used to ask the neighbour to listen out for you. It was different times then,' she admitted.

Maybe, but nothing was going to fill the well of guilt Jasmine felt leaving Simon so much and it was only going to get more complicated for him when she added a babysitter to the mix.

Still, she did her best not to worry about next week or next month, just concentrated on giving him his dinner, and when he spat it out she headed to her mum's freezer and, yes, there were chicken nuggets. He could eat them till he was eighteen, Jasmine thought, and let go of worrying about the small stuff for five minutes, just enjoyed giving him his bath and settling him, and then got herself ready for work.

There really wasn't time to stress about facing Jed, especially when her mum didn't get back till after eight, and by the time she raced into work the clock was already nudging nine but, of course, he was one of the first people she saw.

It was a bit awkward but actually not as bad as she'd feared.

As she headed to the lockers Jasmine met him in the corridor and screwed up her face as she blushed and mouthed the word, 'Sorry.'

'Me too,' Jed said, and possibly he too was blushing just a little bit.

'Upset, you know,' Jasmine said.

'I get it.'

'So it's forgotten?' Jasmine checked.

'Forgotten,' he agreed.

Except it wasn't quite so easy to forget a kiss like that, Jasmine knew, because through a restless sleep she had tried.

So too had Jed.

He was a master at self-recrimination, had been furious with himself all day, and that evening, getting ready for work, he'd braced himself to face her, to be cool and aloof, yet her blush and her grin and her 'sorry' had sideswiped him—had actually made him laugh just a little bit on the inside.

'I got you a present.' Vanessa smiled as, still blushing, Jasmine walked into the locker room and peered into the bag being handed to her. It was a bottle with ribbons tied to the neck. 'I think it should be real champagne, but sparkling wine will have to do. You can open it when you're ready to celebrate.'

'Thank you!' Jasmine was touched. 'I'll have a drink at the weekend.'

'I mean properly celebrate.' Vanessa winked. 'You can't pop that cork till...'

'It will be vintage by then.' Jasmine grinned.

It was a very different night from the one before.

It was quiet and the staff took advantage. Greg, the charge nurse, put some music on at the work station and when at four a.m. there were only a few patients waiting for beds or obs, instead of telling them to restock or reorder, he opened a book as Jasmine and Vanessa checked each other's blood sugars. They were low enough to merit another trip to the vending machine, they decided. Then they came back and checked each other's BP.

'It's so low!' Vanessa pulled a face as she unwrapped the cuff and Jasmine grinned, proud of herself for keeping her pulse and blood pressure down, with Jed sitting at the station.

He noticed how easily she laughed.

She noticed him, full stop.

Noticed that this time when she cracked open her chocolate he took a piece.

'Do you want your blood pressure checked, Jed?' Vanessa asked.

'No, thanks.'

Vanessa pulled a face at his grumpy tone. 'Do you work on it, Jed?' It was ten past four, well into the witching hour for night nurses, a quiet night, lights blazing, the humour becoming more wicked. 'Do you work on being all silent and moody?'

'No,' he said. 'I just work.'

'And that beard you're growing,' Vanessa pushed as Greg looked up and grinned, 'is it designer stubble?'

'No,' Jed said patiently. 'I went for a run when I got in from work and I was too tired to shave afterwards, and then I overslept.'

'You're sure about that?' Vanessa said. 'You're sure you're not a male model on the side?'

Jed had forgotten those times of late. He hadn't partaken in chit-chat and fun for a very long time, he'd been too busy concentrating only on work. Maybe he needed a coffee, maybe *his* blood sugar was down, because he was kind of remembering the harmless fun he had once had at work before it had all become a nightmare.

He sat there recalling the laughs that had been part of the job and he was almost smiling as Vanessa chatted on. There was such a difference between playing and flirting. Jed had always known that, he'd just forgotten how to mix the two of late, had lost one for fear of the other, but the atmosphere tonight was kind of bringing it back.

'When you go to the hairdresser's, do you ask them to leave that bit of fringe?' Vanessa teased. 'Just so it can fall over your eye?'

As he turned, Jasmine waited for a frown, for a sharp word, for a brusque put-down, but her smirking grin turned to a delighted one as he flopped his fringe forward, pouted his lips and looked over their shoulders in a haughty model pose.

And then as they screamed in laughter and even Greg did too, Jed got back to his notes.

Enough fun for one night, Jed told himself.

Except he'd set them off and now they were walking like models.

Greg was joining in too as he filled in the board, standing with one hand on his hip and talking in deliberately effeminate tones. Jed tried not to smile, not notice as he usually managed to—he had just blocked out this side of Emergency, had chosen to ignore the black humour and frivolity that sometimes descended.

And yet somehow it was coming back.

Somehow he was starting to remember that it wasn't all just about work.

And Jed knew why.

It was just that he didn't want to know why.

'I'm going for a sleep.' He stood. 'Call me if anything comes in or at six if it stays quiet.'

He could hear them laughing as he tried to rest.

And whatever they were doing it must be funny because he even heard the po-faced nursing supervisor, who must be doing her rounds, start to laugh.

Jed turned on the white noise machine but still he couldn't sleep.

He could do without this!

'Morning, sunshine!' Greg rapped on the door at six, but Jed was awake. He rolled out of bed and brushed his teeth, headed out, took a few bloods and discharged a couple of patients, and wished the place would pick up.

He got one query appendicitis and one very grumpy old man called Ken Jones. He had a chronically infected leg ulcer, which was being dressed by a visiting nurse twice a week, but he had decided at five-thirty a.m. that it was time to do something about it and had called an ambulance. He was very grubby and unkempt and had his radio with him, which was tuned in to a chat show.

'What's his blood sugar?'

'Eight,' Jasmine said.

'You're taking all your diabetic medication, Ken?' Jed checked.

'I just do what I'm told.'

'Okay.' Jed had already carefully examined the man and his leg and he chatted to him for a little while. 'I'm going to get the medics to come down and have a look at you,' Jed said, 'but it might take a while. We're really quiet down here but I know they're very busy up on the ward, so you might have to stay with us for a while. And we could look at the dressings nurse to come and have a good look at your wound and maybe try something new.'

'Up to you.'

'It could be a few hours,' Jed said.

'I don't make a fuss.'

Jed grinned as he walked out. 'He'll be ringing up the radio station to complain about how long he has to wait soon.'

'Does he really need to see the medics?'

'Probably not,' Jed said. 'Penny will probably clear him out by eight, but…' he gave a shrug, '…the old boy's lonely, isn't he? Anyway, he could do with a good looking over, his chest is a bit rattly and he's a bit dry. I'll run some bloods.'

'I'll order him breakfast,' Jasmine yawned.

She ordered a breakfast from the canteen and then checked on the query appendicitis. His drip was about through so she headed over to the IV room. When she swiped her card and saw that Jed was in there, sorting out his trolley to take the bloods, she nearly turned and ran.

But that would be making a big deal of things so instead she stepped in.

'We need to talk,' Jed said without looking up from his task.

'No we don't,' Jasmine said. 'Really, it's fine.'

'Sure about that?' Jed said, and then looked over.

And, no, she wasn't sure about that because the ghost of their kiss was there in the room. She could see the exact spot where he'd pressed her to the wall, feel again every feeling she had yesterday—except the anger, except the upset.

'What about we meet for coffee after work?' he suggested.

'People will see,' Jasmine said. 'You know what this place is like.' She certainly didn't want a hint of this getting back to Penny.

'I meant away from the hospital. Just to talk.'

She shook her head. She'd hardly slept yesterday and had to work tonight as well as stop by her mum's at five and give Simon his dinner.

'I just want to go to bed.' She opened her mouth to correct herself and thankfully they both actually laughed.

'I really,' Jasmine said slowly, 'and I mean *really* am in no position to start something. I know people say that, but I've got a whole lot of things to sort out before…' She shook her head. 'I'm not going there.'

'I get that,' Jed said. 'Believe me, I had no intention of getting involved with someone at work but yesterday, hell, these past weeks…' He wondered how something he had spent all yesterday regretting should be something he would happily do again right this minute.

'Is that why you've been so horrible?'

'I haven't,' he said, then conceded, 'Maybe a bit. We need to talk, maybe clear the air—because if we don't—'

'If we don't,' Jasmine interrupted, 'we're going to be caught making out in the IV cupboard.' She gave him a grin. 'And I have no intention of going there again.'

Except she was lying.

She was looking at his mouth as she said it.

And he was looking at hers.

Had Greg not come in, that was exactly what would have happened and they both knew it.

Yes, the air needed clearing.

CHAPTER EIGHT

'WHY IS HE waiting for the medics?'

Despite not having to start till eight, Penny was in at a quarter to seven, standing and staring at the admission board and determined to make the most of a rare opportunity to clear the board and start her working day with not a single patient.

'He's brewing something.' Jed shrugged.

'We're not a holding pen,' Penny said. 'I'll get the nurses to order him transport home.'

'Let him have his breakfast at least.'

'Of course he can have his breakfast—by the time transport gets here he'll probably have had lunch as well.' She glanced briefly at a weary Jed. 'You look awful.'

'It's easier when it's busy,' Jed yawned.

'Go home,' she said.

'I might just do that.' And then he looked at Penny, who was rather determinedly not turning round to face him, just staring fixedly at the board. 'Speaking of looking awful...' he waited till she reluctantly turned to face him and he saw her red swollen eye '...what happened?'

'I walked into a branch.'

'Ouch.' Jasmine walked over just as he was taking a look.

'Ooh.' She winced when she saw Penny's red eye. 'Penny,

what happened?' And then she remembered she wasn't supposed to be her sister.

'My neighbour's tree overhangs,' she said darkly. 'Though
it won't be by the time I get home—I've left them a note, telling
them what's happened and that they'd better cut it.'

Jasmine could just imagine she had, and what was in it. And
she could picture the branch, too, and Penny's gorgeous old
neighbours who would be so upset.

Trust Penny to handle things so sensitively!

Of course she said nothing.

'I'll have a look,' Jed said, and went to buzz Reception to get
Penny an admission card.

'I don't need to be registered,' Penny snapped. 'It's just a
scratch.'

'A nasty scratch on your cornea,' Jed confirmed a few minutes later. Penny was sitting at the nurses' station and Jed had
put some fluorescein drops into her eye. It made her eye bright
yellow but any scratches showed up green. 'You need antibi-
otic drops and to keep it covered. When was your last tetanus
booster?'

'I can't remember,' Penny said. 'I'm sure I'm up to date.'

'Penny?' Jed checked, as Jasmine walked in.

'Ken Jones just spiked a temp—his temp's thirty-eight point
nine.'

'I'll do cultures.' Jed grinned, and Penny rolled her tongue in
her cheek because now the old boy would have to be admitted.

'I'll do them,' she sighed.

'Not yet,' Jed yawned. 'I'll just give you your tetanus shot.'

'I'll go to my GP.'

'Don't be ridiculous,' Jed said, already opening a trolley and
pulling out a syringe.

It was then that Jasmine *had* to say something.

'I'll do that.' Jasmine smiled. 'You can do the cultures.'

'I'll do the cultures,' Penny said. 'You go home, Jed, and think about shaving.'

Jasmine said nothing, not a single word as they headed into a cubicle and Penny unbuttoned her blouse. She just handed her a wad of tissues as Penny started crying.

Penny was, as Jasmine knew only too well, petrified of needles.

Not a little bit scared, completely petrified of them, though she didn't blink when sticking them in others.

'If you breathe a word of this…'

She was shaking on the seat as Jasmine swabbed her arm.

'No, wait!' Penny said.

'For what?' Jasmine said, sticking the needle in. 'Done.' She smiled at her. 'You big baby.'

'I know, I know.' Penny shuddered. 'Just give me a minute, would you? Go and set up for those blood cultures.' She had snapped straight back to being Penny, except this time Jasmine was smiling.

Jed didn't think about shaving.

He had a shower and tried not to think about Jasmine.

And then he pulled on some running clothes and ran the length of the beach and told himself to just concentrate on work.

Only this time it didn't work.

And he saw where she lived and her car pull up in her carport and he saw Jasmine minus an armful of Simon but holding a bottle of champagne, which confused him, and he tried to continue to run.

What on earth was he going to say to her if he knocked at her door?

At least nothing would happen, he consoled himself, as ten minutes later he found himself doing just that, because given he wasn't exactly fresh out of the shower, there would be no repeats of yesterday.

Except *she* was fresh out of the shower when she opened

the door and he prided himself on the fact that he did not look down, that he somehow held her eyes, even though her dressing gown did little to hide her womanly shape.

'Bad timing?'

'A bit.'

'Well, I won't keep you from your champagne.' He didn't want to make her laugh, except he did so, only he wasn't here for that.

'It's in the fridge.'

'Good.'

'A present.'

'That's nice.'

'Well?' Jasmine demanded. 'Which Jed am I talking to this morning?' And she looked at him standing there, and she knew who it was—the beachside Jed, the man who made her smile, the Jed who had made his first appearance at work just a few hours ago.

'I like to keep my work and personal life separate,' he offered as way of an explanation, only it didn't wash with Jasmine. Penny did too but she was a cow both in and out of work. Yet with Jed sometimes she felt as if she was dealing with two completely different people.

But she liked this one.

Really liked this one, and, no, maybe they weren't going anywhere, maybe it was just all a bit much for him, she was a mother to one year old after all, but that he was here, that at this hour of the morning he stood at her door, when sensible shift workers should be firmly asleep, proved the undeniable attraction.

'I just wanted to say that I am really sorry and that it won't happen again. There'll be no more inappropriateness.'

'And it won't happen again at this end,' Jasmine said. 'Nothing inappropriate…'

Jed nodded and turned to go, except she didn't want him to.

She was tired of running from the past, tired of saving for the future—she just wanted a little bit of living for now.

'At least, not at work.'

And for two years Jed had kept things separate. Despite some temptations, he had kept fiercely to his rule.

But Jed's rules had never been tested at this level.

Had they not kissed yesterday he might have been able to walk away.

Had he not tasted lips that were exactly suited to his, he might have headed back to the beach and then home.

But more than that, her blush and eye roll and 'sorry' last night, her total lack of pursuit or demands meant more to Jed than Jasmine could possibly know.

Bottom line?

They wanted each other.

Not a little bit of want, it was a morning after a sleepless nights want. It was twenty-five hours since yesterday's kiss and for twenty-five hours it had been on both of their minds.

He walked into the hallway and his mouth met hers.

And his chin was even rougher than yesterday.

And yesterday, though their kiss had been fierce it had been tempered on both sides with bitter restraint.

But now they could have what they wanted.

Each other.

For now, at least, it could be as simple as that.

She didn't care that he was damp from running. He smelt fresh and male and she knew what was under that T-shirt, and as she pulled it up and over his head she didn't just get to glimpse, she got to feel, and, no, he wasn't annoyed at the intrusion this time.

He tugged at her dressing gown as his mouth was every-where—on her lips, on her neck and on her breasts. Meanwhile, she pulled at his shorts, because he was pressed so hard into her, and they pulled apart just enough to get to the bedroom—

they weren't in the treatment room now and they quickly celebrated the fact.

She wanted to see what she had felt and she manoeuvred his shorts and all things unnecessary and he kicked off his running shoes and stepped out of them and they were naked in seconds, and seconds from impact.

'Condoms.' She was on the floor, going through his shorts.

'I don't run with them.' Jed laughed.

She was at eye level with his crotch as she knelt up and pressed her lips to him, pleased with a brief taste. Too selfish to continue, she dashed to her tiny bathroom and pulled the cupboard under the sink apart for condoms that were somewhere in a box she hadn't sorted in ages.

She was uncaring as Jed watched her bottom sticking up as she searched in the cupboard and her breasts jiggling as she turned round and it was safer that he go back into the bedroom.

Oh, my.

It was all Jasmine could think as she walked back towards him, because he was better than anything she had fashioned in her mind. He was incredibly fit and toned. She should have been shy as she walked over, but shy was the furthest thing from her mind and anyway, he didn't wait for her to finish walking—both of them were happy to collide.

He was just so into her body, so wanting, and he didn't need to worry about speed or things moving too quickly for her because as his hands slid between her thighs and met her heat she was moaning and he was pushing her onto the bed, with Jasmine wondering where her inhibitions had gone.

She had hundreds of them, Jasmine reminded herself as he knelt over her and examined every inch of her, his eyes greedy with want.

A telephone book full of them.

Or she had, but they had just all disappeared today.

It was almost impossible to tear the packet for him.

And she found herself licking her lips as he slid it on.

She had never had sex like it.

She had never felt less mechanical in her life.

Thought had been replaced by pure sensation.

Him, she thought as he got back to kissing her.

Her, he thought as he reclaimed her mouth.

And then the power that remained sort of fused into one.

His fingers were there and she was wet and warm and wanted this just as much as he did.

'First time since…' She sort of braced herself and he held back and took a moment to not be selfish, even if she wanted him to be. Instead, he slid deeper into her with fingers that were skilled and frantic, and she left it to him, because he knew what he was doing. If they were quick it was mutual, if they were fast it was with begging consent.

Even with much preparation she was incredibly tense when the moment came and she willed him to ignore her. Slowly he pushed in, and she stretched and resisted and then stretched again, and he gave her a moment of stillness to get used to him inside.

Well, not really a moment because he knew he only had a few left in him but Jed left it for her to initiate movement, felt the squeeze and the pull on him as she tested herself as she moved herself up and down his long length.

Just when she thought she had adjusted, just when she pulled him in, he beat her to it and drove into her, and she met him and then he did it again and she tried to trip into his rhythm, except he was so hard and fast now it was bliss to not try, to simply let him, only it wasn't a passive response, it was more trusting.

Jed could hear Jasmine's moans and her urging, and he wished for a second she'd be quiet, because it made it impossible for Jed not to come, except she was starting to. He felt the lift of her hips and the arch of her into him, the feel of a slow uncurling from the inside, reluctant almost to give in to him, and then as he moaned his release she shattered.

She did, she just gave in in a way she never had, felt and delivered deeper than she ever had, and found out in that moment how much of herself she had always held back, the intensity fusing them for a moment in absolute bliss.

She lay there trying to get her breath back as he rested on top of her, and still they were one as reality slowly started to intrude.

She wasn't ready for a relationship.

He'd sworn to not get involved with someone from work.

Penny.

Promotion.

Simon.

Single mum.

Simultaneously the real world flooded its lights onto them and they both turned looked at each other for a long moment.

'Well,' Jasmine said. 'We must have both needed that.'

He laughed, actually laughed on the inside too as he had when she had mouthed 'sorry', and the doubts that had started hushed.

And they hushed some more as they lay in bed and drank Vanessa's sparkling wine that hadn't even had time to cool, and they congratulated each other on how fantastic that had been, rather than trying to work out where they were, and then she told him not what was on her mind but the truth.

'I have to go to sleep.'

'And me.'

'I hardly slept yesterday.'

'Me neither.'

'Jed, I don't know what happened. I don't really know what to say.' She was as honest as she could be. 'I'm nowhere near ready to get involved with someone, so I don't really know how we ended up here.'

'I do,' Jed admitted. 'Why the hell do you think I've been avoiding you since I found out you weren't married?'

'What?'

He just shrugged.

'Tell me.'

'You just...' He gave an embarrassed grin. 'Well, you know when you're attracted to someone? I suppose when I saw you talking to Penny and then she said you were here for an interview and then someone called you Mrs Phillips, well, I was relieved you were spoken for.'

Jasmine frowned.

'I don't like mixing work with things and thought I might have trouble keeping to that with you—it wasn't a logical thing, just...'

She did know what he meant.

Maybe it hadn't been quite an instant attraction, but that evening on the beach, when he'd lifted his T-shirt... Jasmine pulled back the sheet, looked at his lovely abdomen and bent over and ran her fingers lightly over the line there. He caught her hand as it moved down.

'I thought you wanted to sleep.'

'I do.'

'Then later.'

She set the alarm for that afternoon, before she remembered another potential problem. Penny.

'And no one at work is to know.'

'Suits me.'

'I mean it,' Jasmine said. 'What happened yesterday at work was wrong.'

'I'll carry on being horrible.'

'Good.'

'So much for clearing the air,' Jed said. 'Now it's all the more complicated.'

'Not really,' Jasmine yawned. 'Just sleep with me often and buy me lots of chocolate. My needs are simple.'

For that morning at least it really did seem as straightforward as that.

CHAPTER NINE

JED WAS NICE and grumpy at work and he deliberately didn't look up when she walked past, and Jasmine made sure there were no private jokes or smiles.

Gossip was rife in this place and the last thing she wanted was to be at the centre of it again.

No one could have guessed that their days were spent in bed. She just hoped he understood that it couldn't always be like this—that night shifts and her mother's help had made things far easier than they would be from now on. In fact, Jed got his first proper taste of dating a single mum that weekend.

Ruby was lovely.

'I'm hoping to work overseas as a nanny,' she explained to Jasmine, 'so I'm trying to get as much experience as I can and hopefully by the time I've got my qualification I'll have a couple of good references.'

She was very good with Simon, happy to sit with him as he tried to bang square pegs into round holes, and Jasmine could tell Ruby was very used to dealing with young children.

'My main problem is late shifts,' Jasmine explained.

'The crèche knows me,' Ruby said. 'I pick Liam up and I take him back to Vanessa's. I give him his dinner and bath and I try to get him asleep for Vanessa but Liam likes to wait up for her.'

Jasmine laughed. She and Vanessa had got the boys together a couple of times and Liam certainly had plenty of energy.

'Well, Vanessa and I aren't working the same shifts so much now,' Jasmine explained, 'so if we can try and work opposite late shifts...'

'It will all work out,' Ruby said. 'I can always look after them both some evenings.'

Jasmine was starting to think this could work.

So much so that for a try-out Ruby suggested she look after Simon that night, and for the first time in a very long time Jasmine found herself with a Saturday night free. To her delight, when Jed rang a little bit later she found that she had someone to share it with.

'It went well with Ruby, then?'

He asked about the babysitter as they were seated for dinner.

'She seems lovely,' Jasmine said. 'Simon didn't even get upset when I left.'

They were eating a couple of suburbs away from the Peninsula Hospital in a smart restaurant that overlooked the bay. Jasmine had taken a taxi because she hadn't been out in yonks and she wanted a glass or three of wine.

'I would have picked you up.'

'I know.' Jasmine smiled. 'But I've a feeling Ruby might gossip to Vanessa. I feel like I'm having an affair. It's too confusing to work out...' She looked up from the menu and went cross-eyed and Jed started to laugh.

'I can't do that.'

'It's easy,' Jasmine said. 'You just look at the tip of your nose and then hold it as you look up.'

'You've practised.'

'Of course.' She grinned.

And, cross-eyed or not, she looked stunning, Jed noted.

Her hair was loose as it had been on the day he had met her on her walk on the beach, but it fell in thick glossy curls. Unlike at work, she was wearing make-up, not a lot but just enough to accentuate her very blue eyes and full mouth. 'What do you want to eat?'

'Anything,' Jasmine said. 'Well, anything apart from chicken nuggets.'

So instead of leftover nuggets there was wine and seafood, and conversation was easy, as long as it was just about food, about movies and the beach, but the second it strayed deeper there was a mutual pulling back.

'Will you go back to your maiden name?' Jed asked after a while.

'I don't know,' she admitted. 'I don't know if I should change Simon's…'

'So what is it?'

'Sorry?'

'Your maiden name?'

She didn't answer him, just peeled a prawn. She didn't even get a reprieve when he asked what had happened in her marriage, because for a marriage to break up when someone was pregnant it sounded as if something pretty serious had.

'I've got three hours, Jed.' She smiled, dipping a prawn in lime mayonnaise. 'In fact, two hours and fifteen minutes now. I want to enjoy them, not spend time talking about my ex.'

And later, when they were finishing up their heavenly dessert and he mentioned something about a restaurant in Sydney, she asked why he'd moved. His answer was equally vague and Jasmine frowned when he used her line.

'We've got thirty minutes till you need to be back for Ruby. Do we really want to waste them hearing my woes?'

'No.' She laughed.

But, yes, her heart said, except that wasn't what they were about—they had both decided.

They were going to keep things simple and take things slowly.

But it was difficult to find someone so easy to talk to and not open up, especially when the conversation strayed at one point a little too close to Penny. She'd mentioned something about how good it was to have Ruby, given her mum and sister were so busy with their jobs. As soon as she said it she could have cut out her tongue.

'Your mum's in real estate?' Jed checked, and she nodded. 'What does your sister do?'

It was a natural question but one she'd dreaded.

'She does extremely well at whatever she puts her mind to,' Jasmine evaded, reaching for her glass of wine.

'Ouch.' Jed grinned. 'Sore point?'

'Very.'

So he avoided it.

It was nice and going nowhere, they both knew that. It was an out-of-hours fling, except with each turn it became more complicated because outside work there were Simon and Penny and unbeknown fully to the other the two hearts that were meeting had both been incredibly hurt.

Two hearts that had firmly decided to go it alone for now.

They just hadn't factored in desire.

'It's like being a teenager again.' Jasmine grinned as he pulled the car over before they turned into her street and kissed her. 'My mum lives in this street.'

'We're not outside…?'

'No.'

'Good,' he said, and got back to kissing her.

They were under a huge gum tree that dropped gum nuts everywhere, but Jed risked the paintwork, grateful for the leafy shield, and they were ten minutes into a kiss that was way better than teenage ones she'd partaken in, right on this very spot, especially when Jed moved a lever and her seat went back a delicious fraction.

She could hardly breathe. He was over her and looking down at her, his hand was creeping up between her legs, and she could feel how hard he was. However, they could not take it even a fraction further here and she was desperate to pay Ruby and have her out of there, wanted so badly to have him in her bed.

And it would seem that Jed was thinking the same thing. 'I could wait till Ruby's gone.'

'No.' She hauled the word out, for if she regretted using it now, she knew she would regret it more in the morning if she didn't. 'I don't want that for Simon.' She looked up at those gorgeous eyes and that mouth still wet from her kisses and it killed her to be twenty-six and for it to feel wrong to ask him in. 'We're keeping things light,' Jasmine said. 'Agreed?' she prompted, and he nodded. 'Which is fine for me, but I won't treat his little heart lightly.'

'I know.'

'Next time we'll go to yours,' Jasmine suggested.

He looked down at her and the rules he'd embedded into his brain were starting to fade, because he had enjoyed being out, but now he wanted in.

'We'll see,' he said, because this was starting to be about a whole lot more than sex. He'd more than enjoyed tonight, had loved being in her company. The only bit that was proving difficult was leaving things here. 'Maybe we'll go out but eat more quickly?'

'Confusing, isn't it?' she said, and again she crossed her eyes and he laughed and then one more kiss and it ached to a halt.

Killed to turn on the engine and drive down the street and then turn into her own street and to park two doors down from her home.

To smile and walk out and to rearrange her dress as she let herself in.

To chat and pay Ruby and carry on a normal conversation, saying that, yes, she'd had a great night catching up with an old friend, and maybe she'd ask Ruby to babysit so that they could catch up again, perhaps as soon as next week.

But a week didn't seem so soon once Ruby was gone.

A night felt too long.

It killed her not to text him to come back.

CHAPTER TEN

'HI, JASMINE!'

She looked up at the familiar face of a paramedic who was wheeling a stretcher in.

'I haven't seen you in ages.'

'Hi, Mark.' Jasmine smiled, but there was a dull blush on her cheeks, and as Jed looked over to see how the new patient was, he couldn't help but notice it, couldn't help but see that Jasmine was more than a little flustered as she took the handover. 'What are you doing out here?'

'We're all over the place today,' Mark said. 'I had a transfer from Rosebud that got cancelled and then we were called out to Annie here.' Jasmine smiled at her new patient. 'Annie Clayfield, eighty-two years old, fell at home last night. We were alerted by her security when she didn't respond to their daily phone call. We found her on the floor,' Mark explained. 'Conscious, in pain with shortening and rotation to the left leg.'

He pulled back the blanket and Jasmine looked at the patient's feet and saw the familiar deformity that was an obvious sign of a hip fracture.

Annie was a lovely lady and tough too—she tried to hold back her yelp of pain as they moved her over as gently as they could onto the trolley.

Jed came over when he heard her cry and ordered some analgesic.

'We'll get on top of your pain,' Jed said, 'before we move you too much.' He had a listen to her chest and checked her pulse and was writing up an X-ray order when he saw one of the paramedics leave the stretcher he was sorting out and head over to Jasmine.

'So you're here now?'

'That's right.' Jed noted that her voice was falsely cheerful and he had no reason to listen, no reason not to carry on and see the next patient, except he found himself writing a lot more slowly, found himself wanting to know perhaps more than he should if they were planning to keep things light.

'I heard you and Lloyd split up?'

'We did.'

'What's he doing with himself these days?'

'I've no idea,' Jasmine said. 'We're divorced now. I think he's working in his family's business.'

As Jed went to clip the X-ray slip to Annie's door he saw the paramedic give Jasmine a brief cuddle.

'You had nothing to do with it, Jasmine, we all know that. You don't have to hide.'

'I'm not hiding.'

And there was no such thing as uncomplicated, Jed decided, looking at Annie's X-rays a good hour later and ringing down for the orthopaedic surgeons. They'd both agreed to keep it light, to take things slowly. Neither of them talked much, about families or friends or the past, and it should suit him, and yet the more he knew, or rather the less he got to know...

The more he wanted.

Despite all efforts to take things slowly, things were gathering pace between them. They'd been seeing each other for a few weeks now—at least, whenever they got a chance.

They rang each other a lot, and went out whenever shifts

and babysitters permitted, or more often than not they ended up back at his for a few stolen hours.

It just wasn't enough, though.

Concentrate on work, he told himself as he ran along the beach that night.

Except she was home, he knew it.

And Simon would be in bed.

And she wanted to keep that part of her life very separate.

So too did he, Jed reminded himself.

He caught sight of the city shimmering gold in the distance. Melbourne offered a gorgeous skyline but a different skyline from the one he knew so well.

He'd come here to get away, Jed reminded himself.

To finally focus on his career and get ahead.

Yet he looked at the tall gleaming buildings of Melbourne and as much as he loved Peninsula, there was something about the city, or rather a busy city emergency department.

And still Melbourne Central beckoned.

CHAPTER ELEVEN

JASMINE STARED AT the roster and gritted her teeth.

Jed was filling out blood forms and suitably ignoring her, and Penny was at her annoying best, suggesting that the nurses join her in Resus so that she could run through a new piece of equipment with them.

A new piece of equipment that had been there as long as Jasmine had and had been used often.

Honestly, the second the place was finally quiet Penny found a job or an activity for everyone.

No wonder she was so unpopular.

The roster had finally been revealed for the next eight-week period and as she tapped the shifts into her phone Jasmine could feel her blood pressure rising.

Yes, she was the new girl.

Yes, that meant that she got the rubbish shifts—but she had more late duties coming up than she could count, and lots of weekends too, which she would usually be glad of for the money, but of course the crèche wasn't open on weekends and, even though she'd been told it was only about once every three months, there was *another* stint of nights coming up in two weeks.

Her mum would be on her cruise by then.

'Problem?' Lisa checked.

'Just the nights,' Jasmine said. 'I thought it was every three months.'

'Well, we try and share it, but especially when someone's new I like to get them to do some early, so that was an extra for you.'

Was she supposed to say thanks?

She liked Lisa, Jasmine really did, and she was running a department after all, not Jasmine's childcare arrangements, but the pressure of shift work and single parenting, let alone trying to date, was starting to prove impossible.

Idly flicking through the patient bulletin, her eye fell on the perfect job for a single mum who actually wanted to have a little bit of a life too.

It was in the fracture clinic and was almost nine to five.

It was a level above what she was on now, but with her emergency experience she would stand a pretty good chance at getting it.

'Fracture Clinic!' Vanessa peered over her shoulder. 'You'd go out of your mind.'

'I'm going out of my mind looking at the roster,' Jasmine admitted.

'Don't think about it,' Vanessa said breezily. 'Something always turns up.'

Jasmine rolled her eyes as Vanessa walked out. 'I wish I had her optimism.'

'Jasmine.' She turned and smiled at the sound of Mark's voice. 'How are things?'

'Good.' Jed saw she was uncomfortable, saw she glanced over her shoulder to check whether or not he was there, and it was none of his business, he wanted it that way, yet he wanted to know what the problem was, why Mark thought she was hiding.

'Just giving you the heads up, no doubt you'll be alerted soon, but there's a nasty car versus bike on the beach road. Sounds grim.'

'Do we know how many?' Jed asked.

'That's all I've got but they're calling for backup.'

'Thanks.'

Jasmine let Lisa know and the orthopods were down anyway, looking at a fractured femur, and Lisa said to just wait till they heard more before they started paging anyone but that she'd let Penny and Mr Dean know.

Then Mark's radio started crackling and he listened, translating the coded talk of the operator. 'They're just about to let you know,' Mark said. 'One fatality, one trapped, one on the way—adult male.'

The alert phone went then and Lisa took it just as Penny appeared, looking brusquely efficient as usual.

'Car versus motorbike,' Lisa said. 'We've got the biker coming in, he's conscious, abdominal injuries, hypotensive.' She looked up at the clock. 'He's five minutes away and they've just freed the trapped driver, so he's on his way too.'

'I'll take the first,' Penny said. 'If that's okay with you, Jed?'

'Be my guest,' Jed answered, but Jasmine saw the clenching of his jaw and knew that Penny was seriously rattling him— she was always jumping in, always trying to take over anything that was remotely interesting.

'Have we paged the surgeons?' Penny asked.

'Done,' Jasmine said.

'Blood bank?'

'I've let them know.'

Penny gave no response, but with reason as the blast of a siren told them the ambulance was here. As the paramedics raced the patient in, Jasmine didn't blame Penny a bit for the curse she let out when she asked where the hell the surgeons were.

The patient, though conscious, was beyond pale. His pulse was thin and thready and Jasmine set to work, with Greg cutting his leathers off.

'Can you tell me your name?' Penny asked as she examined him.

'Reece.'

'And do you know where you are?'

He answered the questions when prompted but kept closing his eyes and drifting off. Jasmine could only just palpate his blood pressure manually and Penny wasted no time in drawing blood for an urgent cross-match and telling the porters to run it up.

'And I mean run!' he warned. 'Let's put the O-neg up.'

Penny was possibly up there with the most horrible doctors Jasmine had worked with. She was abrupt to the point of rudeness, gave no thanks, only barked demands, except...

She was brilliant.

'If they can't be bothered to get down here,' Penny shouted as Jasmine tried to locate the surgeons again, 'tell them that I'll meet them up in Theatre.'

The patient had had a spinal and chest X-ray, and despite the O-negative blood being squeezed in, his blood pressure was still barely discernible. It was clear he needed Theatre and Penny wanted him taken straight up.

Jed was dealing with the latest admission, and Jasmine quickly prepared Reece for theatre, loading his clothes into a bag and itemising his valuables—rings, wallet... But as she opened up the wallet Jasmine hesitated. There were loads of hundred-dollar notes—at best guess the wallet contained a few thousand dollars.

'Can someone check this with me?' Jasmine asked.

'I'll check it with you later,' Greg called. 'Just put it in the safe.'

'Can we just check it now?' Jasmine pushed, except Greg wasn't listening, so she popped her head around the curtain to where Vanessa and Lisa were assisting Jed. 'Can someone check this, please? He's got a large amount of cash.'

'Just pop it in the safe,' Lisa called. 'I'll count it when things have calmed down.'

'We're supposed to check it before we put it in the safe.' Jasmine's voice was shrill. 'We're not supposed to sign—'

'Here.' It was Penny who stepped in. 'Give it to me, Nurse. I'll put it in the safe.' She walked over and took the wallet, signed the piece of paper and threw the contents into the safe. Jasmine realised that she was sweating and she could feel Jed's eyes on her.

'Right,' Penny said. 'We need to get him up or he's going to bleed out.' She picked up the phone and told Theatre the same as Jasmine prepared the trolley for an emergency transfer, but her hands were shaking and her heart was thumping as she knew she'd made a bit of a scene.

'All okay, Jasmine?' Lisa checked as Jasmine walked past to get a space blanket to put over Reece on the way up to Theatre.

'We're just about to move him,' Jasmine said, and as Jed briefly looked up she felt the question in his brief gaze, knew she wasn't fooling anyone that everything was okay, least of all Jed.

'Reece.' Jasmine tried to explain things as best she could as she covered him with the space blanket. He was irritable now and struggling to remain conscious, and he wanted to wait till his wife got there before he went up. 'We're going to have to move you to Theatre now. Miss Masters will explain things.'

Which Penny did.

She was efficient, brusque but also terribly kind. 'I know you want to wait for your wife—I completely understand, but you're too sick,' she explained gently but firmly. 'I will talk to your wife myself as soon as she gets here. Is there anything you want me to say to her?' She glanced at Jasmine and Greg and at the anaesthetist who had just arrived. 'Could you all ex- cuse us a moment?'

As Jasmine stepped outside to give Penny and Reece some privacy, there was a strange sting of tears in her eyes. It wasn't that she had seen a different side to her sister, rather she had seen a side to Penny that she had long forgotten.

Sitting on the stairs, hearing her parents argue, had terrified four-year-old Jasmine. It had been Penny who would take her back to bed, Penny who would sit beside her and tell her not to worry, that she would take care of things, that even if things did get bad, that even if Dad did what he was threatening and left, they would be fine.

'But what if we're not?' Jasmine would argue. 'What if we never see him?'

'Then we'll deal with it.'

And in their own ways and albeit not perfectly they had.

And as she ran up to Theatre with her sister, and Penny told her to head back down, that she wanted to speak with surgeons, Jasmine knew that she hadn't just come back for the support of her family, neither had she taken the job here for the reasons she had so determinedly given.

She wanted to be close to Penny again.

CHAPTER TWELVE

'I'LL COME OVER after work.'

Jed was coming out of X-Ray as Jasmine walked back from Theatre and they found themselves walking together towards Emergency.

'It's fine.' Jasmine shook her head. 'I'll see you at the weekend. Ruby said that she could—'

'But you're upset tonight.'

'Don't worry, I'll be fine by Saturday.' She couldn't keep the brittle edge from her voice. Yes, she was happy keeping things light, but sometimes, on days like today, it was hard.

'I'm not expecting to be entertained,' Jed said. 'What happened back there?'

'Nothing.'

'Jasmine? Why did you get all upset over the safe? You know we can't just drop everything—the guy was bleeding out.'

'Just leave it.'

But Jed wouldn't.

It was a very long shift. Vanessa was on a half-day and Jasmine really wished that she herself was—she could feel Jed watching her, especially much later when Lisa came over and asked her to check the cash.

'Four thousand six hundred dollars. Agreed?' Lisa checked.

'Agreed,' Jasmine said, and because Penny had first signed for it, she had to be there too.

'I just rang ICU,' Penny said. 'He's doing much better. His wife told me that he was on his way to put down a deposit on a car—that's why he had so much cash on him.' She added her signature to the valuables book.

'Oh, the irony of it,' Lisa sighed, because in a car his injuries would have been so much less. 'Now, I know this is a lot of money and that it has to be checked,' Lisa continued, 'but it's not always possible to just drop everything. It's better to put it in the safe.'

'That's not what the protocol says,' Jasmine pointed out, and Lisa pursed her lips. 'It's been six hours now.'

'I didn't know you were such a stickler for protocol and guidelines, Nurse,' Penny smirked. 'The irony of it!'

'What was that about?' Lisa grinned when Penny waltzed off.

'I think that might have been Penny's attempt at humour,' Jed said, but she could feel his eyes on her, knew he was trying to talk to her, but as she had all day she did her best to avoid him.

Jasmine actually thought she had when she finally finished for the day and went to pick Simon up. But heading over to the crèche she found Jed at the vending machine outside.

'I'll come over later.'

'You know I don't want that. I don't want to confuse Simon.'

'We're not going to make out on the sofa,' Jed said. 'And I'm not going to stay the night till you think he's ready for that, but I do want to talk to you. You're nearly in tears and I don't get why. What happened at your old job?' He could see the blush on her cheeks but she said nothing, instead walked past him to pick up Simon.

Simon was happy and scruffy after a day in the sandpit and Jasmine knew that it was time to face things, that she and Jed could not keep skirting around the edges.

Here in her hands was the living proof of an exceptionally

difficult relationship, here was the baggage she carried, and yet it felt right in her arms.

She had to be able to talk about it with someone she trusted.

And she had to start trusting Jed.

He was still waiting for her when she headed outside.

'About six?'

'He'll still be up.'

'I don't mind, or I can come over around nine if that's what you'd prefer?' She longed to let Jed closer but she just couldn't take any chances with Simon.

'About nine.'

Simon wasn't at his sunniest and her mum dropped over too. It was just one of those disorganised evenings, not helped by a disorganised brain thanks to the day's events. Jasmine had just got Simon down and was sorting out his bag for the next day when she heard a knock at the door and looked up to see that it was already a quarter past nine.

'I wouldn't have got here at six anyway,' Jed said, following her through to the kitchen. 'I only just got away. It's still busy there.'

'Who's on?'

'Rex!' Jed rolled his eyes. 'And Penny's still hovering. I swear she never sleeps.'

'Do you want something to eat?'

'Are you going to cook for me?' Jed grinned.

'No,' Jasmine said, 'but if you're nice I might defrost something.'

Actually, she did cook. Well, she made some pasta and defrosted some sauce and it was possibly their most normal night together. He ate a large bowl while Jasmine got things ready for the next day. Perhaps realising she wasn't ready to talk yet, he chatted a bit more about himself, telling her a bit about his siblings and their families.

'Don't you miss them?'

'A lot.'

'So how come you moved down here?'

'Just…' Jed shrugged. He knew he had to tell her, but there would be time for all that later—he wasn't here for himself tonight. He could see that she was still upset, see her hands shake a little as she folded some washing and then finally joined him.

'You got upset in Resus today.'

'I didn't.'

'Jasmine?'

'I just get annoyed when people don't check valuables properly,' she attempted. 'Everyone bangs on about how important it is and then if something goes missing…'

'People are busy.'

'I know that.'

'I heard you speaking to that paramedic,' Jed admitted, and he watched as she closed her eyes. 'Jasmine, did something happen at your old job?'

'No,' she broke in. 'Jed, please…' And then she started to cry. 'I found out that my husband was stealing from patients.' It was so awful to say it, to admit to it. She'd made it so huge in her mind that she half expected him to stand up and walk out, but of course he didn't. Instead, he took both her hands.

'Come on.' He was very kind and very firm but he wasn't going to leave it. 'Tell me what happened.'

'I don't know where to start,' she said. 'There was an unconscious patient apparently and there was a lot of money missing.' She knew she wasn't making much sense, so she just told him everything.

'Lloyd,' Jasmine said. 'Simon's father, he was a paramedic. We really got on, but then everyone did with Lloyd. He was very popular. We went out for about three months and—' she couldn't really look at that time properly '—I thought everything was fantastic at first,' she admitted. 'But I know now that it wasn't because I was being lied to even then. I didn't know but there had been a report put in about him.'

'You can't know if someone doesn't tell you,' Jed pointed out.

'I know that, but it wasn't just that he didn't tell me.' She took a deep breath, because if she was going to tell him some of it, then she had better tell him all. 'Remember I told you that I can't take the Pill?' She blushed as she had the first time she'd told him. 'Well, we were careless.' She went really red then, not with embarrassment, more with anger. 'Actually, no, we weren't. I know it takes two, but I think he was the one who was careless.'

'Jasmine.' Jed was completely honest. 'I nearly forgot our first time.'

'I know,' she admitted. 'But even if you had, I've got a coil now, so it wouldn't matter. It was more that I didn't forget.' She looked at Jed, she knew how they had lost it in bed together, but she never had till him. 'I reminded him, I tried to stop him. I don't know, I can't prove that, but there was an accident, and I found I was pregnant and not sure I wanted to be. I was just so confused and yet he was delighted. He insisted we get married and and then we took three months off to see Australia. As he said, to have loads of fun before the baby. I had lots of annual leave saved up.'

She couldn't even look at Jed as she went on. 'What Lloyd hadn't told me was that he was under investigation for stealing from a patient. It was all kept confidential so not even his colleagues knew, but another patient had come forward with a complaint and they'd placed Lloyd on three months' paid suspension. We were swanning around Australia and I had no idea.'

'When did he tell you?'

'He didn't,' Jasmine admitted. 'I went back to work. I was coming up for six months pregnant by then and he told me that he had another month off and then he started to talk about how, given I love my work, why didn't we think about him staying home to look after the baby? Every word that man said to me was a lie.' She could feel her anger rising as it did whenever she thought about him and wondered, as she often did, if he'd got her pregnant deliberately.

'So how did you find out?'

'The other paramedics were a bit cool with me,' Jasmine admitted. 'They're a pretty honourable lot, they don't take kindly to what Lloyd did and there was I, chatting with them like I used to, about our holiday, about things, and then one of my friends pulled me aside and said it might be better if I didn't rub things in.' She started to cry. 'She said it was fine if I could accept what he'd done, but it was a bit much for them to hear about us having fun with his suspension pay. He'd been fired by then and I didn't even know.'

'Oh, Jasmine.'

'He said that as his wife I should have supported him, but the fact is I wouldn't have married him had I known.' She looked at Jed. 'I wouldn't have. I'm not saying someone has to be perfect, I'm not saying you don't stick together through bad times, but I didn't even know that he was in the middle of bad times when we got married, when he made sure I was pregnant.' She was really crying now. 'I moved out and kept working right till the end of my pregnancy, but it was awful. I think my friends believed I had nothing to do with it, that I hadn't had a clue…'

'Of course they did.'

'No.' Jasmine shook her head. 'Not all of them—there was loads of gossip. It was just awful at the time.

'I see some of the paramedics now and we're starting to be friendly again,' she continued. 'I think they really do understand now that I simply didn't know. I'm just trying to get on with my life.'

'Do you speak to him at all?'

'Nothing,' Jasmine said. 'He came and saw Simon a couple of times when we were in the hospital, but there's been nothing since then. He's got a new girlfriend and so much for being a stay-home dad—he doesn't even have a thing to do with his son. He's working in the family business, they're all supporting him, as families do, and making sure it looks like he earns a dollar a week, so I don't get anything.'

'You can fight that.'

'I could, but I don't want to,' Jasmine said. 'I don't want any of his grubby money. I stayed close by for a year because, at the end of the day, I figured that he is Simon's dad and I should make it as easy for him as possible to have access to his son. But when he wanted nothing to do with him...' She was a little more honest than she'd expected to be. 'I was embarrassed to go back to work too. He just completely upended my life.'

And Jed got that, he got that so much, how one person could just walk into your life and shatter it, could make a normal world suddenly crazy, and he could have told her then, but Jed knew that now wasn't the time.

'And I'm the one left holding the baby.' She was the most honest she had been with another person. 'And I know if it hadn't happened then I wouldn't have Simon and I love him more than anything so I can't wish it had never happened, except sometimes I do.'

Of course she heard Simon crying then, just to ram home the guilt of her words.

'I need to go and settle him.'

'Sure.'

Simon didn't want settling, Simon wanted a drink and a play and a conversation.

'He's not going to settle.' She came back into the living room a good twenty minutes later.

'Do you want me to leave?'

'No,' Jasmine said. 'But I'm going to have to bring him in here.'

'Are you sure?' Jed checked.

'It's no big deal,' Jasmine said.

Except they both knew that it was. Jed hadn't seen Simon since that day on the beach when he'd helped get him into the water.

And Jed really didn't want to leave her.

Simon was delighted with the late night visitor, chatting away to him for as long as he could till his eyes were heavy and Jasmine put him back to bed.

'Cute,' Jed said. 'He looks like you—apart from the blond hair. Is his dad blond?'

'No,' Jasmine replied. Simon was a mini, male Penny.

'Have you told Lisa what happened?'

Jasmine shook her head.

'I think you might feel better if you did.' He was very practical. 'You did nothing wrong, but you know what rumours are like and it might be better to just tell Lisa up front what happened,' Jed said. 'And then you can stop worrying about it. If anyone does bring it up, Lisa will just blow them off.

'And...' he gave her a smile '...she might be a bit more understanding when patients land in the department with their life savings stuffed in a carrier bag.'

'I think I might,' Jasmine said. 'Thanks.' It was actually nice to have told someone and telling Lisa was a good idea.

'I'd better go,' Jed said. 'It's one thing having a friend over, but different me still being here in the morning. What are you on tomorrow?'

'I'm on a late,' Jasmine said. 'Ruby's picking Simon up from crèche.'

'How's that working out?'

'Good,' Jasmine admitted. 'She's really sensible and he seems to adore her. Simon's usually in bed by about seven so she gets her homework done.

'Stay if you like,' Jasmine said, 'I mean...'

'I know what you mean.' And he looked over at Jasmine and for the first time things were starting to get serious, and he didn't feel hemmed in. In fact, he wanted more of this and was sure that Jasmine was someone he could open up to about his past. She just didn't need it tonight. 'Are you sure?' Jed checked. 'He might wake up again.'

'He might.' Jasmine looked up at him. 'Look...' She didn't really know how to say it without sounding needy, but she had

Simon to think of so she had to be brave. 'I want to see more of you, Jed.' His eyes never left her face. 'I'm the same as you. I don't want this to carry over to work, which means that if we are going to see more of each other… I'm not asking for for ever, but if you're thinking this isn't working out then say so now.'

'I think it is working out.'

'And I'd like to see you a bit more than a couple of hours once a week.'

'Me, too.'

'Stay, then,' she said.

It was all a bit different having Simon in the house with them.

Like at midnight when they were kissing on the sofa, instead of things leading to wherever they might lead, she had to check on Simon, who was whimpering with his teeth. By the time she'd given him some medicine and rubbed some gel on his gums, Jed was sitting up in her bed, reading his horoscope in one of her trashy magazines.

Except he put it down as she started undressing.

'Don't,' Jasmine said, because he had an unfair advantage, well, two actually. He was already in bed and also with a body like his there was no need to be embarrassed about stripping off in front of another person.

'Why are you shy now?'

'I don't know.' She actually wasn't shy, she felt guilty for what she had said. 'Thanks,' she said as she slipped into bed. 'For hearing me out and what I said about wishing it had never happened.'

'I'd be the same,' Jed said, shuddering at the thought of how much worse things might have been for him—and he closed his eyes for a moment, imagining the last couple of years with a baby added to the mix. And he turned and he almost told her, but he could see her eyes were still swollen from crying and it simply wouldn't be fair to her.

'Imagine if he hadn't stolen the money,' Jed said. 'You could have spent your life married to a guy who was crap in bed.'

He saw the start of a smile.

'Go on,' he said. 'Say it.'

'No.' Jasmine kicked him. 'Anyway, you don't know that he was.'

'Please.' Jed rolled his eyes.

'So much for not getting involved with anyone from work.' He looked down at her before he kissed her. 'I think we should keep it separate, though,' Jed said. 'I really mean that.'

She was incredibly glad to hear it. 'I'm the same.'

'Things are a bit sensitive at the moment,' he said.

'With the promotion?' It was an entirely innocent question, or at least she'd thought it was, but Jed stopped kissing her and frowned.

'You've heard about that?'

'Sorry.' She tried to play for time.

'How did you hear about that?'

She was glad for the lights being off for another reason now. Her face was on fire in the dark from her slip-up.

'I don't know,' she attempted. 'You know what that place is like, there's always talk.'

'I guess.' He let out a long sigh. 'Oh, well, if it's out there's nothing I can do about it. At least I know no one heard it from me.'

He forgot about it then but it took a while for Jasmine to.

He kissed her till she almost had, she kissed him back till she nearly did, but it was there at the back of her mind, just how complicated things were and he didn't even know.

'Are you all right?' He lifted his head.

'Just tense.'

She almost told him, she nearly did.

Except she'd promised her sister that she wouldn't.

'I can fix that.'

And he slid beneath the sheets and she lay there biting her lip, thrashing with her thoughts as his tongue urged her to give in.

He was incredibly patient.

Didn't seem to mind a jot how long it took.

And she tried to relax to the probe of his tongue. To forget her problems, forget Penny and Lloyd and everything really except...

'Jed?'

He didn't answer.

'Jed?' She had to tell him, had to tell him now. 'Things are complicated.'

'Not from where I am,' Jed said, lifting his head just a little. 'You worry too much.'

Maybe she did, Jasmine realised, closing her eyes to the mastery of his mouth.

He gave her no room to think about it anyway. His hands lifted her buttocks so he could concentrate his efforts and he homed in, she pushed on his shoulders, because she should surely tell him, except he pushed back on the pressure she exerted and obliterated her thoughts with his tongue.

He was determined now, felt the shift in her, and it turned him on further. He loved feeling her unbend beneath him, loved the constant fight with her busy mind, and he would win this one and he felt her quiver as he worked on her most tender spot.

He felt her thighs start to tighten and the moans in her throat and he loved the wrestle within in her, loved how her hands moved from his shoulders and to his head, how her body begged him to continue while her mouth urged him to stop.

And then she gave in to him, shocked that he didn't stop there, that when he should surely abate he worked harder, and she throbbed into him and still his mouth cursed her restraint. Still his tongue told her there was more, and there was.

He rose over her in the dark, his hand moved to the bedside and it was hers that stopped him, stopped a man who, very kindly, never forgot.

'I told you,' she said. 'I've got the coil.'

And he smiled down at her as just once she said it. 'And, yes, as I've since found out—he was crap in bed.'

There was nothing to complicate or confuse right now, just the bliss of him sliding inside her, and for Jed he had never been closer to another, just lost himself in her. It was more than sex and they both knew it—it was the most intimate either had ever been. He thrust into her as he wanted to and she tightened her legs around him. He could hear the purr in her throat and feel the scratch of her nails on his back and she knew that, however they denied it, this was fast becoming serious.

And yet there were secrets between them.

For Jed there were no secrets, or there soon wouldn't be. He'd already made the decision to tell her, he just had to find the right time and tonight wasn't it. He felt her tighten around him, loved the intimacy and feeling her without the barrier of a sheath, loved the sob into his shoulder and the sudden demand within her that gave Jed permission to let go, which he did, but not fully. He lifted up on his arms and felt every beat of pleasure that shot out of him, he felt every flicker of hers, except he held back on the words that seemed most fitting right now.

He lay there afterwards and he should have been glad he hadn't said them. Neither of them were ready for love, but for Jed it was starting to feel like it.

And for Jasmine too, she felt as if they were on the edge of something, something that neither had seen, a place they had never intended to go. Except he was in bed beside her and it felt as if he should be, and she knew what to do now.

She wasn't waiting for the interviews, and Penny would just have to deal with it if it confused things.

Tomorrow, or at the very next opportunity, she would tell Penny.

Then she could be completely honest with Jed.

Then, Jasmine decided, there would be no holding back.

CHAPTER THIRTEEN

JED WAS GONE before Simon woke up, but her resolve was the same and once she'd given Simon his breakfast and got him dressed, Jasmine picked up the phone and rang Penny.

'What are you doing, ringing me at work?' Penny sounded irritated at the intrusion.

'It's the only chance I get to speak to you,' Jasmine said. 'Of course I can talk to you there if you prefer.'

'No, this is fine,' Penny sighed. 'What did you want?'

'I was hoping we could catch up away from work. There's something I'd like to talk about, something I need to check with you.'

'Fine,' Penny said.

'Tonight?' Jasmine asked.

'I'm going out tonight.' And she was working the next one. 'I'm going to Mum's on Sunday for dinner—how about then?'

Jasmine really didn't want to discuss this in front of their mother, but maybe they could go for a walk afterwards, or she could suggest that Penny go back to her place for a coffee?

'Sounds good.'

'So, when are you working again?' Penny asked.

'In a couple of hours' time.' Jasmine smiled. 'I promise to keep on ignoring you.'

As she dropped Simon off at crèche, Jasmine realised that things were starting to work out—she was starting to think that this was maybe doable and that nine-to-five job in the fracture clinic might not be necessary after all. Vanessa's mum was looking after Liam this evening, which meant that Ruby would pick Simon up from crèche and take him back to Jasmine's. Her babysitting arrangements were all under control, if a touch too expensive, but it was worth it to be doing a job she loved and for the first time since way before Simon's birth things were starting to look stable.

Well, not stable. Her heart leapt in her throat still at the sight of Jed and she was shaky with all the rush of a new romance, but the rest of her life seemed to be slotting together when just a few weeks ago it had seemed an impossible dream.

There was actually no chance to speak to Lisa about anything personal, or Jed, come to that. The department was incredibly busy and the late shift flew by, so much so that Jasmine blinked in surprise when Lisa caught her on the way up to the ward with a geriatric patient and lightly scolded her for not taking her breaks.

'I had no idea of the time,' Jasmine admitted, surprised to see it was already seven o'clock. 'I'll just take this one up to the ward.'

'Well, make sure that when you get back you take a break,' Lisa said. 'I don't care how busy the place is, I don't want my staff burning out.'

Lisa was always insistent that her staff take their allotted breaks, and often she would ring Admin and have a nurse sent down from the wards during particularly busy periods.

After handing her patient over, Jasmine realised she was actually hungry and stopped at the vending machine for chocolate to take to her break. 'It's crazy out there,' Vanessa greeted her when she got back to the staffroom. 'Did Lisa tell you off for not taking a break?'

'She did,' Jasmine said, slipping off her shoes. 'Maybe it's going to be a full moon tonight. I don't envy the night staff.'

'It will be your turn again soon.'

'I know,' Jasmine groaned.

'Did you speak to Ruby about staying over while you're on nights?'

'I did,' Jasmine said. 'She can do the first week. The problem is with the weekend on the second.'

'I can help you with that,' Vanessa said. 'If you can help out next month when it's my turn?' She gave Jasmine a nice smile. 'It all works out in the end.'

'I know,' Jasmine admitted. 'I think I've got to stop looking too far ahead and take things more day by day.'

'That's all you can do when you've got little ones.'

Right now, Jasmine was looking forward to it being nine o'clock so that she could go home. Jed got off duty at ten and had promised to bring food, which meant she had just enough time to chat with Ruby and then hopefully have a quick shower before Jed arrived.

Yes, she was starting to think that things might work out.

'Are you going to that?' Vanessa broke into her thoughts.

'Sorry?'

'It's the accident and emergency ball in a couple of weeks.' Vanessa pointed to the rather impressive poster up on the staff noticeboard. 'It's the big fundraiser for the department. Apparently there are still some spare tickets.'

Jasmine's eyes widened when she saw the price of the tickets and she wasn't surprised that there were still a few left.

'I doubt I'll be going.' Jasmine shook her head as she broke off some chocolate. Especially when she factored in the price of the new dress, hair, shoes and paying a babysitter. 'Are we expected to go?'

'Not really,' Vanessa said. 'It's really more for the bigwigs. Mind you, it will be a fun night—there's always loads of gossip whizzing around after an emergency do—we can have our fun with that afterwards, even if we can't be there.' Vanessa gave a mischievous smile. 'Still, it's a shame that we won't get to watch Jed and Penny studiously avoiding each other and trying to pretend that they're not together.'

Jasmine felt her blood run cold. She couldn't quite believe what she was hearing. 'Jed and Penny?'

'Didn't you know?' Vanessa was idly watching the television as she spoke and didn't see Jasmine's appalled expression and carried on chatting, blissfully unaware of the impact of her words. 'They've been on and off since Jed started here, not that they would ever admit to it, of course. Heaven forbid that Penny brings her personal life into work and be so reckless as to display human tendencies.' Vanessa's words dripped sarcasm. 'God knows what he sees in her.'

'Maybe he doesn't.' Jasmine was having great trouble speaking, let alone sounding normal. 'Maybe he doesn't see anything in her. It's probably just gossip—you know what this place can be like.'

'I wish,' Vanessa sighed. 'Jed is just gorgeous. He's wasted on that cold fish. But I'm afraid that this time the hospital grapevine is right—Greg walked in on them once and you can hardly miss the tension between them.' She turned and looked at Jasmine. 'I can't believe you haven't noticed. It's an open secret, everyone knows.' Vanessa stood up. 'Come on, we'd better get back out there.'

Except Jasmine couldn't move.

'I'll be along in a moment,' Jasmine said. 'I shan't be long.'

Her hand was clenched around the chocolate so tightly it had all melted, not that she noticed till Vanessa had gone and Jasmine stood up. She headed for the bathrooms—she didn't just feel sick, she actually thought she might vomit as she washed the mess off her hands. She held onto the sink and tried to drag in air and calm her racing thoughts before heading back out there.

Not once had it entered her head that Penny and Jed might be together.

Not one single time.

And Penny had never so much as hinted that she was seeing someone.

But, then, why would she?

Penny never told Jasmine what was going on in her life. Her engagement had ended and Penny had said nothing about it other than it was over. She certainly never invited discussion. Jasmine, in turn, had never confided in Penny. Even when her marriage had been on the rocks, Jasmine had dealt with it herself—telling her mum and Penny that it was over only when her decision had already been made.

She should have listened to Penny, Jasmine realised. She should never have worked in the same department as her sister.

Jasmine scooped water from the sink into her hand and drank it, tried to calm herself down. Somehow she had to get through the rest of her shift.

Jed was coming round tonight.

Jasmine spun in panic at the thought.

She would talk to him… And say what?

If there was anything between him and Penny she would just end it and move to the fracture clinic.

Or back to Melbourne Central, because that sounded quite a good option right now. And if that sounded a lot like running away from her problems, well, at that moment Jasmine truly didn't care. As much as she and Penny didn't get on very well, never in a million years would she do that her sister.

Except it would seem that she already had.

'You seem in a hurry to escape the place,' Penny commented.

'For once, yes,' Jed said. 'It's all yours.'

He had more on his mind tonight than a busy department.

Tonight he was going to tell Jasmine the truth about what had happened with Samantha.

It was an unfamiliar route Jed was considering taking and one he was not entirely comfortable with. He was way too used to keeping things in. He'd avoided anything serious since his last break-up. Sure, he'd had the occasional date, but as soon as it had started to be anything more than that, Jed had found himself backing away. And as if to prove him right, the texts and tears that had invariably followed had only strengthened his resolve not to get attached and to step away. Except for the first time he felt as if he could trust another person. After all, Jasmine had opened up to him.

Jed wasn't stepping away now.

Instead, he was stepping forward.

He rang ahead to his favourite restaurant and ordered a meal for two, but despite confidence in his decision there was more than a touch of nerves as he paid for his takeaway and headed back to the car, as he built himself up to do what he said had sworn he would never do—share what had happened, not just with someone he was starting to get close to…but with someone he was starting to get close to from work.

'Hi.'

Jasmine opened the door and let him in, still unsure what she should say, how best to broach it. Did she really want to know that he was with her sister? Did she really want Jed to find out the truth?

Surely it would better to end it neatly?

To get out before they got in too deep?

Except she was in too deep already.

'I bought Italian,' Jed said, moving in for a kiss, 'but to tell the truth I'm not actually that hungry.'

She'd meant to carry on normally, to sit down and discuss things like adults while they were eating, but as he moved in to kiss her, just the thought that he might have been with Penny had Jasmine move her head away.

'Jasmine?' She saw him frown, heard the question in his voice about her less-than-effusive greeting, but she didn't know how to answer him. Despite three hours trying to work out what she might say to him, how best to approach this, she still didn't know how and in the end settled for the first thing that came into her head.

'I'm not sure that you ought to be here.'

'Sorry?'

'I don't think this is working, Jed.'

'It would seem not.'

Of all the things he had been expecting tonight, this wasn't one of them. Sideswiped, Jed walked through to the lounge and put the takeaway down on her coffee table, completely taken aback by the change in Jasmine. They'd made love that morning, he'd left her smiling and happy, with no hint of what was to come. 'Can I ask what has changed between this morning and tonight?'

'I just think things have moved too fast.'

'And could you not have decided this before you introduced me to Simon?' He didn't get it and he knew she was lying when he saw her blush. 'What's going on, Jasmine?'

'I heard something at work today,' Jasmine admitted. 'Something about you.'

'So it's gospel, then?' was Jed's sarcastic response. 'And while you were listening to this gossip, did you not consider running it by me first, before deciding we that weren't working?'

'Of course I did,' Jasmine attempted. 'That's what I'm doing now.'

'Is it even worth asking?' Jed said. 'Because it sounds to me as if the jury is already in. So, what is it that I'm supposed to have done?'

'I heard…' Jasmine swallowed because it sounded so pathetic, especially with how good he had been with her secret last night, but still she had to find out for sure. 'I heard that you and Penny…'

'Penny?'

'Someone told me that you and Penny…' She couldn't even bring herself to say it, but the implication was clear and Jed stood there and shook his head.

'Jasmine, we agreed from the start that as erratic as things may be for us you and I wouldn't see anybody else so, no, I'm not seeing Penny.'

'But have you?' Jasmine asked. 'Have you dated Penny in the past?'

'What on earth…?' He just looked at her, looked at her as if he'd suddenly put glasses on and was seeing her for the first time and not particularly liking the view. 'I'm being dumped because the hospital grapevine states that I might be or in the past might have slept with a colleague?' He shook his head. 'I never took you for the jealous kind, Jasmine.'

'I just need to know.'

But Jed wasn't about to explain himself. 'Look, I don't need this.' He didn't confirm it and he didn't deny it and she honestly didn't know what to do. She could feel tears pouring down her cheek.

'Jed, please,' she said. 'Just tell me. I need to know if there's ever been anything between you and Penny.' She was starting to cry and she knew she had to tell him, no matter how awkward it made things for them, no matter the hurt to Penny, she just had to come right out and say it, and she was about to, except Jed didn't give her a chance.

'You want a complete itinerary of my past?' Jed said. 'What do you want, a full list of anyone I've ever dated so you can check them out online?'

'Jed, please,' Jasmine attempted, but he wasn't listening to her now.

'You're the one with the past, Jasmine. You're the one who's just had her divorce certificate stamped and has a baby sleeping in the bedroom and an ex who stole from patients. Did I ask for a written statement, did I ask for facts and details?' He turned to go and then changed his mind, but he didn't walk back to her. He picked up his takeaway and took it. 'I'm hungry all of a sudden.'

He headed out to his car and drove off, but only as far as the next street, and it was there that Jed pulled over and buried his head in his hands.

He couldn't believe it.

Could not believe the change in her—the second they'd started to get serious, the moment he'd actually thought this might work, he'd been greeted with a list of questions and accusations and for Jed it all felt terribly familiar.

After all, he'd been through it before.

CHAPTER FOURTEEN

THE WEEK HAD been awful.

Jed was back to being aloof, not just with her but with everyone, and on the occasions they had to work together he said as little as he could to her.

And now, when she'd rather be anywhere else, she sat at her mother's, eating Sunday lunch with Penny and wondering how on earth she could ever tell her and if it would simply be better if Penny never found out.

Which sounded to Jasmine an awful lot like lying.

'You wanted to talk to me.'

'I just wanted a chat,' Jasmine said. 'We haven't caught up lately.'

'Well, there's not really much to catch up on,' Penny said. 'It's just work, work, work.'

'It's your interview soon,' Louise reminded her.

'You haven't mentioned it to anyone?' Penny frowned at Jasmine. 'I told you about that in confidence. I shouldn't have said anything.'

'I haven't,' Jasmine said, but her face burnt as she lied.

'Well, I've heard that there are rumours going around, and if I find out that it's you...' Penny gave a tight shrug. 'Sorry, that was uncalled for. I just hate how gossip spreads in that place.'

'Are you going to the A and E ball?' Jasmine tried to change the subject, attempting to find out what she simply had to know.

Not that it would change anything between her and Jed.

Not just because of the possibility that he and Penny had once been an item, more the way he had been when they'd had a row. He hadn't given her a chance to explain, had just thrown everything she had confided to him back in her face and then walked out.

She didn't need someone like that in her life and certainly not in Simon's—still, she did want to know if the rumours were true, which was why she pushed on with Penny, dancing around the subject of the A and E ball in the hope it might lead to something more revealing.

'I've been asked to put in an appearance,' Penny said, helping herself to another piece of lamb. 'Why?' she asked. 'Are you thinking of going?'

'Not at that price,' Jasmine said. 'I just wondered if you were, that's all.'

'I have to, really. Jed and I will probably take it in turns— someone has to hold the fort and all the consultants will want to be there.'

'Jed?' Louise asked.

'The other senior reg,' Penny explained.

'The one who's going for the same position?' Louise checked, and Penny gave a curt nod.

'You and Jed…' The lovely moist lamb was like burnt toast in Jasmine's mouth and she swallowed it down with a long drink of water. 'Are you two…?' Her voice trailed off as Penny frowned. 'What?'

She should just ask her really, Jasmine reasoned. It was her sister after all—any normal sisters would have this conversation.

Except they weren't like normal sisters.

Still, Jasmine pushed on.

She simply had to know.

'Is there anything between you and Jed?'

'If you're hoping for some gossip, you won't get it from me. I don't feed the grapevine,' Penny said, mopping the last of her gravy from her plate. 'So, what did you want to talk about?'

And really the answer didn't matter.

She and Jed were over. If he had slept with Penny she just wanted to be as far away from them both as possible when the truth came out. 'I'm thinking of taking the job in the fracture clinic.'

Penny looked up.

'Why?'

'Because…' Jasmine shrugged '…it's not working, is it?'

'Actually, I thought it was,' Penny said. 'I was worried at first, thought you'd be rushing to my defence every five minutes or calling me out, but apart from that morning with the baby…' She thought for a moment before she spoke. 'Well, seeing you work, you'd have said the same to any doctor.' She gave her sister a brief smile. 'You don't have to leave on my account. So long as you can keep your mouth shut.'

Her mum had made trifle—a vast mango one with piles of cream—and normally Jasmine would have dived into it, but she'd lost her appetite of late and Penny ate like a bird at the best of times. Louise took one spoonful and then changed her mind.

'I must have eaten too fast,' Louise said. 'I've got terrible indigestion.'

'I'll put it back in the fridge,' Jasmine said, clearing the table.

'Take some home,' her mum suggested. 'I don't fancy it.' She smiled to Simon, who was the only one tucking in. 'He can have some for breakfast.'

'Jasmine.' Penny caught her as she was heading out of the front door. 'Look, I know I kicked up when I found out you were going to be working in Emergency.' Penny actually went a bit pink. 'I think that I went a bit far. I just didn't think we could keep things separate, but things seem to be working out fine.'

'What if you get the consultant's position?' Jasmine checked. 'Wouldn't that just make things more difficult?'

'Maybe,' Penny said. 'But I don't think it's fair that you have to change your career just because of me. You're good at what you do.'

It was the closest she had ever come to a compliment from her sister.

'Look,' Penny said, 'I do want to talk to you if that's okay—not here…not yet.' She closed her eyes. 'It's…' She blew out a breath. 'Look, you know how I bang on about work and keeping things separate? Well, maybe I've being a bit of a hypocrite.'

'Are you seeing someone?'

'It's a bit more complicated than that.' Penny shook her head. 'Let me just get the interview over with. I mustn't lose focus now.' She let out a wry laugh. 'Who knows, I might not even get the job and then there won't be a problem.'

'Sorry?' Jasmine didn't get it. 'I thought you were desperate to be a consultant.'

'Yes, well, maybe someone else might want the role more than I do,' Penny said. 'Forget I said anything. We'll catch up soon.'

And as Jasmine lay in bed that night, she was quite sure she knew what the problem was.

Penny was worried that if she got the position it might hurt Jed.

For the first time in a long time Penny was actually putting another person before herself. She actually cared about another person.

The same person her younger sister had been sleeping with.

Monday morning was busy—it always was, with patients left over from a busy weekend still waiting for beds to clear on the ward, and all the patients who had left things till the weekend had passed seemed to arrive on Emergency's doorstep all the worse for the wait. Jed didn't arrive in the department till eleven and was wearing a suit that was, for once, not crumpled. He was very clean-shaven and she knew he wasn't making any effort on her behalf, especially when Penny came back from a meeting in Admin and her always immaculately turned-out sister was looking just that touch more so.

Clearly it was interview day.

She had to leave.

It really was a no-brainer—she could hardly even bear to look at Penny. She made the mistake of telling Vanessa on their coffee break that she was going to apply for the fracture clinic job.

'You'd be bored senseless in the fracture clinic.' Vanessa laughed as they shifted trolleys to try to make space for a new patient that was being brought over. Unfortunately, though, Vanessa said it at a time when Lisa and Jed were moving a two-year-old who had had a febrile convulsion from a cubicle into Resus.

'I'd be glad of the peace,' Jasmine said, and she would be, she told herself, because she couldn't go on like this. It wasn't about the workload, more about having to face Jed and Penny every day and waiting for the bomb to drop when he found out that she and Penny were sisters.

She could not face her sister if she ever found out that she and Jed had been together, even if it had been over for ages.

But then she looked over and saw that Lisa and Jed were there and, more, that they must have heard her talking about the fracture clinic job.

She wasn't so much worried about Jed's reaction—no doubt he was privately relieved—but Lisa gave her a less-than-impressed look and inwardly Jasmine kicked herself.

'Sorry,' Vanessa winced. 'Me and my mouth.'

'It's my fault for saying anything,' Jasmine said, but there wasn't time to worry about it now. Instead, she took over from Lisa.

'Aiden Wilkins. His temp is forty point two,' Lisa said. 'He had a seizure while Jed was examining him. He's never had one before. He's already had rectal paracetamol.'

'Thanks.'

'He's seizing again.' Just as Lisa got to the Resus door, Aidan started to have another convulsion. Jed gave him some diazepam and told Jasmine to ring the paediatrician, which she did, but as she came off the phone Jed gave another order. 'Fast-page him now, also the anaesthetist.'

'Everything okay?' Penny stopped at the foot of the bed as Vanessa took the mum away because she was growing increasingly upset, understandably so.

'Prolonged seizure,' Jed said. 'He's just stopped, but I've just noticed a petechial rash on his abdomen.' Penny looked closely as Jed bought her up to speed. 'That wasn't there fifteen minutes ago when I first examined him.'

'Okay, let's get some penicillin into him,' Penny said, but Jed shook his head.

'I want to do a spinal. Jasmine, can you hold him?'

Speed really was of the essence. Aiden needed the antibiotics, but Jed needed to get some cultures so that the lab would be able to work out the best drugs to give the toddler in the coming days. Thankfully he was used to doing the delicate procedure and in no time had three vials of spinal fluid. Worryingly, Jed noted it was cloudy.

Jasmine wheeled over the crash trolley and started to pull up the drugs when, as so often happened in Resus, Penny was called away as the paramedics sped another patient in.

'Penny!' came Lisa's calm but urgent voice. 'Can I have a hand now, please?'

'Go,' Jed said. 'I've got this.'

The place just exploded then. The paediatrician and anaesthetist arrived just as an emergency page for a cardiac arrest for the new patient was put out.

'Jed!' Penny's voice was shrill from behind the curtain. 'Can I have a hand here?'

'I'm kind of busy now, Penny.' Jed stated the obvious and Lisa dashed out, seeing that Jed was working on the small toddler and picked up the phone. 'I'm fast-paging Mr Dean...' She called out to the anaesthetist, whose pager was trilling. 'We need you over here.'

'Call the second on.' Jed was very calm. 'He's stopped seizing, but I want him here just in case.'

'You call the second on,' Lisa uncharacteristically snapped and looked over at the anaesthetist. 'We need you in here now.'

It was incredibly busy. Jed took bloods and every cubicle in Resus seemed to be calling for a porter to rush bloods and gasses up to the lab. Jed was speaking with the paediatrician about transferring Aiden to the children's hospital and calling for the helicopter when Lisa came in to check things were okay.

'We're going to transfer him,' Jasmine explained.

'I'll sort that,' Lisa said. 'Jasmine, can you go on your break?'

'I'm fine,' Jasmine said. After all, the place was steaming.

'I don't want the breaks left till midday this time. Let's get the breaks started. I'm sending in Greg to take over from you.'

Jasmine loathed being stuck in the staffroom when she knew how busy things were out there, but Lisa was a stickler for breaks and really did look after her staff. That didn't stop her feeling guilty about sitting down and having a coffee when she knew the bedlam that was going on.

'There you are.' Lisa popped her head in at the same time her pager went off. 'I just need to answer this and then, Jasmine, I need a word with you—can you go into my office?'

Oh, God.

Jasmine felt sick. Lisa must have heard her say she was thinking of handing her notice in. She should never have said anything to Vanessa; she should have at least spoken to Lisa first.

Pouring her coffee down the sink, Jasmine was torn.

She didn't want to leave, except she felt she had to, and, she told herself, it would be easier all round, but she loved working in Emergency.

Would Lisa want a decision this morning? Surely this could wait.

She turned into the offices, ready for a brusque lecture or even a telling-off, ready for anything, except what she saw.

The registrar's office door was open and there was Penny.

Or rather there was Penny, with Jed's arms around her, oblivious that they had been seen.

He was holding her so tenderly, his arms wrapped tightly around her, both unaware that Jasmine was standing there. Blinded with tears, she headed for Lisa's office.

Her mind made up.

She had to leave.

CHAPTER FIFTEEN

'I'M SORRY!' LISA walked in just as Jasmine was blowing her nose and doing her best to stave off tears. 'I really tried to speak to you first before you found out.'

So Lisa knew too?

'How are you feeling?' Lisa asked gently. 'I know it's a huge shock, but things are a lot more stable now...' She paused as Jasmine frowned.

'Stable?'

'Critical, but stable,' Lisa said, and Jasmine felt her stomach turn, started to realise that she and Lisa were having two entirely separate conversations.

'I've no idea what you're talking about,' Jasmine admitted. 'Lisa, what am I here for?'

'You don't know?' Lisa checked. 'You seemed upset...just then, when I came in.'

'Because...' Because I just saw my sister in Jed's arms, Jasmine thought, and then she wasn't thinking anymore, she was panicking, this horrible internal panic that was building as she realised that something was terribly wrong, that maybe what she had seen with Penny and Jed hadn't been a passionate clinch after all. 'What's going on, Lisa?' Jasmine stood up, more in panic, ready to rush to the door.

'Sit down, Jasmine.' Lisa was firm.

'Is it Simon?' Her mind raced to the childcare centre. Had something happened and she hadn't been informed? Was he out there now, being worked on?

'Simon's fine,' Lisa said, and without stopping for breath, realising the panic that not knowing the situation was causing, she told Jasmine, 'Your mum's been brought into the department.'

Jasmine shook her head.

'She's very sick, Jasmine, but at the moment she's stable. She was brought in in full cardiac arrest.'

'When?' She stood to rush out there.

'Just hold on a minute, Jasmine. You need to be calm before you speak to your mum. We're stabilising her, but she needs to go up to the cath lab urgently and will most likely need a stent or bypass.'

'When?' Jasmine couldn't take it in. She'd only been gone twenty minutes, and then she remembered the patient being whizzed in, Lisa taking over and calling Mr Dean, Penny calling for Jed's assistance.

'Penny?' Her mind flew to her sister. 'Did Penny see her when she came in?'

'She had to work on your mum.' Lisa explained what had happened as gently as she could. 'Jed was caught up with the meningococcal child and I didn't want you finding out that way either—unfortunately, I needed you to be working.'

Jasmine nodded. That much she understood. The last thing she would have needed at that critical time in Resus was a doctor and a nurse breaking down before help had been summoned.

'And Penny told me to get you out of the way.' Jasmine looked up. 'She told me you were her younger sister and that you were not to find out the same way she had… She was amazing,' Lisa said. 'Once she got over the initial shock, she just…' Lisa gave a wide-eyed look of admiration. 'She worked on your mother the same way she would any patient—she gave her the very best of care. Your mum was in VF and she was defibrillated twice. By the time Mr Dean took over, your mum was back with us.'

'Oh, God,' Jasmine moaned and this time when she stood, nothing would have stopped her. It wasn't to her mother she raced but to next door, where Penny sat slumped in a chair. Jed was holding a drink of water for her. And to think she'd begrudged her sister that embrace. No wonder Jed had been holding her, and Jasmine rushed to do the same.

'I'm so sorry, Penny.'

She cuddled her sister, who just sat there, clearly still in shock. 'It must have been a nightmare.'

Penny nodded. 'I didn't want you to see her like that.'

She had always been in awe of Penny, always felt slightly less, but she looked at her sister through different eyes, saw the brave, strong woman she was, who had shielded the more sensitive one from their parents' rows, had always told her things would be okay.

That she'd deal with it.

And she had. Again.

'It's my fault,' Penny grimaced. 'Yesterday she was ever so quiet and she said she had indigestion. It must have been chest pain.'

'Penny.' Jasmine had been thinking the same, but hearing her sister say it made her realise there and then what a pointless route that was. 'I had indigestion yesterday. We all did. You know what Mum's Sunday dinners are like.'

'I know.'

Jasmine looked up at Jed. His face was pale and he gave her a very thin smile. 'I'm sorry to hear about your mum,' he said, and then he looked from Jasmine to Penny and then back again. 'I had no idea.'

'Well, how could you have?' Penny said, and then turned to Jasmine. 'Can you go and see Mum? I can't face it just yet, but one of us should be there.'

'Of course.'

'She'll be scared,' Penny warned. 'Not that she'll show it.'

'Come on,' Jed said. 'I'll take you round to her.'

Once they walked out of the door he asked what he had to. 'Jasmine, why didn't you say?'

'She'd made me promise not to.'

'But even so…'

'I can't think about that now, Jed.'

'Come on.' He put his arm round her and led her into her mum's room, and even if it was what he would do with any colleague, even if she no longer wanted him, she was glad to have him there strong and firm beside her as she saw her mum, the strongest, most independent person she knew, with possibly the exception of her elder sister, strapped to machines and looking very small and fragile under a white sheet.

'Hey, Mum.'

Jasmine took her hand.

'I'm sorry,' Louise said, but for once her voice was very weak and thin.

'It's hardly your fault. Don't be daft.'

'No.' She was impatient, despite the morphine, desperate to get everything in order before she went to surgery. 'I haven't been much support.'

'Mum!' Jasmine shook her head. 'You've been wonderful.'

'No.' She could see tears in her mum's eyes. 'Most grandmothers drop everything to help with their grandchildren.'

'Mum,' Jasmine interrupted. 'You can stop right there. I'm glad you're not like most mums, I'm glad Penny is the way that she is, because otherwise I'd be living at home even now. I'd be dumping everything onto you and not sorting my own stuff out, which I have,' Jasmine said firmly, and then wavered. 'Well, almost.' She smiled at her mum. 'And that's thanks to you. I don't want a mum who fixes everything. I want a mum who helps me fix myself.'

'Can I see Simon?' She felt her mum squeeze her hand. 'Or will I scare him?'

'I'll go now and get him.' Before she left, Jasmine looked at Jed.

'I'll stay.'

And it meant a lot that he was with her.

Oh, she knew Mr Dean was around and Vanessa was watching her mother like a hawk, but it wasn't just for medical reasons it helped to have Jed there.

She couldn't think of that now.

The childcare staff were wonderful when Jasmine told them what was going on. 'Bring him back when you're ready.'

'Thanks.'

Jasmine really didn't know if it would terrify Simon or how he'd react when he saw his nanny, but she knew that the calmer she was the better it would be for Simon. 'Nanny's tired,' Jasmine said as they walked back to the department. 'She's having a rest, so we'll go and give her a kiss.'

He seemed delighted at the prospect.

Especially when he saw Penny standing at the bed. Then he turned and saw Jed there and a smile lit up his face.

'Jed!'

He said it so clearly, there was absolutely no mistake, and Penny's eyes were wide for a second as she looked at Jed, who stood, and then back at Penny.

'I'll have to put in a complaint,' Penny said. 'The hospital grapevine is getting terribly slack.'

'Tell me about it,' Jed said, but whatever was going on, whatever questions needed answers, it was all put aside as Simon gave his nanny a kiss and a cuddle. He was amazing, not bothered at all by the tubes and machines, more fascinated by them, if anything, pointing to the cardiac monitor and turning as every drip bleeped. But of course after a few moments he grew restless.

'We're going to take your mum up to the catheter lab soon,' Vanessa said. The cardiac surgeon had spoken to them in more detail and her mum had signed the consent form, and it was all

too quick and too soon. Jasmine had just got used to the idea
that she was terribly ill and now there was surgery to face.

'Can I just take Simon back?'

'Of course.' And in the few weeks she'd been here, Jasmine
found out just how many friends she had made, just how well
she was actually doing, thanks to her mum. 'Tell the crèche that
I'll pick up Simon tonight. He can stay at my place.'

'You're sure?' Jasmine checked. 'I can ring Ruby.'

'It's fine tonight. You'll probably be needing Ruby a lot over
the next few days. Let me help when I can.'

The crèche was marvellous too and told Jasmine that she
could put Simon in full time for the next couple of weeks, and
somehow, *somehow* Jasmine knew she was coping with a family emergency and single motherhood and work combined.

And she didn't want to lose her job, no matter how hard it
would be, working alongside Jed.

Except she couldn't think about it now.

Right now, her heart was with her mum, who was being
wheeled out of Emergency, a brusque and efficient Penny beside her, telling the porter to go ahead and hold the lifts, snapping at Vanessa for not securing the IV pole properly, barking
at everyone and giving out orders as she did each and every
day, while still managing to hold her mum's hand as she did so.

And her heart wasn't just with her mum.

It was with her big sister too.

The time sitting in the Theatre waiting room brought them
possibly the closest they had ever been.

'Is that why you were asking about Jed and I?'

They were two hours into waiting for the surgery to finish,
an hour of panic, ringing around friends and family, and then
an hour of angst-filled silence, and then, because you could only
sit on a knife edge for so long, because sometimes you needed
distracting, Penny asked the question that was starting to filter
into both their minds.

'For all the good it did me.' Jasmine smiled. 'How come we don't gossip?'

'I never gossip,' Penny said. 'I don't do the girly thing and...' Her voice trailed off and she thought for a moment, realising perhaps how impossible for her sister this had been. 'You could have asked me, Jasmine.'

'What if I didn't like the answer?' Jasmine's eyes filled with tears and she couldn't start crying again. She'd shed more tears since her mother had gone to Theatre than she had in a long time.

'You're still not asking me.'

Jasmine shook her head, because if the truth were known she was scared to. Not just for what it would do to her but what the truth might mean for her sister.

'Nothing has ever happened between Jed and I.'

Jasmine felt as if a chest drain had been inserted, or what she imagined it must feel like, because it felt as if for the first time in days, for the first time since Vanessa had inadvertently dropped the bomb, her lungs expanded fully, the shallow breaths of guilt and fear replaced by a deep breath in.

'Nothing,' Penny said. 'Not a single kiss, I promise you.' And Jasmine could now breathe out. 'Who said that there was something going on between us?'

'It's common knowledge apparently, though I only heard this week. My friend couldn't believe that I hadn't notice the tension between you two.'

'The only tension between us,' Penny continued, 'is who might get the promotion.'

'I thought you were worried about getting it and upsetting Jed.'

Penny just laughed. 'Worrying about upsetting or upstaging Jed Devlin is the furthest thing from my mind—believe me. Do I look like someone who would step aside from a promotion for a man?' She actually laughed at the very thought.

'No,' Jasmine admitted. 'But you did say you weren't sure if you wanted the job...'

'Right now I'm not even thinking about work, I just want Mum to get well, that's as far as I can think today. You have nothing to worry about with Jed and I.'

'It doesn't matter.'

'It clearly did.'

But Jasmine shook her head. 'I'm just glad I haven't hurt you—Jed and I are finished.'

'Jasmine!'

But Jasmine was through worrying about Jed. She didn't have the head space to even think about him right now. 'Let's just worry about Mum for now, huh?'

'How is she?' Lisa asked when an extremely weary Jasmine made her way down to Emergency the next morning.

'She's had a really good night,' Jasmine said. 'They're going to get her out of bed for a little while this morning, can you believe?'

'They don't waste any time these days.' Lisa smiled. 'How are you?'

'Tired,' Jasmine admitted. 'I'm sorry to mess you around with the roster.'

'Well, you can hardly help what happened. Have you got time to go through it now—did you want the rest of the week off?'

Jasmine shook her head. 'I was actually hoping to come in to work tomorrow—Penny's going to stay with her today and I'll come back this evening, but I'd rather start back at work as soon as possible. I might need some time off when she comes out, though.'

'We'll sort something out,' Lisa said. 'We're very accommodating here, not like the fracture clinic.' Lisa winked.

'Sorry about that.'

'Don't worry about it for now. We'll have a chat when you're up to it.'

'Actually,' Jasmine said, 'do you have time for a chat now?'

She sat in Lisa's office and, because she'd got a lot of her crying out when she'd told Jed, Jasmine managed to tell Lisa what had happened with her ex-husband without too many tears, and was actually incredibly relieved when she had.

'You didn't need to tell me this,' Lisa said. 'But I'm very glad that you did. I'd rather hear it from you first and it's a good lesson to us all about being less careless with patients' property. I can see why you panicked now. Anyway…' she smiled, '…you can stop worrying about it now.'

Finally she could, and only then did Jasmine fully realise how much it had been eating at her, how much energy she had put towards worrying about it, running from it.

'Go home to bed,' Lisa said.

'I will. But I just need to have a quick word with Vanessa, if that's okay?'

Vanessa was one burning blush when they met. 'Simon's been fantastic. He's tucked up in the crèche now and I can have him again tonight if you like.'

'I'll be fine tonight.'

'Well, why don't I pick him when my shift's finished and bring him home to you?' Vanessa offered, and as Jasmine thanked her she suddenly cringed. 'Jasmine, I am so embarrassed.'

'Why?'

'All the terrible things I said about Penny. I could just die. I keep going over and over them and then I remember another awful thing I said.'

Jasmine laughed. 'Believe me, you weren't the only one, and you told me nothing about Penny that I didn't already know—Penny too, for that matter. It's fine, I promise.'

'Me and my mouth!' Vanessa grimaced.

'Forget it.' Jasmine smiled. 'Anyway, I'm going to go home to bed, and thank you so much for your help with Simon. I'm just going to pop in and give him a kiss.'

'Jasmine.' Just as he had on the first day they had met, Jed called her as she went to head out of the department. 'Can I have a word?'

'I'm really tired, Jed.'

'Five minutes.'

'Sure.'

'Somewhere private.'

They settled for one of the interview rooms.

'How is your mum?'

'Getting there.'

'How are you?'

'A lot better than yesterday,' Jasmine said. 'I'm really tired, though.'

'Of course.' He took a breath. 'You should have told me that you and Penny were sisters,' Jed said.

'You didn't exactly give me much chance.'

'Before that.'

'I was working up to it. But if we weren't serious there didn't seem any point.' She gave a tight shrug. 'I told you from the start I was trying to keep work and things separate—you were the same.' She turned to go. 'Anyway, it doesn't matter now.'

'We need to talk.'

'No,' Jasmine said. 'I don't think we do.'

'Nothing happened between Penny and I,' Jed said. 'Absolutely nothing. I can see now why you were upset, why you felt you couldn't ask.'

And now it was, Jasmine realised, time to face things properly, not make an excuse about being tired and scuttle off. 'It's actually not about whether or not you slept with Penny.' Jasmine swallowed. 'I mean, had you, of course it would have mattered.' He saw the hurt that burnt in her eyes as she looked up at him.

'You gave me no chance to explain,' Jasmine said. 'I was struggling—really struggling to tell you something, and you just talked over me, just decided I was too much hard work.

You didn't even answer my question. You just threw everything back in my face.'

She would not cry, she would not. 'It took guts to leave my marriage,' Jasmine said. 'But it just took common sense to end things with you. In any relationship there are arguments, Jed.' She looked right at him as she said it. 'And from the little I've witnessed, you don't fight fair!'

She saw him open his mouth to argue, but got in first.

'That's a no in my book.'

CHAPTER SIXTEEN

HE RANG AND Jasmine didn't answer.

And she stayed at her mum's, ringing and answering the phone to various aunts and uncles so even if he went over to her place, she wouldn't know and more to the point she wasn't there.

'Cold tea bags help,' Penny said when she dropped around that evening and saw her puffy eyes. 'You don't want him to see that you've been crying.'

'I could be crying because Mum's in ICU.'

'She's been moved to Coronary Care,' Penny said, 'so you don't have that excuse.'

'They've moved her already?'

'Yes. Great, isn't it? And you've got the night off from visiting. She was sound asleep when I left her. Still, if you want to go in I can watch Simon.' She must have seen Jasmine's blink of surprise. 'I *am* capable.'

'I'm sure you are.' Jasmine grinned. 'I might just pop in, if you're sure.'

'Of course.'

'He's asleep,' Jasmine said. 'You won't have to do anything.'

'I'm sure I'll cope if he wakes,' Penny said. 'And if you are going to see Mum then you need to put on some make-up.'

It didn't help much, not that her mum would have noticed.

She was, as Penny had said, asleep. Still, Jasmine felt better for seeing her, but that feeling faded about five minutes after visiting when she saw Jed coming out of X-Ray.

'Hi,' he said.

'Hi.'

'I tried to call,' Jed said, but Jasmine wasn't interested in talking.

'I need to get home.'

'Run off, then,' Jed said, and Jasmine halted for a second.

'Sorry?'

'You said you had to go.'

She opened her mouth to argue. Had he just accused her of running off? But instead of challenging him, she threw him a very disparaging look, and as she marched off, Jasmine knew she didn't need cold tea bags on her eyes—she was through crying.

Her mum was right—it was completely hereditary.

The Masters women had terrible taste in men!

Still, even if she would have liked to avoid him it was impossible at work. Everywhere she went she seemed to be landed with him, but she refused to let him get to her, refused to give him the satisfaction that she was running off.

But worse than the department being busy was the times it was quiet and though she had no idea who knew what, she nearly bit on her gums when Lisa gave her a very sweet smile.

'Could you give Jed a hand, please?' Lisa said, even though there were five other nurses sitting around. 'He's stitching a hand and she won't stay still on the trolley.'

'Her name's Ethel,' Lisa added. 'You'll get to know her soon, she's one of our regulars.'

'Sure.'

She painted on a smile and walked into Theatre.

'Hi, there, Ethel, I'm Jasmine.'

'Who?'

She was an angry old thing, fuelled on sherry and conspiracy theories, and she made Jasmine laugh.

'Why would they knock the hospital down?' Jasmine asked patiently, when Ethel told her the plans were already in and had been approved by the council.

'Prime real estate,' Ethel said. 'Imagine how many town-houses they could put up here.'

'Have you been talking to my mum?' Jasmine grinned.

'All money, isn't it?' Ethel grumbled for a while and then spoke about her children, who, from the age of Ethel, must be in their sixties at least. 'They're just waiting for me to go,' Ethel said bitterly. 'Worried I'm spending their inheritance.' She peered at Jasmine. 'Have you got children?' she asked.

'None,' Jasmine happily lied.

'Husband?'

'Nope.'

'Good for you,' Ethel said. 'Dating?'

'Nope.'

'Quite right, too.' Ethel said. 'They're no good, the lot of them.' And she ranted for a few minutes about her late husband. 'They're all liars and cheats and if they're not now then they're just waiting to be. Nasty, the lot of them—except for the lovely doctor here.'

She caught Jed's eye and they actually managed a slightly wry smile.

'No, we're all horrible, Ethel,' Jed said. 'You're quite right not to listen to their sorry excuses.'

And if he'd looked up then he'd have seen Jasmine poke her tongue out.

'How's your mum?' Jed asked, when Ethel gave in and started snoring.

'Doing well,' Jasmine said. 'She should be home on Monday.'

'How are you?'

'Good,' Jasmine said, and hopped off the stool. 'It looks like she's sleeping. Just call out if you need a hand.'

'Sure,' Jed said, and carried on stitching as Jasmine went to wash her hands.

She knew he was just trying to irritate her as he started humming, knew he was just trying to prove he was completely unbothered working alongside her.

And then she realised what he was humming.

A little song that was familiar, a little song about a little runaway, and when he looked up at her furious face he had the audacity to laugh.

'You'd better go,' Jed said. 'It sounds busy out there.'

There were maybe five patients it the department.

'Or do you need to pop up to visit your mum?'

He teased her with every excuse she had ever made over the last couple of days whenever he had tried to talk to her.

'Or is it time to pick up Simon?'

And then he got back to humming his song.

'I'm not avoiding you or running away.'

'Good,' Jed said. 'Then I'll be over about eight.'

'I don't want to argue.'

As soon as she opened the door to him, Jasmine said it. 'I don't want raised voices…'

'I didn't come here for that,' Jed said. 'And I wouldn't do that to Simon and I certainly wouldn't do that to you.' He saw her frown of confusion as she let him in. 'You are right, though—I didn't fight fair.' He said it the moment he was inside. 'And I'm not proud of that. I didn't give you a chance to explain. I didn't give us a chance.'

He took a seat. 'And I get it that there were things that you couldn't talk about easily. I've thought about it a lot and I can see how impossible it was for you—after all, if you and Penny had agreed not to tell anyone…' He looked up at her. 'You could have told me—I would never have let on.'

'Perhaps not,' Jasmine said, 'but when I thought you two

might have been seeing each other…' She looked at him. 'Penny insists nothing ever happened.'

'It didn't.'

'Apparently Greg walked in on you two once?' She wanted to believe her sister, but deep down she was still worried that it was Penny protecting her all over again.

'Greg walked in on us?' Jed gave a confused shake of his head, raked his fingers through his hair and pulled on it for a moment, then he gave a small smile as realisation hit. 'We had words once.'

'Words.'

'A lot of words. It was a couple of months ago,' Jed said, 'before you were around. In fact…' he frowned in recall, '…it was the same day as your interview. We had a busy afternoon and there was a multi-trauma that I was dealing with and Penny just marched in and tried to take over.'

'I can imagine.' Jasmine gave a tight smile.

'And then she questioned an investigation I was running—Mr Dean was there and I think she was trying to…' he shrugged, '…score points, I guess. I don't do that.' Jasmine knew already that he didn't. 'And I don't mind being questioned if it's merited, but, as I told Penny, she's never to question me like that in front of a patient again or try and take over unless she thinks I'm putting a patient at risk.' Jed looked up at her. 'Which I certainly wasn't and I told her that.'

'Oh!'

'And I asked her to explain her thought process, her rationale behind questioning me,' Jed said. 'Which Penny didn't take to too well.'

'She wouldn't.'

'Your sister's lousy at confrontation, too.' Jed smiled.

'I don't think so.'

'Oh, she is,' Jed assured her. 'She only likes confrontation when it's on her terms. You should remember that next time she starts.'

And Jasmine found she was smiling.

'Greg walked in on us, actually, we were in the IV room, and, yes, I guess he picked up something was going on, but it certainly wasn't that.'

'So why wouldn't you answer me that day?' Jasmine asked. 'Why couldn't you just say that there was nothing going on between the two of you?'

'Because I've spent the last two years convincing myself I'd be mad to get involved with anyone at work.'

'Especially a single mum?'

'You could come with ten kids,' Jed said. 'It was never about that.'

'Then why?'

'Jasmine, please.' He put up his hand. 'This is difficult.' And she knew then he had something to tell her, that she was as guilty as he'd been that night, because she was the one now not letting him speak.

'I left my last job, not because...' He really was struggling with it. 'I got involved with a colleague,' Jed said. 'And there's no big deal about that, or there wasn't then. She worked in the labs in research and, honestly, for a couple of months it was great.' He blew out a breath. 'Then she started talking about children...'

Jasmine opened her mouth and then closed it.

'I wasn't sure. I mean, it was early days, but it wasn't even on the agenda. I told her that. She got upset and that weekend I went out with some friends. I was supposed to go over to hers on the Sunday and I didn't, no excuse, I just was out and got called into work and I forgot.' Jasmine nodded. She completely got it—she forgot things all the time.

'She went *crazy*,' Jed said. And it wasn't so much what he said but the way that he said it, his eyes imploring her to understand that this was no idle statement he was making. 'I got home that night and she was sitting outside my flat and she went berserk—she said that I was lying to her, that I'd met someone else.' He took a long breath.

'She hit me,' Jed said. 'But we're not talking a slap. She scratched my face, bit my hand.' He looked at Jasmine. 'I'm six-foot-two, she's shorter than you and there was nothing I could do. I could have hit her back, but I wouldn't do that, though, looking back, I think that was exactly what she wanted me to do.'

'Did you report it?'

He shook his head. 'What? Walk into a police station and say I'd been beaten up? It was a few scratches.'

'Jed?'

'I thought that was it. Obviously, I told her that we were done. She rang and said sorry, said that she'd just lost her head, but I told her it was over and for a little while it seemed that it was, but then she started following me.'

'Stalking?'

Jed nodded. 'One evening I was talking to a friend in the car park, nothing in it, just talking. The next day I caught up with her in the canteen and she'd had her car keyed—there were scratches all down the side. I can't say for sure that it was Samantha...'

'What did you do?'

'Nothing for a bit,' Jed said. 'Then my flat got broken into and then the phone calls started. It was hell.'

He had never been more honest, had been so matter-of-fact about it when he'd discussed it with others, but he wasn't feeling matter-of-fact now, because for the first time he was properly reliving that time. The flat tyres he'd come out to, the phone ringing in the night, that he didn't even want to think of dating, not because he didn't want to but because of what she might do to any woman he went out with.

'It all went from bad to worse. In the end she just unravelled—she ended up being admitted to Psych and nearly lost her job.'

'It's not your fault.' She saw the doubt in his expression. 'Jed, the same way I wasn't responsible for what my ex did.'

'That doesn't stop you looking back,' Jed said. 'I go over and over the time we were together and maybe I did let her think I was more serious than I felt.'

'Oh, come on, Jed. She clearly had issues. If it hadn't been you it would have been the next guy.'

'But it *was* me,' Jed said. 'I had more than a year of it. She's getting help now, apparently, but I just couldn't stay around,' Jed admitted. 'I don't think it was helping either of us to work in the same hospital and in the end I didn't want to even be in the same city. That's why I moved.'

'That's awful.'

'It was,' Jed said. 'I wasn't scared for myself, I could stop her physically, but when she started messing with people I knew, that was enough. And,' Jed added, 'I was scared for her too. It was awful to see someone who was basically nice just going to pieces.' He managed his first smile since he'd arrived that evening. 'Do you believe me now when I say I had no intention of getting involved with anyone at work?'

'Yes.'

'And do you understand why, when you got so upset that I might have once dated Penny, I thought it was all just happening again? I mean, the second we got serious, and we did get serious, you know that we did…' He waited till she nodded. 'Well, the next night I come round and you're standing there, crying and begging to know if I've ever hooked up with Penny, if anything, *anything* had ever happened between us.'

'I get it.' Jasmine even managed to laugh. 'I'd have freaked too, if I were you.' She went over to him and he pulled her onto his knee. 'I promise not to stalk you when we break up.'

'Maybe we won't.'

'We'll see,' Jasmine said.

'I know that you wouldn't now, anyway. You handled the

break-up brilliantly,' Jed added. 'I mean, a couple of late night phone calls wouldn't have gone amiss—a few tears...'

Jasmine held her finger and thumb together. 'Just a smidge of obsession?'

'Careful what you wish for, huh?' Jed smiled back. 'I think I dreaded a break-up more than a relationship—and you...' He smiled at her. 'You just carried right on.'

'Not on the inside.'

She'd never admitted it to anyone, not just about Jed but about her fears and her thoughts and how more than anyone in the world she hated confrontation, hated rows, and that, yes, she had been running away. 'I've got to stop avoiding rows...'

'I think it's nice that you do.'

But Jasmine shook her head.

'You're a lot stronger than you think.'

She didn't feel very strong sometimes and she told him a little of how it felt to be related to two very strong women who were so accomplished in everything they did.

'Jasmine,' Jed asked. 'What do you want?'

'Meaning?'

'What do you want?'

She thought for a moment, about Simon safe and warm and sleeping in his cot and her job that she loved and her little home right on the beach and a relationship that looked like it might be working.

'What I've got,' Jasmine said.

'And you've worked for it,' Jed pointed out. 'You could have listened to your mum and sister and been some high-powered lawyer or doctor and hating every minute of it, or you could be working in the fracture clinic because the hours are better, but instead you've stood your ground and you do a job you love... And,' Jed added, 'despite a lousy relationship you've got an amazing son and your heart's back out there. I'd say you're pretty strong.'

And he was right. She had everything she wanted, even if

wasn't what her mother or sister might choose. She did, even if it was misguided at times, follow her heart.

'I do want a little bit more,' Jasmine said.

'What?' He moved in for a kiss.

'White walls,' Jasmine whispered. 'I'm on my fourth coat.'

And he looked at walls that were still green tinged and he started to laugh. 'Did you put on an undercoat?'

He saw her frown.

'Jasmine,' he groaned. 'I'll do it at the weekend. But for now...'

It was bliss to be kissed by him again, bliss to be back in his arms and to know there were no secrets between them now, nothing more to know.

Except...

'How did your interview go?' She wriggled out of his kiss—there was so much she had missed out on.

'Don't worry about that now.'

'But how did it go?'

'Very well,' Jed said. 'I should know tomorrow.'

'How did Penny go?'

'Just leave it, huh? Suffice it to say I'm quietly confident but I'll be fine if it doesn't come off.'

'Sure?'

'Sure.'

And then he got back to kissing her and this time she didn't halt him with questions. This time it was just about them, at least until Simon woke up. This time she didn't hesitate, and brought him straight through.

'Jed!' Simon smiled when he saw him.

'You outed us to Penny!' Jed grinned and then he looked at Jasmine. 'We need to go out.'

'I know,' she said. 'I'll speak to Ruby. I can't just...'

'I didn't mean it like that,' Jed said. 'I mean that we need to announce ourselves to the world before Simon does.'

'I think he already has,' Jasmine said. 'Can't you feel them all watching us?'

He just grinned and then he said what he was thinking and it was far nicer than having to censor every word and thought, so much better than having to hold back. 'Do you want to come to the A and E ball?'

'It's too soon.'

'Not for me,' Jed said. 'Though I will probably only be able to stay till ten, so you might be deposited home early, but I want people to know about us. It isn't too soon for me.'

'I meant…' Jasmine laughed '…that it's too soon for me to organise anything. The ball's tomorrow—and I'm working till four and I haven't got anything to wear.'

'You'll look lovely whatever you wear.'

'That's the most stupid thing I've ever heard…' Did he have not a clue as to how much went into getting ready for this sort of thing? Everyone who was going had the afternoon off and had been talking about dresses and shoes for weeks.

'I'm not going to argue with you.' Jed smiled. 'After all, I know how much you hate it. So I'm just going to tell you instead that we're going to the ball tomorrow and I expect you to be ready when I get here.'

CHAPTER SEVENTEEN

A BIT MORE notice would have been nice.

Lisa and Penny were bright orange, thanks to their spray tans, which they would shower off before their hairdresser appointments, Jasmine thought darkly, or after they'd picked up their thousand-dollar dresses from the dry cleaner's.

They were working on a head injury—their newly extended and painted nails hidden under plastic gloves. Penny wanted him admitted to ICU, except there weren't any beds at Peninsula, though they had been told there *might* be one available later on in the afternoon.

'Nope.' Penny shook her head. 'He'll have to be transferred.'

'Okay,' Lisa said. 'Do you want me to do a ring around?' She looked at Jasmine. 'You go and have your break.' As Jasmine opened her mouth to argue, Lisa overrode her. 'You might have to transfer him,' she pointed out, 'so go and have a break now.'

Jasmine didn't have time for a break.

Instead, she raced up to CCU. She was incredibly nervous about tonight and terribly aware of the lack of anything suitable in her wardrobe and she was determined to dash to the shops at lunchtime. She knew it might be her only chance to visit her mum but as she swept in to see her, Jasmine halted when she saw Jed standing there beside her bed.

'Hi, there.' Jasmine smiled, but it was a wary one, because Jed wasn't her mother's doctor. He hadn't even been involved in her admission. 'Is everything okay?'

'Everything's fine.' Louise smiled, but Jasmine was still cautious.

'Your mum's temperature was up a bit up this morning,' Jed explained. 'And Penny's stuck in with that head injury and insisted that I check things out…' He rolled his eyes. 'She's got a slight chest infection but they're onto it with antibiotics and your mum's physio has been increased.' He gave Louise a smile. 'Now that I've seen for myself that you'll live and have spoken to your doctor, I'd better get back down there and reassure your elder daughter.'

She hardly waited till he was out of the door and had she looked over her shoulder she would have seen Jed shake his head as Jasmine anxiously picked up her mother's charts and saw that her temperature had indeed been rather high but was on its way down.

'Jasmine.' Her mum was stern. 'I've got a chest infection.'

'I know.'

'It's not a big deal,' her mum said, and saw Jasmine's anxious eyes. 'Okay, it could be, but they're straight onto it. They've taken loads of bloods and they've got me up and walking and coughing on the hour. It's my own stupid fault,' Louise admitted. 'It hurt to take a deep breath and to cough and I didn't really listen when they said to increase my painkillers. I thought I was doing better by having less.'

'Mum.' Jasmine let out a frustrated sigh. 'You're so…'

'Stubborn.'

'I could think of a few other words,' Jasmine said. 'Why wouldn't you take the medication?'

'I just wanted to go home and I thought the sooner I got off the strong stuff the sooner they'd release me.'

'And because of that you'll probably be stuck here for another couple of days.'

'Well, we don't always do what's right for us, do we?' Louise admitted. 'But I am learning.' And to prove it she pushed her pain medication button and the little pump whirred into life. 'See?'

'I spoke with the insurance and the travel agent,' Jasmine said, 'and you shall have your cruise, but not for a few months.' She saw her mum rest back on the pillow. 'I brought in some brochures—you get to choose all over again.'

'That's such a relief,' Louise said. 'That means that I can help you out a bit more.'

'Mum, the only person you need to be concentrating on right now is you. I'm getting in the swing of things now. Vanessa and I are going to work out our nights and our late shifts, and we've got Ruby. I just needed you for the first few weeks.'

'And I made it hard to ask,' Louise said. 'I'm sorry.'

'Don't be sorry.'

'I am.'

'You gave me a push,' Jasmine said. 'I knew what I was going to get when I decided to come home—and you have helped. I couldn't have started back on shifts without you. But...' Jasmine took a deep breath, '... I'm not going to apply to work in the fracture clinic, I'm going to stay in Emergency. It's what I'm good at. And it might be a juggle, but...'

'You'll sort it.'

'I will,' Jasmine said, feeling far more positive.

'I don't remember much of my time in there, but...' she took her daughter's hand, '... I do know what was done for me and I've seen the nurses hard at it on ICU and in here. I'm proud of what you do, Jasmine, and I'm sorry I haven't been more supportive. I get it now.'

'Good.'

'And it breaks my heart what Penny had to go through, and I am so glad you were spared from that, but apart from that, I can't think of anyone I'd rather have looking after me than you. Don't let your career go.'

'I'm not going to.'

'No matter how easy it is to drop down to part time or—'

'Mum! I've got a one-year-old to support so dropping my hours down isn't even on the agenda. Not for the next seventeen years at least.'

'He seems nice.' Louise's head jerked to the door. 'Jed.'

'He is.'

'Penny said that you two have been seeing each other.'

'Mum!' Jasmine was firm. 'It's early days. Neither of us wants to rush into anything and there's Simon to think of. Still—' she couldn't help but share the news, '—I'm going to the A and E ball with him tonight.'

'What are you wearing?'

'I don't know yet.' Jasmine ignored her mother's horrified expression. 'I'm going to look at lunchtime.'

'In the village?'

Jasmine closed her eyes. There were about two clothes shops near enough to get to in her lunch break and, no, she didn't think they would have a massive selection of ballgowns to choose from.

'I'd lend you something, but...'

'I'm not borrowing something from my mum!'

'I've got very good taste,' Louise said, 'and a black dress is a black dress, but...' she ran an eye over Jasmine '...it wouldn't fit.'

'Just keep pushing that pain medication button, Mum.' Jasmine smiled. 'You might need it soon.'

'What about your wedding dress?'

'Please.'

'Well, it's not really a wedding dress, is it?' Louise pointed out. 'It would look lovely.'

'No.' Jasmine gave her mum a kiss. 'I have to get back.'

'Are you getting your hair done?'

'Yes!' Jasmine lied. 'Don't worry, I'm not going to let the side down.'

'I know. Can you drop by on your way?'

'Mum!' That was too cringy for words.

'Penny is.'

'Oh, Mum,' Jasmine said. 'I think I preferred the old you.'

'Tough.' Louise smiled. 'You've got a new mum now. Right, you have a lovely day and I'll look forward to seeing you this evening.'

Jasmine headed back down to Emergency and gave a brief nod to Penny, who was sitting at the nursing station writing up notes, and beside her was Jed.

'Have you seen Mum?'

Jasmine blinked in surprise. 'I've just been,' Jasmine said. 'She looks well.'

'What's her temp?'

'Down to thirty-seven point five.'

'Good.'

'Well, she's certainly changed her tune,' Jasmine said to Jed as Penny was called back into Resus. 'I'm actually being acknowledged.' She made sure no one was listening. 'Have you heard?'

'What?'

'Jed!' He was so annoying sometimes. 'About the job,' she mouthed.

'Not yet!' he mouthed back. And then she remembered something. 'This is too embarrassing for words, but on the way to the ball Mum wants me to pop in.'

'No problem.'

'For two minutes.'

'It's no big deal,' Jed assured her.

'For you maybe,' Jasmine grumbled. 'I think they bypassed the old mum when they did surgery.'

'Jasmine.' She heard a rather familiar call from Greg and, jumping off her seat, she dashed into Resus to see the head injury Penny had been working on looking significantly worse.

His arms were extending to painful stimuli and Penny was sedating him and getting ready to intubate.

Penny was marvellous, barking out her orders as always, but she actually called for Jed's help when the anaesthetist didn't arrive. Whatever way you looked at it, she was fantastic at her job, just a cow around the staff. That was to say, all the staff, so she didn't deliberately take it personally when Penny told her none too politely to hurry up as Jasmine loaded a syringe with propofol, an oily drug that was a bit slow to draw up. And she really was confident in her work. Penny's hands weren't even shaking as she intubated the patient, Jasmine noticed.

And then Lisa spoke and as Jasmine pulled up some more medication she noticed that her own hands were shaking.

'There's an ICU bed at Melbourne Central. The chopper is already out so I've called for MICA and a police escort.' She told the anaesthetist the same when he arrived and then she told Jasmine to prepare the patient and get herself ready.

'It will be fine,' Jed said just a little while later when Mark and his colleague arrived and transferred the patient to the stretcher. 'Jasmine, it will be.'

'I know.'

'No one's going to say anything.'

'And if they do?'

'They won't,' Jed said. 'But if they do, just tell them to mind their own business.'

He gave her shoulder a squeeze. 'If I don't see you before, I'll pick you up about six-thirty.'

Oh, God... Jasmine would have closed her eyes, except she had to move now, had to follow the stretcher into the ambulance. No, she wasn't going to be buying a dress this lunchtime, neither would she be sorting out her hair.

Instead she was going back to Melbourne Central.

With a police escort they practically flew down the freeway. The patient was stable throughout and Craig, the anaesthetist, was very calm, as were the paramedics. It was Jasmine whose heart was hammering as they approached the hospital she had loved and the place it had hurt so much to leave.

'Are you okay, Jasmine?' Mark asked, before they climbed out.

'Sure.'

'No one's going to eat you.'

'I know.'

Of course, it was a bit of an anticlimax. The hospital didn't suddenly stop just because she was back. In fact, she didn't recognise any of the staff on ICU as she handed the patient over.

The paramedics were going to be taking Jasmine and Craig back to Peninsula, but Mark wanted to take a break before the return journey.

'We'll just grab some lunch at the canteen,' Mark told her.

'I'll meet you back at the ambulance,' Jasmine told him. Tempting as it was to hide out in the canteen, Jasmine decided that she was tired of running away from things, tired of feeling guilty over mistakes that weren't even hers, so feeling nervous but brave she walked into Emergency.

'Hi.' She smiled at a face she didn't recognise. 'I was wondering—'

'Jasmine!' She never got to finish her sentence as Hannah, the charge nurse, came rushing over. 'Where have you been?'

'I moved back home.'

'You never even let us know you'd had your baby. Martha said that she heard it was a boy.'

And she was back and her friends were crowding around her, looking at pictures of Simon on her phone. Hearing their enthusiasm, she realised just how badly she had misjudged her friendships and she started crying.

'He was a bastard,' Hannah said when Jasmine told her why. 'Of course nobody thought you were involved.'

'Everybody was so weird around me.'

'We were embarrassed,' Martha said. 'Upset for you.' She gave Jasmine a hug. 'You're better off without him, you know.'

'Oh, God, do I know.'

'Does that mean you're coming back?' Hannah asked.

She thought for a moment, because she could come back and part of her wanted to come back except, Jasmine realised then, just as she had told Jed, she was very happy with what she had now.

'Maybe one day.' Jasmine smiled and then of course they asked if she was seeing anyone and she was through with covering things up and so she said yes.

'His name's Jed,' Jasmine said. 'Jed Devlin.'

'I know that name.' Hannah frowned. 'Where do I know that name from?'

'He came for an interview here,' Jasmine said.

'That's right.' Hannah nodded and then waved in direction of the door. 'I think your transport's ready.' Jasmine turned and there were the paramedics. 'Don't be a stranger,' Hannah warned. Then she laughed. 'Well, I guess you won't be now.'

Jasmine had no idea what Hannah meant, but she was on too much of a high to think about it, and then when she realised she still had nothing to wear tonight and she wasn't going to get to the shops, she was far too panicked to dwell on Hannah's words, especially when they hit traffic on the way home.

'Can't you put on the sirens?' Jasmine grumbled, but the paramedics just laughed. 'Some of us are going out tonight.'

CHAPTER EIGHTEEN

THANK GOD FOR heated rollers and quick-dry nail varnish, Jasmine thought as somehow she cobbled herself together, cringing as she pulled her old wedding dress on.

It didn't look remotely like a wedding dress.

It was a dark blue silk that her mother had said matched her eyes, and the strange thing was, as she looked in the mirror, she looked better in it than she had on the big day.

Then she had been sixteen weeks pregnant and bloated and miserable and not particularly sure that she wasn't making the biggest mistake of her life, and, no, she hadn't been particularly excited at the prospect of her wedding night.

Now she had curves and a smile and couldn't wait for the formalities to be over just to get Jed into bed!

'Wow,' Ruby said when she opened the door. 'You look gorgeous. I love the dress.'

'Thanks.' Jasmine smiled.

'Where did you get it?'

'I've had it for ages.' Jasmine blushed and mumbled something about a boutique in the city as she stuffed her bag with lipstick and keys. 'I don't think I'll be late back,' she told Ruby. 'Jed has to go into work and cover for Penny.'

'All you have to worry about is enjoying yourself,' Ruby said. 'He'll be fine.'

She knew that Simon would be fine.

It was two other people she was more worried about tonight.

Surely they wouldn't tell them about the job today, Jasmine reasoned. It was the A and E ball tonight so they would no doubt wait till next week to give the verdict.

Oh, God, Jasmine thought, putting in her earrings, she was torn.

Family first, she told herself, except she knew about the delays that had been caused in Jed's career. He was older than Penny and he wasn't where he thought he should be in his career.

And here he was at her door.

Her heart was hammering for different reasons when she first saw him in a tux.

'Wow.' Jed gave a whistle of appreciation. 'I told you you'd look lovely.'

'Wow to you too,' Jasmine said.

'I thought you said you had nothing to wear. Jasmine, you didn't go spending a fortune, did you?'

'No, no,' Jasmine said. 'I've had this for ages. I didn't know if it would fit!' Quickly she tried to change the subject. 'Have you heard about the job?'

'We'll talk about it later.' He sort of nodded his head in the direction of Ruby. 'We ought to go, especially if you want to drop in to see your mum.'

'I feel stupid walking through the hospital dressed like this.'

'It will be nice for her,' Jed said. 'And knowing that place, Penny will get called just as she gets into her dress and have to do something urgent and be swanning around Resus in pink satin.'

'I guess,' Jasmine said. 'Though I can't see her in pink satin.' Jed smiled, but she could tell he was a little on edge. Maybe he was having second thoughts about them being seen out together so soon and she told him so.

'You're being daft.'

It was worth going in just to see the smile on her mum's face.

'You look great.' Louise smiled. 'You both do.'

'I'm just going to go and ring the unit and check it's okay,' Jed said, and she knew it was because staff were a bit thin on the ground, but it also gave her a chance for a little bit longer with her mum.

'You look so much better.'

'I feel it,' Louise said. 'I told you your wedding dress would be perfect!'

'Shhh!' Jasmine warned. 'I don't want him knowing.'

'Now.' Louise was back to practical. 'Your sister's got something to tell you, some big news.' And her heart should have surged for Penny, except first it sank for Jed and then it surged back up because she was truly torn. 'It's big news and even if it's a bit hard to hear it, I think it's really important that you be pleased for her.'

'Of course I'll be pleased.'

'I know,' Louise said. 'I can't say anything, I don't want to spoil things for her, and I guess that it's her news to share, but just keep that smile fixed on.'

'I will.'

She gave her mum a kiss and then walked out to where Jed was just hanging up the phone.

'Let's get going.'

He was quiet on the car ride there and if he was just a touch tense, at least Jasmine knew why, but he took her hand and they walked in together and she knew that if he was being a bit quiet it had nothing to do with her.

'Hi, there!' Penny came over all smiles, and kissed Jed's cheek and then Jasmine's too.

'You look amazing,' Jasmine said, because Penny did. There was a glow in her cheeks and a smile that was just a little bit smug, and she didn't blame Jed when he excused himself to have a word with Mr Dean.

'Why are you wearing your wedding dress?' Penny asked the second he was out of earshot.

'Because I had about ten minutes' warning about tonight,' Jasmine said. 'And don't tell anyone.'

'Isn't that a bit twisted?' Penny wrinkled her nose. 'Doesn't that make you a bit of a saddo?'

'Stop it!' Jasmine said, but she started to laugh. Penny was such a cow at times, but she was also very funny.

'Any news?' Jasmine asked.

'Not here, Jasmine,' Penny warned.

'Oh, stop it,' Jasmine said. 'No one can read my lips. You got the job, didn't you? I know you did.' She looked at her sister. 'I thought we were going to be more honest from now on.'

'Jasmine,' Penny warned.

'Well, I'm thrilled for you.' She really was. 'Honestly.'

'Jasmine, will you please shut up?' Penny gave a sigh of irritation then beckoned her towards the ladies. Of course it was crowded, so they went outside and Penny waited till they were about twenty metres from anyone before she spoke,

'I did get offered the job,' Penny said, 'and before you jump up and down on the spot and get all emotional and then start worrying about Jed...'

Jasmine took a deep breath.

'I withdrew my application.'

Jasmine literally felt her jaw drop. 'Why would you do that?'

'Because,' Jasmine said, 'and I never thought I'd hear myself say this, but some things are more important in life.'

'Your career is...' Jasmine buttoned her lip but Penny just laughed.

'Exactly,' she said. 'There needs to be more. I've been a terrible aunt,' Penny said, 'and an appalling sister, because I've been so incredibly jealous of you. I always have been. And I guess I still am. I want what you have.' And she smiled as Jasmine frowned. 'Not Jed, you idiot. The other guy in your life.'

'A baby?'

'It seems Mr Dean was right. They train you up and what do you go and do…?'

'You're pregnant?'

'Not yet,' Penny said. 'But I'm hoping to be in the not-too-distant future, and from everything I've heard about IVF, well, I'm not going to be the sunniest person.'

'Penny!' Jasmine was stunned.

'I'm in my mid-thirties and I just…' Penny gave a tight shrug. 'At the moment I have about sixty-three minutes a week to devote to a relationship. There are not many men who would put up with that.'

'There might be.'

'Well, I want my baby,' Penny said. 'And I've thought long and hard and I'll work right up to the last minute and then—'

'But IVF?' Jasmine queried. 'Don't you just need a donor?'

'I tried for a baby with Vince.' Jasmine watched her sister's eyes, which were always so sharp, actually fill with tears. 'We had a few problems.' She looked at her sister. 'Or rather I had a few problems in that department. It meant IVF and Vince and I…' She swallowed her tears down. 'Well, I think we weren't really up to the challenge.'

'Is that why you broke up?'

'In part.'

'Why couldn't you talk to me?'

'I am now,' Penny said, and Jasmine realised what her mum had meant about some big news. But, no, she didn't need to be told to keep her smile on, she was genuinely thrilled for her sister. 'You have to give me my injections, though.'

'I can't wait to stick another needle in you.' Jasmine grinned and gave Penny a hug.

'And I'm not giving up my career,' Penny said. 'I'm just not complicating things for now. I have no idea how I'm going to work things out.'

'You will,' Jasmine said.

'I think I'll have to get a nanny.'

'We can share one.' Jasmine grinned.

'I want this,' Penny said. 'And I'm not waiting around for Mr Right. Anyway, I've seen both you and mum stuff up—we have terrible taste in men.'

'I guess.'

'Not this time, though.' Penny smiled. 'Mind you, don't you go telling him I got offered the job.'

'Penny! I'm sick of lying.'

'I mean it. If he has got the job and that's what he's all worked up about, the last thing he needs is to be told I turned it down. Just be all happy and celebrate when he gets the news.'

'Do you think he's got it?' Jasmine wasn't so sure— Jed seemed really tense.

'I'm pretty sure. There was an external applicant who was pretty impressive but I think Mr Dean wants to keep it in-house. He should hear any time soon.'

She had a terrible feeling that he already had.

Jed was lovely as they drove back from the ball a couple of hours later, but she could tell that he had something on his mind—it had stung when she had thought he had lost the job to Penny. She knew how his career had been sidetracked dealing with what he had, but losing it to an outsider would really hurt.

'Where are we going?'

Only then had she noticed they were driving to the city.

'Somewhere nice.'

'But you have to work.'

'Nope.' He grinned. 'Mr Dean arranged a locum, well, not really a locum—he's going to be working there in a few weeks so it's good if he gets a feel for the place.'

She looked over and tried to read his expression.

'Working there?'

'The new consultant.' He gave a small grimace.

'Oh, Jed.' She really didn't know what to say. 'I know it's hard for you…'

'Hard on me?' He turned and looked at Jasmine. 'It's hard on you, though Penny didn't look as upset as I thought she'd be,' Jed admitted. 'I thought she'd be savage.' He shook his head. 'She seemed fine.'

Jasmine looked out of the window to the bay. Penny had been right. Working in the same department was way too complicated. She could hardly tell Jed the real reason Penny was so delighted and she definitely didn't want to tell him that Penny had actually turned down the job.

They chatted about this and that but she could feel his tension and she was so irritated that they had told the applicants today of all days. Couldn't they just have enjoyed tonight?

'We can't stay out too long.' Jasmine glanced at her watch—half an hour really, if she was going to be back by midnight, though maybe she could stretch it till half past. It was hardly his fault. He just wanted to go out somewhere nice and wasn't used to factoring in a one-year-old and his babysitter.

'What are we doing here?' she asked as they pulled up at a very nice hotel.

'I told you I wanted to take you somewhere nice.'

'Just a drink at the bar, then.' She hoped he hadn't booked for dinner. He popped the boot and as Jasmine stepped out of the car, she frowned as he gave his name to park it and frowned even more at the sight of her rather tatty case being hauled out.

'Jed?'

'Ruby packed it,' Jed said. 'It's all sorted.'

'Oh.'

They went to check in. It was the nicest thing he could have done for her, but she felt terrible because surely he had been planning a celebration, or maybe he hadn't factored in that he'd know.

It was like holiday where it was raining and everyone was pretending it didn't matter, all grimly determined to enjoy themselves, and she would…she was. Jasmine was thrilled to have a night away with him, she just knew how hard this must be for him.

'Wow!' She stepped into the hotel room and tried not to notice the champagne and two glasses. Instead, she stared out at the view but Jed poured two glasses and it tasted fantastic and, yes, it was fantastic to be together.

'I am sorry about the job,' Jasmine said.

'Shhh,' he said. 'Let's just celebrate.'

'Cheers!'

'You don't know what we're celebrating,' Jed said.

'That we're here's good enough for me.'

'And me,' Jed said, and then he smiled. '"Oh, ye of little faith".'

She didn't understand. 'Sorry?'

He pulled back one of the curtains. 'Have a look over there. What do you see?' It was just a busy city. 'Over there.' He pointed to a tall building. 'That's where I'm going to be working. I got offered a consultant's position on Thursday, so I withdrew my application.'

'Oh!' She could have thumped him. 'You let me drive all that way thinking you were disappointed!'

'No,' Jed said. 'I knew that you *were* disappointed—it's awful for Penny. I really thought when I took the position at Melbourne Central that Penny was a certainty for the job. I think Mr Dean's really got it wrong. The new guy seems great by all accounts, but it's going to be tough on your sister.'

'No, you don't understand.' She opened her mouth, but again she couldn't say anything.

'What?'

Jasmine shook her head. 'Leave it.'

'I can't.'

'You can.'

'I can't.'

Jasmine was firm. 'She's my sister.'

She looked over to where he'd be working. 'I thought you were happy at Peninsula.'

'I've been incredibly happy,' Jed said. 'I applied to a few hospitals when I first thought of moving here and it was a close-run thing. I love big city hospitals but when Mr Dean hinted at a consultancy... Anyway, Central rang me last week and asked if I'd be interested in a more senior position than the one I interviewed for last year, and given the tension at work, given a lot of things, the choice was actually easy.'

'That's good,' Jasmine said, trying to mask the little edge of disappointment in her voice, that just when they were finding each other he was upping sticks, but, still, it was just an hour or so away.

'I like to keep work and home separate,' Jed said.

'I know that.'

'And I haven't been doing a very good job of it of late.'

He started to kiss her and then pulled his head back. 'You're sulking.'

'No.' She looked up at him and she was too scared to admit it, because he meant so much more than she dared reveal. They'd agreed they were going to take things slowly and, yes, they were back on track, but maybe once he got to a big hospital, maybe when things were more difficult, when Simon was sick and he was on call and it all became too hard to have a single mum as a girlfriend who lived a good hour away, maybe then things would go wrong for them.

'It's been a hell of a week.'

'And now it's over,' Jed said. 'Now you can enjoy being spoiled.' He gave her a smile. 'Come on, tell me, how come Penny's looking so pleased if she didn't get the job.'

Jasmine closed her eyes. 'Actually, come to think of it, it's a good job that you're going to Melbourne Central. I'm not breaking my sister's confidence.' She looked at him.

'Fair enough.'

'She's family.'

'I'm not arguing.' Jed grinned. 'I think you want to, though.'

'I don't.'

Jasmine didn't. She didn't want anything to spoil this night. 'So...' She forced her voice to be upbeat. 'When do you start?'

'Four weeks,' Jed said. 'It's going to be fantastic—it's a great hospital.'

'Good.'

'It's everything I want.'

He pulled her into his arms and he was smiling. She would not ruin this night, would not nit-pick, but how come he was so happy to be leaving? How come he had been so tense all night? Though he wasn't tense now, he was *delighted* with his good news, thrilled to be moving an hour away, and she swallowed down her tears.

'I can't wait to start,' Jed said. 'And tomorrow I thought I might go and look for somewhere to live.'

Some bachelor city apartment, Jasmine thought bitterly, but she kept her smile there.

'The staff there seem really friendly,' he added.

She thought of Hannah, who was gorgeous and flirted like crazy, and Martha, and the wild parties they often had, and he would be there and she would be home with Simon.

'And I can't wait...'

'Okay.' Her lips were taut with smiling. 'I'm thrilled for you.'

She reached for her glass as she did not want to argue; she took a sip of champagne and swallowed down a row, but it was fizzing. Yes, she was happy for him, yes, she was thrilled, but... 'Do you have to keep rubbing it in?'

She didn't get why he was smiling.

'Sorry?'

'Do you have to keep telling me how *thrilled* you are to be leaving, how fantastic it is to be moving away?'

'Come on, Jasmine.' He grinned. 'Don't spoil tonight with a row.'

'I want one!' She did. For the first time in her life she wanted her row and stuff it if it was an expensive one. So what if she

was spoiling a wonderful night? Did he have to be quite so insensitive?

'Go for it.'

'I will,' Jasmine said. 'I'm thrilled for you. I really am, but
do you have to keep going on about it?' She just said it. 'Do
you have to keep telling me how delighted you are to be going
away and all the parties...'

'I never said anything about parties.'

'Oh, but there will be.'

And he just grinned.

'And I'll be home with Simon and you'll be an hour away
and, yes, I am happy for you and, no, I didn't expect you to take
Simon and me into consideration, but I can't keep grinning like
an idiot when the fact is you're moving away.' She started to
cry. 'And I don't understand why you're laughing.'

'Because I love how you row.'

And he pulled her into him. 'I've been goading you.'

'Why?'

'Because.'

'Because what?'

'I want just a smidge of obsession.'

'Well, you've got it.' And he kissed her and it was lovely.
She'd said what she thought, had had a good row and no one was
any the worse for it. Then he stopped kissing her and looked at
her for a very long time.

'I am pleased for you. I honestly am. I know you'll love it
there.' And she realised then what Hannah had meant when
she'd said that she'd see her around. If she was going out with
Jed she'd be with him at times. 'I'm just sad you're leaving,
that's all.'

'I have to,' Jed said. 'Because I'm not working alongside a
woman who turned down my proposal.' And he took out a box
containing a ring but she didn't even look at it properly, just
looked straight back at him. 'And if she doesn't turn it down
then I'm working in the same department as my wife and sister-

in-law. That would be way too complicated and I already have trouble enough concentrating on work when you're around. So which one is it?'

'The complicated one,' Jasmine said, and watched as he put a ring on her finger.

'It won't be complicated for long,' he assured her. 'I'm taking time off before I start my new job and for the next few weeks I'm going to take some time to get to know that son of yours and you're going to get to know me properly. We'll go to Sydney and meet my family. We'll just take some time. I don't want you to feel you're being rushed into anything again. We'll wait as long as it takes for you to feel okay with it.'

'I already am.' She had never been more sure of anything in her life. 'And I don't feel as if I'm rushing into things this time. I know.'

'I know too,' Jed said. 'And you're coming to look for somewhere to live with me. Midway, maybe? Or we can just carry on as we are and I'll sort out the travel, but I promise you that you and Simon will always be my first consideration.'

She believed him, she really did, and her heart filled not just for her own happiness but because her son was going to have such an amazing man to help raise him, for all the happy times to come.

'Mum's going to have another heart attack when she finds out.'

'She already knows,' Jed said. 'What, do you think I'd ask you to marry me without asking for her permission?'

'You asked her?' So that was what her mum had been banging on about not dropping her hours or losing her career—she already knew.

'Of course I asked her.'

'You're an old-fashioned thing, aren't you?'

'Yep,' Jed said. 'But I'm filthy-minded too. I want to do you in your wedding dress.'

She blinked.

'I'm sure you will.'

'I mean this one.'

She just about died of embarrassment, right there on the spot. 'You knew?'

'Your mum told me.' He smiled, and then pulled her back into his arms. 'And now, seeing as I'm almost family, you can tell me what's going on with Penny.' She started to, but he stopped her.

'Not yet.' He was kissing her face, kissing her mouth, and making her feel wanted and beautiful in her wedding dress for the very first time, as he told her just how much the future was theirs. 'We've got ages.'

* * * * *

The Billionaire
Of Coral Bay
Nikki Logan

Nikki Logan lives on the edge of a string of wetlands in Western Australia with her partner and a menagerie of animals. She writes captivating nature-based stories full of romance in descriptive natural environments. She believes the danger and richness of wild places perfectly mirror the passion and risk of falling in love. Nikki loves to hear from readers via nikkilogan.com.au or through social media. Find her on Twitter, @ReadNikkiLogan, and Facebook, NikkiLoganAuthor.

Books by Nikki Logan

Harlequin Romance

The Larkville Legacy

Slow Dance with the Sheriff

Their Miracle Twins
Mr Right at the Wrong Time
Once a Rebel...
His Until Midnight
Awakened by His Touch
Her Knight in the Outback
Bodyguard...to Bridegroom?
Stranded with Her Rescuer

Harlequin KISS

How to Get Over Your Ex
My Boyfriend and Other Enemies
The Morning After the Night Before

Visit the Author Profile page
at millsandboon.com.au for more titles.

Dear Reader,

Say "Australia" and "reef" and minds naturally turn to the Great Barrier Reef a few kilometers off tropical Queensland. But there is another Australian reef system that gives the famous tourist spot a serious run for its money—Ningaloo Marine Park, a spectacular shore-hugging fringing reef out in the middle of a whole lot of nowhere in outback Western Australia. It is a heart-stopping mix: step off scorched red earth into the electric blue waters of tidal lagoons, and a moment later you're floating over a thriving, bustling underwater ecosystem rippling with life. As soon as I saw it, I knew I'd be setting a book amid the stoic corals, the vivid little fish and the gargantuan whale sharks.

Mila Nakano is a unique heroine—part Japanese, part Irish, part Saltwater People. It meant she never really identified as one or the other. It meant she never really *fit*. Add to that a medical condition that makes her experience things differently from everyone else and it's really no surprise that Mila doesn't feel like she belongs anywhere.

Except on her reef...where every day brings someone new who wants to monetize one of nature's most spectacular natural wonders. Who wants to threaten the world she loves.

Welcome to Coral Bay, Western Australia. I hope you enjoy your week there as much as I did.

May love always find you,

Nikki

For Pete

Who came when I needed him most.

CHAPTER ONE

THE LUXURY CATAMARAN had first appeared two days ago, bobbing in the sea off Nancy's Point.

Lurking.

Except Mila Nakano couldn't, in all fairness, call it lurking since it stood out like a flashing white beacon against the otherwise empty blue expanse of ocean. Whatever its crew were doing out there, they weren't trying to be secretive about it, which probably meant they had permission to be moored on the outer fringes of the reef. And a vessel with all the appropriate authorisation was no business of a Wildlife Officer with somewhere else to be.

Vessels came and went daily on the edge of the Marine Park off Coral Bay—mostly research boats, often charters and occasionally private yachts there to enjoy the World Heritage reefs. This one had 'private' written all over it. If she had the kind of money that bought luxury catamarans she'd probably spend it visiting places of wonder too.

Mila peeled her wetsuit down to its waist and let her eyes flutter shut as the coastal air against her sweat-damp skin tinkled like tiny, bouncing ball bearings. Most days, she liked to snorkel in just a bikini to revel in the symphony of water against her bare flesh. Some days, though, she just needed to get things done and a wetsuit was as good as noise-cancelling headphones to someone with synaesthesia—or 'superpower' as her brothers had always referred to her cross-sensed condition—because she couldn't *hear* the physical sensation of swimming over the reef when it was muted by thick neoprene. Not that her condition was conveniently limited to just the single jumbled sensation; no, that would be too pedestrian for Mila Nakano. She *felt* colours. She *tasted* emotion. And she attributed random personality traits to things. It might make no sense to anyone else but it made total sense to her.

Of course it did; she'd been born that way.

But today she could do without the distraction. Her tour-for-one was due any minute and she still needed to cross the rest of the bay and clamber up to Nancy's Point to meet him, because she'd drifted further than she meant while snorkelling the reef. A tour-for-one was the perfect number. *One* made it possible for her to do her job without ending up with a thumping headache—complete with harmonic foghorns. With larger groups, she couldn't control how shouty their body spray was, what mood the colours they wore would leave her in, or how exhausting they were just to be around. They would have a fantastic time out on the reef, but the cost to her was sometimes too great. It could take her three days to rebalance after a big group.

But one… That was doable.

Her *one* was a Mr Richard Grundy. Up from Perth, the solitary, sprawling metropolis on Australia's west coast, tucked away in the bottom corner of the state, two days' drive—or a two-hour jet flight—from here. From *anything*, some visitors thought because they couldn't see what was right in front of them. The vast expanses of outback scrub you had to pass through to get here.

The nothing that was always full of something.

Grundy was a businessman, probably, since *ones* tended to arrive in suits with grand plans for the reef and what they could make it into. Anything from clusters of glamping facilities to elite floating casinos. Luxury theme parks. They never got off the ground, of course; between the public protests, the strict land use conditions and the flat-out *no* that the local leaseholder gave on development access through their property, her tour-for-one usually ended up being a tour-*of*-one. She never saw them, their business suit or their fancy development ideas again.

Which was fine; she was happy to play her part in keeping everything around here exactly as it was.

Mila shed the rest of her wetsuit unselfconsciously, stretched to the heavens for a moment as the ball bearings tinkled around her bikini-clad skin and slipped into the khaki shorts and shirt that identified her as official staff of the World Heritage Area. The backpack sitting on the sand bulged first with the folded wetsuit and then with bundled snorkelling gear, and she pulled her dripping hair back into a ponytail. She dropped the backpack into her work-supplied four-wheel drive then jogged past it and up towards the point overlooking the long, brilliant bay.

She didn't rush. *Ones* were almost always late; they underestimated the time it took to drive up from the city or down from the nearest airport, or they let some smartphone app decide how long it would take them when a bit of software could have no idea how much further a kilometre was in Western Australia's north. Besides, she'd parked on the only road into the meeting point and so her *one* would have had to drive past her to get to Nancy's Point. So far, hers was the only vehicle as far as the eye could see.

If you didn't count the bobbing catamaran beyond the reef.

Strong legs pushed her up over the lip of the massive limestone spur named after Nancy Dawson—the matriarch of the family that had grazed livestock on these lands for generations. Coral Bay's first family.

'Long way to come for a strip-show,' a deep voice rumbled as she straightened.

Mila stumbled to a halt, her stomach sinking on a defensive whiff of old shoe that was more back-of-her-throat *taste* than nose-scrunching *smell*. The man standing there was younger than his name suggested and he wasn't in a suit, like most *ones*, but he wore cargo pants and a faded red T-shirt as if they were one. Something about the way he moved towards her... He still screamed 'corporate' even without a tie.

Richard Grundy.

She spun around, hunting for the vehicle that she'd inexplicably missed. Nothing. It only confounded her more. The muted red of his T-shirt was pumping off all kinds of favourite drunk uncle kind of associations, but she fought the instinctive softening that brought. Nothing about his sarcastic greeting deserved congeniality. Besides, this man was anything but uncle-esque. His dark blond hair was windblown but well-cut and his eyes, as he slid his impenetrable sunglasses up onto his head to reveal them, were a rich blue. Rather like the lagoon behind him, in fact.

That got him a reluctant bonus point.

'You were early,' she puffed.

'I was on time,' he said again, apparently amused at her discomfort. 'And I was dropped off. Just in time for the show.'

She retracted that bonus point. This was *her* bay, not his. If she wanted to swim in it before her shift started, what business was it of his?

'I could have greeted you in my wetsuit,' she muttered, 'but I figured my uniform would be more appropriate.'

'You're the guide, I assume?' he said, approaching with an out-thrust hand.

'I'm *a* guide,' she said, still bristling, then extended hers on a deep breath. Taking someone's hand was never straightforward; she never knew quite what she'd get out of it. 'Mila Nakano. Parks Department.'

'Richard Grundy,' he replied, marching straight into her grasp with no further greeting. Or interest. 'What's the plan for today?'

The muscles around her belly button twittered at his warm

grip on her water-cool fingers and her ears filled with the gentle brush of a harp. That was new; she usually got anything from a solo trumpet to a whole brass section when she touched people, especially strangers.

A harp thrum was incongruously pleasant.

'Today?' she parroted, her synapses temporarily disconnected.

'Our tour.' His lagoon-coloured eyes narrowed in on hers. '*Are* you my guide?'

She quickly recovered. 'Yes, I am. But no one gave me any information on the purpose of your visit—' except to impress upon her his VIP status '—so we'll be playing it a bit by ear today. It would help me to know what you're here for,' she went on. 'Or what things interest you.'

'It all interests me,' he said, glancing away. 'I'd like to get a better appreciation for the…ecological value of the area.'

Uh-huh. Didn't they all…? Then they went back to the city to work on ways to exploit it.

'Is your interest commercial?'

The twin lagoons narrowed. 'Why so much interest in my interest?'

His censure made her flush. 'I'm just wondering what filter to put on the tour. Are you a journalist? A scientist? You don't seem like a tourist. So that only leaves Corporate.'

He glanced out at the horizon again, taking some of the intensity from their conversation. 'Let's just say I have a keen interest in the land. And the fringing reef.'

That wasn't much to go on. But those ramrod shoulders told her it was all she was going to get.

'Well, then, I guess we should start at the southernmost tip of the Marine Park,' she said, 'and work our way north. Can you swim?'

One of his eyebrows lifted. Just the one, as if her question wasn't worth the effort of a second. 'Captain of the swim team.'

Of course he had been.

Ordinarily she would have pushed her sunglasses up onto her head too, to meet a client's gaze, to start the arduous climb from *stranger* to *acquaintance*. But there was a sardonic heat coming off Richard Grundy's otherwise cool eyes and it shimmered such a curious tone—like five sounds all at once, harmonising with each other, being five different things at once. It wiggled in under her synaesthesia and tingled there, but she wasn't about to expose herself too fully to his music until she had a better handle on the man. And so her own sunglasses stayed put.

'If you want to hear the reef you'll need to get out onto it.'

'Hear it?' The eyebrow lift was back. 'Is it particularly noisy?'

She smiled. She'd yet to meet anyone else who could perceive the coral's voice but she had to assume that however normal people experienced it, it was as rich and beautiful as the way she did.

'You'll understand when you get there. Your vehicle or mine?'

But he didn't laugh—he didn't even smile—and her flimsy joke fell as flat as she inexplicably felt robbed of the opportunity to see his lips crack the straight line they'd maintained since she got up here.

'Yours, I think,' he said.

'Let's go, then.' She fell into professional mode, making up for a lot of lost time. 'I'll tell you about Nancy's Point as we walk. It's named for Nancy Dawson…'

Rich was pretty sure he knew all there was to know about Nancy Dawson—after all, stories of his great-grandmother had been part of his upbringing. But the tales as they were told to him didn't focus on Nancy's great love for the land and visionary sustainability measures, as the guide's did, they were designed to showcase her endurance and fortitude against adversity. *Those* were the values his father had wanted to foster in his son and heir. The land—except for the profit it might make for West-Corp—was secondary. Barely even that.

But there was no way to head off the lithe young woman's spiel without confessing who his family was. And he wasn't about to discuss his private business with a stranger on two minutes' acquaintance.

'For one hundred and fifty years the Dawsons have been the leaseholders of all the land as far as you can see to the horizon,' she said, turning to put the ocean behind her and looking east. 'You could drive two hours inland and still be on Wardoo Station.'

'Big,' he grunted. Because anyone else would say that. Truth was, he knew exactly how big Wardoo was—to the square kilometre—and he knew how much each of those ten thousand square kilometres yielded. And how much each one cost to operate.

That was kind of his thing.

Rich cast his eyes out to the reef break. Mila apparently knew enough history to speak about his family, but not enough to recognise his surname for what it was. Great-Grandma Dawson had married Wardoo's leading hand, Jack Grundy, but kept the family name since it was such an established and respected name in the region. The world might have known Jack and Nancy's offspring as Dawsons, but the law knew them as Grundys.

'Nancy's descendants still run it today. Well, their minions do...'

That drew his gaze back. 'Minions?'

'The family is based in the city now. We don't see them.'

Wow. There was a whole world of judgement in that simple sentence.

'Running a business remotely is pretty standard procedure these days,' he pointed out.

In his world everything was run at a distance. In a state this big it was both an operational necessity and a survival imperative. If you got attached to any business—or any of the people in it—you couldn't do what he sometimes had to do. Restructure them. Sell them. Close them.

She surveyed all around them and murmured, 'If this was my land I would never ever leave it.'

It was tempting to take offence at her casual judgement of his family—was this how she spoke of the Dawsons to any passing stranger?—but he'd managed too many teams and too many board meetings with voices far more objectionable than hers to let himself be that reactive. Besides, given that his 'family' consisted of exactly one—if you didn't count a bunch of headstones and some distant cousins in Europe—he really had little cause for complaint.

'You were born here?' he asked instead.

'And raised.'

'How long have your family lived in the area?'

'All my life—'

That had to be…what…? All of two decades?

'And thirty thousand years before that.'

He adjusted his assessment of her killer tan. That bronze-brown hue wasn't only about working outdoors. 'You're Bayungu?'

She shot him a look and he realised that he risked outing himself with his too familiar knowledge of Coral Bay's first people. That could reasonably lead to questions about why he'd taken the time to educate himself about the traditional uses of this area. Same reason he was here finding out about the environmental aspects of the region.

He wanted to know exactly what he was up against. Where the speed humps were going to arise.

'My mother's family,' she corrected softly.

Either she didn't understand how genetics worked or Mila didn't identify as indigenous despite her roots.

'But not only Bayungu? Nakano, I think you said?'

'My grandfather was Japanese. On Dad's side.'

He remembered reading that in the feasibility study on this

whole coast: how it was a cultural melting pot thanks to the exploding pearling trade.

'That explains the bone structure,' he said, tracing his gaze across her face.

She flushed and seemed to say the first thing that came to her. 'His wife's family was from Dublin, just to complicate things.'

Curious that she saw her diversity as a *complication*. In business, it was a strength. Pretty much the first thing he'd done following his father's death was broaden WestCorp's portfolio base so that their eggs were spread across more baskets. Thirty-eight baskets, to be specific.

'What did Irish Grandma give you?' Rich glanced at her dark locks. 'Not red hair…'

'One of my brothers got that,' she acknowledged, stopping to consider him before sliding her sunglasses up onto her head. 'But I got Nan's eyes.'

Whoa…

A decade ago, he'd abseiled face-first down a cliff for sport—fast. The suck of his unprepared guts had been the same that day as the moment Mila's thick dark lashes lifted just now to reveal what they hid. Classic Celtic green. Not notable on their own, perhaps, but bloody amazing against the richness of her unblemished brown skin. Her respective grandparents had certainly left her a magnetising genetic legacy.

He used the last of his air replying. 'You're a walking billboard for cultural diversity.'

She glanced away, her mocha skin darkening, and he could breathe again. But it wasn't some coy affectation on her part. She looked genuinely distressed—though she was skilled at hiding it.

Fortunately, he was more skilled at reading people.

'The riches of the land and sea up here have always drawn people from around the world,' she murmured. 'I'm the end result.'

They reached her modest four-wheel drive, emblazoned with

government logos, halfway down the beach she'd first emerged from, all golden and glittery.

'Is that why you stay?' he asked. 'Because of the riches?'

She looked genuinely horrified at the thought as she unlocked the vehicle and swung her long sandy legs in. 'Not in the sense you mean. My work is here. My family is here. My heart is here.'

And clearly she wore that heart on the sleeve of her Parks Department uniform.

Rich climbed in after her and gave a little inward sigh. Sailing north on the *Portus* had been seven kinds of awesome. All the space and quiet and air he needed wrapped up in black leather and oiled deck timber. He'd even unwound a little. But there was something about driving... Four wheels firm on asphalt. Owning the road.

Literally, in this case.

At least for the next few months. Longer, if he got his way.

'Is that why you're here?' she asked him, though it looked as if she had to summon up a fair bit of courage to do it. 'Drawn by the riches?'

If he was going to spend the day with her he wasn't going to be able to avoid the question for long. Might as well get in front of it.

'I'm here to find out everything I can about the area. I have... business interests up here. I'd like to go in fully informed.'

Her penetrating gaze left him and turned back to the road, leaving only thinned lips in its wake.

He'd disappointed her.

'The others wanted to know a bit about the history of Coral Bay.' She almost sighed. 'Do you?'

It was hard not to smile at her not so subtle angling. He was probably supposed to say *What others?* and she was going to tell him how many people had tried and failed to get developments up in this region. Maybe he was even supposed to be deterred by that.

Despite Mila's amateurish subterfuge, he played along. A few friendly overtures wouldn't go amiss. Even if she didn't look all that disposed to overtures of any kind—friendly or otherwise. Her job meant she kind of had to.

He settled into the well-worn fabric. 'Sure. Take me right back.'

She couldn't possibly maintain her coolness once she got stuck into her favourite topic. As long as Mila was talking, he had every excuse to just watch her lips move and her eyes flash with engagement. If nothing else, he could enjoy that.

She started with the ancient history of the land that they drove through, how this flat coast had been seafloor in the humid time before mammals. Then, a hundred million years later when the oceans were all locked up in a mini ice age and sea levels had retreated lower than they'd ever been, how her mother's ancestors had walked the shores on the edge of the massive continental drop-off that was now five kilometres out to sea. Many of the fantastical creatures of the Saltwater People's creation stories might well have been perfectly literal, hauled out of the deep sea trenches even with primitive tools.

The whole time she talked, Rich watched, entranced. Hiring Mila to be an ambassador for this place was an inspired move on someone's part. She was passionate and vivid. Totally engaged in what was obviously her favourite topic. She sold it in a way history books couldn't possibly.

But the closer she brought him to contemporary times, the more quirks he noticed in her storytelling. At first, he thought it was just the magical language of the tribal stories—evocative, memorable…almost poetic—but then he realised some of the references were too modern to be part of traditional tales.

'Did you just call the inner reef "smug"?' he interrupted.

She glanced at him, mid-sentence. Swallowing. 'Did I?'

'That's what I heard.'

Her knuckles whitened on the steering wheel. 'Are you sure I didn't say warm? That's what I meant. Because it's shallower inside the reef. The sand refracts sunlight and leads to—' she paused for half a heartbeat '—warmer conditions that the coral really thrives in.'

Her gaze darted around for a moment before she continued and he got the distinct feeling he'd just been lied to.

Again, though, amateurish.

This woman could tell one hell of a tale but she would be a sitting duck in one of his boardrooms.

'Ten thousand years from now,' she was continuing, and he forced himself to attend, 'those reef areas out there will emerge from the water and form atolls and, eventually, the certainty of earth.'

He frowned at her augmented storytelling. It didn't diminish her words particularly but the longer it went on the more overshadowing it became until he stopped listening to *what* she was saying and found himself only listening to *how* she said it.

'There are vast gorges at the top of the cape that tourists assume are made purely of cynical rock, but they're not. They were once reef too, tens of millions of years ago, until they got thrust up above the land by tectonic plate action. The enduring limestone is full of marine fossils.'

Cynical rock. *Certain* earth. *Enduring* limestone. The land seemed alive for Mila Nakano—almost a person, with its own traits—but it didn't irritate him because it wasn't an affectation and it didn't diminish the quality of her information at all. When she called the reef *smug* he got the sense that she believed it and, because she believed it, it just sounded…possible. If he got to lie about in warm water all day being nibbled free of parasites by a harem of stunning fish he'd be pretty smug too.

'I'd be interested to see those gorges,' he said, more to spur her on to continue her hyper-descriptive storytelling than anything else. Besides, something like that was just another string in his bow when it came to creating a solid business case for his resort.

She glanced at him. 'No time. We would have had to set off

much earlier. The four-wheel drive access has been under three metres of curi—'

She caught herself and he couldn't help wondering what she'd been about to say.

'Of sea water for weeks. We'd have to go up the eastern side of the cape and come in from the north. It's a long detour.'

His disappointment was entirely disproportionate to her refusal—sixty seconds ago he'd had zero interest in fossils or gorges—but he found himself eager to make it happen.

'What if we had a boat?'

'Well, that would be faster, obviously.' She set her eyes back on the road ahead and then, at this silent expectation, returned them to him. '*Do* you have one?'

He'd never been prouder to have the *Portus* lingering offshore. But he wasn't ready to reveal her just yet. 'I might be able to get access…'

Her green gaze narrowed just slightly. 'Then this afternoon,' she said. 'Right now we have other obligations.'

'We do?'

She hit the indicator even though there were no other roadusers for miles around, and turned off the asphalt onto a graded limestone track. Dozens of tyre-tracks marked its dusty white surface.

'About time you got wet, Mr Grundy.'

CHAPTER TWO

BELOW THE SLIGHTLY elevated parking clearing at Five Fingers Bay, the limestone reef stretched out like the splayed digits in the beach's name. They formed a kind of catwalk, pointing out in five directions to the outer reef beyond the lagoon. Mila led her *one* down to it and stood on what might have been the Fingers' exposed rocky wrist.

'I was expecting more *Finding Nemo*,' he said, circling to look all around him and sounding as disappointed as the sag of his shoulders, 'and less *Flintstones*. Where's all the sea life?'

'What you want is just out there, Mr Grundy.'

He followed her finger out beyond the stretch of turquoise lagoon to the place the water darkened off, marking the start of the back reef that kept most predators—and most boats—out, all the way up to those gorges that he wanted to visit.

'Call me Richard,' he volunteered. 'Rich.'

Uh, no. 'Rich' was a bit too like friends and—given what he was up here for—even calling them acquaintances was a stretch. Besides, she wasn't convinced by his sudden attempt at graciousness.

'Richard…' Mila allowed, conscious that she represented her department. She rummaged in the rucksack she'd dragged from the back seat of the SUV. 'I have a spare mask and snorkel for you.'

He stared at them as if they were entirely foreign, but then reached out with a firm hand and took them from her. She took care not to let her fingers brush against his.

It was always awkward, taking your clothes off in front of a stranger; it was particularly uncomfortable in front of a young, handsome stranger, but Mila turned partly away, shrugged out of her work shorts and shirt and stood in her bikini, fiddling with the adjustment straps on her mask while Richard shed his designer T-shirt and cargo pants.

She kept her eyes carefully averted, not out of any prudishness but because she always approached new experiences with a moment's care. She could never tell how something new was going to impact on her and, while she'd hung out with enough divers and surfers to give her some kind of certainty about what senses a half-naked person would trigger—apples for some random guy peeling off his wetsuit, watermelon for a woman pulling hers on—this was a *new* half-naked man. And a client.

She watched his benign shadow on the sand until she was sure he'd removed everything he was going to.

Only then did she turn around.

Instantly, she was back at the only carnival she'd ever visited, tucking into her first—and last—candyfloss. The light, sticky cloud dissolving into pure sugar on her tongue. The smell of it, the taste of it. That sweet, sweet rush. She craved it instantly. It was so much more intense—and so much more humiliating—than a plain old apples association. But apparently that was what her synaesthesia had decided to associate with a half-naked Richard Grundy.

The harmless innocence of that scent was totally incompatible with a man she feared was here to exploit the reef. But that was how it went; her associations rarely had any logical connection with their trigger.

Richard had come prepared with navy board shorts beneath his expensive but casual clothes. They were laced low and loose on his hips yet still managed to fit snugly all the way down his muscular thighs.

And they weren't even wet yet.

Mila filled her lungs slowly and mastered her gaze. He might not be able to read her dazed thoughts but he might well be able to read her face and so she turned back to her rummaging. Had her snorkelling mask always been this fiddly to adjust?

'I only have one set of fins, sorry,' she said in a rush. 'Five Fingers is good for drift snorkelling, though, so you can let the water do the work.'

She set off up the beach a way so that they could let the current carry them back near to their piled up things by the end of the swim. Her slog through sun-soaked sand was accompanied by the high-pitched single note that came with a warmth so everyday that she barely noticed it anymore. When they reached the old reef, she turned seaward and walked into the water without a backward glance—she didn't need the sugary distraction and she felt certain Richard would follow her in without invitation. They were snorkelling on his dollar, after all.

'So coral's not a plant?' Richard asked once they were waist-deep in the electric-blue water of the lagoon.

She paused and risked another look at him. Prepared this time. 'It's an animal. Thousands of tiny animals, actually, living together in the form of elk horns, branches, plates, cabbages—'

He interrupted her shopping list ramble with the understated impatience of someone whose time really was money. Only the cool water prevented her from blushing. Did she always babble this much with clients? Or did it only feel like babbling in Richard Grundy's presence?

'So how does a little squishy thing end up becoming rock-hard reef?' he asked.

Good. Yes. Focusing on the science kept the candyfloss at

bay. Although as soon as he'd said 'rock-hard' she'd become disturbingly fixated on the remembered angles of his chest and had to severely discipline her unruly gaze not to follow suit.

'The calcium carbonate in their skeletons. In life, it provides resilience against the sea currents, and in death—'

She braced on her left leg as she slipped her right into her mono-fin. Then she straightened and tucked her left foot in with it and balanced there on the soft white seafloor. The gentle waves rocked her a little in her rooted spot, just like one of the corals she was describing.

'In death they pile up to form limestone reef,' he guessed.

'Millions upon millions of them forming reef first, then limestone that weathers into sand, and finally scrubland grows on top of it. We owe a lot to coral, really.'

Mila took a breath and turned to face him, steadfastly ignoring the smell of carnival. 'Ready to meet the reef?'

He glanced out towards the reef break and swallowed hard. It was the first time she'd seen him anything other than supremely confident, verging on arrogant.

'How far out are we going?'

'Not very. That's the beauty of Coral Bay; the inside reef is right there, the moment you step offshore. The lagoon is narrow but long. We'll be travelling parallel to the beach, mostly.'

His body lost some of its rigidity and he took a moment to fit his mask and snorkel before stepping off the sandy ridge after her.

It took no time to get out where the seafloor dropped away enough that they could glide in the cool water two metres above the reef. The moment Mila submerged, the synaesthetic symphony began. It was a mix of the high notes caused by the water rushing over her bare skin and the vast array of sounds and sensations caused by looking down at the natural metropolis below in all its diversity. Far from the flat, gently sloping, sandy sea bottom that people imagined, coral reef towered in places, dropped away in others, just like any urban centre. There were valleys and ridges and little caves from where brightly coloured fish surveyed their personal square metre of territory. Long orange antenna poked out from under a shelf and acted as the early warning system of a perky, pincers-at-the-ready crayfish. Anemones danced smooth and slow on the current, their base firmly tethered to the reef, stinging anything that came close but giving the little fish happily living inside it a free pass in return for its nibbly housekeeping.

Swimming over the top of it all, peering down through the glassy water, it felt like cruising above an alien metropolis in some kind of silent-running airship—just the sound of her own breathing inside the snorkel, and her myriad synaesthetic associations in her mind's ear. The occasional colourful little fellow came up to have a closer look at them but mostly the fish just went about their business, adhering to the strict social rules of reef communities, focusing on their eternal search for food, shelter or a mate.

Life was pretty straightforward under the surface.

And it was insanely abundant.

She glanced at Richard, who didn't seem to know where to look first. His mask darted from left to right, taking in the coral city ahead of them, looking below them at some particular point. He'd tucked his hands into balls by his hips and she wondered if that was to stop him reaching out and touching the strictly forbidden living fossil.

She took a breath and flipped gently in the water, barely flexing her mono-fin to effect the move, swimming backwards ahead of him so that she could see if he was doing okay. His mask came up square onto hers and, even in the electric-blue underworld, his eyes still managed to stand out as they locked on hers.

And he smiled.

The candyfloss returned with a vengeance. It was almost overpowering in the cloistered underwater confines of her mask. Part of her brain knew it wasn't real but as far as the other part was concerned she was sucking her air directly from some carnival tent. That was the first smile she'd seen from Richard and it was a doozy, even working around a mouthful of snorkel. It transformed his already handsome face into something really breath-stealing and, right now, she needed all the air she could get!

She signalled upwards, flicked her fin and was back above the glassy surface within a couple of heartbeats.

'I've spent so much time on the water and I had no idea there was so much going on below!' he said the moment his mouth was free of rubbery snorkel. 'I mean you know but you don't… *know*. You know?'

This level of inarticulateness wasn't uncommon for someone seeing the busy reef for the first time—their minds were almost always blown—but it made her feel just a little bit better about how much of a babbler she'd been with him.

His finless legs had to work much harder than hers to keep him perpendicular to the water and his breath started to grow choppy. 'It's so…structured. Almost city-like.'

Mila smiled. It was so much easier to relate to someone over the reef.

'Coral polyps organise into a stag horn just like a thousand humans organise into a high-rise building. It's a futuristic city… with hovercraft. Ready for more?'

His answer was to bite back down onto his snorkel's mouthpiece and tip himself forward, back under the surface.

They drifted on for another half-hour and she let Richard take the lead, going where interest took him. He got more skilled at the suspension of breath needed to deep snorkel, letting him get closer to the detail of the reef, and the two of them were like mini whales every time they surfaced, except they blew water instead of air from their clumsy plastic blowholes.

There was something intimate in the way they managed to expel the water at the same time on surfacing—relaxed, not urgent—then take another breath and go back for more. Over and over again. It was vaguely like...

Kissing.

Mila's powerful kick pushed her back up to the surface. That was not a thought she was about to entertain. He was a *one*, for a start, and he was here to exploit the very reef he was currently going crazy over. Though if she did her job then maybe he'd change his mind about that after today.

'Seen enough?' she asked when he caught up with her.

His mask couldn't hide the disappointment behind it. 'Is it time to go in?'

'I just want to show you the drop-off, then we'll head back to the beach.'

Just was probably an understatement, and they'd have to swim out of the shallow waters towards the place the continental shelf took its first plunge, but for Richard to understand the reef and how it connected to the oceanic ecosystem he needed to see it for himself.

Seeing was believing.

Unless you were her, in which case, seeing came with a whole bunch of other sensations that no one else experienced. Or necessarily believed.

She'd lost enough friends in the past to recognise that.

Mila slid the mouthpiece back into her snorkel and tooted out of the top.

'Let's go.'

Richard prided himself on being a man of composure. In the boardroom, in the bedroom, in front of a media pack. In fact, it was something he was known for—courage under fire—and it came from always knowing your strengths, and your opponents'. From always doing your homework. From controlling all the variables before they even had time to vary.

This had to be the least composed he'd been in a long, long time.

Mila had swum alongside him, her vigilant eyes sweeping around them so that he could just enjoy the wonders of the reef, monitoring their position to make sure they didn't get caught up in the current. He'd felt the change in the water as the outer reef had started to rise up to meet them, almost shore-like. But it wasn't land; it was the break line one kilometre out from the actual shore where the reef grew most abundant and closest to the surface of anywhere they'd swum yet. So close, the waves from the deeper water on the other side crashed against it relentlessly and things got a little choppier than their earlier efforts. Mila had led him to a channel that allowed them to propel themselves down between the high-rise coral—just like any of the reef's permanent residents—and get some relief from the surging waves as they'd swum out towards a deeper, darker, more distant kind of blue. The water temperature had dropped and the corals started to change—less of the soft, flowy variety interspersed with dancing life and more of the slow-growing, rock-hard variety. Coral mean streets. The ones that could withstand the water pressure coming at them from the open ocean twenty-four-seven.

Rich lifted his eyes and tried to make something out in the deep blue visible beyond the coral valley he presently lurked in. He couldn't—just a graduated, ill-defined shift from blue to deep blue to dark blue looking out and down. No scale. No end point. Impossible to get a grip on how far this drop-off actually went.

It even had the word 'drop' in it.

His pulse kicked up a notch.

Mila swam on ahead, rising briefly to refill her lungs and sinking again to swim out through the opening of the coral valley straight into all that vast blue…nothing.

And that was where his courage flat ran out.

He'd played hard contact sports, he'd battled patronising boardroom jerks, he'd wrangled packs of media wolves hell-bent on getting a story, and he'd climbed steep rock faces for fun. None of those things were for the weak-willed. But could he bring himself to swim past the break and out into the place the reef—and the entire country—dropped off to open, bottomless ocean?

Nope.

He tried—not least because of Mila, back-swimming so easily out into the unknown, her dark hair floating all around her, mermaid tail waving gently at him like a beckoning finger—but even that was not enough to seduce him out there. The vast blue was so impossible to position himself in, he found himself constantly glancing up to the bright surface where the sunlight was, just to keep himself oriented. Or back at the reef edge to have the certainty of it behind him.

Swimming out over the drop-off was as inconceivable to him as stepping off a mountain. His body simply would not comply.

As if it had some information he didn't.

And Richard Grundy made it his priority always to have the information he needed.

'It's okay,' Mila sputtered gently, surfacing next to him once they'd moved back to the side of the reef protected from the churn of the crest. 'The drop-off's not easy the first time.'

No. What wasn't easy was coming face to face with a limitation you never knew you had, and doing it in front of a slip of a thing who clearly didn't suffer the same disability. Who looked as if she'd been born beneath the surface.

'The current...' he hedged.

As if that had anything to do with it. He knew Mila wouldn't have taken him somewhere unsafe. Not that he knew her at all, and yet somehow...he did. She just didn't seem the type to be intentionally unkind. And her job relied on her getting her customers back to shore in one piece.

'Let's head in,' she said.

There was a thread of charity in her voice that he was not comfortable hearing. He didn't need anyone else's help recognising his deficiencies or to be patronised, no matter how well-meant. This would always be the first thing she thought of when she thought of him, no matter what else he achieved.

The guy that couldn't swim the drop-off.

It only took ten minutes to swim back in when he wasn't distracted by the teeming life beneath them. Thriving, living coral turned to rocky old reef, reef turned to sand and then his feet were finding the seafloor and pushing him upwards. He'd never felt such a weighty slave to gravity—it was as indisputable as the instinct that had stopped him swimming out into all that blue.

Survival.

Mila struggled a little to get her feet out of her single rubber fin and he stepped closer so she could use him as a brace. She glanced at him sideways for a moment with something that looked a lot like discomfort before politely resting her hand on his forearm and using him for balance while she prised first one and then the other foot free. As she did it she even held her breath.

Really? Had he diminished himself that much? She didn't even want to *touch* him?

'That was the start of the edge of Australia's continental shelf,' she said when she was back on two legs. 'The small drop-off slopes down to the much bigger one five kilometres out—'

Small?

'And then some of the most immense deep-sea trenches on the planet.'

'Are you trying to make me feel better?' he said tightly.

And had failing always been this excruciating?

Her pretty face twisted a little. 'No. But your body might have been responding instinctively to that unknown danger.'

'I deal with unknowns every day.'

Dealt with them and redressed them. WestCorp thrived on *knowns*.

'Do you, really?' she asked, tipping her glance towards him, apparently intent on placating him with conversation. 'When was the last time you did something truly new to you?'

Part of the reason he dominated in business was because nothing fazed him. Like a good game of chess, there was a finite number of plays to address any challenge and once you'd perfected them the only contest was knowing which one to apply. The momentary flare of satisfaction as the challenge tumbled was about all he had, these days. The rest was business as usual.

And outside of business…

Well, how long had it been since there was anything outside of business?

'I went snorkelling today,' he said, pulling off his mask.

'That was your first time? You did well, then.'

She probably meant to be kind, but all her condescension did was remind him why he never did anything before learning everything there was to know about it. Controlling his environment.

Open ocean was not a controlled environment.

'How about you?' he deflected as the drag of the water dropped away and they stepped onto toasty warm sand. 'You don't get bored of the same view every day? The same reef?'

She turned back out to the turquoise lagoon and the deeper blue sea beyond it—that same blue that he loved from the comfort and safety of his boat.

'Nope.' She sighed. 'I like a lot of familiarity in my environment because of—' she caught herself, turned back and changed tack '—because I'm at my best when it's just me and the ocean.'

He snorted. 'What's the point of being your best when no one's around to see it?'

He didn't mean to be dismissive, but he saw her reaction in the flash behind her eyes.

'I'm around.' She shrugged, almost embarrassed. 'I'll know.'

'And you reserve the best of yourself *for* yourself?' he asked, knowing any hope of a congenial day with her was probably already sunk.

Her curious gaze suggested he was more alien to her than some of the creatures they'd just been studying. 'Why would I give it to someone else?'

She crossed to their piled-up belongings and began to shove her snorkelling equipment into the canvas bag.

Rich pressed the beach towel she'd supplied to his chest as he watched her go, and disguised the full-body shiver that followed. But he couldn't blame it on the chilly water alone—there was something else at play here, something more...disquieting.

He patted his face dry with the sun-warmed fabric to buy himself a moment to identify the uncomfortable sensation.

For all his success—for all his professional renown—Rich suddenly had the most unsettling suspicion that he might have missed something fundamental about life.

Why *would* anyone give the best of themselves to someone else?

CHAPTER THREE

MILA NEVER LIKED to see any creature suffer—even one as cocky as Richard Grundy—but, somehow, suffering brought him closer to her level than he'd yet been. More likeable and relatable Clark Kent, less fortress of solitude Superman. He'd taken the drop-off experience hard, and he'd been finding any feasible excuse not to make eye contact with her ever since.

Most people got no phone reception out of town but Richard somehow did and he'd busied himself with a few business calls, including arranging for the boat he knew of to meet them at Bill's Bay marina. It was indisputably the quickest way to get to the gorges he wanted to see. All they had to do was putter out of the State and Federal-protected marine park, then turn north in open, deregulated waters and power up the coast at full speed, before heading back into the marine park again. They could be there in an hour instead of the three it would take by road. And the three back again.

It looked as if Richard would use every moment of that hour to focus on business.

Still, his distraction gave her time to study him. His hair had only needed a few strategic arrangements to get it back to a perfectly barbered shape, whereas hers was a tangled, salt-crusted mess. Side on, she could see behind his expensive sunglasses and knew just how blue those eyes were. The glasses sat comfortably on high cheekbones, which was where the designer stubble also happened to begin. It ran down his defined jaw and met its mirror image at a slightly cleft chin. As nice as all of that was—and it was; just the thought of how that stubble might feel under her fingers was causing a flurry of kettledrums, of all things—clearly its primary role in life was to frame what had to be his best asset. A killer pair of lips. Not too thin, not too full, perfectly symmetrical. Not at their best right now while he was still so tense, but earlier, when they'd broken out that smile...

Ugh...murder.

The car filled with the scent of spun sugar again.

'Something you need?'

He spoke without turning his eyes off the road ahead or prising the phone from his ear, but the twist of the mouth she'd just been admiring told her he was talking to her.

She'd meant to be subtle, glancing sideways, studying him in her periphery, yet apparently those lips were more magnetic than she realised because she was turned almost fully towards him. She snapped her gaze forward.

'No. Just...um...'

Just obsessing on your body parts, Mr Grundy...

Just wondering how I could get you to smile again, sir...

'We're nearly at the boat launch,' she fabricated. 'Just wanted you to know.'

If he believed her, she couldn't tell. He simply nodded, returned to his call and then took his sweet time finishing it.

Mila forced her mind back on the job.

'This is the main road in and out of Coral Bay,' she said as soon as he disconnected his call, turning her four-wheel drive at a cluster of towering solar panels that powered streetlights at the only intersection in the district. 'It's base camp for everyone wanting access to the southern part of the World Heritage area.'

To her, Coral Bay was a sweet, green little oasis existing in the middle of almost nowhere. No other town for two hundred kilometres in any direction. Just boundless, rust-coloured outback on one side and a quarter of a planet of ocean on the other.

Next stop, Africa.

Richard's eyes narrowed as they entered town and he saw all the caravans, RVs, four-by-fours and tour buses parked all along the main street. 'It's thriving.'

His interest reminded her of a cartoon she'd seen once where a rumpled-suited businessman's eyes had spun and rolled and turned into dollar signs. It was as if he was counting the potential.

'It's whale shark season. Come back in forty-degree February and it will be a ghost town. Summer is brutal up here.'

If he wanted to build some ritzy development, he might as well know it wasn't going to be a year-round goldmine.

'I guess that's what air-conditioning is for,' he murmured.

'Until the power station goes down in a cyclone, then you're on your own.'

His lips twisted, just slightly. 'You're not really selling the virtues of the region, you know.'

No. This wasn't her job. This was personal. She forced herself back on a professional footing.

'Did you want to stop in town? For something to eat, maybe? Snorkelling always makes me hungry.'

Plus, Coral Bay had the best bakery in the district, regardless of the fact it also had the only bakery in the district.

'We'll have lunch on the *Portus*,' he said absently.

The *Portus*? Not one of the boats that frequented Coral Bay. She knew them all by sight. It hadn't occurred to her that he might have access to a vessel from outside the region. Especially given he'd only called to make arrangements half an hour ago.

'Okay—' she shrugged, resigning herself to a long wait '—straight to Bill's Bay, then.'

They parked up on arrival at the newly appointed mini-marina and wandered down to where three others launched boats for a midday run. Compared to the elaborate 'tinnies' of the locals, getting their hulls wet on the ramp, the white Zodiac idling at the end of the single pier immediately caught her attention.

'There's Damo.' Rich raised a hand and the Zodiac's skipper acknowledged it as they approached. 'You look disappointed, Mila.'

Her gaze flew to his, not least because it was the first time he'd called her by her name. It eased off his lips like a perfectly cooked salmon folding off a knife.

'I underestimated how long it was going to take us to get north,' she said, flustered. 'It's okay; I'll adjust the schedule.'

'Were you expecting something with a bit more grunt?'

'No.' *Yes.*

'I really didn't know what to expect,' she went on. 'A boat is a boat, right? As long as it floats.'

He almost smiled then, but it was too twisted to truly earn the name. She cursed the missed moment. A tall man in the white version of her own shorts and shirt stood as they approached the end of the pier. He acknowledged Richard with a courteous nod, then offered her his arm aboard.

'Miss?'

She declined his proffered hand—not just because she needed little help managing embarkation onto such a modest vessel, but also because she could do without the associated sounds that generally came with a stranger's skin against hers.

The skipper was too professional to react. Richard, on the other hand, frowned at her dismissal of a man clearly doing him a favour.

Mila sighed. Okay, so he thought her rude. It wouldn't be the first time someone had assumed the worst. And she wouldn't be seeing him again after today, so what did it really matter?

The skipper wasted no time firing up the surprisingly throaty Zodiac and reversing them out of the marina and in between the markers that led bigger boats safely through the reef-riddled sanctuary zone towards more open waters. They ambled along at five knots and only opened up a little once they hit the recreation zone, where boating was less regulated. It took just a few minutes to navigate the passage that put them in open water, but the skipper didn't throttle right up like she expected; instead he kept his speed down as they approached a much larger and infinitely more expensive catamaran idling just beyond the outer reef. The vessel she'd seen earlier, at Nancy's Point. Slowing as they passed such a massive vessel seemed a back-to-front kind of courtesy, given the giant cat would barely feel their wake if they passed it at full speed. It was only as their little Zodiac swung around to reverse up to the catamaran that she saw the letters emblazoned on the big cat's side.

Portus.

'Did you think we were going all the way north in the tender?' a soft voice came to her over the thrum of the slowly reversing motor.

'Is this yours?' she asked, gaping.

'If she's not, we're getting an awfully accommodating reception for a couple of trespassers.'

'So when you said you were "dropped off" at Nancy's Point…?'

'I didn't mean in a car.'

With those simple words, his capacity to get his mystery development proposal through where others had failed increased by half in Mila's mind. A man with the keys to a vessel like this in his pocket had to have at least a couple of politicians there too, right?

The tender's skipper expertly reversed them backwards, right up to the stern of the *Portus,* where a set of steps came down each of the cat's two hulls to the waterline. A dive platform at the bottom of each served as a disembarkation point and she could see where the tender would nest in snugly under its mother vessel when it wasn't in use. Stepping off the back of the tender and onto the *Portus* was as easy as entering her house.

Where the upward steps delivered them—to an outdoor area that would comfortably seat twelve—the vessel was trimmed out with timber and black leather against the boat's white fibreglass. Not vinyl... Not hardy canvas like most of the boats she'd been on. This was *leather*—soft and smooth under her fingers as she placed a light hand on the top of one padded seat-back. The sensation was accompanied by a percussion of wind chimes, low and sonorous.

Who knew she found leather so soothing!

The colour scheme was conflicting, emotionally, even as it was perfect visually. The tranquillity of white, the sensuality of black. Brown usually made her feel sad, but this particularly rich, oiled tone struck her more specifically as...isolated.

But it was impossible not to also acknowledge the truth.

'This is so beautiful, Richard.'

To her left, timber stairs spiralled up and out of view to the deck above.

'It does the job,' he said modestly, then pulled open two glass doors into the vessel's gorgeous interior, revealing an expansive dining area and a galley twice as big as her own kitchen.

She just stared at him until he noticed her silence.

'What?'

'Surely, even in your world this vessel is something special,' she said, standing firm on the threshold, as though she needed to get this resolved before entering. False humility was worse than an absence of it, and she had a blazing desire to have the truth from this man just once.

On principle.

'What do you know about my world?' he cast back easily over his shoulder, seemingly uncaring whether she followed him or not.

She clung to *not* and hugged the doorway.

'You wouldn't have bought the boat if you didn't think it was special.'

He turned to face her. 'It wouldn't be seemly to boast about my own boat, Mila.'

'It would be honest.' And really, what was this whole vessel but big, mobile bragging rights? 'Or is it just saying the words aloud that bothers you?'

He turned to face her, but she barrelled on without really knowing why it affected her so much. Maybe it had something to do with growing up on two small rural incomes. Or maybe it had something to do with starting to think they might be closer to equals, only to be faced with the leather and timber evidence very much to the contrary.

'I'll say it for you,' she said from the doorway. 'The *Portus* is amazing. You must be incredibly relaxed when you're out on her.' She glanced at the massive dining table. 'And you must have some very happy friends.'

'I don't really bring friends out,' he murmured, regarding her across the space between them.

'Colleagues, then. Clients.'

He leaned back on the kitchen island and crossed his ankles. 'Nope. I like silence when I'm out on the water.'

She snorted. 'Good luck with that.' He just stared at her. 'I mean it's never truly silent, is it?'

He frowned at her. 'Isn't it?'

No. Not in her experience.

She glanced around as the *Portus*' massive engines thrummed into life and they began to move, killing any hope of silence for the time being. Although they weren't nearly as loud as she'd expected. How much did a boat have to cost to get muted engines like that?

Richard didn't invite her in again. Or insist. Or cajole. Instead, he leaned there, patience personified until she felt that her refusal to step inside was more than just ridiculous.

It was as unfriendly as people had always thought her to be.

But entering while he waited felt like too much of a concession in this mini battle of wills. She didn't want to see the flare of triumph in his eyes. Her own shifted to the double fridge at the heart of the galley.

'I guess lunch won't be cheese sandwiches out of an Esky, then?'

The moment his regard left her to follow her glance, she stepped inside, crossing more than just a threshold. She stepped wholly into Richard's fancy world.

He pulled the fridge doors wide. 'It's a platter. Crayfish. Tallegio. Salt and pepper squid. Salad Niçoise. Sourdough bread.'

She laughed. 'I guess I was wrong, then. Cheese sandwich it is.' Just fancier.

He turned his curiosity to her. 'You don't eat seafood?'

'I can eat prawns if I have to. And molluscs. They don't have a strong personality.'

That frown just seemed to be permanently fixed on his face. 'But cray and squid do?'

Her heart warmed just thinking about them and it helped to loosen her bones just a little. 'Very much so. Particularly crayfish. They're quite…optimistic.'

He stared—for several bemused moments—clearly deciding between *quirky* and *nuts*. Both of which she'd had before with a lot less subtlety than he was demonstrating.

'Is it going to bother you if I eat them?'

'No. Something tells me I won't be going hungry.' She smiled and it was easier than she expected. 'I have no strong feelings about cheese, either way.'

'Unlucky for the Tallegio then,' he murmured.

He pulled open a cabinet and revealed it as a small climate-controlled wine cellar. Room temperature on the left, frosty on the right. 'Red or white?' he asked.

'Neither,' she said regretfully. Just looking at the beading on the whites made her long for a dose of ocean spray. 'I'm on the clock.'

'Not right now you're not,' he pointed out. 'For the next ninety minutes, we're both in the capable hands of Captain

Max Farrow, whose jurisdiction, under international maritime law, overrules your own.'

He lifted out one of the dewy bottles and waved it gently in her direction.

It was tempting to play at all this luxury just for a little while. To take a glass and curl up on one of those leather sofas, enjoy the associated wind chimes and act as if they weren't basically complete strangers. To talk like normal people. To pretend. At all of it.

'One glass, then,' she said. 'Thank you.'

He poured and handed her a glass of white. The silent moments afterwards sang with discomfort.

'Come on, I'll give you a tour,' he eventually offered.

He smiled but it didn't ring true and it certainly didn't set off the five-note harmony or the scent of candyfloss that the flash of perfect teeth previously had. He couldn't be as nervous as she was, surely. Was he also conscious of how make-believe this all was?

Even if, for him, it wasn't.

She stood. 'Thank you, Richard.'

'Rich,' he insisted. 'Please. Only my colleagues call me Richard.'

They were a good deal less than colleagues, but it would be impossible now to call him anything else without causing offence. *More* offence.

'Please, Mila. I think you'll like the *Portus*.' Then, when she still didn't move, he added, 'As much as I do.'

That one admission… That one small truth wiggled right in under her ribs. Disarming her completely.

'I would love to see more, Rich, thank you.'

The name felt awkward on her lips and yet somehow right at the same time. Clunky but…okay, as if it could wear in comfortably with use.

The tour didn't take long, not because there wasn't a lot to look at in every sumptuous space but because, despite its size, the *Portus* was, as it happened, mostly boat. As Rich showed her around she noted a jet ski securely stashed at the back, a sea kayak, water skis—everything a man could need to enjoy some time *on* the water. But she saw nothing to indicate that he enjoyed time *in* it.

'No diving gear?' she commented. 'On a boat with not one but two dive decks?'

His pause was momentary. 'Plenty to keep me busy above the surface,' he said.

Something about that niggled in this new environment of truce between them. That little glimpse of vulnerability coming so close on the heels of some humble truth. But she didn't need super-senses to know not to push it. She carried on the tour in comparative silence.

The *Portus* primarily comprised of three living areas: the aft deck lounge that she'd already seen, the indoor galley and the most incredibly functional bedroom space ever. It took up the whole bow, filling the front of the *Portus* with panoramic, all-seeing windows, below which wrapped fitted black cupboards. She trailed a finger along the spotless black surface, over the part that was set up as a workspace, complete with expensive camouflaged laptop, hip-height bookshelves, a disguised mini-bar and a perfectly made up king-sized bed positioned centrally in the space, complete with black pillow and quilt covers. The whole space screamed sensuality and not just because of all the black.

A steamy kind of heat billowed up from under Mila's work shirt. It was way too easy to imagine Rich in here.

'Where's the widescreen TV?' she asked, hunting for the final touch to the space that she knew had to be here somewhere.

Rich leaned next to the workspace. 'I had it removed. When I'm in here it's not to watch TV.'

She turned to face him. 'Is that because this is an office first, or a bedroom first?'

The moments the words left her lips she tried to recapture

them, horrified at her own boldness. It had to be the result of this all-consuming black making her skin tingle, but talking about a client's bedroom habits *with* said client was not just inappropriate, it was utterly mortifying.

'I'm so sorry…' she said hurriedly.

Rich held up a hand and the smile finally returned, lighting up the luxurious space.

'My own fault for having such a rock star bedroom,' he joked. 'I didn't buy the *Portus* for this space, but I have to admit it's pretty functional. Everything I need is close by. But who needs a TV when you have a wraparound view like this, right?'

She followed his easy wave out of the expansive windows. There was something just too…perfect about the image he created. And she just couldn't see him sitting still long enough to enjoy a view.

'You work when you're on board, don't you?'

Those coral-coloured lips twisted. 'Maybe.'

Mila hunted around for a topic of discussion that would soak up some of the cotton candy suddenly swilling around the room. 'Where do your crew sleep?'

The business of climbing down into one of the hulls, where a small bed space and washing facility were, gave her the time she needed to get her rogue senses back in order.

'…comfortable enough for short trips,' Rich was saying as she tuned back in.

'What about long ones?'

He glanced out of the window. 'WestCorp keeps me pretty much tethered to the city. This is shaping up to be the longest trip I've taken since I got her. Three days.'

Wow. Last of the big spenders.

'Come on.' He straightened, maybe seeing the judgement in that thought on her face. 'Let's finish the tour.'

The rest of the *Portus* consisted of a marble-clad *en suite* bathroom, appointed with the same kind of luxury as everywhere else, and then a trip back out to the aft deck and up a spiral staircase to the helm. Like everything else on the vessel, it was a wonder of compact efficiency. Buttons and LED panels and two screens with high-tech navigation and seafloor mapping and a bunch of other equipment she didn't recognise. The *Portus'* captain introduced himself but Mila stood back just far enough that a handshake would be awkward to ask for. She'd rather not insult a second man today. Maybe a third.

'Two crew?' she murmured. The vessel was large enough for it, but for just one passenger…?

'It's more efficient to run overnight. Tag-teaming the skippering. Get up from the city faster. I left the office at seven two nights ago and woke up here the next morning. Same deal tonight. I'll leave before sunset and be back in Perth just in time for my personal trainer.'

Imagine having a boat like this and then rushing every moment you were on her. This gorgeous vessel suddenly became relegated to a water taxi. Despite the wealth and comfort around her, she found herself feeling particularly sorry for Richard Grundy.

Captain Farrow pressed a finger to his headset and spoke quietly, then he turned to Rich.

'Lunch is served, sir.'

'Thanks, Max.'

They backtracked and found the sumptuous spread and the remainder of the wine set out on the aft deck. The deckhand known as Damo lowered his head respectfully then jogged on tanned legs up the spiral stairs to the helm and was gone.

Rich indicated for her to sit.

The first thing she noticed was the absence of the promised crayfish. In its place were some pieces of chicken. The little kindness touched her even as she wondered exactly how and when he'd communicated the instruction. Clearly, his crew had a talent for operating invisibly.

'This is amazing,' she said, curling her bare legs under her on the soft leather. The deep strains of wind chimes flew out of the back of the boat and were overwhelmed in the wash, but they endured. Mila loaded her small plate with delicious morsels.

'So how long have you worked for the Department?' Rich asked, loading a piece of sourdough with pâté and goat's cheese.

It wasn't unusual for one of her tour clients to strike up a personal conversation; what was unusual was the ease with which she approached her answer.

She normally didn't *do* chatty.

'Six years. Until I was eighteen, I instructed snorkelers during the busy season and volunteered on conservation projects in the off-season.'

'While most other teens were bagging groceries or flipping burgers after school?'

'It's different up here. Station work, hospitality or conservation. Those are our options. Or leaving, of course,' she acknowledged. Plenty of young people chose that.

'Waiting on people not your thing?'

She studied her food for a moment. 'People aren't really my thing, to be honest. I much prefer the solitude of the reef system.'

It was the perfect *in* if he wanted to call her on her interpersonal skills. Or lack of.

But he didn't. 'What about working on the Station? Not too many people out there, I wouldn't have thought.'

'I would have worked on Wardoo in a heartbeat,' she admitted. 'But jobs there are very competitive and the size of their crew gets smaller every year as the owners cut back and back.' She looked out towards the vast rust-coloured land on their port side. 'And back.'

He shifted on the comfortable cushions as though he was perched on open reef flat.

'Vast is an understatement,' he murmured, following the direction of her eyes. And her thoughts.

That was not awe in his voice.

'Remote living is not for everyone,' she admitted, refocusing on him. 'But it has its perks.'

He settled back against the plush cushions but his gaze didn't relax with him. If anything, it grew more focused. More intense. 'Like what?'

'You can breathe up here,' she started, remembering how cloistered she'd felt on her one and only visit to the capital when she was a teen. 'The land sets the pace, not someone else's schedule. It's…predictable. Ordered.'

She forked up a piece of chicken and dipped it in a tangy sauce before biting into it and chewing thoughtfully.

'Some people would call that dull…' he started, carefully.

Meaning he would? 'Not me. Life has enough variability in it without giving every day a different purpose.'

'And that's important…why, exactly?'

His gaze grew keen. Too keen, as if he was poking around in a reef cave for something.

Oh…

She should have known he would notice. A man didn't get a boat like this—or the company that paid for it—without being pretty switched on. A deep breath lifted her shoulders before dropping them again. For a moment, Mila was disappointed that he couldn't just…let it lie. She understood the curiosity about her crossed senses, but all her life she'd just wanted someone to *not* be interested in her synaesthesia. So that she could feel normal for a moment.

Apparently, Richard Grundy wasn't going to be that someone.

She sighed. 'You're asking about…'

Funny how she always struggled to broach the subject. He helped her out.

'About crayfish with optimism and the smug reef.' She held her tongue, forcing him to go on. 'You seem very connected to the environment around you. I wondered if it was a cultural thing. Some affinity with your ancestors…?'

Was that what he thought? That it was *cultural*? Of all the things she'd ever thought were going on with her, it had truly never occurred to her that it had anything to do with being

raised Bayungu. Probably because no one else on that side of
the family had it—or any of the community.

It was just one more way that she was different.

'It's not affinity,' she said simply.

It was *her*.

'If anything, it probably comes from my Irish side. My grandmother ended up marrying a Japanese pearler because other
people apparently found her—'

*Unrelatable. Uncomfortable. Any of a bunch of other 'un's
that Mila lived with too.*

'Eccentric.'

But not Grandfather Hiro, with his enormous heart. A Japanese man in outback Australia during the post-war years would
have known more than a little something about not fitting in.
Pity he wasn't still around to talk to...

Rich laid his fork down and just waited.

'I have synaesthesia,' she blurted. 'So I hear some sensations. I taste and smell some emotions. Certain things have
personalities.'

He kept right on staring.

'My synapses are all crossed,' she said in an attempt to clarify. Although even that didn't quite describe it.

'So...' Rich looked utterly confounded. '...the crayfish has
an *actual* personality for you?'

'Yes. Kind of...perky.'

'All of them?'

'No. Just the dead one in your fridge.'

It was impossible not to ruin her straight face with a chuckle.
Force of habit; she'd been minimising her condition with laughter for years. Trying to lessen the discomfort of others. Even if
that meant taking it on herself. 'Yes, all of them, thank goodness. Things are busy enough without giving them *individual*
traits.'

He sat forward. 'And the reef is actually—'

'Smug,' she finished for him. 'But not unpleasantly so. Sky, on the other hand, is quite conceited. Clouds are ambitious.' She glanced around at things she could see for inspiration. 'Your stainless steel fridge is pleasantly mysterious.'

He blinked. 'You don't like sky?'

'I don't like conceit. But I don't pick the associations. They just...are.'

He stared, then, so long and so hard she grew physically uncomfortable. In a way that had nothing to do with her synaesthesia and everything to do with the piercing intelligence behind those blue eyes.

Eventually his bottom lip pushed out and he conceded, 'I guess sky is kind of pleased with itself. All that over-confident blue...'

The candyfloss surged back for a half-moment and then dissipated on the air rushing past the boat. She was no less a spectacle but at least he was taking it in his stride, which wasn't always the case when she confessed her unique perception to people.

'What about the boat?' he asked after a moment. 'Or is it just natural features?'

Her lips tightened and she glanced down at the rapidly emptying platter. 'I'm not an amusement ride, Rich.'

'No. Sorry, I'm just trying to get my head around it. I've never met a...'

'Synaesthete.'

He tested the word silently on his lips and frowned. 'Sounds very sci-fi.'

'My brothers did call it my *superpower,* growing up.' Except that it wasn't terribly super and it didn't make her feel powerful. Quite the opposite, some days. 'I didn't even know that other people didn't experience the world like I did until I was about eleven.'

Before that, she'd just assumed she was flat-out unlikeable.

Rich dropped his eyes away for a moment and he busied himself topping up their glasses. 'So you mentioned sensation? Is that why you tensed up when you shook my hand?'

Heat rushed up Mila's cheeks. He'd noticed that? Had he also noticed every other reaction she'd had to being near him?

That could get awkward fast.

'Someone new might feel okay or they might…not.' She wasn't about to apologise for something that just…was…for her.

Rich studied her. 'Must be lonely.'

Her spine ratcheted straight. The only thing she wanted more than to be treated normally was *not* to be treated with pity. She took her time taking a long sip of wine.

'Are my questions upsetting you?'

'I don't… It's not something I usually talk about with strangers. Until I know someone well. People generally react somewhere on a spectrum from obsessive curiosity to outright incredulity. No one's ever just shrugged and said, *All right, then. More sandwiches?*'

Oh, how she longed for that.

'Thank you for making an exception, then.' His eyes stayed locked on hers and he slid the platter slightly towards her. 'More sandwiches?'

It was so close, it stole her breath.

'Why are you really up here, Rich?' she asked, before thinking better of it. It shouldn't matter why; she was paid to show him the area, end of story. His business was as much his own as hers was. But something pushed her on. And not just the desire to change the subject. 'I'm going to look you up online anyway. Might as well tell me. Are you a developer?'

He shifted in his seat, took his time answering. 'You don't like developers, I take it?'

'I guide a lot of them. They spend the day banging on about their grand plans for the area and then I never see them again. I'm just wondering if you'll be the same.'

Not that she was particularly hoping to see him again. *Was she?*

His body language was easy but there was an intensity in his gaze that she couldn't quite define.

'None of them ever come back?'

'Some underestimate how remote it is. Or how much red tape there will be. Most have no idea of the access restrictions that are in place.'

He tipped his head as he sipped his wine. 'Restrictions? Sounds difficult.'

'Technically,' she went on, 'the land all the way up to the National Park is under the control of three local pastoralists. Lifetime leaseholds. In Coral Bay, if anyone wants to get a serious foothold in this part of the Marine Park, they have to get past the Dawsons. No one ever has.' She shifted forward. 'Honestly, Rich? If you do have development plans, you might as well give up now.'

Why was she giving him a heads-up? Just because he'd been nice to her and given her lunch? And looked good in board shorts?

Blue eyes considered her closely. 'The Dawsons sound like a problem.'

The boiled eggs of loyalty materialised determinedly at the back of her throat. 'They're the reason the land around Coral Bay isn't littered with luxury resorts trying to position themselves on World Heritage coast. They're like a final rampart. Yet to be breached. That makes them heroes in my book.'

Rich studied her for a long time before lifting his glass in salute. And in thanks. 'To the Dawsons, then.'

Had she said too much? Nothing he probably didn't already know, or wouldn't find out soon enough. But still...

She ran her hands up and down arms suddenly bristling with goose pimples.

'Cold?' Rich asked, even though the sun was high.

Mila shook her head. 'Ball bearings.'

CHAPTER FOUR

RICH WANTED TO believe that 'ball bearings' referred to the breeze presently stirring wisps of long, dark hair around Mila's face, but what if she sensed ball bearings when she was feeling foreboding? Or deception. Or distrust.

What if she had more 'extra-sensory' in her 'super-sensory' than she knew? He *was* keeping secrets and she *should* feel foreboding. But that wasn't how Mila's condition worked. Not that he had much of an idea how it *did* work, and he didn't want to pummel her with curious questions just for his own satisfaction. He'd just have to use the brain his parents had spent a fortune improving to figure Mila out the old-fashioned way—through conversation.

A big part of him wished that the heroic Dawsons *were* an impediment to his plans—a good fight always got his blood up. But Mila would be dismayed to discover just how easy it was going to be for him to build his hotel overlooking the reef. The handful of small businesses running here might have had mixed feelings about the percentage that WestCorp took from their take—the motel, the café, the fuel station, even the hard-working glass-bottom boat tours—but they couldn't honestly expect not to pay for the privilege of running a business on

Wardoo's land, just as Wardoo had to pay the government for the privilege of running cattle on leasehold land.

Money flowed like an ebbing tide towards the government. It was all part of the food chain.

Except now that same government was shifting the goalposts, looking to excise the coastal strip from the leasehold boundaries. The only part that made any decent profit. And his analysts agreed with him that the only way to get them to leave the lucrative coastal strip in the lease was to make a reasonable capital investment in the region himself—put something back in.

Governments liked to see potential leveraged and demand met.

And—frankly—he liked to do it.

WestCorp needed the lucrative coastal strip to supplement the Station's meagre profits. Without it, there was nothing holding Wardoo in any half-competent finance holdings and, thanks to his father's move to the big smoke forty years ago, there was nothing holding *him* to Wardoo. His heritage.

That was why he'd hauled himself out of the office—out of the city—and come north, to see for himself the place that had been earmarked for development. Just so he could be as persuasive as possible when he pitched it to the responsible bureaucrat. He'd lucked out with a guide who could also give him a glimpse of community attitudes towards his business—forewarned absolutely was forearmed.

It didn't hurt that Mila was such a puzzle—he'd always liked a challenge. Or that she was so easy on the eye. He'd always liked beautiful things. Now she was just plain intriguing too, courtesy of her synaesthesia. Though he'd have to temper his curiosity, given how touchy she was about it. Had someone made her feel like a freak in the past?

The *Portus'* motor cut out and they slowed to a drift. Mila twisted and stared at the ancient rocky range that stretched up and down the coast, red as far as they could see. She knew where they were immediately.

'We'll have to take the tender in; there's only a slim channel in the reef.'

It was narrow and a little bit turbulent where the contents of the reef lagoon rushed out into open water but they paused long enough to watch a couple of manta rays rolling and scooping just there, clearly taking advantage of the fishy freeway as they puttered over the top of it. Damo dropped them close enough to wade comfortably in, their shoes in one hand and sharing the load of the single kayak they'd towed in behind the tender in the other. They hauled it up to the sandbar that stretched across the mouth of Yardi Creek. Or once had.

'This is why we couldn't just drive up here,' she said, indicating the mostly submerged ridge. 'Thanks to a ferocious cyclone season earlier in the year, the sandbar blew out, taking the four-wheel drive access with it. It's only just now reforming. It'll be good to go again at the end of the year but for now it makes for a convenient launch point for us.'

And launch they did. His sea kayak was wider and flatter than a regular canoe, which made it possible for two of them to fit on a vessel technically designed for half that number. He slid down into the moulded seat well and scooted back to make room for Mila, spreading his legs along the kayak's lip so she could sit comfortably between them at the front of the seat well, with her own bent legs dangling over each side. Once she was in, he bent his knees up on either side of her to serve as some kind of amusement park ride safety barrier and unlocked his double paddle into a single half for each of them.

They soon fell into an easy rhythm that didn't fight the other, though Mila's body stayed as rigid and unyielding as the hard plastic of the kayak against his legs. Given what he now knew about her, this kind of physical contact had to be difficult for her. Not that she was snuggled up to him exactly, but the unconventional position wasn't easy for either of them. Though maybe for different reasons. *He* was supposed to be paying attention to everything around him yet he kept finding his gaze returning to the slim, tanned back and neck of the young woman seated between his knees, her now-dry ponytail hanging not quite neatly down her notched spine. She'd shrugged out of her uniform shirt and folded it neatly into her backpack but somehow—in this marine environment—the bikini top was as much of a uniform as anything.

She was in her mid-twenties—nearly a decade younger than he was—but there was something about her... As if she'd been here a whole lot longer. Born of the land, or even the sea. She just...belonged.

'Looks like we have the creek to ourselves.' Mila's soft words came easily back to him. courtesy of the gorge's natural acoustics.

Sure enough, there was not another human being visible anywhere—on the glassy water, up on the top of the massive canyon cliffs, in the car park gouged out of the limestone and dunes. Though it was easy to imagine a solitary figure, dark and mysterious, silhouetted against the sun, spear casually at hand, watching their approach far below.

It was just that kind of place.

Mila stopped paddling and he copied her, the drag of his paddle embedded in the water slowing them to almost nothing. Ahead, a pair of nostrils and a snub-nosed little face emerged from the water, blinking, checking them out. The kayak drifted silently past him on inertia. Only at the last moment did he dip back underwater and vanish to the depths of the deep canyon creek.

'Hawksbill turtle,' Mila murmured back to him once they were clear. 'Curious little guy.'

'You get curiosity for turtles?'

She turned half back, smiled. 'No. I mean he was *actually* curious. About us. I get bossy for turtles.'

They paddled on in silence. Rich battled with a burning question.

'Does it affect how you feel about some things?' he finally asked, as casually as he could. 'If your perception is negative?'

'It can.'

She didn't elaborate and he wondered if that question—or any question—held some hidden offence, but her voice when she finally continued wasn't tight.

'I'm not a huge fan of yellow fish, for instance, through no fault of their own. I read yellow as derisive and so...' She shrugged. 'But, similarly, people and things can strike me positively because of their associations too.'

'Like what?' he asked.

She paused again, took an age to answer. 'Oak moss. I used to get that when I was curled in my mother's arms as a child. I get it now when I'm wrapped up in my softest, woolliest sweater on a cold night, or snuggled under a quilt. It's impossible not to feel positive about oak moss.'

Her love came through loud and clear in her low voice and he was a bit sorry that he was neither naturally oaky nor mossy. It threw him back to a time, long ago, when he'd done the same with his own mother. Before he'd lost her at the end of primary school. Before he'd been dumped into boarding school by his not-coping father.

There'd been no loving arms at all after that.

She cleared her throat and kept her back firmly to him.

'Once, I met someone who registered as cotton candy. Hard not to respond positively to such a fun and evocative scent memory. I was probably more predisposed to like and trust him than, say, someone who I read as diesel smoke.'

Lucky cotton candy guy. Something told him that being liked and trusted by Mila Nakano was rarer than the mysteries in this gorge.

'What's the worst association you've ever made?' Curious was as close to 'accepting' as she was going to let him get.

'Earwax,' she said softly.

'Was that a person or a thing?'

The kayak sent out ripples ahead of them but it was easy to imagine they were soundwaves from her laughter. It was rich and throaty and it got right in between his ribs.

'A person, unfortunately.' She sighed. 'The one kid at primary school that gave me a chance. Whenever they were around I got a strong hit of earwax in the back of my throat and nose. Now, whenever my heart is sad for any reason at all, I get a delightful reminder...'

Imagine trying to forge a friendship—or, worse, a relationship—with someone who struck you so negatively whenever they were around. How impossible it would be. How that would put you off experimenting with pretty much anyone.

Suddenly, he got a sense of how her superpower worked. He was going to find it difficult to go out on this kayak ever again without an image of Mila's lean, long back popping into his head. Or to watch ripples radiate on still water anywhere without hearing her soft voice. The only difference was that her associations didn't need to have a foundation in real life.

Mila dug the paddle hard into the water again and turned her face up and to the right as the kayak slowed. 'Black-flanked rock wallaby.'

Rich followed her gaze up the towering cliffs that lined both sides of the deep creek and hunted the vertical, rust-coloured rock face. 'All I see are some shadowy overhangs. What am I missing?'

'That's where the wallabies like to lurk. It's why they have evolved black markings.'

He scanned the sheer cliffs for camouflaged little faces. 'What are they, half mountain goat? Don't they fall off?'

'They're born up there, spend their lives leaping from claw-hold to claw-hold, nibbling on the plants that grow there, sleeping under the overhangs, raising their own young away from most predators. They're adapted to it. It's totally normal to them. They would be so surprised to know how impossible we find it.'

He fell back into rhythm with her gentle paddling. Was she

talking about wallabies now or was she talking about her syn-aesthesia?

The more he looked, the more he saw, and the further he pad-dled, the more Mila showed him. She talked about the prehis-toric-looking fish species that liked the cold, dark depths of the creek's uppermost reaches, the osprey and egrets that nested in its heights, the people who had once lived here and the ancient sites that were being rediscovered every year.

It was impossible not to imagine the tourist potential of build-ing something substantial down the coast from a natural re-source like this. An eco-resort in eco-central. Above them, small openings now occupied by wallabies hinted at so much more.

'The cavers must love it here,' he guessed. He knew enough about rocks to know these ones were probably riddled with holes.

'One year there was a massive speleologist convention and cavers from all over the world came specifically to explore the uncharted parts of the Range. They discovered nearly twelve new caves in two days. Imagine what they might have found if they could have stayed up here for a week. Or two!'

'Why couldn't they?'

'There just aren't any facilities up here to house groups of that size. Or labs to accommodate scientists or…really anything. Still, the caves have waited this long, I guess.' Her shoulders slumped. 'As long as the sea doesn't rise any faster.'

In which case the coastal range where the rock wallabies clung would go back to being islands and the exposed rock they were exploring would eventually be blanketed in corals again.

The circle of life.

They took their time paddling the crumbled-in end of the gorge, looking closely at the make-up of the towering walls, the same shapes he'd seen out on the reef here, just fossilised, the synchronised slosh of their oars the only sounds between them.

The silence in this beautiful place was otherwise complete.

It soaked into him in a way he'd never really felt before and he finally understood why Mila might have thought that open ocean wasn't really that quiet at all.

Because she had *this* to compare it to.

'So, I'm thinking of coming back on the weekend,' he said when they were nearly done, before realising he'd even decided. 'For a couple more days. I've obviously underestimated what brings people here.'

They bumped back up against the re-establishing sand bar and Mila clambered out then turned to him with something close to suspicion on her pretty face. After the connection he thought they'd just made it was a disappointing setback.

'I'm only booked for today,' she said bluntly. 'You'll have to find someone else to guide you.'

Denial surged through him.

'You have other clients?' He could get that changed with one phone call. But pulling rank on her like that would be about as popular as...earwax.

'No, but I've got things on.'

'What kind of things?'

'An aerial survey of seagrasses and some whale shark pattern work. A tagging job. And the neap tide is this weekend so I'll be part of the annual spawn collection team. It's a big deal up here.'

Rich felt his chance at continuing to get quality insider information—and his opportunity to get to know Mila a bit better—slipping rapidly away.

'Can I come along? Two birds, one stone.' Then, when she hesitated awkwardly, he added, 'Paid, of course.'

She winced. 'It's not about money. I'm just not sure whether that's okay. Most of our work isn't really a spectator sport.'

It was a practical enough excuse. But every instinct told him it was only half the truth. Was she truly so used to only ever seeing developers the one time? Well, he liked to be memorable.

'Put me to work, then. I can count seagrass or study the… spawn.'

Ten minutes ago that would have earned him another throaty laugh. Now, she just frowned.

'Come on, Mila, wasn't it you who asked when I'd last done something completely new to me? This is an opportunity. A bunch of new experiences.' He found the small tussle of wills disproportionately exhilarating. 'I'll be low-maintenance. Scout's honour.'

She shrugged as she bent to hike her side of the kayak up, but the lines either side of her flat lips told him she wasn't feeling that casual at all.

'It's your time to waste, I guess.'

He only realised he'd been holding his breath when he was able to let it out on a slow, satisfied smile. More time to get a feel for this district and more time to get his head around Mila Nakano.

The return trip felt as if it took half the time, as return trips often did. But it was long enough for Mila to carefully pick her way out to the front of the *Portus* and slide down behind the safety barrier on one of the catamaran hulls. Rich did the same on the other and—together but apart—they lost themselves in the deep blue ocean until they reached the open waters off Coral Bay again. Over on her side, the water whooshing past sang triumphantly.

Regardless, she shifted on the deck and let her shoulders slump.

She'd been rude. Even she could see that. Properly, officially rude.

But the moment Rich had decided to return to Coral Bay for a more in-depth look she'd felt a clawing kind of tension start to climb her spine. Coming back meant he wasn't a *one* any more. Coming back meant that none of the remoteness or the politics or the environmental considerations had deterred him particularly.

Coming back meant he was serious.

She'd guided Rich today because that was her job. But she'd let herself be disarmed by his handsome face and fancy boat and his apparently genuine interest in the reef and cape. Her only comfort was that he still had to get past the Dawsons—and no one had ever managed that—but she still didn't want him to think that she somehow endorsed his plans to develop the bay.

Whatever they were.

Regardless of the cautious camaraderie that had grown between them, Richard Grundy was still her adversary. Because he was the reef's adversary.

She cast her eyes across the deep green ocean flashing by below the twin hulls. Rich sat much as she did, legs dangling, spray in his face, but his gaze was turned away from her, his focus firmly fixed on the coast as they raced south parallel to it. No doubt visualising how his hotel was going to look looming over the water. Or his resort.

Or—perish the thought—his casino.

Knowing wouldn't change anything, yet she had to work hard at not being obsessed by which it would be.

They met on the aft deck as the catamaran drew to an idling halt off Bill's Bay an hour later. Behind them, the sun was making fairly rapid progress towards the horizon.

'It was good to meet you,' she murmured politely, already backing away.

Rich frowned. 'You say that like I won't be seeing you again…'

The weekend was four days away. Anything could happen in that time, including him losing his enthusiasm for returning. Just because he was eager for it now didn't mean he'd still be hot for it after the long journey back to the city and his overflowing inbox. Or maybe she'd have arranged someone else to show him around on Saturday. That would be the smart thing to do. This could quite easily be the last she ever saw of Richard Grundy.

At the back of her throat the slightest tang began to climb over the smell of the ocean.

Earwax.

Which was ridiculous. Rich was virtually a stranger; why would her heart squeeze even a little bit at the thought of parting? But her senses never lied, even when she was lying to herself. That was unmistakably earwax she could taste.

Which made Saturday a really bad idea.

She hurried down to the dive platform on one of the *Portus'* hulls when Rich might have kissed her cheek in farewell, and she busied herself climbing aboard the tender when he might have offered her a helpful outstretched hand. But once she was aboard and the skipper began to throttle the tender out from under the *Portus* she had no real excuse—other than rudeness—not to look back at Rich, his hands shoved deeply into his pockets, still standing on the small dive platform. It changed the shape of his arms and shoulders below the T-shirt he'd put on when they'd got back aboard, showing off the sculpted muscles she'd tried so hard not to appreciate when they were snorkelling. Or when they brushed her briefly while they were paddling the kayak.

'Seven a.m. Saturday, then?' he called over the tender's thrum and nodded towards the marina. It would have sounded like an order if not for the three little forks between his blue eyes.

Doubt.

In a man who probably never second-guessed himself.

'Don't look for me,' she called back to him. 'Look for the uniform.' Just in case. Any one of her colleagues could show him the area.

She should have scrunched her nose as the tender reversed through a light fog of its own diesel exhaust, but all she could taste and smell in the back of her throat was candyfloss. The flavour she was rapidly coming to associate with Rich.

The flavour she was rapidly coming to crave like a sugary drug.

She was almost ashore before she realised that the presence of candyfloss in her mind's nose meant she'd already decided to be the one who met him on Saturday.

The first thing Mila did when she got back to her desk was jump online and check out the etymology of the word *portus*. She'd guessed Greek—some water god or something—but it turned out it was Latin…for port. *Duh!* But it also meant sanctuary, and the imposing vessel certainly was that—even up here, where everything around them was already nine parts tranquil. She'd felt it the moment she'd stepped aboard Rich's luxurious boat. She could only imagine what it was like for him to climb aboard and motor away from the busy city and his corporate responsibilities for a day or two.

No…only ever one. Hadn't he told her as much?

What were those corporate responsibilities, exactly?

It took only moments to search up WestCorp and discover how many pies the corporation had its fingers in. And a couple of media stories that came back high in the search results told her that Richard Grundy was the CEO of WestCorp and had been since the massive and unexpected heart attack that had taken his father. Rich had been carrying the entire corporation since then. No wonder he'd been on the phone a lot that morning. No wonder he didn't have time to use his boat. The Internet celebrated the growth of WestCorp in his few short years. There were pages of resource holdings and she lost interest after only the first few.

Suffice to say that Mr Richard Grundy was as corporate as they came.

Despite that, somewhere between getting off the *Portus* and setting foot back on land she'd decided to definitely be the one to meet him on Saturday. Not just because of the candyfloss, which she reluctantly understood—biology was biology and even hers, tangled as it was with other input, was working just fine when it came to someone so high up on the Mila Nakano Secret Hotness Scale—but because of the earwax.

Her earwax couldn't be for Rich—she just didn't know him well enough—it had to be for the reef. For what a company like WestCorp could do to it. If she left him in the hands of anyone else, could she guarantee that they'd make it as abundantly clear as she would how badly this area did not need development? How it was ticking along just fine as it was?

Or should she only trust something that important to herself?

She reached for her phone.

'Hey, Craig, it's Mila…'

A few minutes later she disconnected her call, reassured that the pilot of Saturday's aerial survey could accommodate an extra body without compromising the duration of the flight. So that was Rich sorted; he would get to see a little more of the region he wanted to know about, and she…

She, what?

She'd bought herself another day or two to work on him and convince him exactly why this region didn't need his fancy-pants development. It happened to also be another day or two for Rich to discover how complicated she and her synaesthesia were to be around but, at the end of the day, the breathy antic-ipation of her lonely heart had to mean less than the sanctity and security of her beloved reef.

It just had to.

CHAPTER FIVE

'WE'RE MAPPING WHAT?' Rich asked into the microphone of the headset they each wore on Saturday morning as the little Cessna lifted higher and higher. Coasting at fifteen hundred feet was the only way to truly appreciate the size and beauty of the whole area.

Dugongs, Mila mouthed back, turning her face out towards a nook in the distant coast where the landforms arranged themselves into the kind of seagrass habitat that the lumbering animals preferred. 'Manatees. Sea cows.'

When he just blinked, she delved into her pocket, swiped through an overcrowded photo roll and then passed the phone back to him.

'Dugong,' she repeated. 'They feed on the seagrasses. They all but disappeared at the start of the century after a cyclone smothered the seagrasses with silt. The department has been monitoring their return ever since.'

She patted the sizeable camera that was fixed to the open window of the aircraft by two heavy-duty braces. 'Their main feeding grounds are a little south of here but more and more are migrating into these sensitive secondary zones. We're tracking their range to measure the viability of recovery from another incident like it.'

The more she impressed upon him the complexity of the environmental situation, the less likely he would be to go ahead with his plans, right? The more words like 'sensitive' and 'fragile' and 'rare' that she used, the harder development would seem up here. Either he would recognise the total lack of sense of developing such delicate coast or—at the very least—he would foresee how much red tape lay in his future.

It couldn't hurt, anyway.

Rich shifted over to sit closer to her window, as if her view was any more revealing than his. This close, she could smell him over the residual whiff of aviation fuel. Cotton candy, as always, but there was something else… Something she couldn't identify. It didn't ring any alarm bells; on the contrary, it made her feel kind of settled. In a way she hadn't stopped feeling since picking him up at the marina after four days apart.

Right.

It felt right.

'Craig comes up twice a day to spot for the whale shark cruises,' she said to distract herself from such a worrying association. To keep her focus firmly on work. She nodded down at the four white boats waiting just offshore. 'If he isn't scheduled to take tourists on a scenic flight then I hitch a lift and gather what data I can while we're up here.'

'Opportunistic,' Rich observed.

'Like the wildlife.' She smiled.

Okay, so he hadn't technically earned the smile, but she was struggling not to hand them out like sweets. What was going on with her today? She hadn't gushed over Craig when she saw him again after a week.

They flew in a wide arc out over the ocean and Rich shifted back to his own window and peered out. Below, areas of darkness on the water might have been the shadow of clouds, reef or expansive seagrass beds.

'We're looking for pale streaks in the dark beds,' Mila said. 'That's likely to be a dugong snuffling its way along the seafloor, vacuuming up everything it finds. Where there's one, hopefully there'll be more.'

Until you saw it, it was difficult to explain—something between a snail's trail and a jet stream—but, as soon as you saw it, it was unmistakable in the bay's kaleidoscopic waters.

They flew lower, back and forth over the grasses, eyes peeled. When she did this, she usually kept her focus tightly fixed on the sea below, not only to spot an elusive dugong but also to limit the distracting sensory input she was receiving from everything else she could see in her periphery. Today, though, she was failing at both.

She'd never been as aware of someone else as she was with Rich up here. If he shuffled, she noticed. If he smiled, she felt it. If he spoke, she attended.

It was infuriating.

'Is that one?' Rich asked, pointing to a murky streak not far from shore.

'Sure is!' Mila signalled to Craig, who adjusted course and took them closer. She tossed a pair of binoculars at Rich and locked onto his eyes. 'Go you.'

Given the animal she was supposed to be fascinated by, it took her a worryingly long time to tear her eyes away from Rich's and focus on the task at hand.

Through the zoom lens of her camera it was possible to not only get some detail on the ever-increasing forage trail of a feeding dugong but to also spot three more rolling around at the surface enjoying the warmest top layer of the sea and the rising sun. Her finger just about cramped on the camera's shutter release and she filled an entire memory card with images. Maybe a dozen or so would be useful to the dugong research team but until she got back to her office she couldn't know which. So she just kept shooting.

Rich shook his head as they finished up the aerial survey. 'Can't believe you get paid to do this.'

'Technically, I don't,' Mila admitted. 'I'm on my own time today.'

He turned a frown towards her and spoke straight into her ear, courtesy of the headsets. 'That doesn't seem right.'

She looked up at him. 'Why? What else would I do with the time?'

'Uh... Socialise? Sleep in? Watch a movie?'

'This is plenty social for my liking.' She chuckled, looking between Craig and Rich. 'And why watch a movie when I can be watching dugongs feeding?'

'So you never relax? You're always doing something wild-lifey?'

His judgement stung a little. And not only because it was true. 'Says the man who has an office set up on his boat so he doesn't miss an email.'

'I run a *Fortune 100* company.' He tsked. 'You're just—'

'Dude...!' Craig choked out a warning before getting really busy flying the plane. All those switches that needed urgent flipping...

'Just?' Mila bristled, as the cabin filled with the unmissable scent of fried chicken. 'Is that right?'

But he was fearless.

'Mila, one of the few advantages to being an employ*ee* and not an employ*er* is that you get to just...switch off. Go home and not think about work until Monday.'

Wow. How out of touch with ordinary people was he?

'My job title may not be comprised of initials, Rich, but what I do is every bit as important and *as occupying* as what you do. The only difference is that I do it for the good of the reef and not for financial gain.'

Craig shook his head without looking back at either of them.

'I'm out,' she thought she heard him mutter in the headset.

Rich ignored him. 'Oh, you're some kind of philanthropist? Is that it?'

'How many voluntary hours did *you* complete last month?'

His voice crept up, even though the microphone at his throat meant it didn't need to. 'Personally? None; I don't have the time. But WestCorp has six new staff working for us in entry level roles who were homeless before we got to them and that's an initiative *I* started.'

Mila's outrage snapped shut.

'Oh.' She puffed out a breath. 'Well… That's not on your website.'

'You think that's something I should be splashing around? Exposing those people to public scrutiny and comment?'

No, that would be horrible. But would a corporation generally care about that when there was good press to be had?

The Cessna's engines spluttered on.

'So you made good on your threat to check up on me, I see,' he eventually queried, his voice softening.

Sour milk mingled in with the bitter embarrassment of Brussels sprouts for a truly distasteful mix. Though she was hardly the only uncomfortable one in the plane. Rich looked wary and Craig looked as if he wanted to leap out without wasting time with a parachute.

'I was just curious about what you did,' she confessed.

'Find anything interesting?'

'Not really.' But then she remembered. 'I'm sorry about your father.'

The twitch high in his clenched jaw got earwax flowing again and this time it came with a significant, tangible and all too actual squeeze behind her breast. Had she hurt him with her clumsy sympathy?

But he didn't bite; he just murmured, 'Thank you.'

The silence then was cola-flavoured and she sank into the awkwardness and chewed her lip as she studied the ocean below. Craig swung the plane around and headed back towards Coral Bay.

'Okay, we're on the clock,' he said, resettling in his seat, clearly relieved to have something constructive to say. 'Whale sharks, here we come.'

Rich knew enough about this region to know what it was most famous for—the seasonal influx of gentle giants of the sea. Whale sharks. More whale than shark, the massive fish were filter feeders and, thus, far safer for humans than the other big sharks also out there. Swimming out in the open waters with any of them was a tightly regulated industry and a massive money-spinner.

But, frankly, anyone doing it for fun had to be nuts.

The water was more than beautiful enough from up here without needing to be immersed in it and all its mysteries.

'What do you need with whale sharks?' he asked, keen to undo his offence of earlier with some easier conversation.

Mila couldn't know how secretly he yearned to be relieved of the pressure of running things, just for a while. A week. A weekend even. He hadn't had a weekend off since taking over WestCorp six years before. Even now, here, he was technically on the job. Constantly thinking, constantly assessing. While other people dreamed of fancy cars and penthouse views, his fantasies were a little more...*suburban*. A sofa, a warm body to curl around and whatever the latest hit series was on TV.

Downtime.

Imagine that.

He couldn't really name the last time he'd done something just for leisure. Sport was about competitiveness, rock-climbing was about discipline and willpower. If he read a book it was likely to be the autobiography of someone wildly successful. It was almost as if he didn't *want* to be alone. Or quiet. Or thoughtful.

So when he'd commented on Mila's downtime, he hadn't meant it as a criticism. Of everything he'd seen in Coral Bay so far, the thing that had made the biggest impression on him was the way Mila spent her days.

Spectacularly simple. While also being very full.

She patted her trusty camera.

'Whale sharks can be identified by their patterning rather than by invasive tagging. The science employs the same algorithms NASA uses to chart star systems.'

A pretty apt analogy. The whale sharks he'd seen in photos were blanketed in constellations of pale spots on a Russian blue skin.

Mila turned more fully to him and her engagement lit up her face just like one of those distant suns he saw as a star. It almost blinded him with optimism. 'Generally, the research team uses crowd-sourced images submitted by the tourists that swim with them but I try and contribute when I can.'

'You can photograph them from up here?'

'Oh, we'll be going lower, mate,' Craig said, over the rattle of the Cessna's engine. 'We're looking for grey tadpoles at the surface. Shout out if you see any.'

Tadpoles? From up here? He looked at Mila.

Her grin was infectious. 'You'll see.'

He liked to do well at things—that came from results-based schooling, an all-honours university career, and a career where he was judged by his successes—so he was super-motivated to replicate his outstanding dugong-spotting performance. But this time Mila was the first to spot a cluster of whale sharks far below.

'On your left, Craig.'

They banked and the sharks came into view.

'Tadpoles,' Rich murmured. Sure enough: square-nosed, slow-swimming tadpoles far, far below. 'How big are they?'

'Maybe forty feet,' Mila said. 'A nice little posse of three.'

'That'll keep the punters happy,' Craig said and switched channels while he radioed the location of the sharks in to the boats waiting patiently but blindly below.

'We'll stay with this pod until the boats get here,' Mila murmured. 'Circle lower and get our shots while we wait.'

Craig trod a careful line between getting Mila the proximity she needed and not scaring the whale sharks away into deeper waters. He descended in a lazy circle, keeping a forty-five-degree angle to the animals at all times. While Mila photographed their markings, Rich peered down through the binoculars to give him the same zoomed-in views she was getting. Far below, the three mammoth fish drifted in interlocking arcs, their big blunt heads narrowing down into long, gently waving tail fins. As if the tadpoles were moving in slow motion. There was an enviable kind of ease in their movements, as if they had nowhere better to be right now. No pressing engagements. No board meeting at nine. No media pack at eleven.

Hard not to envy them their easy life.

'The plankton goes down deep during the day so the whale sharks take long rests up here before going down to feed again at dusk,' Mila said. 'That's why they're so mellow with tourists, because they have a full belly and are half asleep.'

'How many are there on the whole reef?'

'Right now there's at least two dozen and more arriving every day because they're gathering for the coral spawn this weekend.'

'They eat the spawn?'

'Everyone eats the spawn. It's why the entire reef erupts all on the same night—to increase the chances of survival.' She glanced back at him. 'What?'

'You're pretty impressed with nature, aren't you?'

'I appreciate order,' she admitted. 'And nothing is quite as streamlined as evolution. No energy wasted.'

If his world was as cluttered as hers—with all her extrasensory input—he might have a thing for order too. His days tended to roll out in much the same way day in, day out.

Same monkeys, different circus.

'If it was just about systems you'd be happy working in a bank. Why out here? Why wildlife?'

She gave the whale sharks her focus but he knew he had her attention and he could see her thinking hard about her answer—or whether or not to give it to him, maybe. Finally, she slipped the headset off her head, glanced at an otherwise occupied Craig and leaned towards him. He met her in the middle and turned his ear towards her low voice.

'People never got me,' she said, low. And painfully simple. He got the sense that maybe this wasn't a discussion she had very often. Or very easily. 'Growing up. Other kids, their parents. They didn't hate me but they didn't accept me either, because I saw or heard or smelled things that they couldn't. Or they thought I was lying. Or making fun of them. Or defective. One boy called me "Mental Mila" and it kind of...stuck.'

Huh. He'd never wanted to punch a kid so much in his life.

'I already didn't fit anywhere culturally, then I discovered I didn't fit socially.' She looked down at the reef. 'Out there every species is as unique and specialised as the one next to it yet it doesn't make them exclusive. If anything, it makes them inclusive; they learn to work their specialties in together. Nature cooperates; it doesn't judge.'

Mankind sure did.

She slid the headset back on, returned to her final photos and the moment—and Mila's confidence—passed. He could so imagine her as a pretty, lonely young girl who turned her soft heart towards the non-judgemental wildlife and made them her friends.

The sorrowful image sucked all the joy out of his day.

The Cessna kept on circling the three-strong pod of whale sharks, keeping track of them until the boats of tourists began to converge, then Craig left them to their fun and scoured up the coast for a back-up group in case those ones decided to dive deep. As soon as they found more and radioed the alternate location, their job was done and Craig turned for Coral Bay's airfield, charting a direct line down the landward side of the coast.

As they crossed back over terra firma, Rich peered through

the dusty window of his door at the red earth below. He knew that land more for its features on a map than anything else. The distinctive hexagonal dam that looked like a silver coin from here, but was one of the biggest in the region from the ground. The wagon wheel of stock tracks leading to it. The particular pattern of eroded ridges in Wardoo's northwest quadrant. The green oasis of the waterhole closer to the homestead. When he was a boy he'd accompanied his father on a charter flight over the top of the whole Station and been arrested by its geometry. For a little while he'd had an eight-year-old's fantasies of the family life he might have had there, as a kid on the land with a dozen brothers and sisters, parents who sat around a table at night, laughing, after a long day mustering stock…

'That's the Station I told you about,' Mila murmured, misreading his expression as interest. 'Wardoo isn't just beautiful coastline; its lands are spectacular too. All those fierce arid ripples.'

Fierce. He forced his mind back onto the present. 'Is that what you feel when you look at the Station?'

It went some way to explaining her great faith in Wardoo as a protector of the realm if looking at it gave her such strong associations.

'Isolation,' she said. 'There's an undertone in Wardoo's red… I get the same association with jarrah. Like the timber deck on your boat. It's lonely, to me.'

He stared down at all that red geometry. Fantasy Rich and his enormous fantasy family were pretty much all that had got him through losing his mother and then being cast off in boarding school. But by the time he was old enough to consider visiting by himself, he had no reason and even less time to indulge the old crutch. He'd created a stable, rational world for himself at school and thrown himself into getting the grades he needed to get into a top university. Once at uni he'd been all about killing it in exams so that he could excel in the company he'd been raised to inherit. He'd barely achieved that when his father's heart had suddenly stopped beating and, since then, he'd been all about taking WestCorp to new and strictly governable heights. There'd been very little time for anything else. And even less inclination.

Thus, maps and the occasional financial summary were his only reminder that Wardoo even existed.

Until now.

'Actually, I can see that one.'

Her eyes flicked up to his and kind of...crashed there. As if she hadn't expected him to be looking at her. But she didn't look away.

'Really?' she breathed.

There was an expectation in her gaze that stuck in his gut like a blade. As if she was hunting around for someone to understand her. To connect with.

As if she was ravenous for it.

'For what it's worth, Mila,' Rich murmured into the headset, 'your synaesthesia is the least exceptional thing about you.'

Up front, Craig's mouth dropped fully open, but Mila's face lit up like a firework and her smile grew so wide it almost broke her face.

'That's so lovely of you to say,' she breathed. 'Thank you.'

No one could accuse him of not knowing people. And people the world over all wanted the same thing. To belong. To fit. The more atypical that people found Mila, the less comfortable she was bound to be with them. And, even though it was a bad idea, he really wanted her to be comfortable with him for the few short hours they would have together. He turned and found her eyes—despite the fact that his voice was feeding directly to her ears courtesy of the headphones—and pumped all the understanding he could into his gaze.

'You're welcome.'

The most charged of silences fell and Craig was the only one detached enough to break it.

'Buckle up,' he told them both. 'Airstrip's ahead.'

* * *

Mila shifted towards the open door of the Cessna, where Rich had just slid out under its wing. As long as his back was to her she was fine, but the moment he turned to face her she knew she was in trouble. Normally she would have guarded against the inevitable barrage of crossed sensations that being swung down bodily by someone would bring. But, in his case, she had to steel herself against the pleasure—all that hard muscle and breadth against her own little body.

Tangled sensations had never felt so good.

Twenty-four hours ago she would have found some excuse to crawl through to the other door and exit far away from Rich, or accepted his hand—*maybe*—and limit the physical skin-on-skin to just their fingers, but now... She rested her hands lightly on his shoulders and held her breath. He eased her forward, over the edge of the door, and supported her as she slid his full length until her toes touched earth. Even then he didn't hurry to release her and the hot press of his body sent her into a harpy, sugary overdrive.

Your synaesthesia is the least exceptional thing about you.

To have it not be the first thing someone thought about when they thought about her... The novelty of that was mind-blowing. And it begged the question—what *did* he associate first with her? Not something she could ever ask for shame; ridiculous to be curious about and dangerous to want, given what he did for a living.

But there it was. As uncontrollable and illogical as her superpower. And she'd learned a long time ago to accept the inevitability of those.

Her nostrils twitched as her feet found purchase on the runway; alongside the usual carnival associations there was something else. Some indefinable...closeness. She felt inexplicably drawn to Richard Grundy. She'd been feeling it all morning.

It took a moment for her to realise.

She spun on him, eyes wide. 'What are you wearing?'

He didn't bother disguising his grin. He reached up with one arm and hooked it over the strut holding the Cessna's wing and fuselage to each other. The casual pose did uncomfortable things to her pulse.

'Do you have any idea how hard it is to find a cologne with oak moss undertones on short notice?' he said.

Mila stared even as her chest tightened. 'You wore it intentionally?'

'Totally. Unashamedly,' he added, as the gravity of her expression hit him. 'I wasn't sure it was working. You seemed unaffected at first.'

That was because she was fighting the sensation to crawl into his lap in the plane and fall asleep there.

Oak moss.

'Why would you do that?' she half whispered, thinking about that murmured discussion without their headsets. The things she'd confessed. The access she'd given him into her usually protected world.

He shrugged the shoulder that wasn't stretched up towards the plane's wing. 'Because you associate it with security.'

She fought back the rush of adrenaline and citrus that he'd cared at all how she felt around him and gave her anger free rein. 'And you thought manipulating the freak would somehow make me feel safe with you?'

He lowered his arm and straightened, his comfortable expression suddenly growing serious. 'Whoa, no, Mila. That's not what—'

'Then what? Why do I need to feel safe with you?'

She'd not seen Rich look anything but supremely confident since he'd first come striding towards her with his hand outstretched at Nancy's Point. Now he looked positively bewildered. And a little bit sick. It helped ease the whiff of nail varnish that came with the devastation.

This whole conversation stank more than an industrial precinct.

'Because you're so wary and I...' He greyed just a little bit more as his actions dawned on him. 'Oh, God, Mila—'

'Way to go, bro!' Craig called as he breezed past them with a hand raised in farewell and marched towards the little shed that served as the airfield's office.

Rich was way too fixated on her face to acknowledge his departure, but it bought them both a moment to take a breath and think. Mila fought her natural inclination to distrust.

Richard Grundy was not a serial killer. He hadn't just spiked her drink in a nightclub. He wasn't keeping strangers locked up in a basement somewhere.

He'd worn something he thought would make her comfortable around him.

That was all.

Mila could practically see his mind whirring away in that handsome head. He dropped his gaze to the crushed limestone runway and when it came back up his eyes were bleak. But firm. And she registered the truth in them.

'I wanted to ask you to dinner,' he admitted, low. 'And I wanted you to feel comfortable enough around me to say yes.'

'Do I look comfortable?'

He sagged. 'Not even a little bit.'

But every shade paler Rich went helped with that. He saw his mistake now and something told her that he very rarely made them. Old habits died hard, yet something in his demeanour caused a new and unfamiliar sensation to shimmer through her tense body.

Trust.

She wanted to believe in him.

'Why would you care whether I come to dinner or not?' Which was coward-speak for, *Why do you want to have dinner at all?*

With me.

'You intrigue me,' he began. 'And not because of the synaesthesia. Or not *just* because of it,' he added when she lifted a sceptical brow. 'I just wanted to get to know you better. And I wanted you to get to know *me* better.'

'I'm not sure you improve on repeat exposure, to be honest.'

Conflict shone live in his intense gaze. He battled it for moments. Then he decided.

'You know what? This was a mistake. *My* mistake,' he hurried to clarify.

'Big call from a man who never makes mistakes.'

His laugh was half-snort. And barely even that.

'Apparently, I save them up to perpetrate in one stunning atrocity.' His chest broadened with one breath. 'I succeed in business because of my foresight. My planning. Because I anticipate obstacles and plan for them. But I'm completely out of my depth with you, Mila. I have no idea where the boundaries are, never mind how I can control them. But that's a poor excuse for trying to game you.' He stepped out from under the shade of the Cessna's wing. 'Thank you for everything you've shown me and I wish you all the best for the future.'

He didn't try and shake her hand, or to touch her in any way. He just delivered an awkward half-bow like some lord of a long-ago realm and started to back away. But at the last moment he stopped and turned back.

'I meant what I said, Mila, about you being exceptional for a whole bunch of reasons that have nothing to do with your synaesthesia. There's something about how you are on that reef, in this place... I think you and your super-connectedness to the world might just hold the secret to life. I don't understand it, but I'm envious as hell and I think I was just hoping that some of it might rub off on me.'

He nodded one last time and strode away.

A slam of freshly made toast hit her. *Sorrow.* Rich was saying goodbye just as she'd finally got to meet the real him. Just as he'd dropped his slick veneer and let her in through those aquamarine eyes—the colour that always energised her. She would never again know the harp strains of his touch, or the coffee of his easy company or the sugar-rush of his sexy smile. He would be just like every other suited stranger she'd ever guided up here.

A *one*.

She wasn't ready to assign him to those dreaded depths just yet. And not just because of the rapidly diminishing oak moss that made her feel so bereft. She'd spent her life being distanced by people and here was a man trying to close that up a little and she'd gone straight for the jugular.

Maybe she needed to be party to the distance-closing herself.

Maybe change started at home.

'Wait!'

She had to call it a second time because Rich had made such long-legged progress away from her. He stopped and turned almost as he stepped off the airfield onto the carefully reticulated grass that lined it. Some little voice deep down inside urged her that once he'd stepped onto that surface it would have been too late, that he'd have been lost to her.

That she'd caught something—barely—before it was gone for ever. 'What about the coral spawn?'

He frowned and called back. 'What about it?'

'You can't leave before you've seen it, surely? Having come all this way.'

His face grew guarded and she got toast again as she realised that she'd made him feel as bad about himself as others had always made her feel.

'Is it that spectacular?' he called back warily.

'It's a miracle,' she said, catching up. Puffing slightly. More aware of someone than ever before in her life. 'And it should start tonight.'

He battled silently with himself again, and she searched his eyes for signs of an angle she just couldn't find.

'It would be my first miracle…' he conceded.

'And the moon has to be high to trigger it so, you know,

we could grab something to eat beforehand.' She huffed out a breath. 'If you want.'

His smile, when it came, was like a Coral Bay sunrise. Slow to start but eye-watering when it came up over the ridge. It was heralded by a tsunami of candyfloss.

'That won't be weird? After...' He nodded towards the plane. *Cessna-gate?*

'No,' she was quick to confirm. 'It wasn't the brightest thing you've done but I believe that you meant no harm.'

His handsome face softened with gratitude. But there was something else in there too, a shadow...

'Okay then,' he said, pushing it away. 'I'll meet you at the marina at six?'

Her breath bunched up in her throat like onlookers crowding around some spectacle. It made it hard to say much more than, 'Okay.'

It was only at the last moment that she remembered to call out.

'Bring your fins!'

CHAPTER SIX

RICH BRACED HIS feet in the bottom of the tender as it puttered up to the busy pier, then leapt easily off onto the unweathered timbers without Damo needing to tie up amongst the dozen boaters also coming ashore for the evening.

Mila had been on his mind since he'd left her earlier in the day, until the raft of documents waiting for him had forced her out so that he could focus on the plans.

I believe that you meant no harm, she'd said.

Purposefully wearing one of her synaesthesia scents was only a small part of the hurt he feared he might be gearing up to perpetrate on this gentle creature. A decent man would have accepted another guide, or gone back to the city and stayed there. Made the necessary decisions from afar. A decent man wouldn't be finding reasons to stay close to Mila even as he did the paperwork that would change her world for ever. A driven man would. A focused man would.

He would.

Was there no way to succeed up here *and* get the girl?

Deep down, he knew that there probably wasn't.

Mila wouldn't be quite so quick to declare her confident belief in him if she knew that he had the draft plans for a reef-front resort sitting on his desk on board the *Portus*. Or why he was so unconcerned about any eleventh-hour development barriers from the local leaseholders.

Because he *was* that final barrier.

He *was* Wardoo.

And Wardoo's lease was up for renewal right now. There was no time to come up with another strategy, or for long-winded feasibility testing. *Someone* was going to develop this coast—him, the government, some offshore third party—and if he didn't act, then he would lose the coastal strip or the lease on Wardoo. Possibly both.

Then where would Mila and her reef be?

Better the devil and all that.

He waved Damo off and watched him putter past incoming boats, back out towards the *Portus*' holding site beyond the reef. As the sun sank closer to the western horizon, it cast an orange-yellow glow over everything, reflected perfectly in the still, mirrored surface of the windless lagoon. Did Mila dislike golden sunsets the way she distrusted yellow fish? He couldn't imagine her disliking anything about this unique place.

'Beautiful, isn't it,' a soft voice said behind him. 'I could look at that every day.'

Rich turned to face Mila, standing on the marina. He wanted to comment that she *did* look at it every day but the air he needed to accomplish it escaped from his lungs as soon as he set eyes on her.

She wasn't wet, or bedraggled, or crunchy-haired. She wasn't in uniform. Or in a bikini. Or any of the ways he'd seen her up until now. She stood, weight on one leg, hands twisted in front of her, her long dark hair hanging smooth and combed around her perfectly made-up face. All natural tones, almost impossible to see except that he'd been remembering that face without its make-up every hour of the day since he'd left on Tuesday and comparing it subconsciously to every other artfully made-up female face he'd seen since then. That meant he could spot the earthy, natural colours, so perfect on her tanned skin. A clasp of shells tightly circled her long throat while a longer strand hung down across the vee of smooth skin revealed by her simple knitted dress, almost the same light brown as her skin. The whole thing was held up by the flimsiest of straps, lying over the bikini she wore underneath. She looked casual enough to walk straight out into the glassy water, or boho enough to dine in any restaurant in the city. Even the best ones.

'Mila. Good to see you again.' *Ugh, that was formal.* He held up the snorkelling gear he'd purchased on his way back to the *Portus* that morning. 'Fins.'

Her smile seemed all the brighter in the golden light of evening and some of the twist in her fingers loosened up. 'I thought you might have left them on the boat by-accident-on-purpose. To get out of tonight.'

'Are you kidding? Miss out on such a unique event?'

She chewed her lip and it was adorable. 'I should confess that not everyone finds mass spawning as beautiful as I do.'

'Seriously? A sea full of floating sex cells. What's not to love?'

She stood grinning at him long enough for him to realise that he was standing just grinning at her too.

Ridiculous.

'Want me to drive?' he finally managed to say. 'It's such a long way.'

His words seemed to break Mila's trance and her laugh tinkled. 'I think I can handle it.'

He rolled around in that laugh, luxuriating, and his mind went again to the stack of plans on his desk.

Jerk.

It only took three minutes to drive around into the heart of Coral Bay. On the way, she asked him about his day at large in town and he asked her about hers. They filled the three minutes effortlessly.

And then they ran flat out of easy conversation.

As soon as they stepped out of her four-wheel drive in front of the restaurant, Mila's body seemed to tighten up. Was she anticipating the sensory impact of sharing a meal with dozens of others, or the awkwardness of sharing a meal with him? Whichever, her back grew rigid as her hand lifted to push the door open.

'Would it be crazy to suggest eating on the beach instead?' he asked before the noise from the restaurant reached more fully out to them. 'The lagoon is too beautiful not to look at tonight.'

As was Mila.

And he didn't really feel like sharing her with a restaurant full of people.

He watched her eagerness to seek the solace of the beach wrestle with her reluctance to be so alone with him. After what he'd pulled earlier, who could blame her? Sharing a meal in a crowded restaurant was one thing; sharing it on a moonlit beach made it much harder to pretend this was all just…business.

'I'm scent-free tonight,' he assured her, holding his hands out to his sides. Trying to keep it light.

'If only,' he thought he heard her mutter.

But then she spoke louder. 'Yes, that would be great; let's order to go.'

And go they did, all of one hundred metres down to the aptly named Paradise Beach, which stretched out expansively from the parking area. The tide was returning but, still, the beach was wide and white and virtually empty. A lone man ran back and forth with a scrappy terrier, white sand flying against the golden sunset. The dog barked with exuberant joy.

'This looks good,' Rich said, unfolding the battered fish and potato scallops.

'Wait until you taste it,' she promised as the man and dog disappeared up a sandy track away from the beach. 'That fish was still swimming a couple of hours ago. They source locally and daily.'

Talking about food was only one step removed from talking

about the weather and it almost pained him to make such inane small talk when his time with Mila was so limited.

He wanted to see the passion in her eyes again.

'Speaking of swimming, why exactly are we heading out into spawn-infested waters?' he encouraged. 'More volunteering?'

'This one's work-related. My whole department heads out at different points of the Northwest Cape on the first nights of the eruption to collect spawn. So we have diverse genetic stock.'

'For what?'

'The spawn bank.'

He just blinked. 'There's a spawn *bank*?'

'There is. Or…there will be, one day. Right now it's a locked chest freezer in Steve Donahue's fish shed, but some day the fertilised spawn will help to repopulate this reef if it's destroyed. Or we can intentionally repopulate individual patches that die off.' She turned to him, her eyes glowing as golden as the sunset. 'Tonight we collect and freeze, and in the future they'll culture and release the resulting embryos to wiggle their way back onto the reef and fix there.'

'That sounds—' *Desperate? A lost cause?* '—ambitious.'

'We have to do something.' She shrugged. 'One outbreak of disease or a feral competitor, rising global temperatures or a really brutal cyclone… All of that would be gone.'

His eyes followed hers out to the darkening lagoon and the reef no longer visible anywhere above it. The water line was nearly twice as far up the beach as it had been when the *Portus* set him ashore. He didn't realise there were so many threats to the reef's survival.

Threats that didn't include him, anyway.

'And how do you know it will be tonight?'

'It's usually triggered by March's full moon.'

He glanced up at the crescent moon peeking over the eastern horizon. 'Shouldn't you have done this last week, then?'

'By the time they've grown for ten days, the moonlight is dim enough to help hide the spawn bundles from every other creature on the reef waiting to eat them.' She glanced out to the horizon. 'It will probably be more spectacular tomorrow night but I like to be in the water for the first eruptions. Not quite so soupy.'

'Sounds delicious,' he drawled.

But it didn't deter his enjoyment of his seafood as he finished it up.

'How far out are we going this time?'

He hated exposing himself with that question but he also liked to be as prepared as possible for challenges, including death-defying ones. Preparedness was how you stayed alive— in the boardroom and on the beach. There was nothing sensible about swimming out onto a reef after dark.

He'd seen the documentaries.

'The species we're after are all comfortably inside the break.'

Comfortably. Nothing about this was comfortable. It was testament to how badly he wanted to be with Mila that he was entertaining the idea at all.

They fell to silence and talked about nothing for a bit, Mila glancing now and again out to the lagoon to check that the spawning hadn't commenced while they were making small talk.

'Can I ask you something?' she eventually said, bringing her eyes back to him. 'How come the captain of the swim team doesn't like water? And don't mention your jet ski,' she interrupted as he opened his mouth. 'I'm talking about being *in* water.'

Given how she'd opened herself up to him about her synaesthesia, not returning the favour felt wrong. Yet going down this path scarcely felt any better, because of where he knew it led. And how she might judge him for that.

'I'm hurt that you've forgotten our first snorkel already...'

Her green eyes narrowed at his evasion.

He leaned forward and rested his elbows on his knees. 'I

like to be the only species in the water. Swimming pools are awesome for that.'

'Spoken like a true axial predator. You don't like to share?'

'Only child,' he grunted. But Mila still wasn't satisfied. That keen gaze stayed locked firmly on his until he felt obliged to offer up more. 'I like to know what I'm sharing with.'

'You know there's more chance of being killed by lightning than a shark, right?'

'I'd like to see those odds recalculated in the middle of an electrical storm.' Which was effectively what swimming out into their domain was like. Doubly so at night. On a reef.

He could stop there. Leave Mila thinking that he was concerned about sharks. Or whales. Or Jules Verne–type squid. She looked as if she was right on the verge of believing him. But he didn't want to leave her with that impression. Sharks and whales and squid mattered to Mila. And it mattered to *him* what she thought.

He sighed. 'Open ocean is not somewhere that mankind reigns particularly supreme.'

'Ah…' Awareness glowed as bright as the quarter-moonlight in Mila's expression. 'You can't control it.'

'I don't expect to,' he pointed out. 'It's not mine to control. I'm just happier not knowing what's down there.'

'Even if it's amazing?'

Especially if it was amazing. He was better off not knowing what he was missing. Wasn't that true of all areas of life? It certainly helped keep him on track at WestCorp—the only times he wobbled from the course he'd always charted for himself was when he paused to consider what else might be out there for him.

'As far as I'm concerned, human eyes can't see through ocean for a reason. Believing that it's all vast, empty nothing fits much better with my understanding of the world.'

Though that wasn't the world that Mila enjoyed, and it had nothing to do with her superpower.

'It is vast,' she acknowledged carefully. 'And you've probably become accustomed to having things within your power.'

'Is that what you think being CEO is about? Controlling things?'

'Isn't it?'

'It's more like a skipper. Steering things. And I've worked my whole life towards it.'

'You say that like you were greying at the temples when you stepped up. What are you now, mid-thirties? You must have been young when it happened.'

He remembered the day he'd got the call from the hospital, telling him about his father. Telling him to come. The sick feeling of hitting peak-hour traffic. The laws he'd broken trying to get there in time. Wishing for lights or sirens or *something* to help him change what was so obviously happening.

His father was dying and he wasn't there for it.

It was his mother all over again. Except, this time, he couldn't disappear into a child's fantasy world to cope.

'Adult enough that people counted on me to keep things running afterwards.'

'Was it unexpected?' she murmured.

'It shouldn't have been, the way he hammered the liquor and the cigarettes. The double espressos so sweet his spoon practically stood up in the little cup. But none of us were ready for it, him least of all. He still had lots to accomplish in life.'

'Like what?'

He hoped the low light would disguise the tightness of his smile. 'World domination.'

'He got halfway there, at least,' she murmured.

'WestCorp and all its holdings are just an average-sized fish on our particular reef.'

'I've seen some of those holdings; they're nothing to sneeze at.'

Rich tensed. That's right; she'd done her homework on him.

He searched her gaze for a clue but found only interest. And compassion.

So Mila hadn't dug so deep that she'd found Wardoo. She wasn't skilled enough at subterfuge to have that knowledge in her head and be able to hide it. Of course it wouldn't have occurred to her to look. Why would it? And Wardoo—big as it was—was still only a small pastoral holding compared to some of WestCorp's mining and resource interests. She'd probably tired of her search long before getting to the smaller holdings at the end of the list.

'For a woman who hangs out with sea stars and coral for a living you seem to know a lot about the Western Australian corporate scene. I wouldn't have thought it would interest you.'

He saw her flush more in the sweep of her lashes on her cheeks in the moonlight than in her colour. 'Normally, no—'

Out on the water, a few gulls appeared, dipping and soaring, only to dip again at the glittering surface. The moon might not be large but it was high now.

'Oh! We're on!' Mila said, excitement bubbling in her voice.

Compared to the last time she'd stripped off in front of him, this time she did it with far less modesty. It only took a few seconds to slide the strings holding up her slip of a dress off her shoulders and step out of the pooled fabric, leaving only bare feet and white bikini. Her shell necklace followed and she piled both on the table with the same casual concern that she'd balled up the paper from their fish and chips. She gathered her snorkelling gear as Rich shed a few layers down to his board shorts and he followed her tensely to the high tide mark. Their gear on, she handed him a headlamp to match her own and a calico net.

There was something about doing this together—as partners. He trusted Mila not to put him in any kind of danger, and trusting her felt like an empowered decision. And empowerment felt a little like control.

And that was all he needed to step into the dark shallows.

'What do I do with this?' he asked, waving the net around his head, as if it was meant for butterflies.

'Just hold it a foot above any coral that's erupting. Ten seconds maximum. Then find a coral that looks totally different to the first and repeat the process.'

'This is high stakes.'

He meant that glibly but he knew by the pause as she studied him that, for her, it absolutely was.

'You can't get it wrong. Come on.'

She waded in ahead of him and his headlamp slashed across her firm, slim body as she went. Given they were on departmental business, it felt wrong to be checking out a fellow scientist. It would have helped if she'd worn a white lab coat instead of a white bikini.

Focus.

The inky water swallowed them up, and its vastness demanded his full attention even as his mind knew it wasn't particularly deep. He fought to keep a map of the lagoon in his head so that his subconscious had something to reference when it was deciding how much adrenaline to pump through his system.

They were on the shallow side of the drop-off, where everything was warm and golden and filled with happy little sea creatures during the day. There was no reason that should change just because it was dark. Robbed of one of his key senses, his others heightened along with his imagination. In that moment he almost understood how Mila saw the reef. The water was silky-smooth and soft where it brushed his bare skin. Welcoming.

Decidedly un-soupy.

He kept Mila's fins—two of them this time—just inside the funnel of light coming from his headlamp. Beyond the cone of both their lights it was the inkiest of blacks. But Mila swam confidently on and the sandy lagoon floor fell away from them until the first corals started to appear a dozen metres offshore.

'They need a good couple of metres of water above them to do this,' she puffed, raising her head for a moment and pushing out her snorkel mouthpiece. Her long hair glued to her neck and shoulders and her golden skin glittered wet in his lamplight. 'So that the receding tide will carry their spawn bundles away to a new site while the embryos mature. Get ready...'

He mirrored her deep breath and then submerged, kicking down to the reef's surface. At first, there was nothing. Just the odd little bit of detritus floating across his field of light, but between one fin-kick and the next he swam straight into a plume of spawning coral. Instantly, he was inside a snow dome. Hundreds of tiny bundles wafted around him on the water's current, making their way to the surface. Pink. White. Glowing in the lamplight against the endless black background of night ocean. As each one met his skin, it was like rain—or tiny reverse hailstones—plinking onto him from below then rolling off and carrying on its determined journey to the surface. As soft as a breath. Utterly surreal. All around them, tiny bait fish darted, unconcerned by their presence, and picked off single, unlucky bundles. The bigger fish kept their distance and gorged themselves just out of view and, though he knew that *even bigger* fish with much sharper teeth probably watched them from the darkness, he found it difficult to care in light of this once-in-a-lifetime moment.

Mila was right.

It was spectacular.

And he might have missed it if not for her.

He surfaced for air again, glanced at the lights of the beach car park to stay oriented and then plugged his snorkel and returned to a few metres below. Just on the edge of his lamp, Mila back-swam over a particularly active plate coral and held her net aloft, letting the little bundles just float right into its mesh embrace. He turned to the nearby staghorn and did the same. On his, the spawn came off in smoky plumes and it was hard to know which was coral and which was some local fish timing its own reproductive activity within the smokescreen of much more obvious targets. He scooped it all up regardless. For every spawn bundle he caught, thousands more were being released.

Besides, the little fish were picking off many more than he was.

Ten seconds...

A sea jelly floated across the shaft of his lamp, glowing, but it was only when a cuttlefish did the same that he stopped to wonder. He'd only ever seen them dead on the seashore—as a kid he'd used them to dig out moats on sandcastles—like small surfboards. Live and lamplit, the cuttlefish glowed with translucent beauty and busied itself chasing down a particular spawn bundle, with a dozen crazily swimming legs.

But, as he raised his eyes, the shaft of his light filled with Mila, her limbs gently waving in a way the cuttlefish could only dream of, pink-white spawn snowing in reverse all around her, her eyes behind her mask glinting and angled. He didn't need to see her smile to feel its effect on him.

She was born to be here.

And he was honoured to be allowed to visit.

The reef at night reminded him of an eighties movie he'd seen. A dying metropolis, three hundred years from now, saturated with acid rain and blazing with neon, the skies crowded with grungy air transport, the streets far below pocked with dens and cavities of danger and the underbelly that thrived there.

This reef was every bit as busy and systematic as that futuristic world. Just far more beautiful.

She surfaced for a breath near to him.

'Ready to go in?' she asked.

'Nope.' Not nearly.

She smiled. 'It's been an hour, Rich.'

He kicked his legs below the surface and realised how much thicker the water had become in that time. 'You're kidding?'

'Time flies...'

Yeah. It really did. He couldn't remember the last time he'd felt this relaxed. Yet energised at the same time.

'I'm happy with that haul,' she said. 'I missed the *Porites* coral last year so they'll be awesome for the spawn bank.'

'Is that what I can smell?' he said, nostrils twitching at the pungent odour.

'It's probably better not to think about exactly what we're swimming in,' she puffed, staying afloat. 'But trust me when I say it's much better being out here in freshly erupted spawn than tomorrow in day-old spawn. Or the day after.'

She deftly twisted her catch net and then his so that the contents could not escape and then they turned for shore. They had drifted out further than he'd thought but still well within the confines of the lagoon. He could only imagine what a feeding frenzy this night would be beyond the flats where the outer reef spread. In the shallow water, she passed him the nets and then kicked free of her fins to jog ashore and collect the big plastic tub waiting there. She half filled it with clear seawater and then used her snorkelling mask to pour more over the top of her reversed net, swilling out the captured spawn into their watery new home. Maskful after maskful finally got all of his in too. They wrestled the heavy container up to their table together.

After the weightlessness of an hour in the dystopian underworld his legs felt like clumsy, useless trunks and he longed for the ease and effectiveness and freedom of his fins.

Freedom...

'So what did you think?' Mila asked, straightening.

Because they'd carried the tub together, she was standing much closer to him than she ever had before and her head came to just below his shoulder, forcing her to peer up at him with clear green eyes. Even bedraggled and wet, and with red pressure marks from her mask around her face, he wasn't sure he'd ever seen anything quite as beautiful. Except maybe the electric snowfield of spawning coral rising all around her as she did her best mermaid impersonation.

He'd never wanted to kiss someone so much in his life.

'Speechless,' he murmured instead. 'It was everything you said it would be.'

'Now do you get it?'

Somehow he knew what she was really asking.

Now do you get me?

He raised a hand and brushed her cheek with his knuckles, tucking a strand of soggy hair behind her ear. She sucked in a breath and leaned, almost easily, into his touch. It was the first time she hadn't flinched away from him.

His chest tightened even as it felt as if it had expanded two-fold with the pride of that.

'Yeah,' he breathed. 'I think I do. What is it like for you?'

'A symphony. So many sounds all working together.' Her eyes glittered at the memory. 'Not necessarily in harmony—just a wash of sound. The coral bundles are like tiny percussions and they build and they build as the sea fills with them and the ones that touch my skin are like—' she searched around her as if the word she needed was hovering nearby '—a mini firework. Hundreds of tiny explosions. The coral itself is so vibrant under light it just sings to me. Seduces. Breathtaking, except that I'm already holding my breath.' She dropped her head and her wet locks swayed. 'I can't explain it.'

He brought her gaze back up with a finger beneath her chin. His other hand came up to frame her cheek. 'I think I envy you your superpower right now.'

Lips the same gentle pink as the coral spawn parted slightly and mesmerised his gaze just as the little bundles had.

'It has its moments,' she breathed.

Mila was as much a product of this reef as anything he saw out there. Half-mermaid and easily as at home in the water as she was on land. Born of the Saltwater People and she would die in it, living it, loving it.

Protecting it.

This land was technically his heritage too, yet he had no such connection with it and no such protective instincts. He'd been raised to work it and maximise its yield. To exploit it.

For the first time ever he doubted the philosophy he'd been raised with. And he doubted himself.

Was he exploiting Mila too? Mining her for her knowledge and expertise? Wouldn't kissing her when she didn't know the truth about him just be another kind of exploitation? As badly as he wanted to lower his mouth onto hers, until he rectified *that*, any kiss he stole would be just that...

Stolen.

'You have spawn in your hair,' he murmured as she peered up at him.

It said something about how used to the distance of others Mila was that she was so unsurprised when he stepped back.

'I'm sure that's the least of it,' she said. 'Let's get this all back to my place and we can both clean up.'

He retreated a step, then another, and he lifted the heavy spawn-rich container to save Mila the chore. Her dress snagged on her damp skin as she wriggled back into it but then she gathered up the rest of their gear and followed him up to her truck.

CHAPTER SEVEN

IT ONLY OCCURRED to Mila as she pulled up out the front that Rich was the first person she'd ever brought into this place. When she needed to liaise with work people she usually drove the long road north to the department's branch office or met them at some beach site somewhere. She never came with them here, to the little stack of converted transport modules that served as both home and office.

Safe, private spaces.

Rich stood by her four-wheel drive, looking at the two-storey collection of steel.

'Are those…shipping containers?'

The back of her mouth filled with something between fried chicken and old leather. She looked at the corrugated steel walls in their mismatched, faded primary colours as he might see them and definitely found them wanting.

'Up here the regular accommodation is saved for the tourists,' she said. 'Behind the scenes, everyone lives in pretty functional dwellings. But we make them homey inside. Come on in.'

She led him around the back of the efficient dwelling where a weathered timber deck stretched out between the 'U' of sea containers on three sides—double-storey in the centre and single-storey adjoining on the left and right. He stumbled to a halt at the sight of her daybed—an old timber dinghy, tipped on an angle and filled with fat, inviting cushions. A curl of old canvas hung above it between the containers like a crashing wave. He stood, speechless, and stared at her handiwork.

'You're going to see a bit of upcycling in the next quarter-hour...' she warned, past the sour milk of self-consciousness.

Mila pushed open the double doors on the sea container to her left and stepped into her office. Despite the unpromising exterior, inside, it looked much like any other workspace except that her furniture was a bit more eclectic than the big city corporate office Rich was probably used to. A weathered old beach shack door for a desk, with a pair of deep filing cabinets for legs. An old paint-streaked ladder mounted lengthways on the wall served as bookshelves for her biology textbooks and her work files. The plain walls were decorated with a panoramic photograph she had taken of her favourite lagoon, enlarged and mounted in three parts behind mismatched window frames salvaged from old fishing shacks from down the coast.

Rich stared at the artwork.

'My view when I'm working,' she puffed, fighting the heat of a blush. 'Could you put that by the door?'

He positioned the opaque tub by the glass doors so that the moonlight could continue to work its magic on the coral spawn within until she could freeze them in the morning. Those first few hours of moonlight seemed critical to a good fertilisation result; why else had nature designed them to bob immediately to the surface instead of sink to the seafloor?

She killed the light and turned to cross the deck. 'I inherited this stack from someone else when I first moved out of home, but it was pretty functional then. I like to think I've improved it.'

She opened French windows immediately opposite her office and led Rich inside. His eyes had barely managed to stop bulging at her makeshift office before they were goggling again.

'You did all this?' he asked, looking around.

Her furniture mostly consisted of another timber sailing boat cut into parts and sanded within an inch of its life before being waxed until it was glossy. The stern half stood on its fat end at the end of the room and acted as a bookshelf and display cabinet, thanks to some handiwork flipping the boat's seats into shelves; its round little middle sat upturned at the centre of the space and held the glass that made it a coffee table, and its pointed bow was wall-mounted and served as a side table.

'I had some help from one of Coral Bay's old sea dogs, but otherwise, yes, I made most of this. I hate to see anything wasted. Feel free to look around.'

She jogged up polished timber steps to the bedroom that sat on top of the centremost sea container—the one that acted as kitchen, bathroom and laundry. She rustled up some dry clothes and an armful of towels and then padded back down to take a quick shower. Rich hadn't moved his feet but he'd twisted a little, presumably to peer around him. Was it in disbelief? In surprise?

In horror?

To her, it was personalised expression—her little haven filled with things that brought her pleasure. But what did Rich see? Did he view it as the junkyard pickings of some kind of hoarder?

His eyes were fixed overhead, on the lighting centrepiece of the room. A string of bud lights twisted and wove back on itself but each tiny bulb was carefully mounted inside a sea urchin she'd found on the shore outside of the sanctuary zone. Some big. Some small. All glowing their own delicate shades of pinks and orange. The whole thing tangled around an artful piece of driftwood she'd just loved.

The room filled with sour milk again and it killed her that she could feel so self-conscious about something that had brought her so much joy to create. And still did. She refused to defend it even though she burned to.

'I'll be just five minutes,' she announced, tossing the towel over her shoulder. 'Then you can clean up too.'

She scurried through the kitchen to the bathroom at the back of the sea container. If you didn't know what you were standing in you might think you were in some kind of upmarket beach shack, albeit eclectically furnished. Rich had five minutes to look his fill at all her weird stuff and then he'd be in here— her eyes drifted up to the white, round lightshade to which she'd attached streaming lengths of plaited fishing net until the whole thing resembled a cheerful bathroom jellyfish—for better or worse.

When she emerged, rinsed and clean-haired, Rich was studying up close the engineering on a tiered wall unit made of pale driftwood. She moved up next to him and lit the tea lights happily sitting on its shelves. They cast a gentle glow over that side of the room.

'Will I find an ordinary light fitting anywhere in your house?' he murmured down at her.

She had to think about it. 'The lamp in the office is pretty regular.' If you didn't count the tiny sea stars glued to its stand. 'This is one of my favourites.'

She lit another tea light sitting all alone on the boat bow side table except for a tiny piece of beach detritus that sat with it. It looked like nothing more than a minuscule bit of twisted seaweed. But, as the flame caught behind it, a shadow cast on the nearby wall and Rich was drawn by the flickering shape that grew as the flame did.

'I found the poor, dried seahorse on the marina shore when it was first built,' she said. 'Took me ages to think how I could celebrate it.'

He turned and just stared, something rather like confusion in his blue gaze.

Mila handed him a small stack of guest towels and pointed him in the direction of the bathroom. 'Take your time.'

As soon as he was safely out of view, she sagged against the kitchen bench. Nothing should have upstaged the fact that there was a naked man showering just ten feet away in her compact little bathroom, but Rich had given her spectacular fodder for distraction.

That kiss...

Not an actual kiss, but nearly. Cheek-brushing and chest-heaving and lingering looks. Enough that she'd been throbbing candyfloss while her pulse had tumbled over itself like a crashing wave. Lucky she'd built up such excellent lung capacity because she'd flat-out forgotten to breathe during the whole experience. Anyone else might have passed out.

'An almost-kiss isn't an actual kiss,' she lectured herself under her breath.

Even if it was the closest she'd come in a long, long time. Rich had been overwhelmed by his experience on the reef and had reached out instinctively, but—really—who wanted to kiss a woman soaked in spawn?

'No one.'

She rustled up a second mug and put the kettle on to boil. It took about the same time to bubble as the ninety seconds Rich did to shower and change back into his black sweater and jeans. When he emerged from the door next to her, all pink and freshly groomed, the bathroom's steam mingled with the kettle's.

'I made you tea,' she murmured.

He smiled as he took the mug. 'It's been a long time since I've had tea.'

Her eyes immediately hunted for coffee. 'You don't like it?'

'It's just that coffee's more a thing in the corporate world. I've fallen out of practice. It was a standard at boarding school until eleventh form, when we were allowed to upgrade to a harder core breakfast beverage.'

She started rummaging in the kitchen. 'I have some somewhere…'

He met her eyes and held them. 'I would like to drink tea with you, Mila.'

She couldn't look away; she could barely breathe a reply. 'Okay.'

He looked around her humble home again. 'I really like your place.'

'It's different to the *Portus*.'

He laughed. 'It's not a boat, for one thing. But it suits you. It's unique.'

Unique. Yep, that was one word for her.

'I hate to see anything wasted,' she said again. Her eyes went to her sea urchin extravaganza. 'And I hate to see beautiful things die. This is a way I can keep them alive and bring the reef inside at the same time.'

He studied her light art as if it was by a Renaissance sculptor, his brows drawn, deep in thought.

'What is your home like?' she went on when he didn't reply.

The direct question brought his gaze back to her. 'It's not a *home*, for a start. I don't feel like I've had one of those since... A long time.' He peered around again. 'But it's nothing like this.'

No. She couldn't imagine him surrounded by anything other than quality. She sank ahead of him onto one of two sofas made out of old travelling chests. The sort that might have washed up after a shipwreck. The sort that was perfect to have upholstered into insanely comfortable seats.

Rich frowned a little as he examined the seat's engineering.

'Home is something you come back to, isn't it?' he went on. 'About the only thing I have that meets that definition is the *Portus*. I feel different when I step aboard. Changed. Maybe she's my home.'

Mila sipped at her tea in the silence that followed and watched Rich grow less and less comfortable in her company.

'Is everything all right, Rich?' she finally braved.

He glanced up at her and then sighed. Long and deep.

'Mila, there's something I haven't told you.'

The cloves made a brief reappearance but she pushed through the discomfort. Trust came more easily with every minute she spent in Rich's company.

'Keeping secrets, Mr Grundy?' she quipped.

'That's just it,' he went on, ignoring her attempt at humour. 'I'm not Mr Grundy. At least... I am, and I'm not.'

She pressed back into the soft upholstery and gave him her full attention.

He lifted bleak eyes. 'Nancy Dawson married a Grundy.'

Awareness flooded in on a wave of nostalgia. 'Oh, that's right. Jack. I forgot because everyone up here knows them as Dawson. Wait...are you a relative of Jack Grundy? Ten times removed?'

'No times removed, actually.' Rich took a long sip of his tea. As if it were his last. 'Jack was my great-grandfather.'

Mila just stared. 'But that means...'

Nancy's Point. She'd stood there and lectured him about his own great-grandmother. The more immediate ramification took a little longer to sink in. She sat upright and placed her still steaming mug onto the little midships coffee table. The only way to disguise the sudden tremble of her fingers was to lay them flat on the thighs of her yoga pants. Unconsciously bracing herself.

'Are you a Dawson? Of the Wardoo Dawsons?'

Rich took a deep breath. 'I'm *the* Dawson. The only son of an only son. I hold the pastoral rights on Wardoo Station and the ten thousand square kilometres around it.'

Mila's hands dug deeper into her thighs. 'But that means...'

'It means I hold the lease on the land that Coral Bay sits on.'

The back of her throat stung with the taste of nail varnish and it was all she could do to whisper, 'You own my town?'

Rich straightened. 'The only thing I *own* is the Station infrastructure. But the lease is what has the value. And I hold that, presently.'

Her brain finally caught up and the nail varnish dissipated. 'Wardoo is yours.'

Because there was no Wardoo without the Dawsons. Just as there was no Coral Bay without them either.

Rich took a deep breath before answering. 'It is.'

Her eyes came up. 'Then you've been stopping the developers in their tracks! I thought you were one!'

His skin greyed off just a bit. Maybe he wasn't comfortable with overt gushing, but the strong mango of gratitude made it impossible for her to stop.

'WestCorp has been denying access for third-party development, yes—'

Whatever that little bit of careful corporate speak meant. All she heard was that *Rich* was the reason there were no towering hotels on her reef. *Rich* had kept everyone but the state government out of the lands bordering the World Heritage Marine Park. *Rich* was her corporate guardian angel.

Despite herself, despite everything she knew about people and every screaming sense she knew she'd be triggering, Mila tipped herself forward and threw her arms wide around his broad shoulders.

'Thank you,' she gushed, pressing herself into the hug. 'Thank you for my reef.'

CHAPTER EIGHT

RICH COULDN'T REMEMBER a time that he'd been more comfortable in someone's arms yet so excruciatingly uncomfortable as well.

Mila had only grasped half the truth.

Because he had only told half of it.

He let his own hands slide up and contribute to Mila's fervent embrace, but it was brief and it took little physical effort to curl his fingers and ease her slightly back from him. The emotional effort was much higher; she was warm and soft under his hands and she felt incredibly right there—speaking of going *home*—yet he felt more of a louse than when he'd nearly kissed her earlier.

Telling her had been the right thing to do but, in his head, this moment was going to go very differently. He'd steeled himself for her shock, her disappointment. Maybe for an escaped tear or two that he'd been keeping the truth from her. Instead, he got…this.

Gratitude.

He'd confessed his identity now but Mila only saw half the picture… The half that made him a hero, looking out for the underdog and the underdog's reef. She had no sense for the politics and game playing behind every access refusal. The prioritising.

It wasn't noble… It was corporate strategy.

'Don't be too quick to canonise me, Mila,' he murmured as she withdrew from the spontaneous hug, blushing. The gentle flush matched the colour she'd been when she came out of the bathroom. 'It's business. It's not personal. I hadn't even seen the reef until you showed me.'

Even now he was avoiding putting the puzzle fully together for her. It would only take a few words to confess that—yeah, he was still a developer and he was planning on developing her reef. But he wasn't strong enough to do that while he was still warm from her embrace.

'How could you go to Wardoo and not visit such a famous coast?' she asked.

'Actually, I've never been to Wardoo either,' he confessed further. 'I flew over it once, years ago.'

The quizzical smile turned into a gape. 'What? Why?'

'Because there's no need. I get reports and updates from the caretaking team. To me, it's just a remote business holding at the end of one of my spreadsheets.'

The words on his lips made him tense. As though the truth wasn't actually the truth.

Her gape was now a stare. 'No. Really?'

'Really.' He shrugged.

'But… It's *Wardoo*. It's your home.'

'I never grew up there, Mila. It holds no meaning for me.'

A momentary flash of his eight-year-old self tumbled beneath his determination for it to *be* the truth.

She scrabbled upright again and perched on her seat, leaning towards him. 'You need to go, Rich.'

No. He really didn't.

'You need to go and see it in its context, not in some photograph. Smell it and taste it and…'

'Taste it?'

'Okay, maybe that's just me, but won't you at least visit the people who run it for you? Let them show you their work?'

It was his turn to frown. Her previous jibe about *minions* hit home again.

'I'm sure they'd be delighted with a short-notice visit from their CEO,' he drawled.

She considered him. 'You won't know if you don't ask.'

He narrowed his eyes. 'You're very keen for me to visit, Mila. What am I missing?'

Her expression grew suspiciously innocent. 'I *might* be thinking about the fact that you don't have a car. And that I do—'

'And you're offering to lend it to me?' he shot back, his face just as impassive. 'Thanks, that's kind of you.'

Which made it sound as if he was considering going. When had that happened?

'Actually, it's kind of hinky to drive. I'd better take you. Road safety and all.'

'You don't know the roads. You've never been out there.'

Hoisted by her own petard.

'Okay, fine. Then take me in return for the coral spawn.' She shuffled forward. 'I would give anything to see Wardoo.'

Glad one of them was so keen. 'You know there's no reef out there, right? Just scrub and dirt.'

'Come on, Rich, it's a win-win—I get to see Wardoo and you get to have a reason to go there.'

'I don't need a reason to go there.'

And he didn't particularly *want* to. Though he did, very much, want to see the excited colour in Mila's cheeks a little bit longer. It reminded him of the flush as he'd stroked her cheek. And it did make a kind of sense to check it out since he was up here on an official fact-finding mission. After all, how convincing was he going to be if that government bureaucrat discovered he'd never actually been to the property? Photos and monthly reports could only do so much.

'What time?' he sighed.

Mila's eyes glittered like the emeralds they were, triumphant.

'I have a quickish task to do at low tide, but it's on the way to Wardoo so… Eight?'

'Does this *task* involve anything else slimy, soupy or slippery?' he worried.

'Maybe.' She laughed. 'It involves the reef.'

Of course it did.

'How wet will I be getting?'

'You? Not at all. I might, depending on the tide.'

'Okay then.' He could happily endure one last opportunity to see Mila in her natural habitat. Before he told her the full truth. And he could give her the gift of Wardoo, before pulling the happy dream they were both living out from under her too.

The least he could do, maybe.

'Eight it is, then.'

Her gaze glowed her pleasure and Rich just let himself swim there for a few moments. Below it all, he knew he was only delaying the inevitable, but there really was nothing to gain by telling her now instead of tomorrow.

'I should get back to the *Portus*,' he announced, reaching into his pocket for his phone. 'Need my beauty sleep if I'm going to wow the minions tomorrow.'

Her perfect skin flushed again as she remembered her own words and who she'd been talking about all along. But she handled the embarrassment as she handled everything—graciously. She crossed the small room to get her keys off their little hook.

'I'll drive you to the marina.'

Not surprisingly, given the marina was only a few minutes away, there was no sign of Damo when they climbed out of the four-wheel drive at the deserted ramp, although Mila could clearly see the *Portus* waiting out beyond the reef. Had it done laps out there the whole night, like a pacing attendant waiting for its master?

'He won't be long,' Rich murmured as a floodlight made its way steadily across the darkness that was the sea beyond the reef. The speed limits still applied even though no one else was using the channel. They weren't there to protect the boats.

'Did you enjoy dinner?' Rich asked after a longish, silence-filled pause. He turned closer to her in the darkness.

She'd totally forgotten the eating part of the evening. All she'd been fixating on was the looking part, the touching part. The just-out-of-the-shower part.

'Very much,' she said, looking up to him. 'Always happy not to go into a crowded building.'

'Thank you for letting me tag along on the spawn; it really was very beautiful.'

It was impossible not to chuckle but—this close and in this much darkness—it came out sounding way throatier than she meant it. 'I'm pretty sure I bullied you into coming.'

Just like she'd talked her way into Wardoo tomorrow.

'Happy to have been bullied then. I never could have imagined...'

No. It really was *un*imaginable until you'd seen it. She liked knowing that they had that experience in common now. Every shared experience they had brought them that little bit closer. And now that she knew he was a Dawson...every experience would help to secure the borders against developers even more.

A stiff breeze kicked up off the water and reminded Mila that she was still in the light T-shirt and yoga pants she'd shrugged into in her steamy little bathroom inside her warm little house. Gooseflesh prickled, accompanied by imaginary wings fluttering as the bumps raced up her skin.

'You should head home,' Rich immediately said as she rubbed her arms. 'It's cold.'

'No—'

She didn't want to leave. She didn't want to wait until eight a.m. to see him again. She wasn't ready to leave this man who turned out to have had the back of everything she cared about for all these years. If he asked her back to his boat to spend the night she was ready to say yes.

'I'm good.'

Large hands found her upper arms in the light from the silvered moon and added their warmth to her cold skin. Harps immediately joined the fluttering wings.

'Here...'

Rich moved around close behind her and then rubbed his hands up and down her arms, bringing her back against his hard, warm, sweater-clad chest. He'd shifted from a client to an acquaintance somewhere around the visit to Yardi Creek, and from acquaintance to a friend when she'd agreed to have dinner. But exactly when did they become *arm-rubbing* kinds of friends? Was it when they'd stood so close by the shore this evening? When they'd shared the majesty of the spawn event? The not-quite kiss?

Did it even matter? The multiple sensations of his hands on hers, his body against hers was a kind of heaven she'd secretly believed she would never experience.

It was only when she saw the slash of the tender's arriving floodlight on the back of her eyelids that she realised they'd fluttered shut.

Rich stepped away and the harps faded to nothing at the loss of his skin on hers.

'I'll see you here at eight,' he said, far more composed than she felt. But then his big frame blocked the moonlight as he bent to kiss her cheek. His words were a hot caress against her ear and the gooseflesh worsened.

'Sleep well.'

Pfff... As if.

Before she could reply, he had stepped away and she mourned not only the warmth of his hands but now the gentle brush of his lips too. Too, too brief. He stepped down onto the varnished pier out to the tender and left her. Standing here, watching him walk away from her, those narrow jeans-clad hips swinging even in the dim moonlight, was a little too much like self-harm and so she turned to face her truck and took the few steps she needed to cross back to it.

At the last moment she heard a crunch that wasn't her own feet on the crushed gravel marina substrate.

'Mila…'

She pivoted into Rich's return and he didn't even pause as he walked hard up against her and bent again, to her lips this time. His kiss was soft but it lingered. It explored. It blew her little mind. And it came with a sensation overload. He took her too much by surprise to invoke the citrus of anticipation but it kicked in now and mingled with the strong, candy surge of attraction as a tiny corner of her mind wondered breathlessly how long his kiss could last. Waves crashed and she knew it wasn't on the nearby shore; it was what kissing gave her, though not always like this… Not always accompanied by skin harps and the crackle of fireplace that was the heat of Rich's mouth on her own. And all that oak moss…

Her head spun with want as much as the breathless surprise of Rich's stealthy return.

'I should have done that hours ago,' he murmured at last, breathing fast. 'I wanted to right after the coral.'

'Why didn't you?' Belatedly, she realised she was probably supposed to protest his presumption, or say something witty, or be grown up and blasé about it. But really, all she wanted to know was why they hadn't been kissing all evening.

'I wanted you to know about me. Who I was. So you had the choice.'

Oh, kissing him was a *choice*? That was a laugh, and not because he'd sneaked up on her and made the first move. She'd been thinking about his mouth for days now.

There was no choice.

But she was grateful for the consideration.

'I like who you are,' she murmured. 'Thank you for telling me.'

Besides, she was the last person who could judge anyone else for keeping themselves private.

He dipped his head again and sent the harps a-harping

and the fire a-crackling for more precious moments. Then he straightened and stepped back.

'Tomorrow then,' he said and he and his conflicted gaze were gone, jogging down the pier towards the *Portus'* waiting tender.

Mila sagged against her open car door and watched until he was out of sight. Even then, she stared at the inky ocean and imagined the small boat making its way until it reappeared as a shadow against the well-lit *Portus*. Impossible to see Rich climb aboard at this distance but she imagined that too; in her mind's eye she saw him slumping down on that expansive sofa amid the polished chrome and glass. She tried to imagine him checking his phone or picking up a book or even stretching out on that king-sized bed and watching the night sky through the wraparound windows, but it was easier to imagine him settling in behind his laptop at the workstation and getting a few more hours of corporate in before his head hit any kind of pillow.

That was just who he was. And it was where he came from.

A whale shark couldn't change its spots.

Except this one—just maybe—could.

CHAPTER NINE

MILA TOOK A careful knife to the reef and carved out a single oyster from a crowded corner, working carefully not to injure or loosen the rest. Then she did it again at another stack. And again. And again. On the way out to this remote bay, she'd told Rich that her department's licence called for five test oysters every month and a couple of simple observational tests to monitor oyster condition and keep them free of the disease that was ravaging populations down the east coast of the country.

Rich held the little bag for her as she dropped them in one by one.

She smiled shy thanks, though not quite at him. 'For a CEO you make an excellent apprentice ranger.'

So far this morning the two of them had been doing a terrific job of ignoring exactly what it was that had gone down between them last night. The kissing part, not the sharing of secrets part. One was planned, the other... Not so much. He hadn't even known he was going to do it until he'd felt his feet twisting on the pier and striding back towards her.

'Now I understand your fashion choice,' he murmured, nodding at her high-vis vest emblazoned with the department logo.

It wasn't the most flattering thing he'd seen her in since they'd met yet she still managed to make it seem…intriguing.

'Don't want anyone thinking they can just help themselves to oysters here,' she said. 'This is inside the sanctuary zone.'

Not that there was a soul around yet. The tide was way too low to be of interest to snorkelers and the fishermen had too much respect for their equipment to try tossing a line in at this razor-ridden place.

They waded ashore and Mila laid the five knotted shells out on the tailgate of her four-wheel drive. She placed a dog-eared laminated number above each, photographed it and then set about her testing. All that busyness was a fantastic way of not needing to make eye contact with him.

Was she embarrassed? Did she regret participating quite so enthusiastically in last night's experimental kiss? Or was she just as focused on her work as he could be when he was in the zone? Given how distracted he'd been last night, going over and over the proposal, it was hard to imagine ever being in the zone again.

Mila picked one oyster up and gently knocked its semi-open shell. It closed immediately but with no great urgency.

'That's a four,' she told him, and he dutifully wrote it down on the form she'd given him.

The others were all fours too, and one super-speedy five. That made her happy. She'd clearly opened an oyster or three in her time and she made quick work of separating each one from its top shell by a swift knife move to its hinge. She wafted the inner scent of each towards her nostrils before dipping her finger in and then placing it in her mouth to taste its juices. He wrote down her observations as she voiced them.

'If these five exemplars are responsive, fresh and the flesh is opaque then it's a good sign of the health of the whole oyster community,' she said.

'What do you do with them, then—toss them back?'

'These five are ambassadors for their kind. I usually wedge

the shells back in to become part of the stack, but I don't waste the meat.'

'And by that you mean…?'

'I eat them,' she said with a grin. 'Want to help?'

Rich frowned. 'Depends on whether you have any red wine vinegar on hand.'

She used the little knife to shuck the first of them and flip it to study its underside. Then she held up the oyster sample in front of her lips like a salute. *'Au naturel.'*

Down it went. She repeated the neat move and handed the finished shuck to him.

His eyebrows raised as soon as he bit down on the ultra-fresh mollusc. 'Melon!'

'Yeah, kind of. Salty melon.'

'Even to you?'

She smiled. 'Even to me. With a bonus hit of *astute*.'

Rich couldn't really see how a hibernating lump of muscle could have any personality at all but he was prepared to go with 'astute'. He'd never managed to taste the 'ambition' in vintage wine either, but he was prepared to believe that connoisseurs at the fancy restaurants he frequented could.

Maybe Mila was just a nature connoisseur.

Oyster number three and four went the same way and then there was only the one left. He offered it to Mila. 'You know what they say about oysters…'

She blinked at him. 'Excellent for your immune system and bone strength?'

He stared at her, trying to gauge whether she was serious. He loved not being able to read her. How long had it been since someone surprised him?

'Yeah, that's what they say.'

It was only when she smiled, slow and sexy, that he knew *she* knew. But obviously she wasn't about to mention it in light of last night's illicit kiss.

She gasped, scribbling in her log what she'd found on the oyster's underside. 'A pearl.'

Rich peered at the small cream mass. It wasn't much of one but it undoubtedly *was* a pearl. 'Is that a good sign?'

'Not really.' Mila poked at it carefully. 'It could have formed in response to a parasite. Too much of that would be a bad sign for these stacks.'

'Pearls are a defect?' he asked.

'"Out of a flaw comes beauty",' Mila quoted.

She might as well have been describing herself.

She lifted it out with her blade and rinsed it in the seawater, then swallowed the last of the oyster flesh.

'Here,' she said, handing it to him. 'A souvenir.'

'Because you have so many littering your house?'

Just how many had she found in her time?

'It's reasonably rare to find a wild one,' she said, still smiling. 'This is only my second in all the time I've been working here. But I don't feel right about keeping them; I'm lucky enough just to do this for a living without profiting from it further. I gave the last one away to a woman with three noisy kids.'

Rich stared. She was like a whole different species to him. 'Do you know what they're worth?'

'Not so much when they're this small and malformed, I don't think.' She laid it out on her hand and let the little lump flip over on her wet palm. 'But I prefer them like this. Rough and nature-formed. Though it's weird, I don't get any kind of personality off them. I wonder why.'

She studied it a moment longer, as if *willing* it to perform for her.

'Here…' She finally thrust her hand out. 'Something to remember Coral Bay by. Sorry it's not bigger.'

Something deep in his chest protested. Did she imagine he cared about that? When he looked at the small, imperfect pearl he would remember the small, imperfect woman who had given it to him.

And how perfect her imperfections made her.

He closed his hand around the lumpy gem. 'Thank you.'

She took the empty shell parts and jogged back into the water to wedge them back into the stacks as foundation for future generations, then she returned and packed up. Rich took the opportunity to watch her move, and work, without making her self-conscious.

He found he quite liked to just watch her.

'Okay,' she finally puffed. 'All done for the month. Shall we get going? Did you tell Wardoo you were coming?'

'Panic duly instigated, yes.'

She smiled at him and he wondered when he'd started counting the minutes between them. She'd smiled more at him in the last hour than she had in the entire time he'd known her. It was uncomfortably hard not to connect it to her misapprehension that he was some kind of crusading, conservation good guy.

'I think you'll like it. This country really is very beautiful in its own unique way.'

As he followed her up the path to her car all he could think about was an old phrase…

Takes one to know one.

Their arrival at Wardoo was decidedly low-key. If not for the furtive glance of a man crossing between one corrugated outbuilding and the next she'd have thought no one was all that interested in Rich's arrival. But that sideways look spoke volumes. It was more the kind of surreptitious play-down-the-moment peek reserved for politicians or rock stars.

Or royalty.

Some of the men who had worked Wardoo their whole adult lives might never have seen a Dawson in person. *Grundy*, she reminded herself.

A wide grin in a weathered, masculine face met them, introduced himself as the Station foreman and offered to show them, first, through the homestead.

'Jared Kipling,' he said, shaking Rich's hand. 'Kip.'

She wasn't offended that Kip had forgotten to shake her hand in the fluster of meeting his long-absent boss. It saved her the anxiety of another first-time touch.

It was only when she watched Rich's body language as he stepped up onto the veranda running the full perimeter of the homestead that she realised he'd slipped back into business mode. She recognised it from that first day at Nancy's Point. Exactly when he'd stopped being quite so…corporate she wasn't as sure.

'It's vacant?' Mila asked as she stepped into the dust-free hall of Wardoo homestead ahead of the men. Despite being furnished, there was something empty about it, and not just because the polished floorboards exuded isolation the way jarrah always did for her.

Wardoo was…hollow. And somehow lifeless.

How incredibly sad. Not what she had imagined at all.

'Most of our crew live in transportables on site or in town. We keep the house for the Dawsons,' Kip said. 'Just in case.'

The Dawsons who had never visited? The hollowness only increased and she glanced at Rich. He kept his gaze firmly averted.

She left the men to their discussions and explored the homestead. Every room was just as clean and just as empty as the one before it. She ran her fingertips along the rich old surfaces and enjoyed the myriad sensations that came with them. When she made her way back to the living room, Rich and the foreman were deep in discussion on the unused sofas. She heard the word 'lease' before Rich shot to his feet and brought the conversation to a rapid halt.

'If you've seen enough—' Kip floundered at the sudden end to their conversation '—I can show you the operations yards and then the chopper's standing by for an aerial tour.'

Rich looked decidedly awkward too. What a novelty—to be the least socially clumsy person in a room.

'You have your own chopper?' Mila asked him, to ease the tension.

It did the trick. He gifted her a small smile that only served to remind her how many minutes it had been since the last one.

Because apparently she counted, now.

He turned for the door as if she'd been the one keeping him waiting. 'It seems I do.'

'It's a stock mustering chopper,' Kip went on, tailing them. 'There's only room for two. But it's the only way to get out to the perimeter of Wardoo and back in a day.'

'The perimeter can wait,' Rich declared. 'Just show us the highlights within striking distance by road.'

Us. As if she were some kind of permanent part of the Richard Grundy show.

She trotted along behind Rich as he toured the equipment and sheds closest to the Homestead. Of course, on a property of this scale 'close' was relative. Then they piled into a late model Land Cruiser and set off in a plume of red-brown dust to the north. Mila lost herself in the Australian scrub and let time flow over her like water as Rich and Kip discussed the operations of the cattle station. She was yet to actually see a cow.

'The herds like to range inland this time of year,' Kip said when she asked. 'While the eastern dams are full. We'll see some soon.'

She lost track of time again until the brush of knuckles on her cheek tingled her out of a light doze.

'Lunchtime,' Rich murmured.

'How long have…?' Lord, how embarrassing.

'Sorry, there was a lot of shop-talk.'

And she'd only slept fitfully last night. Something to do with being kissed half to death at the marina had left her tossing and turning and, clearly, in need of some decent sleep. Mila scurried to climb out of the comfortable vehicle ahead of him.

'The missus made you this,' Kip said, passing Rich a hamper. 'She wasn't expecting two of you but she's probably over-catered so you should be right. Follow the track down that way and you'll come to Jack's Vent. A nice spot to eat,' he told them and then raised Rich's eyebrows by adding, 'No crocs.'

'No crocs...' Rich murmured as they set off. 'Good to know.'

His twisted smile did the same to her insides, and she'd grown to relish the pineapple smell when he gave her that particular wry grin. Pineapple—just when she thought she'd had every fruit known to man.

They walked in silence as the track descended and the land around them transformed in a way that spoke of regular water. Less scrub, more trees. Less brown, more colours peppering the green vegetation. Even the surface of the dark water was freckled with oversized lily pads, some flowering with vibrant colour. Out of cracks in the rock, tall reeds grew.

They reached the edge of Jack's Vent and peered down from the rocky ledge.

Mila glanced around. 'A waterhole seems out of place here where it's so dry.'

Though it certainly was a tranquil and beautiful surprise.

'I've seen this on a map,' Rich murmured. 'It's a sinkhole, not a waterhole. A groundwater vent.'

Golden granite ringed the hole except for a narrow stock trail on the far side where Wardoo's cattle came to drink their fill of the icy, fresh, presumably artesian water, and a flatter patch of rock to their right. It looked like a natural diving platform.

'Wish I'd brought my snorkelling gear,' she murmured. 'I would love to have a look deeper in the vent.'

'You're off the clock, remember?'

'I could do that while you and Kip talk business.'

He gave her his hand to step down onto the rocky platform, which sloped right down to the water's edge. She moved right down to it and kicked off her shoes.

'It's freezing!' she squealed, dipping a toe in. 'Gorgeous.'

Rich lowered the hamper and toed off his own boots, then

rolled his jeans up to his knees and followed her down to a sitting position. He gingerly sank his feet.

'There must be twenty sandwiches in here,' Mila said, looking through the hamper's contents and passing him a chilled bottle of water to match her own. 'All different.'

'I guess they were covering all bases.'

'Eager to impress, I suppose. This is a big moment for them.'

Rich snorted then turned his gaze out to the water. They ate in companionable silence but Mila felt Rich's focus drift further and further from her like the lily pads floating on the sinkhole's surface.

'For someone sitting in such a beautiful spot, you look pretty unhappy to be here,' she said when his frown grew too great. Guilt swilled around her like the water at her feet; she had nagged him to bring her. To come at all.

'Sorry,' he said, snapping his focus back to the present. 'Memories.'

She kept her frown light. 'But you haven't been here before.'

'No.' And that was all he gave her. His next words tipped the conversation back her way. 'You were the one panting to come today. How's it living up to your expectations?'

She looked around them. 'It's hard to sit somewhere like this and find fault. Wardoo offers the best of both worlds—the richness of the land and the beauty of the coast. I feel very—'

What? What was the quality she felt?

'*Comfortable* here,' she said at last. 'Maybe it's some kind of genetic memory doing its thing. Oh!'

He glanced around to see what had caught her eye.

'I just realised that both our ancestors could have sat right on this spot, separated by centuries. And now here we are again. Maybe that's why I feel so connected to you.'

Those words slipped out before she thought of the wisdom of them.

Eyes the colour of the sky blazed into her. 'Do you? Feel connected?'

Sour milk wafted around them but Rich's nostrils didn't twitch the way hers wanted to. 'You don't?'

He considered her, long and hard. 'It's futile but... I do, yes.'

Her breath tightened in a way that made her wonder whether her sandwich was refusing to go down.

'Futile?' she half breathed.

'We have such different goals.' His eyes dropped away. 'You're Saltwater People and I'm...glass-and-chrome people.'

She'd never been more grateful to not fit any particular label. That way anything felt possible.

'That's just geography, though. It doesn't change who we are at heart.'

'Doesn't it? I don't know anyone like you back home. So connected to the land...earth spirit and mermaid all at once. That's nurture, not nature. You're as much a product of this environment as those waterlilies. You wouldn't last five minutes in the city, synaesthesia or not.'

Did he have so little faith in her? 'You think I wouldn't adapt?'

'I think you'd *wither*, Mila. I think being away from this place would strip the best of you away. Just like staying here would kill me.'

'You don't like the Bay?'

Why did that thought hurt so very much?

'I like it very much but my world isn't here. I don't know how long I would be entertained by all the pretty. Not when there's work to be done.'

Did he count her in with that flippant description? She had no right to expect otherwise, yet she was undeniably tasting the leather of disappointment in the back of her throat.

'Is that what I've been doing? Entertaining you?'

The obvious answer was yes, because she was paid to show him the best of the Marine Park, but they both knew what she was really asking.

'Mila, that was—' He glanced away and back so quickly she

couldn't begin to guess what he was thinking. 'No. That wasn't entertainment. I kissed you because...'

Because why, Rich?

'It was an impulse. A moment. I couldn't walk off that marina without knowing whether the attraction was mutual.'

Given she'd clung to him like a remora, he'd certainly got his answer. Heat billowed up under the collar of her Parks uniform.

'It was,' she murmured. Then she sighed. 'It *is*. I'm awash in candyfloss twenty-four-seven. I'd be sick of it if it didn't smell—' *and feel* '—so good.'

'I'm candyfloss guy?' he breathed. 'I was sure I was earwax.'

He'd eased back on one strong arm so he could turn his body fully to her for this delicate conversation. It would be so easy to lean forward and find his lips, repeat the experiment, but...to what end? She would eventually run out of things to show him in Coral Bay and then he'd be gone, back to the city, probably for good, and the kissing would be over. And he was right. She wouldn't cope in the city. Not long-term.

'Candyfloss is what I get for...' *attraction* '...for you.'

If Rich was flattered to get a scent all to himself, he didn't show it. He studied her and seemed to glance over her shoulder, his head shaking.

'The timing of this sucks.'

'Would six months from now make a difference?'

'Not a good one,' she thought she heard him mutter.

But he leaned closer, bringing his face within breathing distance, and Mila thought that even though these random kisses confused the heck out of her she could certainly get used to the sensation. Pineapple went quite well with candyfloss, after all. But his lips didn't meet hers; his right shoulder brushed her left one as he leaned beyond her for a moment. When he straightened, he had a flower in his hand, plucked with some of its stem still attached. The delicate pink blossom fanned out around a thatch of golden-pink stamens. On its underside it was paler and waxier, to help it survive the harsh outback conditions.

'One of my favourites,' she said, studying it but not taking it. If she took it he might lean back. 'Desert rose.'

'It matches your lips,' he murmured. 'The same soft pink.'

She couldn't help wetting them; it was instinctive. Rich brushed her cheek with the delicate flower, then followed it with his bare knuckles. Somewhere, harps sang out.

'Pollen,' he explained before folding her fingers around the blossom's thick-leaved stem.

But he didn't move back; he just stayed there, bent close.

'I need you to know something—' he began, a shadow in his gaze.

But no, she wasn't ready to have this amazing day intruded upon by more truths. If it was bad news it could wait. If it wasn't...it could wait too.

'Will you still be here tomorrow?'

He took her interruption in his stride. 'I'm heading back overnight. I have an important meeting at ten a.m.'

Panic welled up like the water in this vent.

Tonight... That was just hours away. A few short hours and he would be gone back to his in-tray, twelve hundred kilometres south of here. After which there were no more reasons for him to return to Coral Bay, unless it was to visit Wardoo, which seemed unlikely given he'd never had the interest before.

And they both knew it.

Mila silenced any more bad news with her fingers on his lips. 'Tell me later. Let's just enjoy today.' Then, when the gathering blue shadows looked as if they weren't going to be silenced, she added, 'Please.'

There wasn't much else to do then than close up the short distance between them again. Mila sucked up some courage and took care of that herself, leaning into the warmth of Rich's cheek, brushing hers along it, seeking out his mouth.

Their kiss was soft and exploratory, Rich brushing his lips back and forth across hers, relearning their shape. She inhaled his heated scent, clung to the subtle smell of *him* through the almost overpowering candyfloss and pineapple that made her head light. He tasted like the chutney in Kip's wife's sandwiches but she didn't care. She could eat pickle for the rest of her days and remember this place. This kiss.

This man.

Long after he'd gone.

'Have dinner with me,' he breathed. 'On the *Portus*. Tonight before I leave.'

Dinner... Was that really what he was asking? Or was he hoping to cap off his northern experience with something more... satisfying? Did she even care? She should... She'd only just begun to get used to the sensations that came with kissing; how could she go from that to something so much more irrevocable in just one evening?

Rich watched her between kisses, his blue eyes peering deeply into hers. He withdrew a little. 'Your mind is very busy...'

This moment would probably be overwhelming for anyone— even those without a superpower. She'd never felt more...normal.

'I'm going out on the water this afternoon,' she said. 'Come with me. One last visit onto the reef. Then I'll have dinner with you.'

Because going straight from this to dinner to goodbye just wasn't an option.

'Okay,' he murmured, kissing her softly one last time.

She clung to it, to him, then let him go. In the distance, the Land Cruiser honked politely.

'Back to work,' Rich groaned.

Probably just as well. Sitting here on the edge of an ancient sinkhole, older than anything either of them had ever known, it was too easy to pretend that none of it mattered. That real life didn't matter.

She nodded and watched as he pushed to his feet. When he lowered a strong hand towards her she didn't hesitate to slide her smaller fingers into his. The first time ever she didn't give a moment's thought before touching someone.

Pineapple wafted past her nostrils again.

CHAPTER TEN

'ARE YOU KIDDING ME?' Rich gaped at her. 'How dangerous is this?'

'It's got to be done,' Mila pointed out.

Right. Something about baselines for studying dugong numbers. He understood baselines; he worked with them all the time. But not like this.

'Why does it have to be done by *you*?' he pointed out, pretty reasonably he thought, as he did his part in the equipment chain, loading the small boat.

'It's not just me,' she said, laughing. 'There's a whole team of us.'

Yeah, there was. Four big, strong men, experienced in traditional hunting methods. It was the only bit of comfort he got for this whole crazy idea.

'You hate teams,' he pointed out in a low voice. She loved working solo. Just Mila and the reef life. A mermaid and her undersea world.

'I wouldn't do it every day,' she conceded. 'But I'm way too distracted to think about it until it's over. You don't have to come…'

Right. If a gentle thing like Mila could get out there and tackle wild creatures he wasn't about to wuss out. Besides, if anything went wrong he wanted to be there to help make sure she came out of it okay. Finally, those captain-of-the-swim-team skills coming in useful. Though it wasn't likely she'd be doing this in the comfortable confines of Coral Bay's shallows.

The team loaded up the fast little inflatable and all five of them got in—Mila and her ranger quarterbacks—then the documentary crew that were capturing the dugong tagging exercise for some local news channel loaded into their own boat and Rich got in with them. Not close enough, maybe, but as close as he was going to get out on the open water. And the documentary crew would make sure they had a good view of the activities—which meant he would have a good view of Mila's part in it.

I'm just the tagger, she'd said and he'd thought that was a good thing. Until he realised she'd be in the open ocean down the thrashing end of a wild, defensive dugong fitting that tag.

Rich held on as they headed out. The inflatable wasted no time getting well ahead and the film crew did their thing as Rich watched.

'They've spotted a herd,' the documentary producer called to her crew. 'Twenty animals.'

Twenty? Rich swore under the engine noise and his gut fisted. Anything could happen in a herd that size.

As soon as they reached the herd, the little inflatable veered left to cut an animal off the periphery and chase it away rather than drive it into the herd and risk scattering them. Or, worse, hurting them. They ran it in a wide arc for ten minutes, wearing it down, preventing it from re-entering the herd and then he watched as three of the four wetsuit-clad Rangers got to their feet and balanced there precariously as the fourth veered the inflatable across the big dugong's wake. Mila held on for her life in the back of the little boat.

'Get ready!' the producer called to her two camera operators. Rich tensed too.

When it happened, it all happened in a blinding flash. The puffed animal came up for a breath, then another, then a third.

As soon as they were sure it had a good lungful of air, the first dugong-wrangler leapt over the edge of the inflatable and right onto the dugong's back. The two others followed suit and, though he couldn't quite see what was happening in the thrashing water, he did see Mila toss them a couple of foam tubes, which seemed to help keep the hundred-kilogram dugong incredulously afloat while the men kept its nose, flippers and powerful tail somewhat contained.

Then Mila jumped. Right in there, into that surging whitewater of death, with the tracking gear in her tiny hands. Rich's heart hammered almost loud enough to hear over the engine of the documentary boat and he leapt to his feet in protest. Her bright red one-piece flashed now and again above the churning water and kept him oriented on her. The video crew were busy capturing the rest of what was happening, but he had eyes for only one part of that animal—its wildly thrashing back end and Mila where she clung to it, fitting the strap-on tracker to the narrowest point of its thick tail. How that could possibly be the lesser of jobs out there...

She and the dugong both buffeted against the small boat and he realised why they used an inflatable and not a hard shell like the one he was in. Its cushioned impact protected the animal and bounced Mila—equally harm-free—back onto the dugong's tail and helped keep her where she needed to be to finally affix the tracker.

While he watched, they measured the animal in a few key spots and shouted the results to the inflatable's skipper, who managed to scrawl it in a notebook while also keeping the boat nice and close.

Then...all of a sudden, it was over. The whole thing took less than three minutes once the first body hit the water. The aggravated dugong dived deep the moment it was released and the churning stopped, the water stilled and the five bodies tumbling around in its turbulence righted themselves and then swam back to the inflatable. The men hauled Mila in after them and they all fell back against the rubber, their chests heaving. One of the neoprene-suited quarterbacks threw up the stomachful of water he'd swallowed in the melee.

Rich's own heart was beating set to erupt from his chest. He couldn't imagine what theirs were like.

Of all the stupid things that she could volunteer to help with...

Mila fell back against the boat's fat rim and stared up into the blue sky. Then she turned and sought out his boat. His eyes. And as soon as he found them she laughed.

Laughed!

Who was this woman leaping into open ocean with a creature related more closely to an elephant than anything else? What had she done with gentle, mermaid Mila? The woman who took such exquisite care of the creatures on the reef, who didn't even tread on an ant if she could avoid it. Where was all this strength coming from?

He sank back down onto his seat and resigned himself to a really unhappy afternoon. This activity crossed all the boxes: dangerous, deep and—worst of all—totally uncontrollable. Beyond a bit of experience and skill, their success was ninety per cent luck.

It occurred to him for a nanosecond that experience, skill and luck were pretty much everything he'd built his business on.

All in all, they tagged six animals before the team's collective exhaustion called a halt to the effort. Science would glean a bunch of something from this endeavour but Rich didn't care; all he cared about was the woman laid out in the back of the inflatable, her long hair dangling in the sea as the inflatable turned for shore and passed the film crew's boat.

Rich was the first one off when it slid up onto the beach, but Mila was the last one off the inflatable, rolling bodily over its fat edge, her fatigued legs barely holding her up. In between, he stood, fists clenched, bursting with tension and the blazing need to wrap his arms around Mila and never let her go.

Ever.

'Rich!' she protested as he slammed bodily into her, his arms going around to hold her up. 'I'm drenched.'

'I don't care.' He pressed against her cold ear. 'I *so* don't care.'

What was a wet shirt when she'd just risked her life six times over? Mila stood stiffly for a moment but the longer he held onto her, the more she relaxed into his grip and the more grateful she seemed for the strength he was lending her. Her little hands slid up his back and she returned his firm embrace.

Around them, the beach got busy with the packing up of gear and the previewing out of video and the relocation of vessels but Rich just stood there, hugging her as if his life depended on it.

In that moment it felt like absolute, impossible truth.

'Ugh, my legs are like rubber,' Mila finally said, easing back. She kept one hand on his arm to steady herself as her fatigued muscles took back reluctant responsibility for her standing. She glanced up at him where a Mila-shaped patch clung wetly to his chest.

'Your shirt—'

'Will dry.' He saw the sudden goose pimples rising on her skin. 'Which is what you need to be. Come on.'

'I'm not cold,' she said, low, but moved with him up the beach compliantly.

'You're trembling, Mila.'

'But not with cold,' she said again, and stared at him until her meaning sank in. 'I'm having a carnival moment.'

Oh. Candyfloss.

The idea that his wet skin on hers had set her shivers racing twisted deep down in his guts. He wanted to be at least as attractive to her as she was to him. Though that was a big ask given how keyed-up he was whenever she was around. Yet still his overriding interest was to get her somewhere warm...and safe. Like back into his arms.

That was disturbingly new.

And insanely problematic given he was leaving tonight. And

given that he'd vowed to finish the conversation he'd wanted to have out at the sinkhole.

He stopped at their piled-up belongings on the remote beach and plucked the biggest towel out of the pile, wrapping it around her almost twice. He would much rather be her human towel but right now the heat soaked through it was probably more useful to her. She stood for minutes, just letting the lactic acid ease off in her system and walking off the fatigue. Then she passed him the towel and pulled on her shorts and shirt with what looked a lot like pain. She glanced at her team, still packing up all their gear.

'I should help,' she murmured.

Rich stopped her with a hand to her shoulder. 'You're exhausted.'

'So are they.'

'I'm not. I'll help in your place.'

'I'm not an invalid, Rich.'

'No, but it's something I can do to feel useful. I'd like to do this for you, Mila.' When was the last time he'd felt as... impotent...as he had today? Out on that boat, on all that water, witness to Mila risking her life repeatedly while he just... watched. And there was nothing he could do to help her.

It was like sitting in traffic while his father's heart was rupturing.

His glare hit its target and Mila acquiesced, nodding over mumbled thanks.

Rich turned and crossed to help with the mounded pile of equipment from his boat.

He didn't want her gratitude; a heavy hauling exercise was exactly what he needed to get his emotions back in check. The more gear he carried back and forth across the sand, the saner he began to feel—more the composed CEO and less the breathless novice.

Though maybe in this he *was* a novice. It certainly was worryingly new territory.

He was attracted to everything that was soft about Mila—her kindness, her gentleness; even her quirky superpower was a kind of fragile curiosity. Attraction he could handle. Spin out the anticipation and even enjoy. But this…this was something different. This was leaning towards *admiration*.

Hell, today was downright *awe*.

Gentle, soft Mila turned out to be the strongest person he knew, and not just because she'd spent the day wrestling live dugongs. How much fortitude did it take to engage with a world where everyone else experienced things completely differently to you? Where you were an alien within your own community? Every damned day.

So, *attraction* he could handle. *Admiration* he could troubleshoot his way through. *Awe* he would be able to smile and enjoy as soon as the adrenaline spike of today wore off. But there was something else… Something that tipped the scales of his comfort zone.

Envy.

He was coveting the hell out of Mila and her simple, happy, *vivid* life. Amid all the complexity that her remote lifestyle and synaesthesia brought, Mila just stuck to her basic philosophy—protect the reef. Everything else fell into place behind that. Her goals and her strengths were perfectly aligned. No wonder she could curl up in that quirky little stack-house surrounded by all her treasures and sleep deep, long and easy.

When had he ever slept the night through?

When he'd come to Coral Bay on a fact-finding mission, his direction had been clear. Get a feel for the issues that might hamper his hotel development application. The hotel he needed to build to keep the lucrative coastal strip in Wardoo's lease.

Simple, right?

But now nothing was simple. Mila had more than demonstrated the tourism potential of the place but she'd also shown him how inextricably her well-being was tangled up with the reef. They were like a symbiotic pair. Without Mila, the reef would suffer. Without the reef, Mila would suffer.

They were one.

And he was going to put a hotel on her back.

His eyes came up to her as she joined in on the equipment hauling, finding strength from whatever bottomless supply she had. He could yearn like a kid for Mila's simple, focused life and he could yearn like a grown man for her body—but this *need* for her, this *fear* for her... Those weren't feelings that he could master.

And he didn't do powerless. Not any more.

Mila Nakano never was for him. And he was certainly no good for her. If anything, he was the exact opposite of what was good for her.

And he wasn't going to leave tonight without letting her know how much that was true.

CHAPTER ELEVEN

THE *PORTUS* WAS closer by a half-hour than Mila's little stack-house in Coral Bay town centre and, given she was coming to him for dinner anyway, Rich had called his crew up the coast and had the tender pick them both up at the nearest authorised channel in the reef. The last time she'd been aboard she had done everything she could not to touch either of the men wanting to help her board safely; it was probably wrong to feel so much satisfaction at the fact that she didn't even hesitate to put her hand into his now.

Or that she'd looked at him with such trust as he'd helped her aboard.

It warmed him even as it hurt him.

He'd led her into the *Portus'* expansive bow bedroom, piled her up with big fluffy towels, pointed her in the direction of his bathroom and given her a gentle shove. Then he'd folded back the thick, warm quilt on his bed in readiness so that she could just fall into it when she was clean, warm and dry.

That was two hours ago and he'd been killing time ever since, vacillating between wanting to wake her and spend what little time he could with her, and putting off the inevitable by letting her sleep. In the end, he chose sleep and told himself it wasn't because he was a coward. She'd been almost wobbling on her feet as he'd closed the dark bedroom doors behind him; she needed as much rest as he could give her.

Now, though, it was time for Sleeping Beauty to wake. He'd made sure to bang around on boat business just outside the bedroom door in the hope that the sounds would rouse her naturally, but it looked as if she could sleep through a cyclone—*had he ever slept that well in his life?*—so he had to take the more direct approach now.

'Mila?' He followed up with a quiet knock on the door. Nothing.

He repeated her name a little louder and opened the door a crack to help her hear him. Still not so much as a rustle of bedclothes on the other side. He stepped onto the bedroom's thick carpet and took care to leave the door wide open behind him. If she woke to find him standing over her he didn't want it to be with no escape route. He also didn't want it to be *over* her.

'Mila?' he said again, this time crouched down to bed level.

She twitched but little else, and he took a moment to study her. She looked like a child in his massive bed, curled up small, right on the left edge, as though she knew it wasn't her bed to enjoy. As though she was trying to minimise her impact. Or maybe as though she was trying to minimise its impact *on her*. He studied the expensive bedding critically—who knew what association was triggered by the feel of silk against her skin?

Yet she slept practically curled around his pillow. Embracing it. Would she do that if she wasn't at least a little comfortable in this space? She'd been exhausted, yes, but not so shattered that she couldn't have refused if curling up in a bed other than her own had been in any way disturbing to her. There was no shortage of sofas she could have taken instead.

Rich reached out and tucked a loose lock of hair back in with its still-damp cousins. Mila twitched again but not away from him. She seemed to curl her face towards him before burrowing down deeper into his pillow. Actually, his was on the other side of the bed but he would struggle, after he'd left this place, not to swap it for the one Mila practically embraced. Just to keep her close a little longer. Until her scent faded with Coral Bay on the horizon behind him.

He placed a gentle hand on her exposed shoulder. 'Mila. Time to wake up.'

She roused, shifted. Then her beautiful eyes flickered open and shone at him, full of confused warmth as she tried to remember where she was. It only took a heartbeat before she mastered them, though, and looked around the space.

'How did you sleep?' he asked, just to give her an excuse to look back at him.

She pushed herself up, and brought his quilt with her.

'This bed...' she murmured, all sleepy and sexy.

His chest actually hurt.

'Best money could buy,' he squeezed out.

'How do you even get out of it?' Her voice grew stronger, less dreamy with every sentence she uttered. 'I'm not sure I'm going to be able to.'

That was what he wanted; the kind of sleep the bed promised when you looked at it, lay on it. The kind of sleep that Mila's groggy face said she'd just had. And now that he'd seen his bed with her in it, that was what he wanted too.

But *wanting* didn't always mean *having*.

'Damo will have dinner ready in a half hour,' he said. 'Do you want to freshen up? Maybe come out on deck for some air?'

It was only then that the darkness outside seemed to dawn on her. She pushed up yet straighter.

'Yes, I'm sorry. It was only supposed to be a nap—'

'Don't apologise. After the day you've had, you clearly needed it.' He pushed to his feet. 'I'll see you on deck when you're ready.'

He left her there, blinking a daze in his big bed, and retreated up the steps to the galley, where he busied himself redoing half the tasks his deckhand had already done. Just to keep busy. Just to give Mila the space he figured she would appreciate. He lifted the clear lid on the chowder risotto steaming away beneath it and then, at Damo's frustrated cluck, abandoned the galley, went out on the aft deck and busied himself decanting a bottle of red.

'Gosh, it's even more beautiful at night,' a small voice eventually said from the galley doorway.

His gaze tracked hers across the *Portus'* outer deck. He took it for granted now, but the moody uplights built into discreet places along the gunnel did cast interesting and dramatic shapes along the cat's white surfaces.

'I forget to appreciate it sometimes.'

'Human nature,' she murmured.

But was it? Mila appreciated what she had every single day. Then again, he wasn't at all sure she was strictly human. Maybe all mermaids had synaesthesia.

'What smells so good?'

'No crayfish on the menu tonight,' he assured her. 'I believe we're having some kind of chowder-meets-risotto. What are your feelings about rice?'

Her dark eyes considered that. 'Ambivalent.'

'And clams?'

'Clams are picky,' she said immediately. 'I'm sure they would protest any use you made of them, chowder or otherwise.'

The allusion brought a smile to his lips. 'But you eat them?'

'Honestly? After today, I would happily eat the cushions on your lovely sofa.'

She laughed and he just let himself enjoy the sound. Because it was the last time he ever would.

He led her to the sofa and poured two glasses of Merlot. 'This isn't going to help much with the sleepiness, I'm afraid.'

Mila wafted the glass under her nose and her eyes closed momentarily. 'Don't care.'

He followed her down onto the luxurious sofa that circled the low table on three sides. Her expression made him circle his glass with liquid a few extra times and sip just a little slower.

Craving just a hint of whatever it was that connected Mila so deeply with life.

Pathetically trying to replicate it.

They talked about the dugong tagging—about what the results would be used for and what that meant for populations along this coast. They talked about the coral spawn they'd collected and how little it would take to destroy all that she'd ever collected. One good storm to take out the power for days, one fuel shortage to kill Steve Donahue's generator and the chest freezer they were using would slowly return to room temperature and five years' worth of spawn would all perish. They talked about the two big game fishermen who'd gone out to sea on an ill-prepared boat during the week, and spent a scary and frigid few nights being carried further and further away from Australia on the fast-moving Leeuwin Current before being rescued and how much difference an immediate ocean response unit would have made.

Really he was just raising anything to keep Mila talking.

She listened as well as she contributed and her stories were always so engaging. These were not conversations he got to have back in the city.

He thought that he was letting her talk herself almost out of breath because he knew this might well be the last opportunity he had to do it. But the longer into the night they talked, the more he had to admit that he was letting her dominate their conversation because it meant he didn't have to take such an active part. And if he took a more active part then he knew he would have to begin the discussion he was quietly dreading.

'I'm sorry,' Mila said as she forked the last of the double cream from her dish with the last of her tropical fruit. A gorgeous shade of pink stained her cheeks. 'I've been talking your ear off since the entree.'

'I like listening to you,' he admitted, though *like* wasn't nearly strong enough. But he didn't have the words to describe how tranquil he felt in her presence. As if she were infecting him with her very nature.

That, itself, was warning enough.

'Besides,' he said, beginning what had to be done, 'this might be my last chance.'

Mila frowned. 'Last chance for what?'

'To hear your stories. To learn from you.' Then, as she just stared, he added, 'I have what I need now. There's no reason for me to come back to Coral Bay.'

Yeah, there was. Of course there was. There was Wardoo and there was his proposed development and there was Mila. She was probably enough all by herself to lure him back to this beautiful place. What he meant, though, was that he *wouldn't* be coming back, despite those things.

She just blinked at him as his words sank into her exhausted brain. What kind of a jerk would do this to someone so unprepared?

'No reason? At all?'

He shrugged, but the nonchalance cost him dear. 'I have what I came for.'

It was hard to define the expression that suffused her face then: part-confusion, part-sorrow, part-disappointment. 'What about Wardoo?'

It was impossible not to mark the perfect segue into the revelation he wanted so badly not to make. To hurt this gentle creature in a way that was as wrong as taking a spear gun to some brightly coloured fish just going about its own business on the reef.

But he'd already missed several opportunities to be strong— to be honest—and do the right thing by Mila.

He wasn't about to leave her thinking the best of him.

Not when it was the last thing he deserved.

'Mila, listen—' Rich began.

'I wasn't making any assumptions,' she said in a rush. 'I

know I don't have any claims on you. That I'm necessarily anything more than just...'

Entertainment.

Though the all too familiar and awkward taste of cola forming at the back of her throat suggested otherwise.

*Mila, listen...*was as classic an entrée into the *it's-not-you-it's-me* speech as she'd ever heard. Except she well knew the truth behind that now.

It was *always* her.

Just because she'd found someone that she could be comfortable around—with—didn't necessarily mean Rich felt the same way. Or, even if he did, that it was particularly unique for him. There were probably a lot of women back in the city that he felt comfortable around. More businesslike women with whom he could discuss current affairs. More suitable women that he could take to important functions. More cognitively conventional women that he could just be normal with.

The cola started to transition into the nose-scrunching earwax that she hated so much.

'We've spent days together,' he began. 'We've eaten together and we've kissed a couple of times. It's not unreasonable for you to wonder what we are to each other, Mila.'

He spoke as if he were letting an employee go. Impersonal. Functional. Controlled. It was hard not to admire the leader in him, but it was just as impossible not to resent the heck out of that. He'd clearly had time to prepare for this moment whereas she'd walked into it all sleepy-eyed and Merlot-filled.

Yet, somehow, this felt as prepared as she was ever going to get.

'And what is that, exactly?' she asked.

'There's a connection here,' he said, leaning in. 'I think it would be foolish to try and pretend otherwise. But good chemistry doesn't necessarily make us a good fit.'

She blinked at him. *They* didn't fit? He would fit in anywhere. He was just that kind of a man. Which meant...

'You mean *I'm* not.'

'That's not what I was saying, but you have to admit that you would fit about as well in my world as I've fit in yours.'

'You fit in mine just fine.' Or so she'd thought.

His laugh wasn't for her. 'The man who can't go in open water? That novelty wouldn't last long.'

She refused to let him minimise this moment. 'Do you not like it here?'

'I didn't say I haven't enjoyed it. I said I don't *fit* here.'

Why? Because he was new to it? 'You haven't really given it much of a chance.'

It was so much easier to defend the place she loved than the heart that was hurting.

Rich sighed. 'I didn't come here looking for anything but information, Mila…'

'Why *did* you come, Rich?' she asked. He'd avoided the question twice before but asking that bought her a few moments to get her thoughts in order. To chart some safe passage out of these choppy emotional waters.

He took a deep, slow breath and studied her, tiny forks appearing between his eyes. Then he leaned forward with the most purpose she'd seen in him and she immediately regretted asking.

'The government is proposing a re-draft of the boundaries of the leaseholdings on the Northwest Cape,' he began. 'They want to remove the coastal strip from Wardoo's lease.'

His words were so unlike the extreme gravity in his face it took her a moment to orient. That was not the terrible blow she'd steeled herself for.

'Why?'

'They want to see the potential of the area fulfilled and remove the impediments to tourism coming in.'

Impediments like the Dawsons protecting the region by controlling the access.

'It's a big deal that this is a World Heritage Marine Park,' he went on. 'They want the world to be able to come see it. But until now they haven't been able to act.'

There was a point in all this corporate speak, somewhere. Mila grappled for it. 'What's changed now?'

'Wardoo's fifty-year lease is up. They're free to renegotiate the boundaries as they wish.'

Ironic that the very listing that was supposed to recognise and protect the reef only made it more attractive for tourists. And all those people needed somewhere to stay.

'And redrawn boundaries are bad?'

'The new leasehold terms will make it nearly impossible to turn a reasonable profit from this land. Without the coastal strip.'

Was she still feeling the effects of her not-so-power nap? Somehow, she was failing to connect the dots that Rich was laying out. 'What has the coastal strip got to do with Wardoo's profitability?'

Rich's broad shoulders lifted high and then dropped slowly as he measured his words.

'Every business that operates in Coral Bay pays a percentage to WestCorp for the opportunity to do so. Tourism has been keeping Wardoo afloat for years.'

The stink of realisation hit her like black tar. She sagged against the sofa back. *That* was why the Dawsons were so staunchly against external developers in Coral Bay.

'So…you weren't protecting the reef,' she whispered. 'You were protecting your profits?'

'WestCorp is a business, Mila. Wardoo is just one holding amongst three dozen.'

She pushed her empty dish away. 'Is that why you were up here? To check up on your tenants?' It hit her then. 'Oh, God! A percentage of my rent probably goes to you too. You should have said it was a rental inspection, I would have tidied up—'

'Mila—'

She pushed to her feet as her stomach protested the mix of

yeast and cherry that came with all the anger and confusion—on top of the clam chowder, red wine and utter stupidity, it threatened a really humiliating resurgence.

'Excuse me, I need a moment.'

She didn't wait for permission. Before Rich could even rise to his own feet, she'd crossed the room and started negotiating the steps down to his bedroom. Once in the spacious en suite bathroom, she braced her hands either side of the sink until she was sure that her churning stomach was not going to actually broil over. Then she pressed a damp cloth to her face and neck until the queasiness eased off.

This was not the first time she'd had synaesthesia-prompted nausea. Her body really couldn't discriminate between actual tastes and imagined, so some combinations, usually reserved for really complicated moments, ended up in long sojourns to a quiet, cool place.

She sagged down onto her elbows on the marble vanity and pressed the cloth to her closed eyes.

If she'd given it any real thought she wouldn't have been surprised to discover Wardoo was getting kickbacks from the local businesses. If they were in the city they'd definitely have been paying rent to someone.

No, the churning cherry was all about how stupid she had been to just assume that Rich would find the *reef* the most valuable part of the Bay. If he liked the reef at all, it was secondary to the income that the tenants could bring him. He was still here for the money.

He was all about the money.

WestCorp is a business, Mila...

He'd even hinted at as much, several times. But she hadn't listened. She and Rich saw the world completely differently. She had no more right to judge him for the way he perceived the world than he had to judge her synaesthesia.

They just came at life from very different places.

Too different.

Leveraging a bunch of cafés and caravan parks and glass-bottom boat operators for a percentage did not make him a bad person.

It just meant he was no white knight to her reef after all.

She'd have to carry on doing her own white knighting.

She patted her face dry, pinched her cheeks to encourage a little colour into them and switched off the fancy lights as she stepped back into the bedroom. Such a short time ago she'd curled up in that bed—in amongst Rich's lingering scent—and thought drowsily how nice it would be to stay there for ever. Now, that moment felt as dreamlike as the past few days.

When viewed with the cold, hard light of reality.

She'd stumbled against Rich's office chair as she'd staggered into the bedroom a few minutes earlier and she took a moment now to right it, sliding it back into the cavity under the workstation and setting to rights the documents she'd splayed across the desktop with her falter. As she did, her eyes slashed across a bound wad of pages that had slipped out from under a plain file.

The word 'Coral Bay' immediately leapt out at her.

She glanced at the empty doorway and then lifted the corner on the cover page like a criminal.

Words. Lots and lots of words. Some kind of summary introduction. She flipped to the next page and saw a map of the coast—as familiar to her as the shape of her own hand. A large area was shaded virtually across the coast road from Nancy's Point.

That was where she stopped being covert.

Mila pulled out the chair, let her wobbly legs sink her into it and unclipped the binder so she could turn the pages more fully. Another plan showing massive trenching down from Coral Bay township—water, power, sewer. Over the page another, showing side elevations of a mass-scale construction—single, two and three storeys high in different places. Swathes of parking. Irrigation. Gardens.

A helipad, for crying out loud.

Her fingers trembled more with every page she turned. Urgent eyes scanned the top of every plan and found the WestCorp logo. Waves of nausea rolled in again and Mila concentrated on slowing her patchy breathing. She bought herself more time by tidying the pages and fixing the binding. Just before she stood, she glanced again at the summary introduction and her eyes fell to the page bottom. An elaborate signature in ink. Rich's signature.

And that was yesterday's date beside it.

The *Portus* seemed to lurch beneath her as if it had been hit by some undersea quake.

Rich was developing the reef—a luxury resort on the coast of Wardoo's land. No wonder he protested the government's plans to excise the coastal strip.

He had *this* under development.

And he'd signed off on it after he'd seen the coral spawn. After he'd first kissed her.

She wobbled to her feet and pressed the incriminating evidence to her chest as she returned to the aft deck. Rich rose politely as she came back out but if he noticed what she was clinging to he showed no sign.

Mila dropped the report on the table between them and let it lie there like some dead thing.

Rich's eyes fell shut briefly, but then found hers again—one hundred per cent CEO. 'WestCorp isn't a charity, Mila. I have shareholders and other ventures to protect.'

No. That wasn't what he was supposed to protect.

'You're forsaking the reef?' she cut in. 'And the Bay.'

And me, a tiny, hurt voice whimpered.

'I admit it is beautiful, Mila. And diverse. UNESCO obviously agreed to give it World Heritage status. But without the revenue from tourism activity, without the coastal strip, I can't see how I can justify maintaining Wardoo.' His chest rose high and then fell.

Couldn't justify it? Did every part of his world have to pay for itself? Did life itself come with a profit margin?

Her voice fell to a hoarse whisper. 'It's your heritage, Rich. Your roots are here. You're a Dawson. Does that not matter?'

'That's like me saying that your roots are in Tokyo because your surname is Nakano. Do you *feel* Japanese, Mila?'

She'd never fully identified with any one culture in her crazy patchwork quilt family. That had always been part of her general disconnection with the world until the day she'd woken up and realised that where she belonged was *here*. The reef was her roots. Regardless of the many where-elses she had come from.

She identified as *Mila*. Wildlife was her people.

And she would defend them against whoever came.

'You're Saltwater People too, Rich. You just don't know it. Look at who you become on the *Portus*. Look at where you go to find peace.'

'Peace doesn't put food on the table.'

'Does everything have to revolve around the almighty dollar?'

'We can't all live in shipping containers and spend our days frolicking with sea life, Mila. Money matters. Choosing it isn't a bad choice; it's just not your choice.'

Her beautiful little home had never sounded so tawdry—nor her job so unimportant—and when those two things formed at least half of your world believing in them mattered.

A lot.

She pushed to her feet. Words tumbled up past the earwax taste of heartbreak and she had to force them over her tight lips so they could be heard up on the fly bridge. Though there was no chance on earth that the crew hadn't heard their most recent discussion.

'Damo? I would like to go to shore, please.'

Rich rose too. 'Mila, we're not done...'

'Oh, yes. We are.' *Completely.* 'As soon as you're free, Damo.'

There was enough anxiety in her voice to get anyone's attention.

'Mila,' Rich urged, 'you don't understand. If it's not me, it will be someone else...'

'I understand better than you think,' she hissed. 'You used me and you lied to me. About why you were here. About who you are. I squired you around the district like some royal bloody tour and showed you all its secrets, and I thought I was making a difference. I thought you saw the Bay the way I do. And maybe you actually did, yet you're *still* happy to toss it all away with your trenches and your pipes and your helipads.'

Her arms crept around her middle. 'That was my mistake for letting my guard down for you; I won't be so foolish again.'

She stepped up to him as he also rose to his feet.

'But if you think for one minute that I am going to let anyone hurt the place and people that I love, then you—' she pushed a finger into his chest '—don't understand me. I will whip up a PR nightmare for WestCorp. I'll get every single tourist who visits this place to sign my petition and every scientist I know to go on record with the damage that commercialisation does to reefs. You go ahead and throw the Bay to the wolves. You go make your money and spend it on making more money and don't worry about any of us. But I want you to think on something as you sit on your big stockpile of cash, tossing it over your head and letting it rain down on you...'

She flicked her chin up.

'What are you keeping the money for, exactly, if not to allow you to have ten thousand square kilometres of gorgeous, red, barely productive land in your life? Or an ocean. Or a reef. Or a luxury catamaran. Things that might not make any money but are completely priceless because of what they bring you. Money is a means to an end; it's not the end itself. Surely wealth is meaningless unless it buys you freedom or love or—'

She stumbled on the word as soon as it fell across her lips

because she hadn't meant to say it. And she hadn't meant to feel it. But the subtlest undertones of pineapple told her that she did.

Richard Grundy, of all people…

She took a steadying breath.

'Or sanctuary! It won't keep you warm at night and it won't fill the great void inside you that you try so hard to disguise.'

'I don't have a void—'

'Of course you do. You pack your money down into it like a tooth cavity.' She frowned and stepped closer. 'What if wealth is the thing that people like you are raised to believe matters in lieu of the things that actually matter?'

'People like me?' he gritted.

'Disconnected people. Empty people. Lonely people.'

Rich's strong jaw twitched and he paled a little. 'Really, Mila? The poster-child for dysfunction wants to counsel me on being disconnected?'

His hard words hit home, but she could not deny the essential truth in them.

'Has it not occurred to you yet that I am far richer than you could ever be? *Will* ever be? Because I have all of this.' She held her hands out to the moonlight and the ocean and the reef they couldn't see and the wonders they both knew to be on it. 'And I have my *place* within it. The certainty and fulfilment of that. All of this is more wealth than anyone could ever need in a dozen lifetimes.'

Damo appeared at the bottom of the steps down from the bridge, looking about as uncomfortable as she suddenly felt. Here, in this place that she'd already started to think of as a second home.

Mila turned immediately to follow him down to the tender.

'If WestCorp opts not to renew the lease then who knows who would come in or what they might do with it? The only thing that will keep the government from excising the coastal strip is significant capital investment in the area,' he called after her. 'I need to build something.'

She called back over her shoulder. 'Why don't you build an undersea hotel? That would be awesome.'

She refused to think of what she'd seen on his desk as a reasonable compromise. And she refused to let herself believe that the project was still open to amendment, any more than she could believe that *she* made the slightest difference to his secret plans.

He'd *signed* it. In ink.

'Or, better yet, don't build anything. Just let Wardoo stand or fall on its own merits.'

'It will fall.'

'Then give up the lease, if that's what it takes.'

'I don't *want* to give it up. I'm trying to save it.'

She stared at him, her chest heaving. Even he looked confused by that.

'If I surrender the lease,' he went on after the momentary fumble, 'then anyone could take it up. You could end up with a million goats destroying the land. If I keep the lease and don't develop then the government will excise the strip and someone else will come in and do it. Someone who doesn't care about the reef at all.'

'Funny,' she spat. 'I thought that was you.'

For a moment she thought that Rich was going to let her go with the last word still tasting like nail varnish on her lips. But he was a CEO, and people with acronyms for titles probably never surrendered the final word. On principle.

'Mila, don't go. Not like this.'

But final words could sometimes be silent. And she was determined that hers should be. Besides which, her lungs were too full of the scent of earwax for adequate speech and the last thing she wanted was for Richard Grundy to hear her croak. So she kept moving. Her feet reached the timber dive platform. The jarrah deck's isolation practically pulsed through her feet. Resonating with a kindred spirit, perhaps. She accepted Damo's hand without thought and stepped into the tender, sinking down with her back firmly to the man she'd accepted so readily into her life.

Nothing.

No solo trumpet at Damo's touch. No plinking ball bearings at the breeze rushing under the *Portus*. No fluttering of wings as her skin erupted in gooseflesh.

It was as if every part of her was as deadened as her heart.

Had he not taken enough from her this night? Now he'd muted her superpower.

Behind her, Rich stood silent and still. Had she expected an eleventh-hour apology? Some final sense of regret? An attitudinal about-face?

Just how naive was she, really?

Richard Grundy was making decisions based on the needs and wants of his shareholders. She couldn't reasonably expect him to put anyone else's needs ahead of his own. And certainly not hers. She was his tour guide, nothing more. A curiosity and an entertainment. A woman he'd known only days in the greater scheme of things. It was pure folly to imagine that she would— or even could—affect any change in his deep-seated attitudes.

Then again, folly seemed to be all Rich thought she was capable of here. In her quaint little shack with her funny little job...

Damo had the good sense to stay completely silent as he ran her back to the marina and dropped her onto the pier. She gave him the weakest of smiles in farewell and didn't wait to watch him leave, climbing down onto the beach and turning towards town. The tide was far enough out that she could wade around the rocks to get back to town and, somehow, it felt critical that she put her feet back in the water, that she prove to herself that Rich had not muted her senses for good.

That he had not broken her.

But there was no symphony as the water swilled around her bare feet. And as she turned to look out to the reef, imagining what was down there, there was no sound or sensation at all.

Everything was as deadened as her heart.

It was impossible to imagine a world without her superpower to help her interpret it. Or without her reef to help her breathe. And, though she hated to admit it after such a spectacularly short time, she was struggling to even imagine a world without Rich in it.

To help her live.

How had he done that? So quickly. So deeply. And—knowing what he'd done—how could she ever trust any of her senses ever again?

CHAPTER TWELVE

'I'VE GOT NEWS,' her supervisor said down the telephone, his voice grave. 'But you're not going to like some of it.'

Mila took a deep breath. There had been much about the past nine weeks that she didn't like, least of all her inability to get the treacherous Richard Grundy completely from her mind. Whether she was angry at herself for failing to heed her own instincts or angry at him for turning out to be such a mercenary, she couldn't tell.

All she knew was that time had not healed that particular wound, no matter what the adage promised. And no matter how many worthy distractions she'd thrown at it.

It was her own stupid fault that many of her favourite places were now tainted with memories of Rich in them. She had to go showing them off...

'Go ahead, Lyle.'

'First up... Wardoo's lease has been renewed.'

Her stomach clenched. *Renewed*, Lyle had said. Not *refilled*.

Part of the emotional swell she'd been surfing these past months—up, down, up, down—was due to the conflict between wanting Rich to keep his heritage and wanting him to surrender his resort plans. If Rich kept Wardoo it meant he must have kept the coastal strip, which meant going ahead with the resort.

But if he dropped the resort, it meant he must have given up Wardoo. And giving up Wardoo meant there was no conceivable reason for Rich to ever be in Coral Bay again.

So, secretly craving an opportunity to see Rich again meant secretly accepting commercialisation of her beloved coast.

'By the Dawsons?'

How her stomach could leap quite that high while still fisted from nerves she didn't know but it seemed to lurch almost into her throat, accompanied by the delicious hot chocolate of hope behind her tongue.

'Looks like they're staying.'

He's staying. Impossible to think of Wardoo as WestCorp's. Not when she'd eaten sandwiches with and stood in the living room with—and *kissed*—the the man who owned it.

'I'm looking at a copy of an agreement that I'm probably not supposed to have,' Lyle admitted. 'Friends in high places. It's not the whole thing, just highlights.'

'And the coastal strip?'

Please… There was still a chance that Rich had negotiated a different outcome. That he'd dropped the resort plans. Or that he'd found a way to keep Wardoo profitable without the coastal strip.

Not the perfect outcome, but one she only realised in this moment that she would accept. As long as it wasn't *Rich* trashing her reef…

'It's staying in the leasehold,' Lyle admitted and her heart sank. 'Not without conditions, though. That's what I want to talk to you about.'

She'd been the one to tell her boss about the government's plans for the coastal strip, but she never told him about Rich's development. Or that she was on a first name basis with the Dawsons.

The hopeful hot chocolate wavered into a cigarettey kind of mocha.

'What kind of conditions?' she asked suspiciously. Though, really, she knew.

The helicopters were probably circling Coral Bay right now, waiting for that helipad.

'Government has approved a development for the Bay,' he said.

Courtesy of a two-month head start, that news didn't send her to water, but it still hurt hearing it. Had she really imagined he would change his multi-million-dollar plans…?

For her?

The hot chocolate completely dissipated and Mila wrapped the arm not holding the phone around her middle and closed her eyes. She asked purely because she was not supposed to already know.

'What kind of development, Lyle?'

'Like I said, I've only got select pages,' he started. 'But it's big, some kind of resort or hotel. Dozens of bathrooms or kitchens; it's hard to tell. No idea why they'd need quite that many, so far from the accommodation,' Lyle flicked through pages on his end of the phone, 'but there's lots of that too. Looks like a theatre of some kind, and a massive wine cellar, maybe? Underground, anyway, temperature-controlled. And a helipad of all things. It's hard to say what it is. But it's not small, Mila. And it can't be a coincidence that it's coming up just as Wardoo's lease is resolved.'

No. It was no coincidence.

'Do you know where it's approved for?' she breathed.

This was her last hope. Maybe he'd shifted its site further south, out of the Marine Park. Though really, wouldn't that defeat the purpose?

'There is a sketch map. Looks like it's about a half-hour south of you. Nancy's Point, maybe?'

Ice began to crystallise the very cells in her flesh.

So it was done. And at his great-grandmother's favourite point, of all places.

'Lyle, look through the documents. Is there any reference to a company called WestCorp anywhere in them?'

Lyle shuffled while Mila died inside.

'Yeah, Mila. There is a WestCorp stamp on one of the floor plans. Who are they?'

Mila stared at the blank space on the wall opposite her.

'WestCorp is the Dawsons,' she breathed down the line.

Lyle seemed as speechless as she was. 'Dawsons? You're kidding. They're the last ones I would have thought—'

'We don't know them,' Mila cut in. 'Or what they're capable of. They're just a family who loved this land once. They haven't lived here for decades.'

'But still—'

'They're not for the reef any more, Lyle.' She realised she was punishing him for Rich's decisions. 'I'm sorry, I have to go. Can you send me those documents?'

This time his hesitation was brief. 'I can't, Mila. I'm not even supposed to have seen them. This was just a heads-up.'

Right. Like a five-minute warning siren that a tsunami was coming. What was she supposed to do with that?

'I understand,' she murmured. 'And I appreciate it. Thank you, Lyle.'

It took no time to lock up her little office and get into her four-wheel drive. Then about a half-hour more to get down to Nancy's Point, half expecting to see site works underway—survey pegs, vehicle tracks, a subterranean wine cellar. But there was nothing, just the same rocky outlook she'd visited a hundred times. The place Rich had first come striding towards her, his big hand outstretched.

Impotence burned as bourbon in her throat. She tried to imagine the site filled with tourists, staff, power stations and treatment plants and found she couldn't. It was simply inconceivable.

And in that moment she decided to tell Rich so.

If she didn't fight for her reef, who would?

There had been no communication between them since he'd left all those weeks ago but this was worth the precedent—now that it was a reality. But she wasn't brave enough to talk to him face to face or even voice to voice. A big part of her feared what it would do to her heart to hear his voice right inside her ear, and what it would do to her soul to have to endure his justification for this monstrosity. She had a smartphone and she had working fingers, and she could tap him one heck of a scathing email telling him exactly what she thought of his plans to put a resort at Nancy's Point. And she could do it right now while she was still angry enough to be honest and brave.

Brave in a way she hadn't been when she'd fled the *Portus* that night.

She climbed back into her car and reached into her dashboard for her phone, then swiped her way through to her email app. She gave a half-moment's consideration to a subject line that he couldn't ignore and then began tapping on letters.

Subject: Nancy will turn in her grave!

'All right, folks, time to get wet!'

Mila sat back and let the excited tourists leap in ahead of her. If they'd been nervous earlier, about snorkelling in open ocean, the anxiety dissipated completely when they spotted their first whale shark, the immense shape looming as a shadow in the water ahead. There were two out here, but the boat chose this one to centre on while another vessel chugged their passengers closer to the other one. But not too close…there were rules. It was up to the tourists to swim the distance and close up the gap between them.

Not everyone was a natural swimmer and so every spare member of crew got in the water with them and shepherded a small number of snorkelers each. Each leader took an underwater whiteboard so they could communicate with their group without having to get alongside them or surface constantly.

Easier when you were navigating an animal as big as a whale shark to be able to keep your eyes on its every move.

The last cluster slipped off the back of the boat and into the open water in an excited, splashy frenzy.

That left Mila to go it alone—just how she liked it. She'd eased herself right out onto the front of the big tourist boat where none of them thought to go and so she hadn't had to sit amongst them with the smells and sounds of unfamiliar people. Now, she gave the captain a wave so he knew she was in, and slid down quietly and gently into the silken water.

It was normally completely clear out here, barring the odd cluster of weed floating along or balls of fish picking at the surface, but the churning engines of two boats and the splashing of the associated snorkelling tourists made the water foggy with a champagne of bubbles in all directions. Easy to forget what was out here with them when she couldn't see it, but Mila swam a wide arc to break out of the white-water. As the boats backed away from the site, the water cleared, darkened and then settled a little. The surface turbulence still rocked her but, with her head under, it was much calmer. Calm enough to get on with the job. She looked around her at the light streaming down into the deep blue, converging on some distant point far below, her eyes hunting for the creature so big it seemed impossible that it could hide out here.

The first clue that it was with them was the frenzied flipper action of the nearby tourists, then a great looming shape materialised in slow motion out of the blue below them straight towards her. The whale shark's camouflage—the very thing she'd come to photograph—made it hard for Mila to define its distinctive shape until it was nearly upon her, but it did nothing more dramatic than cruise silently by, its massive tail fanning just once to propel it the entire distance between the other tourists and her group. Everyone else started swimming to keep up with it while Mila back-pedalled madly to get herself out of its way.

She dived under as it passed her, and she got a good view

of the half-dozen remoras either catching a ride on the shark's underside or using its draught to swim against its pale underbelly. She swung her underwater camera up and took a couple of images of the patterning around its gills—the ones that the star-mapping software needed—and then watched it disappear once again into the deep blue. But she knew it wouldn't be gone long. Whale sharks seemed to enjoy the interaction with people and this one circled around and emerged out of nothing again to swim between them once more. Mila photographed it on the way back through in case it wasn't the same one at all, then set off after its relaxed tail, swimming back towards the main group of tourists. Two boatloads were combined now, all eager to see the same animal.

As she approached, a staff member in dive gear held up a whiteboard with four letters on it.

R U OK?

Mila gave him an easy thumbs-up and he turned and focused on the less certain swimmers. It was more exhausting than many expected, being out here in the open current and trying to swim clear of a forty-foot-long prehistoric creature.

Mila let herself enjoy the shark, the gorgeous light filtering down through the surface and the sensations both brought with them. She attributed whale sharks with regal qualities—maybe her most literal association yet—and this one was quite the prince. Comparatively unscarred, spectacular markings, big square head, massive gaping mouth that swallowed hundreds of litres of seawater at a time. When it wasn't gulping, it pressed its lips together hard to squeeze the headful of water out through its gills and then swallow what solids were left behind in its massive mouth. To Mila, the lips looked like a vaguely wry smirk.

Her chest squeezed and not because of exertion.

She'd seen that smirk before. But not for months.

She back-swam again, to maintain the required safety distance, and watched the swimmers on the far side of the animal move forward as it swam away from them. Another carried a whiteboard, but he wasn't a diver and he wasn't in one of the company wetsuits. Mila tipped her head and looked closer.

The snorkeler wrote something on his board with waterproof marker then held it aloft in the streaming light.

NOT...

She had to wait for the long tail of the whale shark to pass between them before she could read it properly.

NOT EN SUITES... LABS.

What? What did that mean? She straightened to read it again, certain she'd misread some diving instruction. The man wiped it off with his bare arm and wrote again. Something about the way he moved made her spine ratchet straighter than even the circling whale shark did. But she could not take her eyes off his board. He held it up again and the words were longer and so the letters were smaller. Mila had to swim a little closer to read them.

ROOMS NOT 4 TOURISTS.
4 RESEARCHERS.

Her heart began to pound. In earnest. She tried to be alert to what the shark was doing but found it impossible to do anything other than stare at that whiteboard and the man holding it.

'Rich?'

She couldn't help saying it aloud and the little word must have puffed out of the top of her snorkel into the air above the surface to be lost on the stiff ocean breeze.

He held the board up again, the words newly written.

NOT U/GROUND WINE CELLAR...

The whale shark swam back through between them, doing its best to drag her eyes off the man wiping the board clean again and back onto the *true* ocean spectacle, but Mila paid it no heed, other than to be frustrated by the spectacular length of the shark as it blocked her view of Rich. As soon as it passed, she read the two words he'd replaced on the board. Her already tight breath caught altogether.

SPAWN BANK.

She pushed her feet and gasped for air above the surface. Water splashed and surged against her body, buffeting her on two sides. Using the clustered snorkelers for reference, she stroked her way towards them with already weary muscles. Just out of voice range, another snorkeler rose above the splash. The only head other than hers poking out of the water while the massive shark dominated attention below.

Rich.

They swam directly towards each other, oblivious to any monsters of the deep still doing graceful laps below them. But when they got close, Mila pulled up short and slid her mask up onto her head.

'What are you doing here?' Her arms and legs worked in opposition to keep her stable in the undulating water.

'I got your email,' Rich answered, raising his mask too. His thick hair spiked up in all directions.

'You could have just replied,' she gasped as the gently rolling seas pitched her in two directions at once.

Rich swam a little closer and Mila turned to keep some distance between them. As life-preserving as the four metres' clearance she was supposed to give the whale shark. They ended up swimming in a synchronised arc in the heaving swell, circling each other.

'Yeah, I could have. But I wanted to see you.'

Hard enough to speak as all her muscles focused on keeping her afloat without the added complication of a suddenly collapsing chest cavity.

She didn't waste time with coyness. 'Why? To break the news in person?'

His voice was thick as he answered. 'It's not a resort, Mila. It's a technology centre. The Wardoo Northern Studies Centre.'

Labs. Accommodation for researchers.

Incongruous to smell hot chocolate over the smell of fresh seawater and marine diesel, but that was hope for you...

'It has a helipad, Rich.'

He ignored her sarcasm and answered her straight. 'For a sea rescue chopper.'

She just blinked. Hadn't they talked about that the night on the *Portus*? The difference it would make to lives up here?

Her voice was as weak as her breath, suddenly. 'And the spawn bank?'

'Subterranean. Temperature-controlled. Solar-powered. You can't keep that stuff in a fish freezer, Mila. It's too important.'

She circled him warily in the water.

'Why?'

There it was again. Such a simple little word but it loomed as large as the whale shark now swimming away in the distance.

A wave splashed Rich full in the face. 'Is this really where you want to have this discussion?'

'You picked it,' she pointed out.

Mila could see all the tourists making their way back to their respective boats, ready to go and find another shark at another location. But, in the distance between them, she saw something else. The flashing white double hull of the *Portus*. Poised to whisk Rich away from her once again.

He puffed, as the swell bobbed them both up and down.

'A state-of-the-art research and conference facility appealed to the government's interest in improving the region.' He swam around her as he spoke but kept his eyes firmly locked on hers. Effort made every word choppy. 'It satisfies the need for facilities for all the programmes running up here.'

The scientists, the researchers. Even the cavers. They would all have somewhere local to work now.

She wanted to reply but didn't. Breathing was hard enough without wasting air on pointless words. Besides which, she didn't trust herself to speak just yet.

His eyes darted to the *Portus*, to his sanctuary, but it was too far away to provide him with any respite now. 'They didn't have the funding for something like that; it had to be private investment.'

And who else was going to invest in a region like this for something like that, if not a local?

Mila lifted her mouth above the waterline. 'I can't imagine Wardoo will ever make enough to pay for a science centre. Even with kickbacks from your tenants.'

'The centre should pay for itself eventually. With grants. And conference business. The emergency response bit, West-Corp will be covering.'

His breath-stealing revelation was interrupted by the burbling arrival of Mila's charter boat alongside them; it towered above and dozens of strangers' eyes peered over the edge at them. Rich passed the little whiteboard back to whoever he had borrowed it from and waited until she was able to scrabble aboard the dive platform. Gravity immediately made its presence felt in muscles that had been working so hard to keep her afloat and away from the whale sharks. Rich had a quick word with the crew and the charter chugged happily over to the *Portus* and waited as they transferred from one dive deck to the other.

Moments later, the twenty curious tourists were happily heading off after another whale shark sighting signalled by Craig in his Cessna high above them.

A science centre. Rich was planning on building an entire facility so that all the work being done on the reef could be done locally, properly and comfortably. No more long-haul journeys. No more working out of rust-flecked transportables or four-wheel drives. No more vulnerable, fish-filled freezers for her spawn. The researchers of Coral Bay would have facilities at least as good as the visitors who flocked here in the high season.

It was a godsend in so many ways.

But Rich has used it to buy his way to holding onto the revenue-rich coastal strip, a flat inner voice reminded her.

He could have just freed himself of Wardoo and run, a perkier voice said. *He didn't have to come back.*

Is he even 'back'? the cynical voice said. *He's owned and run it for years without ever setting foot on the property. You still might never see him again.*

I'm seeing him now, aren't I...?

Yes. She was. Fulfilling her most secret hopes. The ones she'd pushed down and down until the only place they could be expressed was in her dreams. Mila stripped off her mask and snorkel and dropped them on the dive deck but left her flippered feet dangling in the deep.

Ready for a fast getaway.

'Do you even want Wardoo?' she challenged without looking at him.

'I thought I didn't,' he admitted, casting the words to the sea like she had. 'Not if I couldn't make it profitable. I thought it was just a business like any other to me. A means to an end. A millstone even.'

'But it's not?'

'Turns out I'm more northern than I thought,' he quipped. 'I didn't know how much until that night on the *Portus*. After we'd been there and I was able to conceptualise what I'd be losing.'

Mila studied her waving fins in the undulating water below the *Portus*.

'Wardoo was an emotional sanctuary when my mother died, and I'd forgotten how much. I let myself forget. I painted a picture of what it could be—full of children, full of love—and all of that came rushing back when I faced the reality of losing it. That's why I was reluctant to go out there; I feared it wouldn't make my decision any easier.'

She remembered his quietness at Jack's Vent. Were those the thoughts he'd been struggling with?

'And what about the reef?' she pressed. 'How was discovering that going to help you make your decision?'

'I needed to know what I was up against with the development. See it as the government sees it.'

'Sure.' She looked sideways at him. 'Who better to ask than a government employee?'

'I wasn't expecting you, Mila. Someone with your passion and connectedness. I thought I was just getting a guide to show me around. I didn't mean to exploit your love for the reef.'

'Okay, so you're sorry. Is that what you came all this way to say?'

Rich frowned. 'You likened Wardoo to the *Portus*, that last day I saw you,' he said. 'And I spent a lot of time thinking about that, of all the reasons it wasn't true. Except that, eventually, I realised it was. I don't hesitate to let other areas of WestCorp's operations pay for maintaining and running the *Portus* because she's become a fundamental part of my survival. She makes me...happy. She's important.'

'Except the land isn't important to you,' she reminded him.

He found her eyes. Stared. 'It is to you.'

A whale shark bumping up against her legs couldn't have rocked her more. Cherry-flavoured confusion whirled in her head.

'You signed a fifty-year lease—' she grappled '—you're building an entire science and rescue facility. You're changing all your big corporate plans...to please *me*? Someone you've known for a few days at most?'

No. There had to be another angle here. Some kind of money trail at work.

Rich turned side on to face her.

'Mila, you have a handle on life that I'm only beginning to understand. You are just…in tune. You dive into life with full immersion. Before I met you I would have scoffed at how important that was in life. I'm pretty sure I did scoff at it, until I saw it in action. In *you*.' He brought them closer, but still didn't touch her. 'I envy what you have, Mila. And I absolutely don't want to be the one to take it from you.'

Uneasiness washed around them.

'You're not responsible for me, Rich,' she said tightly.

'I don't feel responsible, Mila. I feel…grateful.' He swung his legs up under him and pushed to standing. 'Come on, let's get warm.'

She was plenty warm looking up at all that hard flesh, thanks very much.

Without accepting his aid, she also stood and used the short, arduous climb up the *Portus'* steps to get her thoughts in order. On deck, Rich patted at his face and shoulders with one of the thick towels neatly piled there.

'I'm a king in the city, Mila. Well-connected, well-resourced. I have colleagues and respect and a diary full to overflowing with opportunity. Busy enough to mask any number of voids inside. But you called me empty and disconnected—' *and lonely* '—and you named all the things I'd started to feel so dramatically when I came here. To this place where none of those city achievements meant squat. A place that stripped me back to the essence of who I am. I hated being that exposed because it meant I couldn't kid myself any more.'

'About what?'

He tucked himself deeper into the massive towel.

'Losing my mother so young hit me hard, Mila. Being sent away to school just added to that. I was convinced then that if I played by life's rules then I would be rewarded with the certainty that had just been stripped away from me. The rules said that if you worked hard you would be a success, and that with success came money and that people with money got the power.'

'And you wanted power?' she whispered.

'As a motherless eight-year-old abandoned in boarding school? Yes, I did. I never wanted life to happen *to* me again.'

Mila could only stand and stare. 'Did it work?'

'Yeah, everything was going great. All my sacrifices were paying off and I was rising through the ranks nicely. And then my father's heart ruptured one day while I was busy taking an international conference call and I couldn't get there in time and he died alone. Life stuck it to me, just to remind me it could. So I worked harder and I earned more. I forsook everything else and I stuck it back to life.'

'And did *that* work?' she breathed, knowing the answer already.

Rich slid her a sideways look and it was full of despair. 'I thought so. And then I came here. And I met you and I saw how you didn't need to compete with life because you just worked with it. Symbiotically. Like the creatures on the reef you told me about with all their diversity, working together, cooperatively. You *owned* life.'

Rich looked towards the coastline—burnished red against the electric blue of the coastal reef lagoons.

'I don't own it, Rich. I just live it. As best I can.'

'I'd worked my whole life to make sure that *I* got life's best, Mila. I upskilled and strategised and created this sanitised environment where everything that happened to me happened *because* of me. Not because of someone else and sure as heck not because of capricious life! And then I discover that you're just getting it organically…just by being you.'

'Rich…'

'This is not a complaint, Mila. Just an explanation. I got back to Perth and I was all set to go ashore for that critical ten a.m., and then it hit me, right between my eyes.'

'What did?'

'That I didn't want to be a Grundy any more.'

Mila frowned. 'What do you want to be?'

His brows dipped and then straightened. His blue eyes cleared and widened with resolve. 'I think I want to be a Dawson.'

She gasped.

'*The* Dawson—the one you described to me that first day we met and spoke of with such respect. Protector of the reef. Part of the land up here. Part of the history. I want you to look at me like someone who built something here, not just…mined it for profits.'

She realised. 'That's why you wanted to keep the Wardoo lease?'

'Now I just have to learn how to run it.'

Mila thought through the ramifications of his words. 'You'd give up WestCorp?'

He shook his head. 'I'll transform it. Play to my own strengths and transition away from the rest. Get back to fundamentals.'

Nothing was quite as fundamental as grazing the animals that fed the country.

'You have zero expertise in running a cattle station,' she pointed out.

'I have expertise in buying floundering businesses and building them back up. That's how WestCorp got its start. About time I applied that to our oldest business, don't you think? See what it could be with some focus. Besides, as you so rightly pointed out, I have minions. Very talented minions.'

She could see it. Rich as a Dawson. Standing on Wardoo's wrap-around verandas, a slouch hat shielding him from the mid-morning sun, even if it was only once a month. But she wasn't in that picture. And, despite saying all the right things, he wasn't inviting her.

This was just a *mea culpa* for everything that had gone down between them. Nothing more.

'If anyone can do it,' she murmured, 'you can.'

Her heart squeezed just to say it. Having him be twelve hundred kilometres away was hard enough. Having him here in

Coral Bay yet not *be* with him would be torture. But she'd done hard things before. And protecting herself was second nature.

'Nancy would be proud of you, Rich.'

It was impossible not to feel the upwelling of happiness for him; that this good man had found his way to such a good and optimistic place.

'I'm glad someone will because the rest of my world is going to be totally and utterly bemused. I'm going to need your help, Mila,' he said, eyes shining. 'To make a go of it.'

Earwax flooded her senses. She knew he didn't mean to be cruel, but what he asked… It was too much. Even for a woman who had hardened herself against so much in the past. She couldn't put herself through that.

She wouldn't.

He would have to find someone else to be his cheer squad as he upturned his life.

'You don't need me,' she said firmly. 'Now that you know what you want to do.'

Confusion stained his handsome face. 'But you're the one that inspired me.'

'I'm not some kind of muse,' she said, pulling her hair up into something resembling a soggy ponytail. 'And I'm not your staff.'

He reeled back a little. 'No. Of course. That's not what I—'

Tying up her hair was like breathing to her—second nature. Yet she couldn't even manage that with her trembling hands. She abandoned her effort and clenched them as the smell of processed yeast overruled the heartbreak.

'I recognise that I'm a curiosity to you and that my *quirky* little life here is probably adorably idyllic from your perspective, particularly at a time when you're facing some major changes, but I never actually invited you to share it. And I'm not obliged to, simply because you've had an epiphany about your own life.'

Rich frowned. Stared. Realised.

'I've lost your faith,' he murmured.

'It's been nine weeks!' Anger made her rash but it was pain

that made her spit. 'And you just roll up out of the blue wanting something from me yet again. Enough to even hunt me down two kilometres off—'

She cut herself off on a gasp. *Offshore*...

'You were in the deep!' she stammered. 'Way beyond the drop-off.'

Rich grimaced. 'I was trying not to think about it.'

'You came out into the open ocean to find me.' Where life was utterly uncontrollable. 'With sharks and whales and... and...'

'Sea monsters,' he added helpfully.

Maybe that was her cue to laugh. Maybe that would be the smart thing to do—laugh it off and move on with her life. But Rich had gone *into the deep*. Where he never, ever went.

The yeast entirely vanished, to make way for a strong thread of pineapple.

Love.

The thing she'd been struggling against since the day she'd sat, straddled between his thighs, on the sea kayak on Yardi Creek. The thing she'd very determinedly not let herself in-dulge since the night she'd motored away from him all those weeks ago.

No one had ever put themselves into danger for her. Or even vague discomfort. All her life *she* was the one who'd endured unease for the ease of others.

Yet Rich had climbed down into the vast unknown of open water and swum with a whale shark...

And he'd done it to get to *her*.

'Why are you really here, Rich?' she whispered.

He'd apologised.

He'd had an epiphany...all over the place.

But he hadn't told her why he'd come in person.

He studied her close, eyes tracking all over her face, and she became insanely self-conscious about what she must look like, fresh out of the water with a face full of mask pressure marks.

'I have something for you, Mila.' He reached for another towel and carefully draped it around her shoulders, tucking it into her cold hands. 'Come on.'

He discarded his own towel and Mila padded silently into the galley behind him as he crossed to a shelf beside the interior sofa and tucked something there into his fist. Gentle hands on her shoulders urged her down onto the sofa as he squatted in front of her. All that bare flesh and candyfloss was incredibly distracting.

'I should have reached out to you, Mila,' he started. 'Not left it nine weeks.' His eyes dropped to his fist momentarily, as though to check that whatever was in there was *still* in there. 'But it took me half of that to get my head around the things that you'd said. To get my head right.'

That still left several weeks...

'And then I didn't want to come back to you until I had something tangible to offer you. Development permission on the Northern Studies Centre. A plan. Something I could give you that would show how much I—'

His courage seemed to fail him just at the crucial moment. He blew a long, slow breath out and brought his gaze back to hers.

'This is harder than stepping into that ocean,' he murmured, but then he straightened. 'I don't have planning approval to give you, Mila. That's still a week or two away. But I have this. And it's something. A place-holder, if you like.'

He opened his white-knuckled hand to reveal a small silk pouch.

Mila stared at it and the tang of curiosity added itself to all the pineapple to create something almost like a delicious cocktail.

'What is it?'

'A gift. An apology.' He took a deep breath, hand outstretched. 'A promise.'

That word stalled her hand just as it hovered over the little pouch. But he didn't expand on it, just held his palm flat and not quite steady.

That made her own shake anew.

But the pouch opened easily and a pale necklace slid out. A wisp of white-gold chain and hanging from it...

'Is that your pearl?'

The one from the oyster stacks that day. The one she'd given him as a memento of the reef. The one that was small and a little bit too malformed to be of actual value.

It hung on its cobweb-fine chain as if it was as priceless as any of its more perfect spherical cousins.

More so because it came from Rich.

'It's your pearl,' he murmured. 'It always was.'

She lifted her eyes to his.

'I should have known better than to try and stage-manage this whole reunion,' he said. 'I guess I have a way to go in giving up control over uncontrollable things.'

Her heart thumped even harder.

This was a *reunion*?

Her eyes fell back to the pearl on its beautiful chain. 'But I gave this to you.'

He nodded. 'To remember you by. I would rather have the real deal.'

She stared at him, wordless.

'I know you've done it tough in the past,' he went on. 'That you consider yourself as much a misfit as your grandmother. And I know that's made it hard for you to trust people. Or believe in them. But you believed in me when we met and I came to hope that maybe you trusted me a little bit too.'

Still she could do nothing but stare. And battle the myriad incompatible tastes swamping the back of her throat and nose.

'I'm hoping we can get that back. With time. And a fair amount of effort on my part.'

'You lied to me, Rich.' There was no getting around that.

'I was lying to me, too. You raised too many *what-ifs* in my nice ordered life, Mila. And I didn't deal in ifs, I only dealt in certainties.'

Did he mean to use the past tense?

'You threw into doubt everything I'd been raised to believe, and I...panicked. I fell back on what I knew best. And what I started to feel for you... It was as uncontrollable as everything I'd ever fought against.'

'You said your world was in the city,' she whispered. Saying it aloud was too scary because what if she reminded him? What if she talked him out of what she was starting to think he was saying?

But she had to know.

And he had to say it.

'That's because I had no idea then that you were about to become my world,' he attested. 'My world is wherever you are.'

Pineapple suffused every other scent trying to get her attention. But every other scent had no chance. Not while she sat here, so near to a half-naked Rich with truth in his eyes and the most amazing miracle on his gorgeous lips.

'We barely know each other.'

Did she need to test him again? Or did she just not trust it?

Rich leaned closer. 'I know everything I need to know about you. And you have a lifetime to get to know me better.'

'What exactly are you saying?'

'I'm saying that you can swim Wardoo's sinkhole whenever you want. And you can use the *Portus* any time you need a ride somewhere. And you'll have your own swipe key for the Science Centre and sole management of the spawn bank.'

He forked his fingers through her hair either side of her face.

'I'm saying that you have a standing welcome in any part of my life. I'm through putting impediments of any kind between myself and the most spectacularly unique and beautiful woman I could ever imagine meeting. I'm saying that your synaesthesia does not entertain me or confuse me or challenge me. It delights me. It reminds me what I've been missing in this world.' His fingers curled gently against her scalp to punctuate his vow. 'I will make it my life's work to understand it—and you—because the Dawson kids are probably going to have it and I'd like them to always feel loved and supported, even by their poor, superpower-deficient dad.'

Dawson *kids*?

Her heart was out-and-out galloping now.

'I'm saying that all of this will happen on *your* schedule, as soon as I've won back your trust and faith in me. You and I are meant to be together, Mila. I don't think it's any coincidence that we first met at a place that was so special to my great-grandmother. Nancy had my back that day.'

He pressed his lips against hers briefly.

'I'm asking you to be with me, Mila Nakano. To help me navigate the great unknown waters ahead. To help me interpret them.' Then, when she just stared at him, still wordless, he added, 'I'm saying that I love you, Mermaid. Weirdness inclusive. In fact, especially for that.'

Mila just stared, overcome by his words, and by the pineapple onslaught that swamped her whole system. It seemed to finally dawn on Rich that she hadn't said a word in a while.

A very long while.

'Have I blown it?' he checked softly, setting himself back from her. 'Misjudged your interest?' She still didn't speak but he braved it out. 'Or am I the creepiest stalker ever to live, right now?'

Mila caressed the smooth undulations of the imperfect pearl resting in her fingers. Grounding herself. She traced the fine chain away from it and then back again. But the longer she did it, the clearer the pearl's personality became.

Rich's soft voice broke into her meditation.

'Is that a happy smile or a how-am-I-going-to-let-him-down-gently smile?'

She found his nervous eyes.

'It's the pearl,' she breathed. 'My subconscious has finally given them a personality.'

'Oh.' The topic change seemed to pain him, but he'd just promised not to rush her. 'What is it?'

Maybe her subconscious had been waiting for him all this time so that she'd know it when she saw it. 'Smitten.'

Her cotton candy stole back in as a cautious smile broke across Rich's face.

'Smitten is a good start,' he said, nodding his appraisal. 'I can work with smitten.'

'You won't need to. It's a small pearl,' she murmured on a deep, long breath. 'It only reflects a small percentage of what I'm feeling.'

This time, the hope in Rich's expression was so palpable it even engendered a burst of hot chocolate on his behalf.

Well, that was a first.

'Mila, you're killing me...'

'Payback.' She smiled, then slipped the pearl chain around her neck and fiddled with the clasp until it was secure. Made him wait. Made him sweat, just a little bit. After nine weeks, it was the least she could do.

And after a lifetime of strict caution, it was almost the best she could do.

'It killed me to walk away from you the last time I was on the *Portus*,' she said. 'I'm not doing it again. I may need to take things slow for a bit, but—' she took a deep breath '—yes, I would love to explore whatever lies ahead. With you,' she clarified, to be totally patent.

Rich hauled her to her feet and whipped the massive towel from around her until it circled him instead. Then he brought her right into its fluffy circle, hard up against him, and found her mouth with his own.

'I think I first fell for you during the coral spawn,' Rich murmured around their kisses. 'Literally in the middle of the snow globe. And then the truth slammed into me like you slammed into that dugong and I was a goner.'

'Yardi Creek for me,' she murmured. 'So I guess I've loved you longer.'

His smile took over his face. 'But I guarantee you I've loved you deeper.'

She curled her arms around his neck and kept him close.

'I guess we can call that a draw then. Although—' she fingered the little pearl on the chain '—I think the oyster might have known before either of us.'

He bent again for another kiss. 'Oysters always were astute.'

* * * * *

The CEO's Baby Surprise
Helen Lacey

Helen Lacey grew up reading *Black Beauty* and *Little House on the Prairie*. These childhood classics inspired her to write her first book when she was seven, a story about a girl and her horse. She loves writing for Harlequin Western, where she can create strong heroes with a soft heart and heroines with gumption who get their happily-ever-after. For more about Helen, visit her website, helenlacey.com.

Books by Helen Lacey

Harlequin Western

The Prestons of Crystal Point

The CEO's Baby Surprise
Claiming His Brother's Baby
Once Upon a Bride
Date with Destiny
His-and-Hers Family
Marriage Under the Mistletoe
Made for Marriage

Visit the Author Profile page at millsandboon.com.au for more titles.

Dear Reader,

Hello, and welcome back to Crystal Point and my seventh book for Harlequin Western, *The CEO's Baby Surprise*.

Since the publication of my first Western book, I've had countless emails from readers asking me when the spirited and feisty Mary-Jayne Preston was going to get her own story. I'm delighted that I've been able to give Mary-Jayne her very own happy ending at last! It's not an easy road—not when she falls for a man who is her complete opposite in every way...except, of course, in the way which counts the most. The hero, Daniel, gets a whole lot more than he bargains for when he meets the free-spirited Mary-Jayne. Including a couple of very big surprises along the way!

I hope you enjoy *The CEO's Baby Surprise* and wish you a few hours of happy reading. For more of my Crystal Point books please visit my author page at millsandboon.com.au.

I love hearing from readers and can be contacted via my website at helenlacey.com.

Warm wishes,

Helen Lacey

For my mother, Evelyn.
Who believes in me no matter what.

PROLOGUE

MARY-JAYNE PRESTON YAWNED, opened her eyes and blinked a few times. The ceiling spun fractionally, and she drew in a soft breath.

I'm not hungover.

She closed her eyes again. The two glasses of champagne she'd drunk the night before weren't responsible for the way she felt. This was something else. An unusual lethargy crept into her limbs and spread across her skin. Her lids fluttered, and she glimpsed a sliver of light from between heavy drapes.

An unfamiliar room.

Her memory kicked in. The Sandwhisper Resort. Port Douglas.

But this isn't my bedroom.

This was a villa suite. And a top-end one, judging by the plush feel of the giant king-size bed and lavish damask drapes. Extravagance personified. Her eyelids drooped before opening again as she stretched her spine—and then nearly jumped out of her skin when she realized she wasn't alone in the big bed.

A man lay beside her. She twisted her head and saw a long, perfectly proportioned back. Smooth skin, like the sheerest satin stretched over pressed steel, broad shoulders, strong arms and dark hair. He lay on his stomach, one arm flung above his head, the other curved by his side. And he was asleep. The soft rhythm of his breathing was oddly hypnotic, and she stared at him, suddenly mesmerized by his bronzed skin and lean, muscular frame.

And then, in stunning Technicolor, it came rushing back.

The party.

The kiss.

The one-night stand.

Her first. Her *last*.

She needed to get up. To *think*. She shimmied sideways but quickly stopped moving when he stirred. She wasn't quite ready for any kind of face-to-face, morning-after awkwardness. Not with *him*. She took a deep breath and tried again, inching her hips across the cool sheet so slowly it was agonizing. Finally one leg found the edge of the mattress and she pushed the cover back. He moved again and she stilled instantly. He made a sound, half groan, half moan, and flipped around, the sheet draping haphazardly over his hips as he came to face her.

But still asleep.

Mary-Jayne's breath shuddered out as she caught sight of his profile. He was ridiculously handsome. No wonder she'd lost her head. The straight nose, chiseled cheeks and square jaw was a riveting combination. And she quickly recalled those silver-gray eyes of his…just too sexy for words. As her gaze traveled lower her fingertips tingled. His body was incredibly well cut, and she fought the urge to touch him just one more time. She spotted a faint mark on his shoulder. Like a love bite.

Did I do that?

Heat surged through her blood when she remembered what they'd done the night before, and again in the small hours of the morning. No sweet wonder her muscles ached and her skin seemed ultrasensitive. She'd never had a night like it before, never felt such intense desire or experienced such acute and mindboggling pleasure.

It was like a dream. A fantasy.

And she needed to wake up from this particular dream. Quickly.

She managed to ease off the bed and quickly looked around for her clothes. Her underwear was by the bed, and she snatched it up with guilty fingers and then quickly dressed into the thong and bra. The shoes were easily spotted—one was by the window, the other under a chair in the corner of the room. But the black dress was nowhere to be seen. The smooth fabric had clung to her curves, and the man in the bed had told her how beautiful and desirable she'd looked. No one had ever said those words quite that way to her before. She found her purse on the chair and continued looking for the dress, keeping a mindful eye on him.

Please don't wake up...

He didn't, thankfully, and a few moments later she found the dress, scrunched in a ball and hidden beneath the quilt that had fallen to the foot of the bed. She stepped into it and slipped it up and over her hips, settling her arms through the bodice before she twisted herself into a pretzel to do up the zipper. Breathless, she cast another look toward the sleeping man.

I'm such a fool...

For weeks she'd stayed resolute, determined to avoid crashing into bed with him. But the moment he'd touched her, the moment he'd made his move she'd melted like an ice cube in hell.

Mary-Jayne pushed her feet into her patent pumps, grabbed her purse and ran.

CHAPTER ONE

PREGNANT.

Not a bout of food poisoning as she'd wanted to believe.

Mary-Jayne walked from the doctor's office and headed for her car. Her head hurt. Her feet hurt. Everything hurt. The snap on her jeans felt tight around her waist. Now she knew why.

She was three months and three weeks pregnant.

She opened the door of the borrowed Honda Civic and got inside. Then she placed a hand over her belly and let out a long, heavy breath.

Twenty-seven. Single. Pregnant.

Right.

Not exactly the end of the world…but not what she'd been expecting, either.

One day she'd imagined she'd have a baby. When she was married and settled, not while she was trying to carve out a career as a jewelry designer and wasn't exactly financially stable.

She thought about calling her older sisters, Evie and Grace, but quickly shrugged off the idea. She needed time to think. Plan. Sort out what she was going to do, before she told anyone. Especially her sisters, who'd want to know *everything*.

She'd have to tell them about that night.

She gripped the steering wheel and let out a long, weary

sigh. She'd tried to put the memory from her mind countless times. And failed. Every time she walked around the grounds of the Sandwhisper Resort she was reminded. And every time she fielded a telephone call from *him* she was thrust back to that crazy night.

Mary-Jayne drove through the gates of the resort and took a left down the road that led to the employees' residences. Her villa was small but well appointed and opened onto the deck and to the huge heated pool and spa area. The Sandwhisper Resort was one of the largest in Port Douglas, and certainly one of the most luxurious. The town of Port Douglas was about forty miles north of Cairns, and its population of over three thousand often doubled during peak vacation times. Living and working at the luxurious resort for the past four and half months hadn't exactly been a hardship. Running her friend Audrey's boutique was mostly enjoyable and gave her the opportunity to create and showcase her own jewelry. Life was a breeze.

Correction.

Life *had* been a breeze.

Until she'd had an uncharacteristic one-night stand with Daniel Anderson.

CEO of Anderson Holdings and heir apparent to the huge fortune that had been made by his grandfather from ore and copper mining years earlier, he owned the Sandwhisper Resort with his two brothers. There were four other resorts around the globe—one in Phuket, another along the Amalfi coast in Italy, another in the Maldives and the flagship resort in the San Francisco Bay Area.

He was rich, successful, uptight and absurdly arrogant.

Everything she'd always abhorred in a man.

He was also reported to be kind, generous and honest.

Well…according to his grandmother.

Eighty-year-old Solana Anderson adored her grandsons and spent her retirement flying between the east and west coasts of Australia and America, living at the resorts during the spring and summer months in alternating time zones. Mary-Jayne liked the older woman very much. They'd met the first day she'd arrived at the resort after the desperate emergency call from her old school friend Audrey had sent her flying up to Port Douglas with barely a packed suitcase. Audrey had moved into Mary-Jayne's small house in Crystal Point so she could be close to her ill mother while Mary-Jayne moved into Audrey's condo at the resort. Once she was in residence, she read the scribbled note with instructions her friend had left and opened the boutique at an unrespectable eleven o'clock. It was meant to be a temporary gig—but Audrey insisted her mother needed her. So her planned three weeks ended up being for six months.

And Solana, straight backed and still vibrant at nearly eighty years of age, had come into the store looking for an outfit to wear to her upcoming birthday party, and within the hour they were chatting and laughing over herbal tea and several outfit changes. It was then she learned that Solana's American-born husband had died a decade earlier and how she'd borne him a son and daughter. Mary-Jayne had listened while Solana talked about her much-loved grandsons, Daniel, Blake and Caleb and granddaughter Renee. One hour ticked over into two, and by three o'clock the older woman had finally decided upon an outfit and persuaded Mary-Jayne to let her see some of her handcrafted jewelry pieces. Solana had since bought three items and had recommended Mary-Jayne's work to several of her friends.

Yes, she liked Solana. But wasn't about to tell the other woman she was carrying her great-grandchild. Not until she figured out what she was going to do. She was nearly four months along, and her pregnancy would be showing itself very soon. She couldn't hide her growing stomach behind baggy clothes forever.

He has a right to know...

The notion niggled at her over and over.

She could have the baby alone. Women did it all the time. And it was not as if she and Daniel had any kind of relationship. If she wanted, she could leave the resort and go home and never see him again. He lived mostly in San Francisco. She lived in Crystal Point, a small seaside town that sat at the southern-most point of the Great Barrier Reef. They had different lives. Different worlds.

And she didn't even like him.

She'd met him three times before the night of Solana's birth-day. The first time she'd been in the store window, bent over and struggling to remove a garment from the mannequin. When she was done she'd straightened, turned to avoid knocking the mannequin over and came face-to-face with him on the other side of the glass. He'd been watching her, arms crossed.

Of course she'd known immediately who he was. There were several pictures of him and his brothers in Solana's villa, and she'd visited the older woman many times. Plus, he looked enough like his younger brother Caleb for her to recognize the family resemblance. Caleb ran the resorts in Port Douglas and Phuket while his twin Blake looked after Amalfi, Maldives and San Francisco. And according to staff gossip Daniel lorded over the resorts, his brothers and the staff from his private jet.

Still, it was hard not to be impressed by his ridiculous good looks, and despite the fact he was not her type, Mary-Jayne was as susceptible as the next woman. The impeccably cut suit, creaseless white shirt and dark tie were a riveting combination on his broad, tall frame, and for a second she'd been rooted to the spot, unable to move, unable to do anything other than stare back, held captive by the look in his gray eyes. For a moment, at least. Until he'd raised one brow and a tiny smile whispered along the edges of his mouth. He'd then looked her over with a kind of leisurely conceit that had quickly sent alarm bells clanging in her head.

There'd been interest in his expression and if he'd been any-one else she might have made some kind of encouraging ges-ture. Like a smile. Or nod. But Daniel Anderson was out of her league. A rich and successful corporate shark with a reputation for having no tolerance for fools in business, and no proclivity for commitment in his private life. He was the kind of man she'd always planned to avoid like the plague. The kind of man that had never interested her before.

But something had passed between them in that first moment. A look... Recognition.

Awareness...

Heat...

Attraction...

When her good sense had returned she'd darted from the window and got back to the customer waiting in the changing room. By the time she'd moved back to the front of the store and began ringing up the sale he was gone.

Mary-Jayne saw him a day later, striding across the resort foyer with his brother at his side. She'd been coming from the day spa, arms loaded with jewelry trays, when Caleb had said her name. She'd met the younger Anderson many times over the previous weeks. He was rich, charming and handsome and didn't do a solitary thing to her libido. Not so his older brother. She'd fumbled with the trays and stayed rooted to the spot as they approached and then managed to nod her way through an introduction. He was unsmiling, but his eyes regarded her with blistering intensity. Caleb's attention had quickly been diverted by the day-shift concierge and she'd been left alone with him, silent and nervous beneath his unfaltering gaze.

Then he'd spoken, and his deep voice, a smooth mix of his American upbringing and Australian roots, wound up her spine like liquid silk. "My grandmother tells me you're here for six months rather than the few weeks you'd originally planned on?"

He'd talked about her with Solana? "Ah, that's right," she'd croaked.

"And are you enjoying your time here?"

She'd nodded, feeling stupid and awkward and not in the least bit like her usual self. Normally she was confident and opinionated and more than comfortable in her own skin. But two seconds around Daniel Anderson and she was a speech-less fool. Übergood looks had never interested her before. But he stirred her senses big time.

"Yes, very much."

"And I trust your friend's parent's health is improving?"

He knew about Audrey's mother? Solana *had* been busy sharing information.

"A little…yes."

A small smile had crinkled the corner of his mouth and Mary-Jayne's gaze had instantly been drawn to his lips. He had seen her reaction and his smile had increased fractionally. There was something extraordinarily hypnotic about him, something she couldn't quite fathom. Something she'd known she had to extricate herself from…and fast.

She'd hastily excused herself and taken off as fast as she could.

And hadn't seen him again for two days.

She'd left the resort for a run along the beach and had come upon him jogging in the other direction. He'd slowed when he was about twenty feet from her and come to a halt right next to her. And the look between them had been electric. Out of this world and all-consuming. She'd never experienced such blatant and blistering physical attraction for anyone before. And it shocked her to the core. He wasn't her usual type. In fact, Daniel Anderson was the epitome of everything she *didn't* want in a man. Money, power, arrogance… They were attributes her small-town, middle-class self had decided long ago were not for her. She dated musicians and out-of-work artists. Not corporate sharks.

His expression had been unwavering and contained hot sexual appreciation. He wanted her. No doubt about it. And the look in his eyes had made it clear he thought he'd get her.

"You know," he'd said with a kind of arrogant confidence that made her tremble. "My villa is only minutes away."

She knew that. The family's quarters were secluded and luxurious and away from the main part of the resort and had a spectacular view of the beach.

"And?" she'd managed to say, despite the way her heart had thundered behind her ribs and her knees wobbled.

He'd half smiled. "And we both know that's where we're going to end up at some point."

Mortified, she'd quickly taken off like a bullet. But her body was thrumming with a kind of intoxicating awareness that stayed with her for hours. For days. Until she'd seen him again two days later at Solana's birthday party. The older woman had insisted she attend the celebration and Mary-Jayne respected Solana too much to refuse the invitation. She'd ditched her usual multicolored skirts and long tops and rummaged through Audrey's wardrobe for a party dress. And she'd found one—a slip of silky black jersey that clung to her like a second skin. The huge ballroom was easy to get lost in…or so she'd thought. But it had only taken ten minutes until she'd felt him watching her from across the room. He'd approached and asked if she wanted a drink. Within half an hour they had been out on the balcony, talking intimately. Seconds later they'd been kissing madly. Minutes later they'd been in his villa tearing each other's clothes off.

But Mary-Jayne wasn't under any illusions.

She knew enough about Daniel Anderson to realize she was simply another notch on his bedpost. He was handsome, successful and wealthy and played the field mercilessly. Something he had done without compunction since the death of his wife and unborn child four years earlier. He certainly wouldn't be interested in her for anything other than a one-night stand. She wasn't his type. Oh, he'd knocked on the door of her villa the day after Solana's party and asked her out. But she'd shut him down. She'd piqued his interest for a moment and that was all. Thankfully, he'd left the resort the following day and returned to San Francisco, exactly as she'd hoped. But she hadn't expected that he'd call the store two weeks later and announce that he wanted to see her again when he returned from California.

See her?

Yeah…right. The only thing he wanted to see was her naked body between the sheets. And she knew that for a man like Daniel Anderson, the chase was all that mattered. She'd refused him, and that was like pouring oil onto a fire.

When he'd called her again two weeks later she'd been in South Dakota for a friend's wedding. Annoyed that he wouldn't take the hint and all out of patience, she'd lost her temper and told him to go to hell. Then she'd returned to the Sandwhisper Resort and waited. Waited for another call. Waited for him to arrive at the resort and confuse and seduce her with his steely-eyed gaze and uncompromising intensity. But he hadn't called. And hadn't returned. As one week slipped into another, Mary-Jayne had slowly relaxed and convinced herself he'd lost interest.

Which was exactly what she wanted.

Only now, the tables had turned. She was having his baby. Which meant one thing—she'd have to see him and tell him she was having his baby. And soon.

Daniel had struggled with the remnants of a headache for two days. The three other suits in the conference room were grating on his nerves. Some days he wanted nothing more than to throw off the shackles of his name, his legacy and everything else and live a simple, quiet life.

Like today.

Because it was his birthday. He was turning thirty-four years old. He had money and power and a successful business at his command. He had apartments in San Francisco, another in London and then there was the family-owned hilltop chateau in France that he hadn't been near for over four years. He also had any number of women willing to warm his bed with minimal notice and who understood he didn't want commitment or anything resembling a serious relationship. He traveled the world but rarely saw anything other than the walls of boardrooms and offices at the resorts he'd helped build into some of the most successful around the globe. Nothing and no one touched him.

Well…except for Mary-Jayne Preston.

She was a thorn in his side. A stone in his shoe. A pain in his neck.

Months after that one crazy night in Port Douglas and he was still thinking about her. She was incredibly beautiful. Her green eyes were luminous; her lips were full and endlessly kissable. But it was her hair that had first captured his attention that day in the store window. She had masses of dark curls that hung down past her shoulders. And of course there were her lovely curves, which she possessed in all the right places.

He'd checked out her history and discovered she came from a middle-class family in Crystal Point, had studied at a local technical college and had an online business selling her hand-crafted jewelry. She rented her home, owned a dog, volunteered at a number of animal shelters, had strong opinions about the environment and politics and liked to dress in colorful skirts or jeans with holes in the knees. She had piercings in her ears and navel and a butterfly tattoo on one shoulder.

She wasn't his type. Not by a long shot.

Which didn't make one ounce of difference to the relentless effect she had on him whenever she was within a twenty-foot radius. And the night of his grandmother's birthday party he'd almost tripped over his own feet when he'd caught a glimpse of her across the room. She'd looked incredible in a dress that highlighted every dip and curve of her body. And with her dark hair cascading down her back in a wave he just about had to cleave his tongue from the roof of his mouth. She looked hot. Gorgeous. Desirable.

And he knew then he wanted to get her in his bed.

It took half an hour to get her alone. Then he'd kissed her. And she'd kissed him back.

And before either of them had a chance to come up for air they were in his villa suite, tearing off clothes with little finesse and more eagerness than he'd felt in years. It had been a hot, wild night, compounded by months of abstinence and the fact he'd had Mary-Jayne Preston very much on his mind since the first time he'd seen her.

"Are you listening?"

Daniel shook off his thoughts and glanced to his left. Blake was staring at him, one brow cocked. "Always."

Blake didn't look convinced and quickly turned his attention to the other suits in the room. After a few more minutes, he dismissed the two other men, and once they were alone his brother moved to the bar and grabbed two imported beers from the fridge.

Daniel frowned. "A little early, don't you think?"

Blake flicked the tops off the bottles and shrugged. "It's after three. And you look as if you need it."

He didn't disagree, and stretched back in his leather chair. "Maybe I do."

Blake passed him a beer and grabbed a seat. "Happy birthday," his brother said, and clinked the bottle necks.

"Thanks," he said but didn't take a drink. The last thing he wanted to do was add alcohol to the remainders of a blinding headache.

His brother, who was probably the most intuitive person he'd ever known, looked at him as if he knew exactly what he was thinking. "You know, you should go home."

"I live *here*, remember?"

Blake shook his head. "I meant *home*…not here. Port Douglas."

Except Port Douglas didn't feel any more like home than San Francisco, Phuket or Amalfi.

Nowhere did. Not since Simone had died. The bayside condo they'd bought still sat empty, and he lived in a villa at the San Francisco resort when he wasn't at any of the other four locations. He'd been born in Australia and moved to California when he was two years old. The San Francisco resort was the first, which made it home, even though he'd spent most of his adult life shifting between the two countries.

He scowled. "I can't do that right now."

"Why not?" Blake shot back. "Caleb's got the Phuket renovation under control. Things are sweet here in San Francisco." His brother grinned. "You're not really needed. CEOs are kind of superfluous to the running of a company anyhow. We all knew that when Gramps was at the helm."

"Superfluous?"

Blake's grin widened. "Yeah...like the foam on the top of an espresso to go... You know, there but not really necessary."

"You're an ass."

His brother's grin turned into a chuckle. "All I'm saying is that you haven't taken a real break from this gig for years. Not even when..."

Not even when Simone died.

Four years, four months and three weeks ago. Give or take a day. She'd been driving back from a doctor's appointment and had stopped at the mall for some shopping. The brakes on a car traveling in the opposite direction had failed. Simone had suffered terrible injuries and died an hour later in hospital. So had the baby she carried. He'd lost his wife and unborn daughter because of a broken brake line. "I'm fine," he said, and tasted the lie on his tongue.

"I'm pretty sure you're not," Blake said, more serious. "And something's been bugging you the past few months."

Something. Someone. *Green eyes... Black curling hair... Red lips...*

Daniel drank some beer. "You're imagining things. And stop fretting. You're turning into your mother."

His brother laughed loudly. They both knew that Blake was more like their father, Miles, than any of them. Daniel's mother had died of a massive brain hemorrhage barely hours after his birth, and their father had married Bernadette two years later. Within six months the twins, Blake and Caleb, were born. Bernie was a nice woman and had always treated him like her own, and wasn't as vague and hopeless as their father. Business acumen and ambition had skipped a generation, and now Miles spent his time painting and sculpting and living on their small hobby farm an hour west of Port Douglas.

Daniel finished the beer and placed the bottle on the table. "I don't need a vacation."

"Sure you do," Blake replied. "If you don't want to go to Australia, take a break somewhere else. Maybe Fiji? Or what about using that damned mausoleum that sits on that hill just outside Paris? Take some time off, relax, get laid," his brother said, and grinned again. "Recharge like us regular folk have to do every now and then."

"You're as tied to this business as I am."

"Yeah," his brother agreed. "But I know when to quit. I've got my cabin in the woods, remember?"

Blake's *cabin* was a sprawling Western red cedar house nestled on forty hectares he'd bought in small town Colorado a few years back. Daniel had visited once, hated the cold and being snowbound for days on end and decided that a warm climate was more his thing.

"I don't need a—"

"Then, how about you think about what the rest of us need?" Blake said firmly. "Or what Caleb and I need, which isn't you breathing down our necks looking for things we're doing wrong because you're so damned bored and frustrated that you can't get out your own way. Basically, *I* need a break. So go home and get whatever's bugging you out of your system and spend some time with Solana. You know you've always been her favorite."

Daniel looked at his brother. Had he done that? Had he become an overzealous, critical jerk looking for fault in everything and everyone? And bored? Was that what he was? He did miss Solana. He hadn't seen his grandmother since her birthday weekend. And it was excuse enough to see Mary-Jayne again—and get her out of his system once and for all.

He half smiled. "Okay."

CHAPTER TWO

"Everything all right?"

Mary-Jayne nodded and looked up from the plate of food she'd been pretending to give way too much attention. "Fine."

"Are you still feeling unwell?" Solana asked. "You never did tell me what the doctor said."

"Just a twenty-four-hour bug," she replied vaguely. "And I feel fine now."

Solana didn't look convinced. "You're still pale. Is that ex-boyfriend of yours giving you grief?"

The *ex-boyfriend*. The one she'd made up to avoid any nosy questions about what was becoming her rapidly expanding middle. The ex-boyfriend she'd say was the father of her baby until she summoned the nerve to tell Solana she was carrying her grandson's child. Raised to have a solid moral compass, she was torn between believing the father of her baby had a right to know, and the fear that telling him would change everything. She was carrying Solana's great-grandchild. An Anderson heir. Nothing would be the same.

Of course, she had no illusions. Daniel Anderson was not a man looking for commitment or a family. Solana had told her enough about him, from his closed-off heart to his rumored no-strings relationships. He'd lost the love of his life and unborn child and had no interest in replacing, either.

Not that she was interested in him in *that* way. She didn't like him at all. He was arrogant and opinionated and as cold as a Popsicle. Oh, she'd certainly been swept away that one night. But one night of hot and heavy sex didn't make them *anything*.

Still…they'd made a baby together, and as prepared as she was to raise her child alone, common courtesy made it very clear to her that she had to tell him. And soon. Before Solana or anyone else worked out that she was pregnant.

She had another two weeks at the store before Audrey returned, and once that was done, Mary-Jayne intended returning to Crystal Point to regroup and figure out how to tell Daniel he was about to become a father.

"I'm going to miss you when you leave," Solana said and smiled. "I've grown very fond of our talks."

So had Mary-Jayne. She'd become increasingly attached to the other woman over the past few months, and they lunched together at least twice a week. And Solana had been incredibly supportive of her jewelry designing and had even offered to finance her work and help expand the range into several well-known stores around the country. Of course Mary-Jayne had declined the offer. Solana was a generous woman, but she'd never take advantage of their friendship in such a way…good business or not.

"We'll keep in touch," Mary-Jayne assured her and ignored the nausea scratching at her throat. Her appetite had been out of whack for weeks and the sick feeling still hadn't abated even though she was into her second trimester. Her doctor told her not to worry about it and assured her that her appetite would return, and had put her on a series of vitamins. But most days the idea of food before three in the afternoon was unimaginable.

"Yes, we must," Solana said warmly. "Knowing you has made me not miss Renee quite so much," she said of her granddaughter, who resided in London. "Of course, I get to see Caleb while I'm here and Blake when I'm in San Francisco. And Daniel when he's done looking after things and flying in between resorts. But sometimes I wish for those days when they were kids and not spread all over the world." The older woman put down her cutlery and sighed. "Listen to me, babbling on, when you must miss your own family very much."

"I do," she admitted. "I'm really close to my sisters and brother and I miss my parents a lot."

"Naturally." Solana's eyed sparkled. "Family is everything."

Mary-Jayne swallowed the lump of emotion in her throat, like she'd done countless times over the past few months. Her hormones were running riot, and with her body behaving erratically, it was getting harder to keep her feelings under wraps. One thing she did know—she wanted her baby. As unplanned as it was, as challenging as it might be being a single mother, she had developed a strong and soul-reaching love for the child in her womb.

Family is everything...

It was. She knew that. She'd been raised by wonderful parents and loved her siblings dearly. Her baby would be enveloped in that love. She *could* go home, and Daniel need never know about her pregnancy. She'd considered it. Dreamed of it.

Except...

It would be wrong. Dishonest. And wholly unfair.

"I should very much like to visit your little town one day," Solana said cheerfully.

Crystal Point. It was a tiny seaside community of eight hundred people. From the pristine beaches to the rich soil of the surrounding farmlands, it would always be home, no matter where life took her.

"I'd like that, too," she said, and pushed her plate aside.

"Not hungry?" Solana asked, her keen light gray eyes watching everything she did.

Mary-Jayne shrugged. "Not really. But it is delicious," she said of the warm mango salad on her plate. "I'm not much use in the kitchen, so our lunches are always a nice change from the grilled-cheese sandwich I'd usually have."

Solana grinned. "Didn't your mother teach you to cook?"

"She tried, but I was something of a tomboy when I was young and more interested in helping my dad in his workshop," she explained.

"Well, those skills can come in handy, too."

Mary-Jayne nodded. "For sure. I can fix a leaking tap and build a bookcase...but a cheese toastie is about my limit in the kitchen."

"Well, you'll just have to find yourself a husband who can cook," Solana suggested, smiling broadly.

"I'm not really in the market for a husband." *Not since I got knocked up by your grandson...*

Solana smiled. "Nonsense. Everyone is looking for a soul mate...even a girl as independent and free-spirited as you."

Mary-Jayne nodded vaguely. Independent and free-spirited? It was exactly how she appeared to the world. And exactly how she liked it. But for the most part, it was a charade. A facade to fool everyone into thinking she had it all together—that she was strong and self-sufficient and happy-go-lucky. She'd left home at seventeen determined to prove she could make it on her own, and had spent ten years treading water in the hope no one noticed she was just getting by—both financially and emotionally. Her family loved her, no doubt about it. As the youngest child she was indulged and allowed to do whatever she liked, mostly without consequence. Her role as the lovable but unreliable flake in the Preston family had been set from a young age. While her older brother, Noah, took over the family business, perennial earth-mother Evie married young and pursued her art, and übersmart Grace headed for a career in New York before she returned to Australia to marry the man she loved.

But for Mary-Jayne there were no such expectations, and no traditional career. She'd gotten her first piercing at fourteen and had a tattoo by the time she was fifteen. When school was over she'd found a job as a cashier in a supermarket and a month later moved out of her parents' home and into a partly furnished cottage three streets away. She'd packed whatever she could fit into her battered Volkswagen and began her adult life away from the low expectations of her family. She never doubted their love…but sometimes she wished they expected more of her. Then perhaps she would have had more ambition, more focus.

Mary-Jayne pushed back her chair and stood up. "I'll take the dishes to the kitchen."

"Thank you. You're a sweet girl, Mary-Jayne," Solana said, and collected up the cutlery. "You know, I was just telling Caleb that very thing yesterday."

It was another not-so-subtle attempt to play matchmaker.

Solana had somehow got it in her head that her younger grandson would be a good match for her. And the irony wasn't lost on Mary-Jayne. She liked Caleb. He was friendly and charming and came into the store every couple of days and asked how things were going, and always politely inquired after Audrey. The resort staff all respected him, and he clearly ran a tight ship.

But he didn't so much as cause a blip on her radar.

Unlike Daniel. He was the blip of the century.

Mary-Jayne ignored Solana's words, collected the dishes and headed for the kitchen. Once there she took a deep breath and settled her hips against the countertop. Her stomach was still queasy, and she took a few deep breaths before she turned toward the sink and decided to make a start on the dishes. She filled the sink and was about to plunge her hands into the water when she heard a decisive knock on the front door, and then seconds later the low sound of voices. Solana had a visitor. Mary-Jayne finished the washing up, dried her hands and headed for the door.

And then stopped in her tracks.

Even though his back was to her she recognized Daniel Anderson immediately. The dark chinos and white shirt fitted him as though they'd been specifically tailored for his broad, well-cut frame. She knew those shoulders and every other part of him because the memory of the night they'd spent together was etched into her brain, and the result was the child growing inside her.

Perhaps he'd tracked her down to confront her? Maybe he knew?

Impossible.

No one knew she was pregnant. It was a coincidence. He'd forgotten all about her. He hadn't called since she'd told him to go to hell. He'd returned to see his grandmother. Mary-Jayne's hand moved to her belly, and she puffed out the smock-style shirt she wore. If she kept her arms to her sides and kept her clothing as loose as possible it was unlikely he'd notice her little baby bump. She lingered by the doorway, her mind racing at a trillion miles an hour.

Solana was clearly delighted to see him and hugged him twice in succession. "What a wonderful surprise," his grandmother said. "Why didn't you tell me you were coming?"

"Then it's not a surprise," he replied. "Is it?"

As they chatted Mary-Jayne moved back behind the architrave and considered her options. Come clean? Act nonchalant? Make a run for it? Running for it appealed most. This wasn't the time or place to make any kind of announcement about being pregnant, not with Solana in the room. She needed time to think. Prepare.

I have to get out of here.

The back door was through the kitchen and off the dining room. But if she sneaked out through the back Solana would want to know why. There would be questions. From Solana. And then from Daniel.

"Show some backbone," she muttered to herself.

She'd always had gumption. Now wasn't the time to ditch her usual resolve and act like a frightened little girl. Mary-Jayne was about to push back her shoulders and face the music when an unwelcome and unexpected wave of nausea rose up and made her suddenly forget everything else. She put a hand to her chest, heaved and swallowed hard, fighting the awful feeling with every ounce of willpower she possessed.

And failed.

She rushed forward to the closest exit, racing past Solana and *him* and headed across the room and out to the patio, just making it to the garden in time.

Where she threw up in spectacular and humiliating fashion.

Daniel remained where he was and watched as his grandmother hurried through the doorway and quickly attended to the still-vomiting woman who was bent over in the garden. If he thought he was needed Daniel would have helped, but he was pretty sure she would much prefer his grandmother coming to her aid.

After several minutes both women came back through the door. Mary-Jayne didn't look at him. Didn't even acknowledge he was there as she walked to the front door and let herself out, head bowed, arms rigid at her sides. But he was rattled seeing her. And silently cursed himself for having so little control over the effect she had on him.

"The poor thing," his grandmother said, hovering in the doorway before she finally closed the door. "She's been unwell for weeks. Ex-boyfriend trouble, too, I think. Not that she's said much to me about it…but I think there's been someone in the picture."

Boyfriend?

His gut twinged. "Does she need a doctor?" he asked, matter-of-fact.

"I don't think so," his grandmother replied. "Probably just a twenty-four-hour bug."

Daniel ignored the twitch of concern. Mary-Jayne had a way of making him feel a whole lot of things he didn't want or need. Attraction aside, she invaded his thoughts when he least expected it. She needled his subconscious. Like she had when he'd been on a date a couple of weeks back. He'd gone out with the tall leggy blonde he'd met at a business dinner, thinking she'd be a distraction. And spent the evening wishing he'd been with someone who would at least occasionally disagree and not be totally compliant to his whims. Someone like Mary-Jayne Preston. He'd ended up saying good-night to his date by nine o'clock, barely kissing her hand when he dropped her home. Sure, he didn't want a serious relationship, but he didn't want boring conversation and shallow sex, either.

And since there had been nothing boring or shallow about the night he'd spent with the bewitching brunette, Daniel still wanted her in his bed. Despite his good sense telling him otherwise.

"So," Solana said, and raised her hands. "Why have you come home?"

"To see you. Why else?"

She tutted. "Always a question with a question. Even as a toddler you were inquisitive. Always questioning everything, always asking *why* to your grandfather. Your brothers were never as curious about things as you were. Do you remember when you were eight and persuaded your grandfather to let you ride that mad, one-eyed pony your dad saved from the animal rescue center?" She shook her head and grinned. "Everyone wanted to know why you'd want to get on such a crazy animal. And all you said was, *why not*?"

Daniel shrugged. "As I recall I dislocated my collarbone."

"And scared Bernie and me half to death," Solana said and chuckled. "You were a handful, you know. Always getting into scraps. Always pushing the envelope. Amazing you turned out so sensible."

"Who say's I'm sensible?" he inquired lightly.

Solana's smile widened. "Me. Your brothers. Your grandfather if he was still alive."

"And Miles?"

His grandmother raised a silvery brow. "I think your dad would like you to be a little *less* sensible."

"I think my father would like me to eat tofu and drive a car that runs on doughnut grease."

"My son is who he is," Solana said affectionately. "Your grandfather never understood Miles and his alternative ways. But your dad knows who he is and what he wants from life. *And* he knows how to relax and enjoy the simple things."

Daniel didn't miss the dig. It wasn't the first time he'd been accused of being an uptight killjoy by his family. "I can relax."

His grandmother looked skeptical. "Well, perhaps you can learn to while you're here."

Daniel crossed his arms. Something about her tone made him suspicious. "You knew I was coming?"

Solana nodded, clearly unapologetic. "Blake called me. And of course it was my idea." She sat down at the table. "Did you know your grandfather had his first heart attack at thirty-nine?"

Daniel sighed. He'd heard it before. Mike Anderson died at sixty-nine from a massive coronary. His fourth. After two previous bypass surgeries the final heart attack had been swift and fatal, killing him before he'd had a chance to get up from his desk. "Gran, I—"

"Don't fob me off with some vague assurance that it won't happen to you," she said, cutting him off. "You work too hard. You don't take time off. You've become as defined by Anderson Holdings as your grandfather was…and all it got him was an early grave. There's more to life than business."

He would have dismissed the criticism from anyone else… but not Solana. He loved and respected his grandmother, and her opinion was one of the few that mattered to him.

"I know that. But I'm not ready to—"

"It's been over four years," Solana reminded him gently. "And time you got back to the land of the living. Simone wouldn't want you to—"

"Gran," Daniel said, hanging on to his patience. "I know you're trying to help. And I promise I'll relax and unwind while I'm here. I'm back for a week so I'll—"

"You'll need more than a week to unwind," she said, cutting him off again. "But if that's all you can manage then so be it. And your parents are expecting you to visit, in case you were thinking you'd fly under the radar while you're here."

Guilt spiked between his shoulder blades. Solana had a way of doing that. And he hadn't considered *not* seeing his father and stepmother. Not really. True, he had little in common with Miles and Bernadette...but they *were* his parents, and he knew they'd be genuinely pleased that he'd come home for a visit.

From a young age he'd known where his path lay. He was who his grandfather looked to as his protégé. At eighteen he'd been drafted into Anderson's, studying economics at night school so he could learn the business firsthand from his grandfather. At twenty-three, following Mike Anderson's death, he'd taken over the reins and since then he'd lived and breathed Anderson's. Blake and Caleb had followed him a few years later, while Daniel remained at the helm.

He worked and had little time for anything resembling a personal life. Simone had understood that. She was a corporate lawyer and worked seventy-hour weeks. Marrying her had made sense. They were a good match...alike in many ways, and they'd been happy together. And would still be together if fate and a faulty brake line hadn't intervened. She'd still be a lawyer and he would still spend his waking hours living and breathing Anderson Holdings. And they would be parents to their daughter. Just as they'd planned.

Daniel stretched his shoulders and stifled a yawn. He was tired. Jet-lagged. But if he crashed in the afternoon he'd feel worse. The trick to staying on top of the jet lag was keeping normal sleep patterns. Besides, there were two things he wanted to do—take a shower, and see Mary-Jayne Preston.

* * *

Mary-Jayne knew that the knock on her door would be Daniel. She'd been waiting for the sound for the past hour. But the sharp rap still startled her and she jumped up from the sofa, where she'd been sitting, hands twisted and stomach churning.

She walked across the living room and down the short hallway, grappling with the emotions running riot throughout her. She ruffled out her baggy shirt and hoped it disguised her belly enough to give her some time to work out how she was going to tell the man at her door he was going to become a father. She took a deep breath, steadied her knees, grabbed the handle and opened the door.

His gray eyes immediately looked her over with unconcealed interest. "How are you feeling?"

His lovely accent wound up her spine. "Fine."

"My grandmother is worried about you."

"I'm fine, like I said."

He tilted his head slightly. "You sure about that?"

Her chin came up. "Positive. Not that I have to explain myself to you."

"No," he mused. "I guess you don't."

"Is there something else you wanted?"

A tiny smile creased one corner of his mouth. "Can I come in?"

"I'd rather you didn't," she said, and stepped back, shielding herself behind the door. "But since you own this resort I guess you can do whatever the hell you want."

There was laughter in his eyes, and she realized the more hostile she got, the more amused he appeared. Mary-Jayne took a deep breath and turned on her heels, quickly finding solace behind the single recliner chair just a few feet away. She watched as he closed the door and took a few easy strides into the room.

"I hear you've been taking my grandmother to see fortunetellers?"

Solana had told him about that? The older woman had sworn

her to secrecy, saying her grandsons would think her crazy for visiting a clairvoyant. "It was *one* fortune-teller," she informed him. "And a reputable one, I might add."

His brows came up. "Really? You believe in all that nonsense?"

She glared at him. "Well, she did say I'd meet a man who was a real jerk...so I'd say she was pretty accurate, wouldn't you agree?"

"Is that a question?" he shot back. "Because I'm probably not the best judge of my own character. Other people's characters, on the other hand, I can usually peg."

"Don't start with—"

"Why did you hang up on me when I called you?"

She was genuinely surprised by his question. And didn't respond.

"You were in South Dakota at your friend's wedding," he reminded her. "I was in San Francisco. I would have flown you to the city."

Into the city. And into his bed. Mary-Jayne knew the score. She might have been a fool the night of Solana's birthday party, but she certainly wasn't about to repeat that monumental mistake.

"I wasn't in the market for another meaningless one-night stand."

His mouth twitched. "Really? More to the point, I guess your boyfriend wouldn't have approved?"

She frowned. "My what?"

"My grandmother can be indiscreet," he said and looked her over. "Unintentionally of course, since she has no idea we had that *meaningless one-night stand*."

Color rose and spotted her cheeks. And for several long seconds she felt a kind of riveting connection to him. It was illogical. It was relentless. It made it impossible to ignore him. Or forget the night they'd spent together. Or the way they'd made love. The silence stretched between them, and Mary-Jayne was drawn deep into his smoky gray eyes.

"I don't have a boyfriend or lover," she said quietly. "I made that up to stop Solana from asking questions about…" Her words trailed off and she moved back, putting distance between them.

"About what?"

She shook her head. "Nothing. I really can't… I can't do this."

"Do what?" he asked.

"I can't do this with you."

"We're not doing anything," he said. "Just talking."

"That's just it," she said, her voice coming out a little strangled. "I'm not ready for this. Not here. Not today. I feel unwell and I—"

"I thought you said you were feeling better?" he asked, cutting her off.

"Well, I'm not, okay? I'm not better. And seeing you here only makes me feel worse."

"Such brutal honesty. I don't know whether to be flattered or offended."

She let out an agonized moan. "That's just it. I am honest. *Always*. And seeing you now makes it impossible for me to be anything else. And I'm not ready for it… I can't do this today. I simply can't—"

"What are you talking about?" he asked impatiently and cut her off again.

"I'm talking about… I mean… I can't…"

"Mary-Jayne," he said, saying her name like he had that night, when he'd said it over and over, against her skin, against her breath. "I'm not sure what's going on with you, but you're not making much sense."

The truth screamed to be told. There was no other way. She couldn't stop being who she was. She was an honest, forthright person who wore her heart on her sleeve. Mary-Jayne stepped out from behind the chair and spread her hands across her stomach, tightening the baggy shirt over her middle. Highlighting the small bump that hadn't been there four months ago.

"I'm talking about *this*."

Daniel quickly refocused his gaze onto her middle and frowned. "You're pregnant?"

She nodded and swallowed hard. "Yes."

"And?"

She shrugged and her hair flipped around her shoulders. Now or never.

"And isn't it obvious? You're the father."

CHAPTER THREE

HE HADN'T MOVED. Mary-Jayne looked at him and took a long breath. "This isn't how I wanted you to find out. I was going to call and tell you and—"

"You're not serious?" he asked, cutting through her words with icy precision.

She nodded. "I'm perfectly serious. I'm pregnant."

He raised a dark brow. "We used protection," he said quietly and held up a few fingers. "Three times, three lots of birth control. So your math doesn't quite work out."

"My math?" She stared at him. "What exactly are you accusing me of?"

"Nothing," he replied evenly. "Simply stating an irrefutable fact."

A fact?

Right. There was no possible way of misunderstanding his meaning. "I'm not lying to you. This baby is—"

"Yours," he corrected coldly. "And probably the ex-boyfriend who my grandmother said is giving you grief at the moment."

She fought the urge to rush across the room and slug him. "I don't have a *boyfriend*. Ex or otherwise."

"You do according to my grandmother," he stated. "Who I trust more than anyone else."

No punches pulled. He didn't believe her. *Okay.* She could handle it. She didn't care what he thought. "I only told Solana that to stop her from asking questions about why I've been unwell."

He crossed his arms, accentuating his broad shoulders, and stood as still as a statue. He really was absurdly good-looking, she thought, disliking him with every fiber in her body. His gray eyes had darkened to a deep slate color and his almost black hair was short and shiny, and she remembered how soft it had been between her fingertips. His face was perfectly proportioned and he had a small cleft in his chin that was ridiculously sexy. Yes, Daniel Anderson was as handsome as sin. He was also an arrogant, overbearing, condescending so-and-so, and if it weren't for the fact he was the biological father of her child, she'd happily *never* see him again.

"Do I really appear so gullible, Miss Preston?"

Miss Preston?

"Gullible? I don't know what you—"

"If you think naming me in a paternity claim will fatten your bank balance, think again. My lawyers will be all over you in a microsecond."

His pompous arrogance was unbelievable. "I'm not after your money."

"Then, what?" he asked. "A wedding ring?"

Fury surged through her. "I wouldn't marry you if you were the last man left on the planet."

Her words seemed to amuse him and he looked at her in such a haughty, condescending way that her palms actually itched with the urge to slap his face. In every way she'd played the scene out in her head, and not once had she imagined he wouldn't believe that her baby was his. Naive perhaps, but Mary-Jayne had been raised to take someone at their word.

"That's quite a relief, since I won't be proposing anytime soon."

"Go to hell," she said quietly as emotion tightened her chest, and she drew in a shuddering breath. He pushed her buttons effortlessly. He really was a hateful jerk.

"Not until we've sorted out this little mix-up."

"Mix-up?" She glared at him. "I'm pregnant and you're the father. This is not a mix-up. This is just how it is."

"Then, I demand a paternity test."

Daniel hadn't meant to sound like such a cold, unfeeling bastard. But he wasn't about to be taken for a ride. He knew the score. A few months back his brother Caleb had been put through the ringer in a paternity suit that had eventually proved the kid he'd believed was his wasn't. And Daniel wasn't about to get pulled into that same kind of circus.

Mary-Jayne Preston's baby couldn't possibly be his...could it? He'd never played roulette with birth control. Besides, now that he could well and truly see her baby bump she looked further along than four months. Simone hadn't started showing so obviously until she was five months' pregnant.

"I'd like you to leave."

Daniel didn't move. "Won't that defeat the purpose of your revelation?"

She scowled, and he couldn't help thinking how she still looked beautiful even with an infuriated expression. "You know about the baby, so whatever you decide to do with the information is up to you."

"Until I get served with child-support demands, you mean?"

She placed her hands on her hips and Daniel's gaze was immediately drawn to her belly. She was rounder than he remembered, kind of voluptuous, and a swift niggle of attraction wound its way through his blood and across his skin. Her curves had appealed to him from the moment they'd first met, and watching her now only amplified that desire.

Which was damned inconvenient, since she was obviously trying to scam him.

"I don't want your money," she said stiffly. "And I certainly don't want a wedding ring. When I get married it will be to someone I actually like. I intend to raise this baby alone. Believe me, or don't believe me. Frankly, I don't care either way."

There was such blatant contempt in her voice that he was tempted to smile. One thing about the woman in front of him— she wasn't afraid to speak her mind. And even though he knew it was crazy thinking, it was an interesting change from the usual lengths some women went to in order to get his attention. How sincere she was, he couldn't tell.

"We spent the night together a little over four months ago," he reminded her. "You look more than four months pregnant."

Her glare intensified. "So it's clearly a big baby. All I know is that the only possible way I got pregnant was from that night I spent with you. I hadn't been with anyone for a long time before that night. Despite what you think of me, I'm not easy. And I don't lie. I have no reason to want this child to be yours. I don't like you. I'm not interested in you or your money or anything else. But I am telling you the truth."

He still wasn't convinced. "So the ex-boyfriend?"

"A figment of my imagination," she replied. "Like I said, Solana was asking questions and I needed a little camouflage for a while."

He kept his head. "Even if there is no boyfriend and you are indeed carrying a supersize baby...we used contraception. So it doesn't add up."

"And since condoms are only ninety-eight percent effective, we obviously managed to slip into the two percent bracket."

Ninety-eight percent effective?

Since when?

Daniel struggled with the unease clawing up his spine. "You cannot expect me to simply accept this news at face value."

She shrugged, as if she couldn't care either way. "Do, or don't. If you want a paternity test to confirm it, then fine, that's what we'll do."

He relaxed a little. Finally, some good sense. "Thank you."

"But it won't be done until the baby is born," she said evenly and took a long breath. "There are risks associated with tests after the fifteen-week mark, and I won't put my baby in jeopardy. Not for you. Not for anyone."

There was such unequivocal resolve in her voice, and it surprised him. She was a flake. Unreliable. Unpredictable. Nothing like Simone. "Of course," he said, and did his best to ignore the stabbing pain in his temple. His shoulders ached, and he could feel the effects of no sleep and hours flying across the globe begin to creep into his limbs. "I wouldn't expect you to put your child at risk."

Her child.

Her baby.

This wasn't what he'd expected to face when he'd decided to come home. But if she was telling the truth? What then? To share a child with a woman he barely knew. It was a train wreck waiting to happen.

And he hated waiting. In business. In his personal life.

He'd waited at the hospital when Simone was brought in with critical injuries. He waited while the doctors had tried to save her and their unborn daughter. He'd waited, and then received the worst possible news. And afterward he'd experienced a heartbreaking despair. After that night he became hollow inside. He'd loved his wife and daughter. Losing them had been unbearable. And he'd never wanted to feel that kind of soul-destroying anguish again.

But if Mary-Jayne *was* carrying his child, how could he turn his back?

He couldn't. He'd be trapped.

Held ransom by the very feelings he'd sworn he never wanted to feel again.

"So what do you want from me until then?"

"Want? Nothing," she replied quietly. "I'll call you when the baby is born and the paternity test is done. Goodbye."

He sighed. "Is this how you usually handle problems? By ignoring them?"

Her cheeks quickly heated. "I don't consider this baby a problem," she shot back. "And the only thing I plan to ignore is you."

He stared at her for a moment, and then when he laughed Mary-Jayne realized she liked the sound way too much. She didn't want to like *anything* about him. Not ever. He had become enemy number one. For the next five months all she wanted to do was concentrate on growing a healthy baby. Wasting time thinking about Daniel and his sexy laugh and gray eyes was off her agenda.

"You don't really think that's going to happen, do you?" he asked, watching her with such hot intensity she couldn't look away. "You've dropped this bombshell, and you know enough about me to realize I won't simply fade away for the next five months."

"I can live in hope."

"I think you live in a fantasyland, Mary-Jayne."

The way he said her name caused her skin to prickle. No one called her that except her parents and her older brother, Noah. Even her sisters and closest friends mostly called her M.J. To the rest of the world she was M. J. Preston—the youngest and much loved sibling in a close-knit middle-class family. But Daniel had always used her full name.

Mary-Jayne took a deep breath. "A fantasyland?" She repeated his words as a question.

"What else would you call it?" he shot back as he looked her over. "You're what, twenty-seven? Never married or engaged. No real career to speak of. And a barely solvent online business. You've rented the same house for nearly ten years. You drive a car that's good for little else but scrap metal. You have less than a thousand dollars in the bank at any given time and a not-so-stellar credit rating thanks to a certain dubious ex-boyfriend who ran up a debt on your behalf over five years ago. It looks very much like you do—"

"How do you know that?" she demanded hotly, hands on hips. "How do you know all that about me? I've not told Solana any of…" She trailed off as realization hit. And then she seethed. "You had me investigated?"

"Of course," he replied, unmoving and clearly unapologetic.

"You had no right to do that," she spat. "No right at all. You invaded my privacy."

He shrugged his magnificent shoulders. "You are working at this resort and have befriended my grandmother—it was prudent to make sure you weren't a fortune hunter."

"Fortune hunter?" Mary-Jayne's eyes bulged wide and she said a rude word.

He tilted his head a fraction. "Well, the jury's still out on that one."

"Jury?" She echoed the word in disbelief. "And what does that make you? The judge? Can you actually hear yourself? Of all the pompous, arrogant and self-important things I've ever heard in my life, you take the cake. And you really do take yourself and the significance of your opinions way too seriously."

He didn't like that. Not one bit. She watched, fascinated as his eyes darkened and a tiny pulse in his cheek beat rapidly. His hands were clenched and suddenly his body looked as if it had been carved from granite. And as much as she tried to fight it, attraction reared up, and heat swirled around the small room as their gazes clashed.

Memories of that night four months ago banged around in her head. Kissing, touching, stroking. Possession and desire unlike any she had known before. There had been a quiet intensity in him that night, and she'd been swept away into another world, another universe where only pleasure and a deeply intimate connection existed. That night, he hadn't been the rigid, unyielding and disagreeable man who was now in her living room. He'd been tender and passionate. He'd whispered her name against her skin. He'd kissed her and made love to her with such profound eagerness Mary-Jayne's entire mind and body had awakened and responded in kind. She'd never been driven to please and be pleasured like that before.

But right now she had to get back to hating him. "I'm going to get changed and go for a walk to clear my head. You know the way out."

He didn't move. And he looked a little pale, she thought. Perhaps the shock that he was going to be a father was finally hitting home. But then she remembered that he didn't believe he actually was her baby's father, so that probably wasn't it.

"We still have things to discuss."

"Not for another…" Her words trailed off and she tapped off five of her fingers in her palm. "Five months. Until then, how about you treat me with the disdain that you've clearly mastered, and I'll simply pretend that you don't exist. That will work out nicely for us both, don't you think?"

Of course, she knew saying something so provocative was like waving a red cape at a bull. But she couldn't help herself. He deserved it in spades. And it was only the truth. She didn't want to see him or spend any more time in his company.

"I don't treat you with disdain."

And there it was again—his resolute belief in the sound of his own voice.

"No?" She bit down on her lip for a moment. "You've admitted you had me investigated and just accused me of being a fortune hunter. Oh, and what about what you said to me on the phone when I was in South Dakota?" She took a strengthening breath. "That I was a flake who dressed like a hippie."

His eyes flashed. "And before you told me to go to hell you called me an uptight, overachieving, supercilious snob, if I remember correctly." He uncrossed his arms and took a step toward her.

"Well, it's the truth. You are an uptight snob."

"And you dress like a hippie."

"I like to be comfortable," she said, and touched her head self-consciously. "And I can't help the way my hair gets all curly in the humidity."

His gaze flicked to her hair and she saw his mouth twitch fractionally. "I didn't say a word about your hair. In fact it's quite…it's…it's…"

"It's what?" she asked.

"Nothing," he said, and shrugged. "I would like to know your plans."

Mary-Jayne stared at him. "I don't have any plans other than to have a healthy baby in five months' time."

He looked around the room. "When are you leaving here?"

"Audrey's back in two weeks. I'll go home then."

"Have you told your family?"

She shook her head. "Not yet."

"Have you told anyone?"

She met his gaze. "You."

His expression narrowed. "And since she didn't mention it while you were throwing up in her garden, I'm guessing you haven't told my grandmother, either?"

"Just you," she replied, fighting the resentment fueling her blood. "Like I said. Incidentally, Daniel, if you're going to disbelieve everything that comes out of my mouth, it's going to be a long five months."

He grinned unexpectedly. "So you do know my name? I don't think you've ever used it before. Well, except for that night we spent together."

Her skin heated. She remembered exactly how she'd said his name that night. Over and over, whispered and moaned, as though it was the only word she'd known.

"Like I said, you know the way out."

He didn't budge. "We still need to talk."

"We've talked enough," she said tensely. "You don't believe me and you need a paternity test. *And* you think I'm after your money. Believe me, I've got your message loud and clear."

"You're angry because I want proof of paternity?"

He actually sounded surprised. Mary-Jayne almost laughed at his absurd sense of entitlement. "I'm angry because you think I'm lying to you. I don't know what kind of world you live in where you have this compulsion to question someone's integrity without cause, but I don't live in that world, Daniel. And I would never want to."

She spun on her heel and left the room, barely taking a breath until she reached the sanctuary of the main bedroom. She leaned against the closed door and shuddered.

It's done now. He knows. I can get on with things.

She pulled herself together, changed into sweats and sneakers and loitered in the room for more than ten minutes to ensure he'd be gone.

She strode into the living room and then stopped in her tracks. The room was empty. He'd left. As if he'd never been there.

A strange hollowness fluttered behind her ribs. She was glad he was gone—arrogant and disbelieving jerk that he was. She was well rid of him. With any luck she'd never have to see him again. Or speak to him. Or have to stare into those smoky gray eyes of his.

She could go home and have her baby.

Simple.

But in her heart she knew she was dreaming to believe he'd just disappear from her life. She was having his baby—and that made it about as complicated as it got.

When Daniel woke up he had a crick in his neck and his left leg was numb. It was dark out. He checked his watch: six-forty. He sat up and stretched. When he'd left her condo, he'd walked around the grounds for a few minutes before heading back to his own villa. Once he'd sat down, the jet lag had hit him with a thud. Now he needed coffee and a clear head.

He got to his feet and rounded out his shoulders. The condo

was quiet, and he walked from the living room and headed for the kitchen. He had to refocus and figure what the hell he was supposed to do for the next five months until the baby came into the world.

The baby.

His baby...

I'm going to be a father.

Maybe?

Daniel still wasn't entirely convinced. Mary-Jayne potentially had a lot to gain by saying he'd fathered her child. He wasn't naive and knew some people were mercenary enough to try to take advantage of others. He remembered how devastated Caleb had been when he'd discovered the boy he'd thought was his son turned out to belong to his *then* girlfriend's ex-husband. And Daniel didn't want to form a bond with a child only to have it snatched away. Not again. Losing Simone and their unborn daughter had been soul destroying. He wasn't going to put himself in a position to get another serving of that kind of loss.

He made coffee and drank it. Damn...he felt as if his head was going to explode. He'd had it all planned out...come back to Port Douglas, reconnect with Mary-Jayne for a week and get her out of his system once and for all.

Not going to happen.

Daniel rounded out his shoulders and sucked in a long breath. He needed a plan. And fast. He swilled the cup in the sink, grabbed his keys and left the villa.

By the time he reached her condo his hands were sweating. No one had ever had such an intense physical effect on him. And he wasn't sure how to feel about it. The crazy thing was, he couldn't ignore it. And now that had amplified a hundredfold.

They needed to talk. There was no way around it. Daniel took another breath and knocked on the door.

When she answered the door she looked almost as though she'd been expecting him to return. He didn't like the idea that he was so transparent to her.

"I'm working," she said, and left him standing in the door-way. "So you'll need to amuse yourself for ten minutes before we get into round two."

The way she dismissed him so effortlessly *should* have made him madder than hell. But it didn't. He liked her spirit, and it was one of the things he found so attractive about her.

He followed her down the hall, and when he reached the dining room she was already standing by a small workbench tucked against the wall in one corner. She was bent over the narrow table, one elbow resting, using a small soldering iron. There was enough light from the lamp positioned to one side for him to see her profile, and despite the protective glasses perched on her nose he couldn't miss the intense concentration she gave her craft. There were several boards fashioned on easels that displayed her jewelry pieces, and although he was no expert, there was certainly style and creativity in her work.

She must have sensed him watching her because she turned and switched off the soldering iron. "So you're back?"

He nodded. "I'm back."

"Did you call your lawyer?"

"What?"

She shrugged a little. "Seems like something you'd do."

Daniel ignored the irritation clawing at his spine. "No, Mary-Jayne, I didn't call my lawyer. Actually, I fell asleep."

She looked surprised and then frowned a little. "Jet lag?"

He nodded again. "Once I sat down it hit me."

"I had the same reaction when I returned from Thailand last year. It took me three days to recover. The trick is to stay awake until bedtime."

There was something husky and incredibly sexy about Mary-Jayne's voice that reached him deep down. After they'd slept together, he'd pursued her and she'd turned him down flat. Even from across an ocean she'd managed to throw a bucket of cold water on his attempts to ask her out. And get her back in his bed. Because he still wanted her. As foolish as it was, as different and unsuitable for one another as they were—he couldn't stop thinking about her.

She knew that. She knew they were from different worlds. She'd accused him of thinking she was an easy mark and that was why he wanted her. But it wasn't that. He wanted her because she stirred him like no other woman ever had. From her crazy beautiful hair to her curvy body and her sassy mouth, Daniel had never known a woman like her. He might not like her…but he wanted her. And it was as inconvenient as hell.

"So what do you want, then?"

Daniel's back straightened. She didn't hold back. She clearly didn't think she had anything to gain by being friendly or even civil. It wasn't a tactic he was used to. She'd called him a spoiled, pampered and arrogant snob, and although he didn't agree with that assumption, it was exactly how she treated him.

"To talk," he replied. "Seems we've got plenty to talk about."

"Do you think?" she shot back. "Since you don't believe that this baby is yours, I can't see what's so important that you felt compelled to come back so soon."

Daniel took a breath. "I guess I deserve that."

"Yeah," she said and plucked the glasses off her nose. "I guess you do."

He managed a tight smile. "I would like to talk with you. Would coffee be too much trouble?"

She placed the soldering iron on the bench. "I guess not."

As she walked past him and through the door to the kitchen it occurred to Daniel that she swayed when she moved. The kitchen seemed small with both of them in it, and he stayed on the outside of the counter.

"That's quite a collection your friend has up there," he remarked and pointed to the cooking pots hanging from an old window shutter frame that was suspended from the ceiling.

"Audrey likes pans," she said without looking at him. "I don't know why."

"She doesn't need a reason," he said and pulled out a chair. "I collect old books."

She glanced up. "Old books?"

"First editions," he explained. "Poetry and classic literature."

One of her eyebrows rose subtly. "I didn't peg you as a reader. Except perhaps the *Financial Times*."

Daniel grinned a little. "I didn't say I read them."

"Then why collect them?"

He half shrugged. "They're often unique. You know, rare."

"Valuable?" she asked, saying the word almost as an insult. "Does everything in your life have a dollar sign attached to it?"

As digs went between them, it was pretty mild, but it still irked him. "Everything? No."

"Good," she said, and held up a small sugar pot. When he shook his head, she continued speaking. "Because I have no intention of allowing my baby to become caught up in your old family money or your sense of self-entitlement."

Daniel stilled. "What does that mean?"

"It means that people like you have a kind of overconfident belief that money fixes everything."

"People like me?" Daniel walked across the small room and moved around the countertop. "Like me?" he asked again, trying to hold on to the annoyance sneaking across his skin. "Like me, how…exactly?"

She stepped back. "You're rich and successful. You can snap your fingers and have any number of minions willing to do whatever you need done."

He laughed humorlessly. "Really? I must try that next time I want someone to bring me my slippers."

Her green eyes glittered brilliantly. "Did you just make a joke? I didn't realize you had it in you."

Daniel's shoulders twitched. "Perhaps I'm not quite the *uptight, overachieving, supercilious snob* you think I am."

"Oh, I wouldn't go that far," she said and pushed the mug along the countertop. "There's milk in the fridge."

"This is fine." Daniel took the mug and leaned a hip against the counter. "Thank you."

"No problem. And you *are* uptight, Daniel. Everything about you screams order and control."

"Because I don't live in chaos?" he asked, deliberately waving a hand around the untidy room. "That doesn't necessarily equate to being a control freak."

She crossed her arms. "Chaos? So now you think I'm a slob?"

He drank some coffee and placed the mug on the counter. "What I think is that it's interesting that you express every opinion you have without considering the consequences."

"Oh, have I offended your sensibilities?"

"Have I offended yours?"

She shrugged. "I'd have to care what you thought, wouldn't I?"

In all his life he'd never met anyone who tried so hard to antagonize him. Or anyone with whom he'd been compelled to do the same. Mary-Jayne got under his skin in ways he could barely rationalize. They were all wrong for one another and they both knew it.

And now there was a baby coming...

His baby.

Daniel glanced at her belly and then met her gaze.

"Mary-Jayne." He said her name quietly, and the mood between them changed almost immediately. "Are you...are you sure?"

She nodded slowly. "Am I sure the baby is yours? Yes, I'm certain."

Resistance lingered in his blood. "But we—"

"I may be a lot of things, Daniel...but I'm not a liar." She drew in a long breath. "The contraception we used obviously failed. Despite what you think of me, I've been single for over twelve months and I haven't slept with anyone since...except you."

A stupid, egotistical part of him was glad to hear it. One part wanted to believe her. And the other…the other could only think about what it meant for them both if what she said was true.

"I need to be sure," he said.

"I understand," she replied. "You can have your proof when he or she is born."

Guilt niggled its way through his blood. "I appreciate you agreeing to a paternity test."

She shrugged lightly. "There's little point in being at odds over this. Be assured that I don't want anything from you, and once you have your proof of paternity you can decide how much or how little time you invest in this."

As she spoke she certainly didn't come across as flighty as she appeared. She sounded like a woman who knew exactly what she wanted. Which was her child…and no interference from him.

Which of course wasn't going to happen.

If the baby *was* his, then he would be very involved. He'd have no choice. The child would be an Anderson and have the right to claim the legacy that went with the name. Only, he wasn't sure how he'd get Mary-Jayne to see it that way.

"If this child is mine, then I won't dodge my responsibility."

She looked less than impressed by the idea. "If you're talking about money, I think I've made it pretty clear I'm not interested."

"You can't raise a child on good intentions, Mary-Jayne. Be sensible."

Her mouth thinned and she looked ready for an argument, but she seemed to change her mind. Some battles, he figured, were about defense, not attack…and she knew that as well as he did.

"We'll see what happens," she said casually as she crossed the small kitchen and stood in front of the refrigerator. She waited for him to stand aside and then opened the door. "I'm heating up lasagna. Are you staying for dinner?"

Daniel raised a brow. "Am I invited?"

She shrugged, as if she couldn't care either way. But he knew she probably wanted to tell him to take a hike in some of her more colorful language.

"Sure," he said, and grabbed the coffee mug as he stepped out of her way. "That would be good."

He caught a tiny smile on her mouth and watched as she removed several items from the refrigerator and began preparing food on the countertop. She placed a casserole dish in the microwave and began making a salad. And Daniel couldn't take his eyes off her. She was fascinating to watch. Her glorious hair shone like ebony beneath the kitchen light, and she chewed her bottom lip as she completed the task. And of course thinking about her lips made him remember their night together. And kissing her. And making love to her. She had a remarkable effect on his libido, and he wondered if it was because they *were* so different that he was so achingly attracted to her. She was all challenge. All resistance. And since very little challenged him these days, Daniel knew her very determination to avoid him had a magnetic pull all of its own.

And he had no idea what he was going to do about it.

Or if he could do actually do anything at all.

CHAPTER FOUR

MARY-JAYNE FINISHED preparing dinner, uncomfortably conscious of the gorgeous man standing by the kitchen table. There was such blistering intensity in his gaze she could barely concentrate on what she was doing. She hated that he could do that to her. If she had her way she'd never see him again.

But the baby she carried bound them together.

He wouldn't, she was certain, simply disappear from her life.

She had five months until the baby came, and she had to figure out how to get through those months with Daniel in the background. Or worse. He wasn't the kind of man who'd simply go away until the baby came…regardless of how much she might wish for things to go that way.

"How long are you staying at the resort?" she asked, hoping he'd say not too long at all. Best he leave quickly.

"I'd planned to only be here a week to visit with my grandmother," he replied, and shrugged slightly. "But now I'm not sure."

She frowned. "Don't you have a company to run or something?"

"Yes."

"Isn't it hard to do that from here? You live mostly in San Francisco, right?"

He placed the mug on the dining table and crossed his arms. "Most of the time. Anderson's corporate offices are there. And the Bay Area resort is the largest."

"Well, I'm sure they need you back."

His mouth twitched. "Eager to see me gone, Mary-Jayne?"

"If I said no I'd be lying," she replied, and brought plates and cutlery to the table. "And as I've repeatedly said, I don't lie. So if you're thinking of extending your stay on my account, there's really no need. The birth is five months away and there's nothing you can do until then."

Mary-Jayne brought the food to the table and gestured for him to take a seat. When he was sitting she did the same and took the lids off the salad and lasagna. She didn't bother to ask what he wanted and quickly piled a scoop of pasta on his plate. Once she'd filled her own plate she picked up the utensils and speared some lettuce and cucumber with a fork.

"What…is…that?"

She looked up and smirked when she saw how Daniel was staring at his food. "Lasagna. With mushroom, spinach, shredded zucchini flowers and goat cheese."

He looked as if she'd asked him to chew broken glass. He took a breath and met her gaze. "You're a vegetarian?"

"Of course."

Mary-Jayne knew his parents were strict vegans. She also knew he and his brothers had made a point from his early teens of *not* following in their footsteps.

"Of course," he repeated with more than a touch of irony. "Looks…delicious."

"I'm not much of a cook," she said frankly. "So don't hold your breath."

"Thanks for the warning."

She smiled to herself as they began to eat. He was being good-humored about her attempts to wind him up and it surprised her. Maybe he wasn't quite as straitlaced and uptight as she'd believed. Which didn't mean anything. He could be nice.

He could be the most charming and agreeable man on the planet and it wouldn't change the one significant fact—they were like oil and water and would never mix. Despite the fact that they'd made a baby together and were now bound by parenthood. They were in different leagues, and she had to remember that every time she was tempted to think about his sexy voice and broad shoulders.

"I have an ultrasound appointment on Tuesday at ten-thirty," she said, and speared some pasta. "My doctor gave me a referral to a medical center in Cairns."

The regional city was forty miles south of Port Douglas.

"And?"

"And you're welcome to come along if you want to," she replied flatly.

He didn't really look as though he wanted to. But he did nod. "I'll pick you up."

"I can drive myself."

He raised a brow. "I'll pick you up."

She was about to argue, but stopped herself. Battling with Daniel over the small stuff was pointless. "Okay," she said, and didn't miss the flash of surprise in his eyes.

For a while the only sound in the room was the clicking of cutlery. He seemed happy not to talk and Mary-Jayne was content to eat her food and not think about how intimate the situation was. Once dinner was done he offered to help wash up, and before she had a chance to refuse his assistance he was out of the chair and in the kitchen, rinsing the plates with one hand while he opened the dishwasher with the other.

"You know your way around a kitchen," she said, surprised.

He shrugged. "Bernie made sure my brothers and I knew how to cook and clean up."

"That's your mother?"

"Stepmother," he replied, and began stacking the dishwasher. "She married my dad when I was two."

Her insides contracted. "Solana told me your mother passed away just after you were born."

"That's right."

Mary-Jayne moved into the kitchen. "You were born in Australia, weren't you?"

"That's right. My dad moved to California when he married Bernie and the twins were born there. They moved back here about ten years ago."

"I like your dad."

He glanced sideways. "I didn't realize you were acquainted."

"He came here to visit your grandmother and Caleb a few weeks ago. I was with Solana at the time and she introduced me to him. He had a very relaxed sense of self, if that makes sense. He was very charismatic and friendly," she said, and smiled a little.

"Not like me, you mean?"

Mary-Jayne grabbed a tea towel. "I'm sure you could be the same if you put your mind to it."

He turned and faced her. "And ruin my image of being an uptight bore?"

She laughed softly. "One thing you're not, Daniel, is boring."

"Just uptight?" he asked.

Mary-Jayne shrugged lightly. "I guess it goes with the territory. Solana told me how you took over the business when you were in your early twenties. That must have been quite a responsibility to shoulder. Duty above all else, right?"

He didn't move. "My grandfather was dead. My father had tried his hand at the business and bailed when he realized he was happier growing organic vegetables and pursuing his art. So yes, being drafted into the business that young had its challenges. But I wasn't about to let my family down. Or the people who rely on Anderson's for their livelihood. I did what I had to do... If that made me an uptight bore in the process, then I guess I'll simply have to live with it."

She took a deep breath. There was something so seductive

about his deep voice it was impossible to move. She could have easily moved closer to him. The heat that had been between them from the start was as vibrant and scorching as it had ever been.

It's just sex...

Of course she knew that. Sex and lust and some kind of manic chemical reaction that had her hormones running riot. She had to get them under control. And fast.

"So I'll see you Tuesday. Around nine o'clock."

His gaze darkened. "Are you kicking me out?"

Mary-Jayne took a tentative step backward. "I guess so."

He laughed. "You know, I've never met anyone quite like you. There are no punches pulled with you, Mary-Jayne—you say exactly what you think."

"Blame it on my middle-class upbringing."

"I'm not criticizing you," he said, and folded his arms. "On the contrary, I find it intriguing. And incredibly sexy."

She stepped back again. "If you're flirting with me, stop right now. Your *charm* has got us into enough trouble already."

He laughed again. "Good night, Mary-Jayne."

"Good night," she whispered as she followed him up the hall, and she didn't take a breath until she closed the front door behind him.

After a restless night spent staring mostly at the ceiling, Daniel went for a long run along the beach around ten o'clock on Sunday morning. He stayed out for over an hour, and when he returned to his villa, took a shower and dressed and was about to head for his grandmother's when there was a tap on his door.

It was Caleb.

His brother walked across the threshold and dropped a set of keys onto the narrow hall table. "The keys to my Jeep," Caleb said and grinned. "In case you want to visit the folks."

Caleb never failed to remind him or Blake about the importance of family.

"Thanks," he said, and walked down the hallway.

His brother followed, and they each dropped into one of the two leather sofas in the living room. "Have you heard from Audrey?" Daniel asked the one question he knew his brother wouldn't want to answer.

Caleb shook his head. "I screwed up, and she's not about to forgive me anytime soon."

"You did what you thought was right."

"I moved my ex-girlfriend and her child into my house without thinking about what it would mean to my *current* girlfriend. I mean, I know Audrey and I had only been together a couple of months…but still…" The regretful look on his brother's face spoke volumes. "I should have done things differently. I shouldn't have taken Nikki's word that he was my kid without getting tested. I should have known Audrey was going to end up bailing. Hell, I probably would have done the same thing had the situation been reversed. When her mother got sick she had just the out she needed to get away from the resort for a while…and from me."

Which had been the catalyst for Mary-Jayne coming to the resort. Daniel was certain that his brother was in love with Mary-Jayne's friend Audrey. But when his ex-girlfriend had arrived on his doorstep, holding a baby she'd claimed was his, Caleb had reacted instinctively and moved them into his home.

"She's coming back in two weeks."

"Audrey?" Caleb's gaze narrowed. "How do you know that?"

He shrugged. "Gran must have mentioned it."

"Gran did?" His brother raised both brows. "You sure about that?"

"I don't know what—"

"Less than twenty-four hours, hey?" Caleb laughed. "I take it you've seen her?"

Her.

He'd told Caleb about spending the night with Mary-Jayne.

He hadn't been able to avoid it since his brother had spotted her leaving his villa early that morning. "Yes, I've seen her."

"You still hung up on her?"

Daniel shrugged one shoulder. Caleb knew him well enough to sniff out a lie. "Things are a little more complicated."

"Complicated?"

He didn't flinch. "She's pregnant."

His brother's eyes bulged. "Hell! And it's yours?"

"So she says."

Caleb let out a long breath. "Do you believe her?"

"Do I have doubts?" He shrugged again. "Of course. But Mary-Jayne isn't like—"

"Like Nikki?" Caleb suggested, cutting him off. "Yeah, you're right. She seems like a real straight shooter. I know Audrey trusted her to run the store in her absence without hesitation. You gonna marry her?"

Daniel's back straightened. "Don't be stupid. I hardly know her."

Caleb grinned. "Well, you'll have plenty of opportunity to get to know her once you start raising a child together."

Raising a child together...

Daniel knew it wouldn't be that simple. She lived in Crystal Point. He lived in San Francisco. There was a hell of a lot of geography separating them. Which would make him what? A once-a-year father? Summer-vacation time or less? He was looking down the barrel at an impossible situation.

"We'll see what happens."

His brother's expression turned serious. "Tell me you're getting a paternity test?"

"Once the child is born," he said, and explained about the risks of doing the test during the second trimester.

Caleb nodded slowly. "And what do you plan to do until then?"

He shrugged a little. "It's not really up to me."

His brother made a disagreeable sound. "I can see that attitude lasting about two days," he said, and smiled. "Until the shock really hits you."

Caleb knew him well. The idea of doing nothing until the baby came sat like a lead weight in his gut. But what choice did he have? Mary-Jayne wasn't the kind of woman to take easily to being watched or hovered over. She was obviously fiercely independent and made it clear she didn't need him for anything.

Which should have put him it at ease.

Instead his insides churned. He was torn between wanting to believe her child was his and knowing it would be much better for them both if it wasn't true. But he had no real reason to disbelieve her. Sure, he thought she was a bit of a flake. But according to Solana she was honest and forthright and exactly as she seemed—a free, independent spirit who answered to no one but herself. Not the kind of woman to claim paternity when she wanted nothing in return.

"I thought I'd visit Gran," Daniel said, and sprang from the sofa. "Feel like joining me?"

Caleb shook his head and grinned as he stood. "I'm not on vacation like you. I have a business to run. And don't forget to go and see the folks this week."

"I won't," Daniel promised, and walked his brother down the hall.

Once Caleb left he locked up the villa, grabbed the keys on the hall stand and headed out. He walked around the grounds for a few minutes, and instead of going directly to Solana's villa made his way to the western side of the resort where the condos were smaller and home to many of the employees. He tapped on Mary-Jayne's door and ignored the interested looks from a few people in corporate shirts who passed him on the pathway that separated the apartments.

The door swung back and she stood in front of him. "Oh... hi."

She sounded breathless, and he was immediately concerned. "Are you okay?"

"Fine," she replied and took a deep breath. "I've been doing Pilates."

Daniel looked her over. Her hair was tied up in a haphazard ponytail and she wore black leggings and a hot pink racer-back tank top that clung to her curves. Her belly looked like it had popped out a little more overnight and he fought the unexpected urge to place his hand on her stomach. Her cheeks were flushed and her lips looked plump and red. There was something wholly healthy and attractive about her that warmed his blood.

"Pilates?" he echoed, and curled his fingers into his palms to stop himself from reaching out to touch her.

"It's good for the baby," she replied. "And me. So did you want something?"

"Only to see how you are feeling today."

"I'm fine," she said, her hand positioned on the door like she couldn't wait to close it. "How are you?"

"Okay," he said.

"Well, thanks for stopping by."

Daniel shifted on his feet. "I thought... I wondered if you would like to have lunch."

Her brows arched. "Lunch? With you? Where?"

He shrugged a little. "There are four restaurants at this resort...take your pick."

Her brows stayed high. "Beneath the prying eyes of wait staff and various employees? Isn't that a little risky? People might start thinking you've been consorting with the help."

Daniel's jaw clenched. She was an argumentative and provocative pain in the neck. And he wanted her anyway.

"First, I don't care what anyone thinks. And second, you are not *the help*, Mary-Jayne. Are you going to be difficult and refuse every request I make? Or accept that you need to eat and since you're a lousy cook anyway, it would—"

"I'm not a *lousy* cook," she retorted and a tiny smile curved her mouth. "Just not a good cook. And while I appreciate your invitation, I'm hardly dressed for anything other than a cheese sandwich in front of the TV."

He looked her over again and his libido twitched. "I'll come back in half an hour. Unless you need help getting out of your clothes?"

For a second he thought she might slam the door in his face. But to his surprise she laughed softly. "I'm sure I can manage. Okay, see you in thirty minutes."

Then she did close the door and Daniel turned on his heels. And as he walked back down the path he realized he was grinning foolishly.

Lunch.

Great idea.

Not...

As she slipped into a knee-length white denim sundress, Mary-Jayne cursed herself repeatedly for being so agreeable and for finding Daniel Anderson charming and attractive and so darn sexy he could ask her to jet to the moon and she probably would.

She had to get a handle on the chemistry between them. There was no other option.

He tapped on her door exactly thirty minutes later and Mary-Jayne scowled as she moved down the short hallway. He was the punctual type. It figured. Everything about him screamed order and control.

She opened the door and faced him. "I'm ready."

"So I see," he said, and stood aside to let her pass.

Mary-Jayne closed the door and dropped the key into the tote draped over her left shoulder. "Where are we going?" she asked.

"Your choice," he replied. "Like I said."

Mary-Jayne took a deep breath. There were four restaurants at the resort: two bistros designed for families, a trendy Japanese teppanyaki bar and an exclusive à la carte restaurant named after his grandmother that Mary-Jayne had never been in because the menu was way out of her price range, even though Solana had offered to take her there several times.

She smiled sweetly. "Solana's. Think you'll be able to get a table at such short notice?"

His mouth turned up a little. "I'm sure they will be able to accommodate us."

Mary-Jayne looked up at him. "No one would dare defy you, would they?"

"Oh, I could think of someone who would."

He was smiling now and it made her smile back. *Keep your head.* The warning voice at the back of her mind told her to ignore the way her insides fluttered. She didn't want to *flutter* around him. She didn't want to have any kind of reaction. He was her baby's father—that was all. Besides, he didn't actually believe he had fathered her baby, so she should keep being madder than hell and resentful that he thought her so deceptive.

"Well, there's no point in going through life thinking you can have everything your own way, is there?" she replied, and started walking down the path.

He caught up with her in a few strides. "Or thinking you can say whatever you like."

Mary-Jayne stopped in her tracks. "Is that a nice way of saying I have a big mouth?"

"Actually," he said as he came to a halt beside her, "you have a very…lovely mouth."

There was something so flagrantly suggestive about his words that heat quickly travelled up her legs, belly and chest and then hit her directly in her cheeks. Memories banged around in her head. Memories of his touch. His kiss. His possession. It was too easy to recall the crazy chemistry they shared and the night they'd spent together.

"I wish you wouldn't…"

Her words trailed off as she met his steely gaze. He had a hypnotic power that was uniquely his and it was something she'd never experienced before. She didn't *like* him. She didn't *want* him in her life. But Daniel had a way of invading her thoughts and plaguing her dreams.

"You wish I wouldn't…what?"

She sucked in a shallow breath and stepped sideways. "Stand so close," she said and crossed her arms.

A grin tugged at his mouth. As if he knew just how profoundly he affected her. And as if it pleased him no end.

"Not everything has to be a battle, Mary-Jayne."

And she wished he'd stop saying her name like that…kind of silky and smooth and sexy and impossible to ignore.

He was wrong. Everything did have to be a battle. It was the only way she'd remain unscathed. "Sure," she said and started walking again.

He stopped to make a phone call and was by the main entrance when he caught up with her. Without saying another word she followed him inside, across the foyer and then toward the elevator. The looks and stares from staff as they passed didn't go unnoticed, and Mary-Jayne suspected she'd quickly be the subject of whispers and conjecture. Since she'd arrived at the resort she'd kept to herself. She hadn't socialized with the staff or other store owners. She managed Audrey's store during the day and worked on her jewelry in the evenings. After Solana's birthday party she'd kept her head down and minded her own business, figuring others would do the same in regard to her. And mostly the staff did. Of course everyone knew about Audrey's disastrous affair with Caleb and speculation was rife that her friend had bailed simply to get away from the resort and him and avoid further humiliation. Only Mary-Jayne knew the truth. Sure, Audrey's mother was unwell…but it *was* exactly the excuse Audrey had needed to salvage her pride and put serious miles between herself and the man who'd hurt her so badly.

Mary-Jayne certainly didn't want to trade one scandal for another.

And she certainly didn't want anyone thinking she was sleeping with the boss!

"Everything all right?"

She glanced sideways and pulled her tote close to her belly. "Peachy."

"Worried what people might think?"

Her mouth tightened. He was too intuitive for her liking. "Couldn't care less."

She stepped into the elevator and he moved in behind her. He stared at her for a second before raising one dark brow. "Perhaps you're not as free-spirited as I thought."

She shrugged. "Maybe not."

The door opened, and Mary-Jayne was about to step out when she realized they weren't on the restaurant level. They were one floor up on the conference suites and boardroom level.

He touched her back and gently urged her forward. "Come on."

"Why are we here? I thought we were—"

"This way," he replied, and kept her moving down the short corridor.

A door opened at the end of the hall and a young man in white chef's gear greeted them. Mary-Jayne had seen him around the resort a few times. Daniel greeted him by name and they were shown directly into a private dining area. It was luxury personified. There were half a dozen tables covered in crisp white linen and the finest dinnerware and crystal. A long panel of windows overlooked the pool area and also offered an incredible view of the ocean.

A waiter emerged from another door and pulled out a seat at a table by the window.

Mary-Jayne rocked back on her heels and looked at Daniel. "Nice view."

"Shall we sit?"

His words were more request than question, and she fought the urge to turn around and leave. Instead she smiled a little and sat down. The waiter offered her some sparkling water, and she gave a grateful nod and only spoke again when the young man and the chef left the room.

She dropped her tote to her feet, stared out the window for a moment before resting her elbows on the table and turning her gaze toward the man sitting opposite. "Clearly I'm not the only one concerned about what people think."

He stilled. "What?"

She waved a hand vaguely. "Up the back elevator and into a secret room?"

"Private," he clarified. "Not secret. I thought you might prefer it. Personally I couldn't care less what people think."

She wondered if that were true. Daniel possessed a kind of confidence she suspected was born from arrogance. He was used to getting his own way. Used to telling people what to do. He called the shots...and she couldn't imagine him tolerating speculation from anyone in his employ.

"Well, they'll be *thinking* plenty once my belly really pops out."

His mouth curled at the edges. "They can think what they like. I should have realized you were pregnant when I first saw you yesterday," he said quietly. "It suits you."

She smirked a little. "Am I glowing?"

He nodded. "Yes."

It was a nice compliment, and her skin warmed. "I'll probably end up the size of a house, though," she said and laughed. "All the women in my family have looked like they've swallowed an elephant when they were pregnant."

His mouth curled at the sides, and it was incredibly sexy. "Tell me about them."

"My family?" She shrugged. "There's not much to tell. We all live in Crystal Point. My parents are both retired. My older brother, Noah, is married to Callie and they have four kids. He builds boats and she's a horse-riding instructor. Then there's my sister Evie, who's an artist and runs a bed-and-breakfast. She's married to Scott—who's actually Callie's brother. He's a firefighter and they have two kids. Then there's Grace, who is married to Noah's best friend Cameron. He's a cop, she's a finance broker and they had their first baby two months ago. And then there's little-old-knocked-up me."

He smiled at her words. "No…not much to tell at all."

Mary-Jayne laughed again. It occurred to her that despite how much he aggravated her, she smiled a lot around Daniel. "They're good people."

"I don't doubt it. I imagine you had a very happy childhood."

"Mostly," she admitted. "Of course it was fraught with the usual teenage-girl angst and rebellion, I suppose. I'm the youngest and therefore it's expected that I would be the most troublesome."

He grinned a little. "What kind of trouble?"

"Oh…crushes on inappropriate boys, late nights, the wrong company…and I got my tattoo at fourteen."

He grimaced. "Brave girl."

"Getting a tattoo? Brave or foolish, you mean, because basically I'm marked for life."

"I mean the pain thing."

"Pain?"

"They use needles…right?"

Mary-Jayne tilted her head. "Well…yes."

"I don't like needles."

She laughed loudly. "Chicken."

"You're mocking me," he said, his mouth twisting a little. "That's something of a habit of yours."

The waiter returned with their drinks and placed a menu on the table. Once the young man left, she returned her attention to Daniel.

"I imagine your ego is healthy enough to take it."

He grinned again. "You're probably right. So…" he said and pushed the glass around the table. "Is there any chance your father is going to come after me with a shotgun?"

She laughed loudly. "Not one. My brother, Noah, on the other hand, is very protective of his sisters." She took a long breath. "Seriously…my family let me live my own life. I'm fully prepared to raise this baby alone, Daniel. Be involved or don't. It's that simple."

His brows rose fractionally. "With me in San Francisco and you in Crystal Point? That's not simple. That's about as complicated as it gets, Mary-Jayne. Because I'm not about to avoid my legal and moral responsibility…no matter how much it seems you would like me to."

She frowned and touched her belly. "If I wanted that I would never have told you I was pregnant. Frankly, I just don't want you to get hung up on what you think you *have* to do. Sure, I'd like my baby to have a father who's involved in his or her life, but I don't want this to turn into some kind of parenting battleground with you on one side and me on the other and our child stuck in the middle."

"Nice speech. Is it meant to put me in my place?"

She shrugged. "Take it how you want. It's all rather moot, anyhow…isn't it? Since you don't actually believe this baby is yours."

His eyes darkened and she was quickly drawn into them. Something passed between them, a kind of relentless energy that warmed her blood.

"It's not that…it's…"

"It's what?" Mary-Jayne asked, and met his gaze and asked the question hovering on her lips. "Is it because of your wife?"

CHAPTER FIVE

DANIEL STILLED. It was the first time the subject had been mentioned since Mary-Jayne had told him she was pregnant. Had he spared Simone more than a fleeting thought in the past twelve hours? The past twenty-four? He'd become so consumed by Mary-Jayne and the idea she was carrying his baby that he could barely think of anything else.

"I gather my grandmother told you what happened?"

She shrugged lightly. "Solana told me she was killed in a car wreck a few years ago."

"Four years," he corrected. "Four years, four months and three weeks."

Her eyes shone. "She was pregnant, wasn't she?"

He nodded slowly as his throat tightened. "Yes. Five months."

"I'm so sorry." Her hand moved across the table and connected with his for a moment before she quickly pulled it back. "It must have been devastating."

"It was the single worst day of my life."

She gathered her hands together in her lap and opened her mouth to speak when the waiter returned. Daniel watched as she studied the menu for a few seconds and then ordered one of the three vegetarian options he'd insisted be included. When she was done he ordered the swordfish, and when the waiter left he grabbed his glass and took a drink.

He put the glass down and spoke. "If you want to ask me about it, go ahead."

Her eyes widened. "You don't mind?"

He shrugged one shoulder.

"How did it happen?"

Daniel closed his eyes for a second as memories banged around in his head. He'd gone over that day countless times in his mind and the pain never lessened. "Simone was driving home from a doctor's appointment and stopped off at the mall to get a birthday gift. She pulled out of the parking lot and into the flow of traffic and a vehicle coming in the opposite direction slammed into her car. The brake line had snapped on the other car and the inexperienced driver panicked, hit the accelerator and crossed over the road."

"Was she killed instantly?"

He shook his head, almost admiring Mary-Jayne's blunt questioning. There was no false pity in her expression. Only curiosity and genuine concern.

"She died in hospital. The doctors tried to save her but her injuries were too severe."

"And the baby?"

"Our daughter died within minutes of Simone passing away."

"That's so sad. Did you have a name picked out for her?"

Daniel pushed down the heat clawing up his throat. "We'd planned on naming her Lana, after my grandmother."

She was quiet for a moment, her gaze lowered, clearly absorbing what he'd said. When she looked up her eyes were bright, almost glistening. He watched as she bit down on her bottom lip as moisture quickly filled her eyes. He'd observed many emotions cross her face in the time they'd known one another—anger, dislike, humor, passion—but this was something else. Sadness. Acute and heartfelt. He didn't like how it made him feel. Dealing with the combative, argumentative Mary-Jayne was easy compared to seeing her in tears.

"I'm sorry," she said, and grabbed the napkin to dab at her eyes. "I didn't mean to…" Her words trailed and she swallowed hard. "It's the baby hormones. They get me at the most unexpected times. Anyway," she said, her voice a little stronger, "thank you for telling me."

"It's not a secret. I'm sure my grandmother or Caleb would have told you the same thing had you asked them. It was an accident…and like all accidents, it was simply a series of events that merged into one terrible outcome."

She looked at him with silent intensity. "You mean, if she'd lingered at the mall a little longer, or if she had taken another exit from the parking lot, or the other driver had gotten out of bed ten minutes later that morning things would have turned out differently?"

"Exactly."

"You said she was buying a birthday gift. Who was it for?"

Daniel hesitated for a moment. "My grandmother."

It took a moment, but her eyes widened as realization dawned. "So…that night…the night of Solana's birthday party…it was the…the…"

"The anniversary of their deaths? Yes, it was."

The waiter returned with their meals before she had a chance to respond, and Daniel watched with keen interest as she took a long breath and stared into her plate. Once the waiter left them she looked up.

"Is that why you…why you…"

"Why I what?" he asked.

"The party, you know…and how we…" Her words trailed and she shrugged lightly.

"We had sex, you mean?"

Sex. He wasn't going to call it anything else. He wasn't going to suggest they'd made love because it would have been a lie. He used to make love to his wife. There was love and heart and passion between them. They'd been friends since college and started dating when Simone had finished law school. What he felt for Mary-Jayne wasn't grounded in that kind of friendship or any measure of deep emotion. It was base and instinctual and fuelled by attraction and sexual desire. And he intended for it to stay that way. She might be under his skin, but he wasn't about to let her get into his heart.

"I thought there might be a connection," she said and arched one brow. "Like you were wanting...to forget about..."

"I could never forget my wife," he said quietly.

She flinched a little. "I didn't mean that. I was thinking perhaps you needed a distraction that night and that's why you were interested in me."

"I was *interested* in you from the moment I saw you in the store window."

He knew she wouldn't be surprised by his admission. There had been heat between them from that first glance. Daniel wasn't conceited, but he knew the attraction he felt for Mary-Jayne was very much reciprocated.

"Oh...okay."

"The fact it was my grandmother's birthday was a coincidence," he said, stretching the truth to avoid her questions or her censure. He wasn't about to admit that the hollow feeling that had haunted him since Simone's death had been amplified that night. Or that for a few incredible hours he'd found solace in the arms of a woman he barely knew. "So have you been well other than the nausea?" he asked, shifting the subject.

"Mostly," she replied. "Both my sisters suffered from gestational diabetes when they were pregnant, so my doctor is keeping watch on my sugar levels. But I feel fine at the moment."

Concern tightened his chest. "Does that mean this pregnancy holds risks for you? Is there something we should talk to your doctor about? Perhaps a second opinion is needed to ensure you get the best possible care. I can arrange an appointment with a specialist if—"

"I'm fine," she said sharply, interrupting him as she picked up the cutlery. "The nausea and appetite issues are a normal part of being pregnant. And I like my current doctor just fine, thank you. Stop interfering."

He bit back a grin at her impatience. "Don't mistake concern for control, Mary-Jayne."

She flashed him an annoyed look. "I don't."

"Oh, I think you do. I think you're so desperate to stay in control here that anything I say will be like waving a red flag at a bull."

She looked as if she wanted to jab him in the forehead with her fork. "You really do love to hear the sound of your own voice."

He laughed. "Hit a nerve, did I?"

"By implying that I value my independence?" she shot back. "Not a nerve...a fact. I'm not about to be lorded over like some spineless minion."

"That's a favorite insult of yours," he said and watched her. "Despite what you've conjured in your colorful imagination, I don't live in a house filled with servants. I cook my own meals, launder my own clothes and even tie my own shoes."

Her green eyes flashed. "Doesn't stop you from being a con-descending horse's ass, does it?"

He laughed again. They had a way of pushing each other's buttons, and watching her fiery expression quickly stirred his blood and libido. "We have five months to get through until the baby comes, and I'd prefer it if we could manage that time with-out constantly goading one another, wouldn't you?"

She shrugged as if she couldn't have cared less. But Daniel wasn't fooled. She was as wound up as he was. "Since you'll be in San Francisco and I'll be in Crystal Point, what differ-ence does it make?"

An ocean. Thousands of miles. A different life. There would be so many things between them. Between him and the child she carried. The child she said was his. Most of the shock had worn off overnight. Sure, he wanted a paternity test, but there were months ahead where he either had to accept the child was his, or not. And, despite everything between them, he realized that he believed Mary-Jayne. His grandmother knew her, trusted her…and although some old cynical instincts banged around in his head, Daniel realized he trusted her, too.

"You could come to San Francisco."

She looked up and made a scoffing sound. "Yeah…right."

Maybe not. "What about here?"

Her gaze sharpened. "Here? At the resort?"

"Yes."

"I can't do that, either," she said, and put down her fork.

"Why not?" he shot back. "Your jewelry business is mostly done online, so you could do that anywhere… San Francisco or here."

"This isn't my home, that's why not. I live in Crystal Point… I've lived there all my life. It's where I was born and it's where my baby will be born."

"Our baby."

Her jaw dropped slightly. "You believe me?"

He took a breath and nodded. "I believe you."

She looked wary. "Why the sudden change of heart?"

"Because *not* believing you essentially means I forfeit any rights to be part of this experience."

Mary-Jayne stilled. Rights? What did he mean by that? He wanted rights? He believed her? It should have put her at ease. Instead her entire body was suddenly on red alert. What had she expected? That once she told him about her pregnancy then he would quietly go away and leave her to raise her child alone?

Naive idiot.

The urge to get up and leave suddenly overwhelmed her, and it took all her strength to remain in her seat. She slowly met his unwavering gaze. "I'll be leaving in less than two weeks," she said. "As soon as Audrey returns I'm going home. My home," she reiterated. "Where I belong."

"Then I'll go with you," he said, so casually that her blood simmered. "We need to tell your folks, anyhow."

"*I'll* tell *my* family when *I* choose," she said, and pushed back her chair a fraction. "Stop bossing me about."

"Stop acting like a child."

It was the kind of verbal gridlock she expected when she was near him. They didn't like one another. They never would. They had sexual chemistry and nothing more. Fatigue and a sudden surge of queasiness shortened her patience and she pushed the seat back.

"Thanks for lunch," she said, and stood. "I'll see my own way out."

"My case in point," he said as he got up. "Run when you don't like what you hear. That's a child's way out, Mary-Jayne."

Her rage sought release. "Go to hell."

His mouth quirked fractionally. "I'll see you Tuesday morning, at nine, for the ultrasound appointment."

"I'd rather—"

"At nine," he insisted, cutting her off.

She didn't respond. Instead she grabbed her tote, thrust back her shoulders and left the room with a pounding heart, more determined than ever to keep him at arm's length.

Back in her condo she calmed down a little, took a shower and called Audrey. Her friend didn't answer her phone so she left a brief message. She spent the remainder of the day staring at her phone, hoping Audrey would call and watching an old movie on the television. By the time she dropped into bed her head was thumping and her rage was festering.

How dare he call her childish? He was an arrogant, pompous jerk! The sooner she was away from him, the better.

On Monday Mary-Jayne lay low. She opened the store and kept away from the front window as much as possible, in case *he* walked by. Or watched her. Or stalked her. But thankfully he didn't show up at the store and didn't call. And since Caleb didn't do his usual midmorning drop in either, Mary-Jayne knew Daniel had told his brother to steer clear.

Puppet master...

Controlling everything and everyone around him.

It made her mad, and got her blood boiling.

On Tuesday morning she set her alarm an hour early, showered and forced herself to eat breakfast. She dressed in a knee-length button-up blue floral dress and tied her hair up in a ponytail. Then she waited on the sofa for him to arrive, hands clasped together. He tapped on the door at nine o'clock with his usual annoying promptness.

He looked so good in jeans and a collared black T-shirt she could barely croak out a greeting when her level gaze met the broad expanse of his chest. She stupidly wished she were taller, more slender, more elegant...and able to meet his eyes without having to look up.

"Good morning."

Mary-Jayne forced out a smile. "Are you always on time for everything?"

"Always."

"It's an annoying trait of yours."

He grinned and motioned for her to pass. Once he pulled the door shut he placed a hand into the small of her back and ushered her forward. "Well, I guess it's one of those things you'll have to get used to."

Not when there's an ocean between us I won't...

By the time they were in his car she was so worked up her teeth chattered. He asked for the address and she replied quietly, staying silent as he punched the information into his GPS. Once they were on their way she dropped her tote to her feet and stared out the side window. But his nearness still rattled her. He was so close and had a kind of hypnotic power she'd never experienced before. Any man she'd ever known paled beside him. Any attraction she'd had in the past seemed luke-warm compared to the heat that simmered between them. The arguments didn't mask anything. It only amplified the under-current of desire and made her remember the passion and plea-sure they'd shared that night four months ago.

She turned her head to glance at his profile. "Have you ever done that before?"

"Done what?"

"Sleep with someone you hardly know."

His mouth curved, but he looked straight ahead. "I don't re-call either of us getting a whole lot of sleep that night."

Her cheeks heated. "You know what I mean." She swallowed hard. "I… It's just that I… Despite how I *seem*… I'm not like that…usually."

"Usually?"

She let out a heavy breath. "I don't sleep around…okay. I might come across as free-spirited and all that…but when it comes to sex I'm not easy. I've had three serious relationships including my high school boyfriend and I've never had a one-night stand before."

"Are you asking how many relationships I've had? Or one-night stands?" He glanced at her for a moment. "Does it really matter?"

His reticence irritated her and she frowned. "Is the subject off-limits for some reason?"

His jaw tightened. "My wife died over four years ago. Have I remained celibate since then? No. Have I had a committed relationship since then? No. Is that enough of an answer, Mary-Jayne?"

She got the message. She was one in a long line of meaning-less one-night stands.

Just as well she didn't like him in the least, or she might have been offended by his admission. "I don't have any kind of ul-terior motive for asking," she said and stared directly ahead. "I was curious, that's all."

"Well, if your curiosity has you imagining I have a different woman in my bed every night, you'll be disappointed."

She didn't want to think about any woman in his bed, different or otherwise. "I'd have to care to feel disappointment, wouldn't I?"

"I guess you would," he said quietly. "But in case you've been having sleepless nights over it—my bed has been empty since you left it so quickly in the small hours of the morning all those months ago."

It was a dig. She'd snuck out of his villa, all right, and he clearly didn't appreciate her efforts to avoid any uncomfortable morning-after postmortems. Obviously he'd been stung by her disappearing act. And it took her a moment to realize what he'd said about his empty bed.

"No one since? Have you already nailed every woman in San Francisco? Is that the problem?"

He laughed humorlessly. "You're the problem."

"Me?" She almost squeaked the word out. "I can't imagine why."

"One night didn't really do us justice, did it? Not with that kind of instant attraction."

She knew what he meant. The store window. The resort foyer. The beach. Solana's party. Every time they'd met the heat had ramped up a notch. Until it had become so explosive the outcome was unavoidable.

"So you want…you still want…"

He chuckled. "You know, you really are a fascinating contradiction. For such a *free-spirited* woman, you can be equally shy and self-conscious."

"Because I think sex should mean something? Because I think one-night stands are empty and pointless and of little importance?"

His profile was unmoving. "Since our night together resulted in this pregnancy, I'd say it's about as important as it gets, wouldn't you?"

She frowned. "You're twisting my words. I meant the sex wasn't important…not the baby."

There was insult in her words, and she was surprised that he stayed silent.

Silent and seething.

He was mad. Perhaps his ego wasn't as rock solid as she thought?

"That's not a complaint, by the way," she said, and pushed the tote around with her feet. "The sex was very…nice."

"It wasn't *nice*, Mary-Jayne. It was hot and incredibly erotic and about as good as it gets."

He was right. They both knew it.

"That, too," she admitted. "And the reason I left," she said, and figured she may as well tell him the truth, "is I didn't want any morning-after awkwardness. I thought it would be easier to bail and forget the whole thing. I mean, it was never going to be any more than one night. I think we both knew that."

"If I believed that I wouldn't have repeatedly asked you out."

It was true. He *had* pursued her. And she'd refused him every time. Because they were too different. As clichéd as oil and water. He wanted her in his bed and he got what he wanted. Only a fool would imagine he was looking for anything more.

"To get me into bed again, right? Which means we would have been back to square one. The point I'm making is men and women generally think about sex differently. I'm not saying I'm after a picket fence quite yet, but I'm not foolish enough to waste time on something or someone where it wouldn't be on the table ever."

"That's quite a judgment."

"Can you deny it?" she asked. "Let's face it, Daniel, you and I are polar opposites in every way. Sure, we have chemistry, but that's all. Most of the time we barely seem to tolerate one another. That's not a recipe for romance. It's a recipe for disaster."

She turned back to look out the side window with a heavy sigh, and they didn't say another word to one another until they'd reached Cairns. With a population of over one hundred thousand, the bustling regional city was a popular tourist spot and served as a starting point for people wanting to visit the Great Barrier Reef.

Within minutes they were pulling into the car park in front of the medical center. She got out of the Jeep, grabbed her tote and waited for him to come around to the passenger side.

"If you like, we can look around town when we're done," he suggested and locked the vehicle. "Maybe have lunch."

"The way you keep trying to feed me, anyone would think I need fattening up."

His brows narrowed. "Well, I have noticed you don't eat enough."

Mary-Jayne put her hands on her thickening waist. "I eat plenty. Have you seen my ever-expanding middle? I told you how the women in my family look when they're pregnant."

"You hardly touched your food the other day."

Mary-Jayne looked up at him. "I was too mad to eat."

"Too hot headed, you mean."

"You were being a bossy, arrogant jerk. It annoyed me."

"Everything I do appears to annoy you," he said and ushered her toward the steps that led into the building. "Perhaps you should consider why that is."

"I know why," she said, and moved up the steps. "Because you're a bossy, arrogant jerk."

He laughed softly and grasped her hand, stopping her before they reached the door. Mary-Jayne looked up and met his gaze. His gray eyes were dark and intense, and for a second she couldn't do anything but stare at him. The pulse in his cheek throbbed and she fought the urge to touch the spot.

He threaded their fingers and drew her closer. "How about you let me off the hook for a little while, hmm?"

Don't do it...

"I can't..."

"Sure you can," he said, and rubbed his thumb inside her

palm. "I'm not your enemy, Mary-Jayne…except perhaps in your lively imagination."

"Daniel…"

"Come on," he said, and gently led her inside. "Let's go and meet this baby."

It took about twenty minutes to find the correct office, see reception and be shown to a small room when she was instructed to lie on the bed and wait for the doctor. A nurse appeared and wheeled the imaging machine close to the bed and told them the doctor would be in soon.

"Are you okay?" he asked from the chair he sat on from across the room.

Mary-Jayne lay back on the table and wiggled. "Fine. Peachy. Never better."

"You look nervous."

She shrugged. "Well, I've never done this before, so of course I'm a little nervous."

As she said the words it occurred to her that Daniel probably *had* done this before. With Simone. With the wife he'd loved and the baby they'd lost. It must have been hard for him to come into the room with her, a woman he hardly knew, and potentially have the same experience he'd shared with his wife.

Shame hit her square between the shoulders.

All morning she'd been thinking of herself and hadn't spared a thought for his feelings. *What's happened to me? When did I become so self-absorbed?*

"I'm sorry."

He looked at her. "For what?"

"For not considering how difficult it must be for you to do this."

His gaze didn't waver. "It's not difficult. Just…different. Simone and I had planned everything, from conception to her due date. She'd had endometriosis for several years and had trouble getting pregnant. Eventually we used IVF and she got pregnant after three attempts. It was all rather clinical and organized and

more about the treatments and processes rather than the baby...
at least in the beginning. So, yes, this is different."

There was heat in her throat. "Okay," she said, and smiled a
little. "You're off the hook."

The doctor came into the room then and Daniel got to his
feet. Mary-Jayne lay back and tried to relax. He moved beside
her and touched her shoulder.

"So," Doctor Stewart said once she'd introduced herself and
perched on a stool at the side of the bed. "Would you like to
know your baby's sex?"

Mary-Jayne looked at Daniel.

He shrugged lightly. "It's up to you."

She swallowed hard. "I think... Yes... I'd like to know."

She glanced at him again and thought he looked relieved.

The doctor got her to unbutton her dress, and Mary-Jayne
tried not to be self-conscious of Daniel's presence in the chair
at her side as her belly was bared. A cool gel was placed on her
stomach and she shivered a little. Daniel took hold of her hand
and squeezed gently.

Once the ultrasound started she was riveted to the image on
the small screen. It didn't look like anything at first, until the
doctor pointed out an arm and the baby's head. Emotion welled
inside her and she bit back a sob.

*Hi there, peanut... I'm your mother...and I love you more
than I thought possible.*

"And there's your baby," the doctor said, and rolled the de-
vice lower. "You have a perfectly lovely boy."

She looked at Daniel and noticed he stared directly at the
screen, clearly absorbed by what they saw. He'd never looked
more attractive to her, and in that moment an unexpected surge
of longing rushed through her entire body.

Longing and desire and something else...something she
couldn't quite fathom.

Something she didn't want to think about.

"Oh..."

The doctor's voice quickly cut through her thoughts.

"What is it?"

Daniel's voice now. Deep and smooth and quicker than usual. It gave her comfort. If something was wrong, he was there, holding her hand, giving her strength. He glanced at her and squeezed her fingers.

Doctor Stewart looked at them both. "Well... I see."

"What?" he asked again, firmer this time. "Is something wrong?" It was the question she was too afraid to ask.

"Nothing's wrong," the doctor said, and smiled broadly. "It's just...there are two of them."

Mary-Jayne stared at the screen. "What do you mean?"

The doctor smiled. "Congratulations to you both...you're having twin boys."

CHAPTER SIX

SOMEONE COULD HAVE told him that he was going to live on the moon for the next fifty years and he wouldn't have been more shocked.

Twin boys...

"You're sure?" he asked the doctor, and noticed how Mary-Jayne hadn't moved. He squeezed her hand reassuringly. "And they're fine?"

The doctor nodded. "Fine. Big, strong and healthy. Would you like to listen to their heartbeats?"

Daniel didn't recall saying yes. But within seconds he had small earphones on and heard the incredible sound of his sons' hearts. Emotion rose up and hit him directly in the solar plexus, polarizing him for a moment. He swallowed hard, fighting the heat in his eyes and throat. Nothing he ever heard again would match the sound of the two tiny heartbeats pounding almost in unison. Longing, absolute and raw, filled his chest with such force he grabbed the side of the chair for support.

The doctor said something about having a picture done for them, but he barely heard. He took off the earphones and gently placed them over Mary-Jayne's head. Watching her expression shift from shock to wonderment was incredible. Her face radiated with a joy so acute it was blinding in its intensity. She'd never looked more beautiful.

The doctor stood. "I'll arrange for a picture and come back in a little while," she said, and quickly left the room.

Daniel tightened his grip on Mary-Jayne's hand. "Are you okay?"

She dropped the earphones onto the bed. "Um… I think so."

"Not what you were expecting, huh?"

She sighed. "Not exactly. But…" Her words trailed off for a moment. "I'm happy." She glanced at the now-blank screen. "I can't quite believe it."

"Are there many twins in your family?" he asked, and rubbed her fingertips. She shrugged. "Not really. I know there are in yours, though."

He nodded and grinned. "Yes. My brothers are twins. My grandfather was a twin, and I have two sets of cousins who are twins. It's like an epidemic in my family."

"This is all your doing, then?" she said and smiled.

"I don't think there's actually a genetic link on the father's side, but I'll happily take the credit if you want," he said softly. "Are you okay with this?"

"I'm happy, like I said. And a little scared. I wasn't expecting two." She looked down at her naked stomach. "I wonder if the nurse will come back to get this goo off my belly."

Daniel released her hand and got up. He found a box of tissues on the counter and came back to her side. "This should do it," he said as he sat down and began wiping the gel off her skin.

It was the most intimate thing they'd done in months, and even though he acted as perfunctory as he could, it didn't stop a surge of desire from climbing up his spine. She lay still, perfectly composed. Until he met her gaze and saw that she was watching him with scorching intensity. When he was done her hand came up and she grabbed his fingertips and then gently laid his palm against her belly. She placed her hand on top of his, connecting them in a way that was mesmerizing. Feeling her, feeling their babies, Daniel had no answer for the sensation banging around in his head.

He'd never wanted to feel this again. Not after Simone.

But it was inevitable. They were his children. His sons. They were part of him. How could he not get drawn into feeling such acute and blinding love for them? He couldn't. And he wanted them. He wanted to be part of their lives. Full-time. A real parent.

A real father.

He looked at Mary-Jayne. Her eyes were bright. Luminous. She chewed on her bottom lip and his gaze immediately went to her mouth. He touched her forehead with his other hand and felt the connection down deep. Soul-deep.

In that moment he could nothing else but kiss her.

And her lips, as new as they were familiar, softened beneath his instantly. Daniel's pulse quickened as the kiss quickly deepened. Her breath was warm, her tongue accepting when he sought it with his own. She sighed deep in her throat, and a powerful surge of desire wound through his blood. He touched her hair, twirling the glorious strands between his fingertips. Her hand came up to his chest and he felt the connection through to his bones. And he kissed her again. And again. With each kiss his need for her grew. As did the knowledge he had one option. One way to make things right.

"Mary-Jayne," he said against her lips, trailing his mouth down her cheek to the sensitive spot by her earlobe. A spot he knew made her quiver. "We should get married."

She stilled instantly. Her mouth drew in a tight line and she pushed his hand off her belly. "What?"

Daniel pulled back and stared into her face. "Married," he said again. "We should get married."

She put a hand on his shoulder and gave him a shove. "Don't be ridiculous."

He straightened and got to his feet. "It's the only solution."

"To what?" she said, and pulled her dress closed over her

stomach as she swung her legs off the bed. "Since there's no problem, we don't need a solution." She swiftly buttoned up her dress.

He crossed his arms. "There *is* a problem. We're having two children together and we live on opposite sides of the world."

"I said you can see the baby... I mean, babies, as much as you want. But I'm not interested in a loveless marriage, Daniel. Not with you or anyone else."

The doctor returned before he had an opportunity to say anything more. She gave them the photo of the twins and advised Mary-Jayne to make another appointment with her obstetrician in the next few weeks. Daniel listened while she briefly explained how she was returning home to Crystal Point in the next fortnight and how she would see her family doctor once she was back home.

Home...

He almost envied the way she spoke about the tiny town where she'd lived all her life. Nowhere felt like home to Daniel. Not Port Douglas. Not San Francisco.

They left a few minutes later and Mary-Jayne didn't say a word as they made their way out of the building toward their vehicle.

"Are you hungry?" he asked as he opened the passenger door. "We could stop somewhere for—"

"I'd prefer to just go back to the resort," she said, cutting him off. "I'm a little tired."

Daniel didn't argue. He nodded and closed the door once she was inside. They were soon back on the road, and he made a quick stop to refuel and grab a couple of bottles of water. She took the water with a nod and tucked it by the seat. Fifteen minutes into their return trip he'd had enough of her unusual silence and spoke.

"Avoiding the subject isn't going to make it go away, Mary-Jayne."

"What subject?"

"My proposal."

She glanced sideways. "I thought you must have been joking."

"I'm perfectly serious. Once you calm down you'll realize it's the only thing we can do."

She huffed. "I'm perfectly calm. And marrying you is the *last* thing I want to do."

"Why not?" he asked, ignoring how much disdain she had in her voice.

"Because I'm not in the market for someone like you."

"Like me?" He smiled at her relentless insults. "Straight, healthy and financially secure?"

"Arrogant, judgmental and a pain in the—"

"Don't you think our children deserve two parents?"

"Our children *will* have two parents," she said, her knuckles white where she clasped her hands together. "Two parents who live in different countries. Two parents who have too much good sense to marry because it's expected they should." She turned her head. "Be honest, Daniel. You don't want to marry me, you just think you *have* to. But you don't. You're off the hook here. So please, don't mention it again."

He pushed down his irritation. She wound him up like no one else ever had. "I take it you're not opposed to marriage entirely…just marriage to me?"

"I'm opposed to marrying someone I don't love," she said bluntly. "And someone who doesn't love me. The thing is, I believe in love…and I want it. I want to be with someone who wants *me* above all others. Who wants only me and sees only me and who carries only me close to his heart."

It was foolish and romantic nonsense. "How can that matter when there are children involved?"

"Because it does," she insisted. "You've had some attack of conscience since you saw them on that screen and think marriage will somehow uncomplicate this…but it won't. We're too different to be tied to one another for life. And I'm not criticizing your motives, I'm simply trying to do what's best for everyone involved…including you."

Daniel wasn't convinced. His father and stepmother had married because Bernie was pregnant, and their marriage had turned out fine. They'd scraped a family together despite their differences. And if he was going to have any chance of being a hands-on father to his sons, Daniel knew he had to do the same.

But he knew Mary-Jayne well enough to recognize she wasn't prepared to discuss it any further. At least for now.

"We'll talk about it later."

"No, we won't," she reaffirmed. "And what was with that kiss?"

"It was a kiss. People kiss, Mary-Jayne."

She pointed to him and then herself. "Well, not *these* people. Don't do it again."

Had he lost his mind?

Marriage? As if she'd ever agree to that? Couldn't he see it was madness? He'd married for love once…how could he be prepared to settle for anything less? He could still be a father to their children. Sure, it would be challenging, considering the miles between them. But they could make it work. Plenty of people did the same. He was simply being bullheaded about it. Wanting his own way. Trying to control her.

Well, she wasn't about to be maneuvered into a loveless marriage.

She didn't care how much chemistry they had.

And he better not try to kiss her again, either!

"I'd like to stop and see my parents and tell them the news, if that's okay with you?"

Mary-Jayne turned her head. "Sure. Whatever."

It was a small detour, but she didn't mind. She liked Miles and figured they had to start telling people about the babies at some point. It took about half an hour to reach their small hobby farm, and Mary-Jayne sat up straight as he turned off into a narrow driveway and drove half a mile down the bumpy road until they reached the house. She saw the lovely timber home with wide verandas and noticed a small structure built in replica.

"My dad's studio," Daniel explained.

She turned her head. He watched her with such intensity for a moment her breath stuck in her throat. There was something riveting about his gaze, and she turned hot all over. She foolishly thought about the kiss again. It had been sweet and hot and had stirred her libido.

People kiss...

His words fluttered around in her head. Of course she knew it had been a spur-of-the-moment thing—they were looking at their babies for the first time, he'd helped remove the gel from her belly... No wonder she'd kissed him back so eagerly. She was only human. But he had an agenda. He'd decided what he wanted and would use whatever method he could to achieve that goal—which included seducing her!

She stared at him. "Please, Daniel...don't..."

"Don't what?" A smile creased the corners of his mouth. "What have I done now?"

"You know what," she said, pretty sure she sounded like a petulant child but not caring. "You kissed me."

"You kissed me back."

Color spotted her cheeks. "Well, I'm not going to be swept up in a whole lot of sex stuff...if that's what you're thinking."

He laughed as though he thought her hilarious. "I guess time will tell."

She seethed. "Just because you got me into bed once doesn't mean you will again. That night was out of character for me. I don't even *like* you."

Daniel sat back and turned the engine off. "Is this your usual mode of defense, Mary-Jayne? Attack first?"

She made a scoffing sound. "That's rich, coming from you. You're the corporate shark, not me."

"What is it exactly that you think I do for a living—steamroll over whoever gets in my way? I hate to disappoint you, but I'm not that mercenary. I'm the CEO of a large business that employs several thousand people around the globe. I'm not sure what it is you find so disagreeable about that or me."

"Everything," she replied. "Your arrogance for one…like right now when you think I'm loopy because I dare to admit that I don't like you."

"I think you're scared," he said quietly. "Not loopy. And I think your emotions are heightened because you're pregnant."

Logically, she knew he was right. But he wound her up in a way that fueled every rebellious streak she possessed. And she was fairly certain he knew it.

"It's not baby brain," she shot back. "This is *me*. Emotional and loopy."

He made an exasperated sound. "Can we put a hold on this conversation? My dad is on his way over."

Sure enough, Miles Anderson was walking toward them from his studio, one strap of his shabby overalls flapping in the breeze. At sixty, he was still handsome and fit, and Mary-Jayne got a snapshot of what Daniel would be like in thirty years. The notion made her insides flutter. *Stupid*. She had to concentrate on now, not some time in the unknown future.

Daniel got out of the vehicle and Mary-Jayne remained where she was for the moment, watching as the two men greeted one another and shook hands. No embrace. No obvious display of affection. It saddened her a little. Would Daniel be like that with his own sons? He spoke to his father for a moment and then turned back toward the Jeep. Mary-Jayne was half out by the time he met her at the door. Miles wasn't far behind, and he watched as his son helped her out of the car.

"Lovely to see you again M.J.," Miles said cheerfully.

"Mary-Jayne," Daniel corrected, as though his father had committed the crime of the century.

She grabbed her tote and looked up at him. "No one really

calls me that," she said quietly as he closed the door. "Except my folks…and you."

His mouth twitched. "It's your name."

"It's an old-fashioned mouthful."

"I think it's very pretty," Miles said, and took her arm. "Let's get up to the house. Bernie will be delighted you're here."

She could feel Daniel behind her as they walked toward the house. Mary-Jayne made a comment about how lovely the gardens were and Miles began chatting about the vegetable patch, the chickens and the new milking goat he'd recently bought who kept getting into the yard and eating the zucchini flowers.

Once they reached the veranda Miles spoke again. "My wife has a client in half an hour, but we have time for coffee and some of her pecan cookies."

Mary-Jayne noticed a door to the left of the main door and the shingle that hung to one side—Homeopath, Masseuse and Acupuncturist. Daniel's stepmother came through the open doorway, wearing a blue-and-gold tunic over white trousers, her blond hair flowing. She rushed toward him with a happy squeal and gave him a long hug.

"I'm so glad to see you," she said, all breathless energy, as they pulled apart. "Your brother told us you were back. Four months in between visits is too long."

He is loved.

It was all Mary-Jayne could think of. And then she realized how lucky her babies would be to have two such lovely people as grandparents. Her hand moved instinctively to her belly, and she noticed how Bernie's gaze immediately shifted toward the movement. She looked as though she was about to say something when Daniel stepped back and introduced them.

"It's lovely to meet you," Bernie said, smiling broadly. "Solana has told me all about you, of course. You've made quite an impression on my mother-in-law, and she's the best judge of character I know."

Mary-Jayne returned the smile. "Thank you."

Bernie tapped her husband's shoulder. "Why don't you take Daniel to the studio and show him the piece you're working on for the Phuket renovation, and Mary-Jayne and I will make coffee," she suggested, and then looked back toward Mary-Jayne. "My talented husband is sculpting an incredible bronze for the resort's foyer," she explained animatedly. "It's a dolphin pod diving through a wave." She sighed and smiled. "Just breathtaking."

Mary-Jayne grinned at the other woman's enthusiasm. She liked her immensely. "How lovely," she said, and noticed Miles looked faintly embarrassed by the praise. Daniel stood beside her, unmoving. She tapped his shoulder lightly, trying not to think about how her fingertips tingled at the connection. "You go, I'll be fine."

"Of course she will be," Bernie said, and linked their arms.

They headed inside and into the huge red cedar kitchen in the center of the house. Mary-Jayne noticed the dream catchers in nearly every window and smiled. A large pebbled water feature took up almost an entire wall, and the sound of the water slipping gently over the rocks created a charming ambience and feeling throughout the house.

"You have a lovely home," she said and perched onto a stool behind the wide kitchen counter.

"Thank you. We've been here for nearly ten years. We wanted somewhere where Miles could work without disturbing the neighbors," she said and grinned as she fiddled with the coffee machine. "Sometimes the soldering and battering goes on for hours. But we love it here and we wanted a place where our boys could call home. You know, for when they get married and have families of their own."

The innuendo wasn't missed and she dropped her gaze, took a breath and then met the other woman's inquisitive look head-on. "Yes, I'm pregnant. And yes, Daniel is the father. And we just learned we're having twin boys."

Bernie's beaming smile was infectious, and she came around

the counter and hugged her close for a few seconds. "I'm so delighted. He deserves some happiness in his life after what he's been through."

Mary-Jayne was pretty sure Daniel wouldn't consider her a tonic for unhappiness.

"He loved his wife a lot, didn't he?" she asked quietly when the other woman moved back around the bench.

Bernie shrugged a little. "Simone? Well, she was easy to love. She was a nice woman, very kind and good-hearted. She was a lawyer, you know, very successful one, too, from all accounts."

As the other woman made coffee for the men and tea for them, Mary-Jayne fiddled with the silver ring on her right hand. She wasn't sure how she felt knowing Daniel had loved his wife so much. Not jealous—that would be plain stupid. Because it would mean she had feelings invested in him. Which she didn't. But displaced. As though she didn't quite belong. She wasn't someone whom Daniel would *choose* to bring home to meet his parents. Or choose to marry. She was there because she was carrying his babies. If she hadn't gotten pregnant that night they spent together then they probably would never have seen one another again.

"I'm sure she was lovely," she said and smiled.

"Daniel doesn't talk much about her," Bernie remarked, and grabbed four mugs. "He's always been a little closed off from his feelings. When Simone and their unborn baby died he kind of turned inward. The only person he really opens up to is Solana—they're very close. He never knew his real mother," she said and sighed. "I've always treated him like my own, of course. He was just a toddler when the twins were born. But I think losing his mother had a profound impact on him. And Miles grieved for a long time," she said candidly. "Even after we married and had our sons he was still mourning her death. I tried not to take it personally. I still don't on those times when he mentions her."

Mary-Jayne didn't miss the message in the other woman's

words. But the situations weren't the same. She was sure Miles Anderson loved Bernadette, even if he had still grieved the wife he lost. Whereas Daniel didn't even *like* her. He might want her in his bed, but that was all it was.

"Thanks for the talk," Mary-Jayne said and smiled. "And the support."

"Anytime," Bernie said just as the men walked in through the back door.

Mary-Jayne swiveled on the stool and looked at Daniel. "How's the sculpture look?"

"Good."

Miles clapped a hand onto his son's shoulder. "Why don't you take her to the studio and show her?" he suggested, then winked at Mary-Jayne. "I should've guessed a brilliantly creative girl like you might want to critique my work. Go easy on this old man, though. My fragile artistic ego can't take too much criticism."

Mary-Jayne laughed. She genuinely liked Miles and understood his self-effacing humor. "Of course," she said and slid off the stool.

Daniel watched the interaction in silence and only moved when she took a few steps toward the door. "Coming?" she asked.

She was through the door and down the back steps quickly and didn't wait for him to catch up as she headed across the yard toward the studio. She was already inside and staring at the huge bronze sculpture when he came up behind her.

"Wow," she said as she stepped around the piece and admired the effort and imagination that had gone into its creation. "This is incredible."

Daniel came beside her. "He'll be delighted you approve."

She looked up and raised a brow. "I suppose you told him, then."

"About the babies?" He nodded. "Yes. He's delighted about

that, too. Told me it was about time I settled down and raised a family."

"I hope you set him straight?"

"You mean did I tell him you've turned down my proposal? No, I thought I'd try my luck again before I admitted that."

Mary-Jayne offered a wry smile. "One marriage proposal in a day is enough, thanks very much."

"Even if I get down on my knee this time?" he asked, his eyes glittering. "Or get you a ring?"

"You're too uptight to get your kneecap dirty," she shot back, saccharine sweet. "And I want to design my own ring when I *eventually* get married."

He laughed, and she liked the sound way too much. "So, how'd Bernie take the news?"

"Very well. Tell me something, why do you call her Bernie? She's the only mother you've known, right?"

"I call her Mom sometimes," he said, looking just a little uncomfortable. "And stop cross-examining me."

"Gotta take the chance when I can. They're very nice," she said and moved around the sculpture some more. "And they love you."

"I know that," he said, and came closer again. "We just live different lives."

"But you had a happy childhood?"

He shrugged loosely. "I guess. Although there were times when I wished they'd stop moving the furniture around the house to accommodate their feng shui beliefs or eat a steak and fries instead of tofu burgers. Or have an aspirin for a headache instead of Bernie's acupuncture jabs to the temple."

Mary-Jayne stilled and looked up at him. "Is that why you don't like needles?"

"Well, I—"

She was mortified when she realized what it meant. "They stuck needles into their child?"

"They thought they were doing the right thing," he said and moved around behind her.

She turned to face him and looked up. "But that's why you don't like needles?"

"I guess," he said and shrugged again. "Seems foolish to make that kind of connection, though. It was a long time ago and it wasn't as if it was some kind of deliberate torture. Bernie's well qualified in her field and she thought she was helping. They were good parents."

"I know. And we'll be good, too," she assured him. "We've had good role models."

"Good parents who live in two different countries?" He reached out and touched a lock of her hair, twirling it between his fingertips. "I want to be their father, Mary-Jayne. All I'm asking for is a chance to do that."

Her heart tugged, and she pushed back a sudden swell of emotion "I can't. It wouldn't work," she implored. "Look, I'm not saying it's going to be easy doing this with the situation being what it is. We both know there will be challenges, especially as the children get older. But I can't and won't commit to a loveless marriage. I want what my parents have, and I want to raise my children in the town I've lived in all my life." She moved back fractionally and his hand dropped. "And I know you think that's all a load of overly romantic hogwash, but I can't change who I am and what I believe any more than you can. I've never really been in love. But I want to be."

"Yeah," he said, and shook his head. "And you want some romantic sap to carry you next to his heart… I heard all that the other day."

"But did you listen? Love isn't an illusion, Daniel. You loved your wife, right? Bernie said she was smart and beautiful and how everyone adored her. So if love was good enough for you back then, why do you think I'm so foolish for wanting the same thing?"

"Because it doesn't last."

"It does," she refuted. "Our parents are testament to that."

"So maybe sometimes it does last. But when it doesn't…
When it's gone it's about as bad as it gets."

There was real pain in his voice, and she unconsciously
reached out and grasped his upper arm. The muscles were tight
and bunched with tension, and she met his gaze head on.

"You're still hurting," she whispered, fighting the need to
comfort him.

He looked down into her face, his expression unmoving. The
pulse in his cheek throbbed, and his gray eyes were as dark
as polished slate. Her fingers tingled where she touched him,
and when he reached up and cupped her cheek Mary-Jayne's
knees wobbled.

"Most days…most days I'm just…numb."

Every compassionate and caring instinct she possessed was
quickly on red alert. "It was an accident, Daniel. A terrible accident. And she wouldn't want you to feel this way, would she?"

"No," he said and traced her cheek with his thumb. "She'd
want me to marry you and raise our sons together. And that's
what we're going to do, Mary-Jayne. We have to get married.
For the sake of our sons. All you need to do is say yes."

CHAPTER SEVEN

SHE DIDN'T SAY YES. She didn't say anything. Instead she pulled away from him and headed back inside. They stayed for another twenty minutes, and when Bernie's client showed up they said their goodbyes and Daniel promised to return to see them in a couple of days. Being around his family made her long for her own, and Mary-Jayne stayed quiet on the trip back to the resort.

All you need to do is say yes...

As if it was so easy.

She almost admired his perseverance. Almost. He was relentless when he wanted something. No wonder he was so successful professionally. Solana had told her that he'd pretty much singlehandedly turned the chain of Sandwhisper Resorts into a flourishing enterprise around the globe. When his grandfather had been at the helm, Anderson's had only recently ventured into the new direction after spending years in copper and ore mining. Most of that was sold off now and the business focused on the resorts. While other empires had failed, Daniel had kept Anderson's afloat by using natural business acumen and innate tenacity. She remembered how he'd told her how so many people relied on the company for their livelihood and that was what made him determined to keep the organization growing.

Once they got back to the resort, he walked her to her door and lingered for a moment. "Can I see you tonight?"

Mary-Jayne shook her head. "I don't think so."

His eyes flashed. "You can't avoid me. I'm not going away, and neither is this situation."

"I'm tired, that's all. It's been a long day. And eventful," she said, and waved the envelope that held the picture of their babies.

He nodded. "All right, Mary-Jayne, I'll back off for tonight. But we have to get this sorted out."

"Yes," she said, and sighed heavily. "And we will. Just not today."

He left her reluctantly, and once he was gone she moved into the living room and slumped into the sofa. She was more confused than ever. *Daniel* confused her. Confounded her. He was relentless about the marriage thing. But she wouldn't change her mind. She couldn't. It would be a complete disaster.

She wanted love...not duty. Maybe he wasn't quite the closed-off corporate shark she'd first thought him to be; maybe there were moments when she enjoyed his company and liked the way they verbally sparred. And maybe there *was* a constant undercurrent of attraction and desire between them that made her head spin. But it still wasn't enough. And it never would be. Attraction alone wasn't enough. And those few unexpected moments where she relaxed around him were unreliable.

She hung around the condo for the remainder of the afternoon and at five o'clock was about to call Audrey again when there was a knock on her door. She groaned, loathing the thought of going another round with Daniel when all she wanted to do was talk to her friend and then curl into bed.

But it wasn't Daniel at her door. It was his grandmother.

"Can I come in?" Solana asked.

Mary-Jayne stepped back and opened the door wider. "Of course."

Once they were both settled in the living room, Solana spoke again.

"My grandson came to see me," she said and smiled. "He told me you were expecting twin boys."

Mary-Jayne wasn't surprised. It was the last thing he'd said to her when he'd walked her to her door earlier that day. He'd announced how he planned telling his grandmother about her pregnancy.

She nodded. "Yes, I am."

"And are you happy about it?"

"Very," she admitted. "I'm sorry I haven't told you earlier. Things were a little complicated and I—"

"You don't need to explain yourself. Daniel told me what happened."

She was relieved Solana understood. "Thank you. I know it must be something of a shock."

The older woman smiled. "Well, I was lining you up for Caleb…but now I think about it, you are definitely much better suited to Daniel. He needs someone who won't let him rule the roost. Caleb is way too easygoing. Whereas Daniel," Solana grinned widely, "is as wound up as a spring. You'll be good for him, I'm sure of it."

Mary-Jayne perched on the edge of the sofa. "Oh, it's not like that. We're not together or anything," she explained, coloring hotly. "I mean, we were *together*…just that once…but not now."

Solana's brows raised. "He said you've refused his marriage proposal."

"I did," she replied. "I had to. Please try to understand."

"I do," Solana said gently. "You want to fall in love and be swept off your feet. You want roses and moonlight and real romance."

"Yes," she admitted. "Exactly."

"And my grandson is too sensible and pragmatic for all that, right?"

Mary-Jayne shrugged. "We're not in love. We never would be. It would be a catastrophe."

Solana got up and moved to sit beside her on the sofa. "My son Miles married his first wife after dating her for two years. They were more in love than I'd ever seen two people in love. When she died so soon after Daniel was born Miles was heart-broken. And then along came Bernie and a few months later she was pregnant. It wasn't a love match at first...but they've made a good marriage together and raised three boys into the finest men I know."

She ignored the heavy thump behind her ribs. It was a nice story. But it's wasn't hers and Daniel's. "I know you want to see your grandson happy, but believe me, I could never be the person to do that. We don't even *like* one another."

Solana's hand came out and she briefly touched her stomach. "Oh, I'd say you liked one another well enough."

"That's not love...that's..."

"It's a place to start, that's all," Solana said. "Don't make a rash decision because you're scared of the future. Work on the present and let the future take care of itself."

It was a nice idea. But Mary-Jayne wasn't convinced.

Once the other woman left, she returned to her pacing. She wasn't about to marry a man she didn't love. She might want him. She might even like him a little bit. Maybe more than a little bit. Maybe she liked him a lot. But it wasn't enough. It would never be enough. And she wasn't about to be railroaded into something she didn't want.

The phone rang and she snatched it up. It was Audrey.

"Thank God," she said, and quickly explained what was happening to her concerned friend.

Fourteen hours later Mary-Jayne was on a flight home.

She was gone.

Gone...

Again.

Daniel's mood shifted between concern and rage and in varying degrees.

How could she leave without a word?

Damn it, they were his children, too. His flesh. His blood.

He'd knocked on her door on Wednesday afternoon after Caleb had called and told him the store was closed again. He knocked and waited, and when she didn't respond he called her cell. It went to message and he hung up. On Thursday morning Audrey Cooper answered the door. And he knew instantly that she'd bailed. Her friend was of little help and regarded him with barely concealed contempt. The pretty redhead stood in the doorway, arms crossed, defiant and clearly willing to go into battle for her friend.

"Is she back in Crystal Point with her family?" he asked, his rage simmering, his patience frayed.

Audrey pushed back her hair, clearly unimpressed. "I'm not saying. But wherever she is, there's no point in going after her. I think it's fairly clear she doesn't want to see or hear from you."

"She said that?"

Audrey, who evidently had as much contempt for him as she did for Caleb, nodded slowly. "If you go after her she'll spook and disappear."

It sounded a little melodramatic. Mary-Jayne wouldn't do that. She wouldn't put their babies at risk. Not for anything. He knew her well enough to realize that. "That doesn't make sense."

Audrey's brows rose sharply. "I know M.J. way better than you do. She doesn't like to be hemmed in, and if you push her she'll react and run. She's got friends all over the place and they and her family would do anything for her...and that includes helping her avoid you at all costs. Just leave her alone."

Run? Jesus...she wouldn't... Would she?

Audrey grabbed the door and closed it a little. "Since you own this place, I should tell you I'm looking for someone to take over the lease on the store. If I can't find anyone in a week I'm closing up and leaving. So if you want to sue me for breach of contract, go right ahead. And tell that lousy brother of yours to stay out of my way."

Then she closed the door in his face.

Daniel was furious by the time he reached Caleb's office. His brother was sitting at his desk, punching numbers into the computer.

"Your redhead is back," he said when the door was shut.

Caleb almost jumped out of his chair. "Audrey?"

"Yeah."

"Is she still…"

"Angry?" Daniel nodded. "She hates you as much as ever and me by association, which is why she wouldn't confirm that Mary-Jayne has gone home."

His brother grabbed his jacket off the back of the chair. "I'm going to see her. Is she at the—"

Daniel pulled the jacket from his brother's hands and tossed it on the desk. "You'd better not. She's leaving the resort, closing up the store if she can't find someone to take on her lease."

Clearly agitated, Caleb grabbed the jacket again. "She can't do that. She signed a contract. We'll get the lawyers to make sure she—"

"Stop being such a hothead," Daniel said, and took the jacket, throwing it onto the sofa by the door. "And leave the lawyers out of it. She's angry and hurt and has every reason to hate you, so if she wants to leave and break the lease agreement then she can do just that…without any interference from you, understand?"

Caleb glared at him. "When did you get so sentimental?"

"When I realized that Audrey has probably already contacted Mary-Jayne and told her I'm looking for her."

His brother's temper calmed a little. "Okay, I get the point. You're concerned Mary-Jayne might do something rash."

"Actually," he said, calmer now, "I think she'll do whatever is best for the babies. Which in her eyes is going home to be around her family."

"And that's where you're going?"

He shrugged. "I have to make this right."

Caleb raised an eyebrow. "You sure you want to make a commitment to a woman you don't love? Hell, you don't even know for sure if those babies are yours."

"I do know," he said. He wound back the irritation he felt toward his brother and tapped his hand to his chest. "I feel it... in here."

And that, he figured, was all that mattered.

Mary-Jayne had been holed up in her small house for four days. Her family knew she was back, but she'd insisted she had a bad head cold and said she needed some time to recover. Her mother had tutted and pleaded to bring her some soup and parental comfort, but Mary-Jayne wasn't prepared for them quite yet. Her sisters called every day and her friend Lauren did the same. Her dog, Pricilla, and parrot, Elvis, were happy she was home and gave her all the company she needed. While she waited for Daniel to turn up. Which she knew he would.

He wasn't the kind of man to give up when he wanted something.

Mary-Jayne had no illusions... His proposal was only about their children. He didn't want to marry *her*. And she didn't want to marry him. He was single-minded in his intent... He wanted the babies. He'd take her, too, if it meant getting full-time custody of their sons.

She wondered what his next move would be. And made herself sick to the stomach thinking about the possibilities. Since she'd refused his outrageous proposal, would he try another tack? Was he thinking about sole custody? Would he fight her in court to get what he wanted? He had money and power, and that equated to influence. He could afford the finest lawyers in the country and they'd certainly be out to prove she was less capable of giving their children the best possible life. Maybe the courts would see it that way, too.

By Sunday morning she was so wound up she wanted to scream. And cry. And run.

But she wouldn't do any of those things. She needed to stay strong and focus on growing two healthy babies. She'd fight the fight she needed to when she faced it head on. Until then, her sons were all that mattered.

When Evie and Grace arrived at her door late on Sunday afternoon she was almost relieved. She hated lying to her sisters, even if it was only by omission.

One look at her and Evie squealed. "Oh, my God, you're pregnant!"

"Well, don't tell the whole neighborhood," she said, and ushered them both inside.

Grace, who was easily the most beautiful woman Mary-Jayne had ever known, was a little less animated. She'd also had her first child two months earlier. But Evie, ever the nurturer, who had a seventeen-year-old son and a toddler daughter, was still chattering as Mary-Jayne closed the door and ushered them down the hallway.

"Tell us everything," Evie insisted as the trio dropped onto the big chintz sofa. "And first the part about how you've managed to keep from spilling the beans about this."

"Forget that," Grace said and smiled. "First, tell us who the baby's father is?"

"Babies," Mary-Jayne said and waited a microsecond before her sisters realized what she meant.

There were more shrieks and laughter and a load of questions before Mary-Jayne had an opportunity to explain. It took several minutes, and when she was done each of her sisters had a hold of her hands.

"And he wants to marry you?" Grace asked.

She shrugged. "That's what he says."

Evie squeezed her fingers. "But you don't want to marry him, M.J.?"

She screwed up her face. "Definitely not."

"Is he that awful?"

She opened her mouth to respond, but quickly stopped herself. She couldn't, in good conscience, make out as if he was some kind of ogre. Once he'd settled into the idea that he was the father he'd been incredibly supportive. And she couldn't forget his caring behavior when she'd had the ultrasound.

And then there was that kiss.

Don't forget the kiss...

Of course she needed to forget the kiss. It shouldn't have happened. It had only confused her. "He's not awful," she said and sat back in the chair. "Most of the time he's quite...nice."

Grace frowned. "Most?"

"Well, he can also be an arrogant jerk," she replied. "You know, all that old money and entitlement."

"Is he tall, dark and handsome to go along with all that old money?" Evie asked and grinned.

"Oh, yeah. He's all that. And more."

"And you *still* don't want to marry him?"

"I want to marry for love," she said and sighed. "Like you both did. I don't want to settle for a man who looks at me as some kind of incubator. We might have a whole lot of chemistry now, but when that goes what's left? An empty shell disguised as a marriage? No, thanks."

"That's a fairly pessimistic view of things," Grace remarked. "And not like you at all."

"I'm tired of being the eternal optimist," she said, feeling stronger. "Being pregnant has changed my thinking. I want to build a good life for my babies—one that's honest and authentic. And if I married Daniel I would be living a lie. Despite how much I..." She stopped and let her words trail.

"Despite how much you *like* him, you mean?" Evie prompted.

She shrugged again. "Sure, I like him. But I dislike him, too, and that's where it gets complicated."

"Maybe you're making it more complicated than it needs to

be," Grace suggested. "I mean, you don't really know him very well. Perhaps over time you will change your mind."

"I doubt it," she said. "I live here and he lives in San Francisco. There's a whole lot of ocean in between. Look, I'm happy for him to see his sons and have a relationship with them. I *want* them to have a father. But when I get married I want it to be with someone who wants *me*...and not just because I'm the mother of his children."

She was about to get to her feet when the doorbell rang.

"That's probably the folks," Evie said and smiled. "They've been worried about you. Which might have something to do with the fake head cold you said you had to keep us all at bay."

"Not that it did any good," Mary-Jayne said and grinned.

"Want me to get it?" Grace asked.

"Nah," she said and pulled herself out of the soft sofa. "I got it."

She walked down the hall and opened the front door, half expecting her mother to be standing there with a big pot of chicken soup. But it wasn't either of her parents.

It was Daniel.

He looked so good. So familiar. In jeans and a blue shirt, everything about him screamed sexy and wholly masculine. She wished she was immune. She wished he didn't set her blood and skin on fire. His steely gaze traveled over her slowly until he finally met her eyes with his own and spoke.

"So you didn't run too far after all?"

"Run?"

Daniel had expected her to slam the door. But she didn't look all that surprised to see him on her doorstep.

"Your friend said you might be tempted to run to get away from me."

"Audrey did?" She laughed loudly. "I'm afraid she's got a vivid imagination and a flair for the dramatic."

"Speaking of which," Daniel said pointedly, "taking off without a word was a little theatrical, don't you think?"

She shrugged and her T-shirt slipped off her shoulder. "I needed some breathing space."

"I wasn't exactly smothering you."

"Maybe not to you," she flipped back.

He grinned a little, even though his insides churned. She had a way of doing that—a way of mixing up his emotions. He was as mad as hell with her for taking off without a word, but he wouldn't show her that. Daniel turned to briefly look at the two cars in her driveway. "You have company?"

She nodded. "My sisters."

His gaze dropped to her belly. "You told them?"

"They told me," she said, and pulled the T-shirt over her middle a fraction. "Hard to hide this from the world now."

"You shouldn't," he said quietly. "You look good."

She shrugged. "So… I guess I'll see you around."

Daniel laughed lightly. "Oh, no, Mary-Jayne, you don't get out of it that easy."

Her gaze narrowed. "You plan on camping on my doorstep?"

"If I have to," he replied. "Or you could invite me in."

His eyes widened. "You want to meet my sisters, is that it?"

"Absolutely."

She exhaled heavily and stepped back. "Okay. Best you come inside."

Daniel crossed the threshold of her small cottage and followed her down the hall. Her house was filled with old furniture and bric-a-brac and was as muddled as he'd expected. The Preston sisters regarded him curiously when he entered the living room and as Mary-Jayne introduced him. They were similar, all with the same dark curling hair and wide green eyes. Evie was down to earth and friendly, while Grace had a kind of ethereal beauty that made her look as though she'd stepped off the set of a Hollywood movie.

The eldest, Evie, asked him if he'd had a good trip and began chatting about flying and vacations, which he figured she was doing to break the ice a little. The other sister was more serious and content to stand back and watch Mary-Jayne and him interact. It didn't bother him. All he cared about was Mary-Jayne.

He cared...

Damn.

He didn't want to think about that. But he couldn't get the vision of her staring up at him in his dad's studio, her hand gently rubbing his arm, all wide-eyed and lovely. In that moment he realized she was kind and considerate, despite the bouts of exuberant bravado.

Her siblings were nice women who were clearly curious about him but were too polite to say too much. They stayed for a few minutes, and he asked about Evie's art and mentioned how his father was an artist, and she said she knew his work. Both women talked about Crystal Point and how much they loved the small town. Daniel hadn't taken much notice as he'd driven along the waterfront. His mind was set on seeing Mary-Jayne, not the beach. Evie suggested he drop by her bed-and-breakfast, and he noticed how Mary-Jayne scowled at her sister. Maybe he had an ally in the Preston sisters? Maybe they agreed that she should marry him? He wasn't averse to using whatever leverage he could if it meant he'd have the chance to be a full-time father to his sons.

Once they left, Mary-Jayne propped her hands on her hips and glared at him.

"I suppose you'd like coffee?"

He smiled. "If it's not too much trouble."

She tossed her incredible hair. "Oh, it is...not that it would make one damn bit of difference to you. And by the way," she said as she walked down the hall, "don't think you can sway me by charming my family. I've already told my sisters what a jerk you are."

He laughed and walked after her. "I don't think they quite believed you, Mary-Jayne."

When he reached the kitchen he stood by the counter for a moment, looking around at the crowded room with its cluttered cabinets, colorful drapes and assortment of pots hanging from hooks above the stove top. But as untidy and overdone as it was, there was something oddly welcoming about the room. With its mismatched table and chairs and the wrought iron stand in the corner jammed with an array of ceramic vases containing a variety of overgrown herbs, it was far removed from the huge ultramodern kitchen in his San Francisco apartment. He never used it these days. Even when he was married, Simone had worked long hours like he did and they preferred to dine out most evenings. But Mary-Jayne's kitchen suited her. It was easy to imagine her sitting at the round scrubbed table, sipping tea from one of the patterned china cups from the collection on the dresser.

"Yes," she said, still scowling. "I'm a slob, remember?"

"Did I say that?"

"Words to the effect. One of my many flaws."

He chuckled and watched her pull a pair of ceramic mugs from the cupboard. She looked so beautiful with her scowl, all fired up and ready to do battle with him. One thing was for sure, life with Mary-Jayne Preston sure wasn't dull!

Daniel came around the counter and stood beside her. She turned and rested her hip against the bench, arms crossed.

"Yes?"

"Nothing," he said and reached for her, curling his hand gently around her neck.

"Don't you dare," she said, but didn't move.

"What are you so afraid of?" he asked, urging her closer. "That I'm going to kiss you? Or that you'll like it?"

"Neither," she said on a shallow breath. "Both."

"You never have to be afraid of me, Mary-Jayne," he said quietly, bringing her against him. The feel of her belly and breasts instantly spiked his libido. "I'd never hurt you. Or make you to do something you didn't want to do."

"Then, stop asking me to marry you," she said, still breathless as she looked up into his face.

"I can't. When I want something I'm—"

"Relentless," she said, cutting off his words. "Yeah, I know. I'm not used to someone like you," she admitted, her mouth trembling a little. "My last boyfriend was—"

"An unemployed musician," he finished for her, not in the mood to hear about the man she'd once dated. "Yes, I had you investigated, remember?"

She frowned and wriggled against him. "Jerk."

Daniel moved his other arm around her waist and gently held her. "Me or him?"

"You."

He chuckled. "You know, I don't think you really mean that."

"Sure I do," she said, and wriggled some more. "And kissing me isn't going to get me to change my mind."

"Maybe not," he said and dipped his head. "But it sure beats arguing about it."

Her lips were soft when he claimed them. Soft and sweet and familiar. Her hands crept up his chest and reached his shoulders and she clung on to him. Daniel pressed closer and she moaned softly. The sweet vanilla scent that was uniquely hers assailed his senses, and he tilted her head a fraction. Their tongues met and danced. And he was pretty sure she knew exactly the effect she had on him and his libido. His hand moved down to her hip, and he urged her closer. Heat flared between them, and suddenly kissing wasn't enough. Her fingertips dug into his shoulders and she arched her back, drawing them closer together.

"Mary-Jayne," he whispered against her mouth and trailed his lips down her cheek and throat. "Let me stay with you tonight."

She shivered in his arms. "I can't," she said on a shallow breath. "Tomorrow…"

"Forget tomorrow," he said, and pushed the T-shirt off her shoulder. Her creamy skin was like tonic for the desire that churned through his blood. "Forget everything but right now."

It was what he wanted. What he needed. Her skin, her mouth, her tender touch. He'd shut off from truly feeling anything for so long, but Mary-Jayne made him feel in ways he could barely understand. They fought; they battled with words and with ideals. But underneath the conflict simmered an attraction and a pull that was the most powerful of his life.

And it also had the power to undo him.

CHAPTER EIGHT

SHE DIDN'T LET him stay. She couldn't. If he'd stayed and they'd made love she wasn't sure she would have had the strength to refuse his marriage proposal. He'd use sex to confuse and manipulate her, even if that wasn't his intention. She was like putty in his arms. One kiss, one touch and being with him was all she could think about.

Idiot...

Mary-Jayne garnered all her strength and sent him packing. And tried to convince herself she couldn't care less where he went. There were plenty of quality hotels in the nearby town of Bellandale. It was barely a twenty-minute drive from Crystal Point. He had a GPS. He'd be fine. She didn't feel bad at all.

She had a shower, made soup and toast and curled up on the sofa to watch TV with Pricilla and pretended she'd put Daniel out of her mind once and for all.

Her dreams, however, were something else altogether. He invaded them. She couldn't keep him out. His touch was like a brand against her skin, and she could still feel the heat of his body pressed against her for hours later. And his kiss... It was like no other. She remembered his comment about her ex-boyfriend. *An unemployed musician?* Toby had been exactly that. He wasn't even much of a musician. They'd dated off and on 'for two years and she often wondered if she'd brought home a tattooed, frequently pierced, dreadlocked boyfriend simply because that was what everyone expected of her. Her teenage willfulness made her rebel against what she'd considered the average or mundane. After she'd left home she'd saved her money and quickly headed overseas. She'd returned feeling even more independent and more determined to live her own life.

And Toby was the end result. A deadbeat, she realized now. Someone who took advantage of her generous nature and swindled her out of her money and her pride. She'd been left with a debt for a car he crashed and a guitar he'd taken with him when he walked out the door. He had no goals, no ambition and no integrity. She'd had one serious relationship since with a man who ended up complaining about her spending too much time worrying about her career. He'd had no ambition, either—except the desire to sit in front of his computer all day playing games. She'd foolishly believed she chose men who were free-spirited and artistic. Now they simply seemed lazy and immature.

She tossed and turned all night and woke up feeling nauseated and unable to stomach the dry crackers and green tea that usually helped most when morning sickness came upon her.

She changed into her favorite overalls and grinned when she discovered she had to leave two of the three side buttons undone to accommodate her rapidly expanding middle. Her workshop needed a cleanup before she got to work on the few back orders she had, so she headed outside and began decluttering the counters. It was midmorning before she took a break and snacked on some apple slices and a cup of tea.

At eleven Daniel rocked up.

In dark jeans and a navy polo shirt he looked effortlessly handsome, and her stomach flipped with familiar awareness. He looked her over and smiled.

"Cute outfit."

Her overalls were paint splattered and had holes in each knee. But they were comfy, and she could care less what he thought about her clothes. "Thanks. Did you want something?" she asked, pushing the memory of his kisses from her mind.

"We're going out."

Bossy, as usual. "Are we? Am I allowed to ask where we're going?"

"To see your parents," he said swiftly. "It's about time they were told they're about to become grandparents again."

"I'd rather tell them myself."

"*We'll* tell them," he said, firmer this time. "Stop being stubborn."

Mary-Jayne turned and sashayed down the hall. "I'd really prefer to do it some other time. Please try to understand."

"Well, I don't. We're in this together," he said, and followed her into the house. "We told my parents together...and now we'll tell yours...together. That's how things are going to be, Mary-Jayne. They have a right to know, don't you think?"

When she reached the living room she turned and propped her hands on her hips. "Of course. I just don't want you to meet them right now."

His brows shot up. "Why the hell not?"

"Because," she said, and dragged out a long breath, "you don't know them. One look at you and they'll get all...thingy."

He stilled. *"Thingy?"*

Her patience frayed. "Excited, okay? Thrilled. Happy. They'll feel as though they've won the lottery in the potential son-in-law department."

He laughed. "They want you to nab a rich husband?"

"No," she corrected. "That's not it. It's just that you're different from anyone I've ever...you know...dated. You're not an *unemployed musician*," she explained, coloring hotly. "Or a beach bum or a lazy good-for-nothing, as my dad would say. You're... *normal*... You're successful and hardworking and come from a nice family. Once they know that, they'll get all worked up and start pressuring me to...to..."

"Marry me?"

"Well, yeah," she admitted. "Probably."

"I thought you said they let you lead your own life?"

"They do," she replied. "But they're still my parents. They still want what's best for me. Once they clap eyes on you, I'll be done for."

His mouth twitched at the edges. "Best you get changed so we can get going."

Mary-Jayne frowned. "Didn't you hear what I said?"

"Every word," he said, and dropped into the sofa. "Hurry up, *dear*."

Impatience snaked up her spine. "You are the most infuriating and—"

"Want me to kiss you again?" he asked as he grabbed a magazine from the coffee table and opened it at a random page. "If not, go and get changed."

Irritated, she turned on her heels and stomped to her bedroom. He was an ass. He didn't give a hoot what she wanted. Or care about how she felt. By the time she'd dressed, Mary-Jayne was so mad she could have slugged his smug face.

Once they were out of the house she pointed to her car. "I'll drive," she said and rattled her keys. "I know the way."

Daniel stopped midstride and looked at the battered VW in the driveway. "In that hunk of junk? I don't think so." He gestured to the top-of-the-range Ford sedan parked alongside the curb. "We'll take my rental car."

"Snob."

He laughed and gently grasped her elbow. "Come on."

"Sometimes I really don't like you much at all."

He laughed again. "And other times?"

She quickstepped it to the car and waited by the passenger door. It was hard to stay mad at him when he was being so nice to her. "No comment."

Once they were in the car she gave him the address. The trip took only minutes, and by the time they pulled into the driveway her temper had lost its momentum.

"You're something of a hothead, aren't you?" he asked as he unclipped his seat belt.

"Around you?" She raised a brow and smiled a little. "Yeah."

He seemed to find that idea amusing and was still chuckling by the time he was out of the car and had come around to her side. "It's one of the things I find captivating about you, Mary-Jayne."

Captivating? That was quite an admission. He usually didn't admit to anything, not when it came to feelings. Oh, sure, she knew he wanted her in his bed, but anything else seemed off his agenda. He'd said he felt numb. The very idea pained her deep down. He'd lost the woman he'd loved and didn't want to love again… That was clear enough.

"What are you thinking about?" he asked as he took her hand.

I'm thinking about how it must feel to be loved by you…

Mary-Jayne's fingers tingled at the connection with his. She didn't want to be so vulnerable to his touch, but her attraction for him had a will of its own. She simply couldn't help herself. That was why she'd become so caught up in the heat and passion between them the night of Solana's birthday party. It was heady and powerful and drove her beyond coherent thought. It was more than attraction. More than anything she'd felt before.

And the very idea scared her senseless.

Her parents, as expected, were delighted, if not a little shocked at their news. Once the shock settled, her mother had countless questions for Daniel and he answered every one without faltering. He was as resilient as the devil when under intense scrutiny. Barbara Preston skirted around the question about marriage and Mary-Jayne was relieved that Daniel didn't mention that she'd refused his proposal. There was time for that revelation later. Her father, she realized, looked as pleased as she'd ever seen him. Bill Preston approved. Daniel was a hit. Her parents were clearly delighted, even with her out-of-wedlock pregnancy. Her mother was all hugs and tears when they explained she was expecting twins.

Over a jug of iced tea her father spoke. "What do you think of our little town, son?"

Son?

Her dad was already calling Daniel "son"?

Great.

"I haven't had a chance to see much of it yet," Daniel replied. "But I'm hoping Mary-Jayne will show me around sometime today."

She smiled sweetly and nodded, and then noticed how her mother seemed to approve wholeheartedly about the way Daniel used her full name. He could clearly do no wrong.

I'm doomed.

They stayed for two hours, and Daniel answered every probing question her parents asked. He talked about his career, his family and even his wife and the baby they had lost. Before they left her father ushered him off to his garage to inspect the Chevrolet Impala that he was restoring, and Mary-Jayne was left to endure her mother's scrutiny.

"Now," Barbara said, hugging her closely once the men had left the room. "What don't I know?"

"Nothing," she replied and began collecting the mugs from the table. "The babies are doing fine and I feel okay other than a little morning sickness."

"I meant with the two of you," Barbara said and raised a brow. "He's awfully handsome, isn't he? And such nice manners."

Mary-Jayne smiled. "I know he isn't what you've imagined I'd bring home to meet you."

"Well, your track record hasn't exactly given us confidence."

"I know. And you're right—he's handsome and nice and has good manners."

"Are you in love with him?"

Love...

She'd not considered the word in regard to him. Falling in love with Daniel was out of the question. He'd never love her back. *He was numb.* There was nothing left in his heart. He'd love their sons and that was all.

"No," she said and heard the hesitation in her own voice. "Definitely not."

Barbara smiled. "It wouldn't be the end of the world, you know... I mean, if you did fall in love with a man like Daniel."

"It would," she corrected, suddenly hurting deep in her chest. "He still loves his wife. And she was very different from me. She was smart and successful and everything I'm not."

There... I said it out loud.

Her mother's expression softened some more. "You're smart, and your dad and I have every faith that your business will be a success one day. And sometimes being *different* is a good thing," Barbara added gently.

"Not in this," she said, her heart suddenly and inexplicably heavy. "I know you only want to see me happy, and I am happy about the babies. Really happy. Even though it's been something of a shock I'm looking forward to being a mother."

Barbara rubbed her arm comfortingly. "You'll be a good one, too, I'm sure of it."

"I hope so," she said. "Although I'm sure some people will think having twin boys is my medicine for being such a difficult child myself."

Her mother smiled. "You were spirited, not difficult."

"That's sweet of you to say so, but I know I caused you and Dad some major headaches over the years. Remember when I ditched school for three days to follow that carnival that had arrived in town?"

Barbara laughed. "Every kid dreams of running away and joining the circus at some point. Especially a strong-willed eleven-year-old."

Mary-Jayne giggled. "I had visions of being a trapeze artist."

They chatted for a few more minutes about her childhood escapades, and by the time her father and Daniel returned her

mood was much improved. Daniel looked his usual self-satis-
fied self and her dad looked pleased as punch. Whatever had
transpired in the garage, she was sure it had something to do
her father giving Daniel his blessing and full support.

Typical...

Once they were back in the car, she strapped on the seat belt
and pasted on a smile.

"Take a left at the end of the street," she instructed.

"Because?"

"You wanted to see my town, my home, right?"

"Well...yes."

"So we'll go to the beach."

He frowned a little. "We're not exactly dressed for the beach."

Mary-Jayne laughed. "Does everything always have to be
done to order with you? Live dangerously, Daniel," she said
and laughed again. "You might surprise yourself and enjoy it."

His mouth tightened. "You know, despite what you think,
I'm not some overworked killjoy."

"Prove it," she challenged. "Get those extrastarched clothes
of yours crumpled for a moment."

"Extrastarched?" he echoed as he started the ignition.

She chuckled. "Oh, come on, even you have to admit that
you're a neat freak. You even folded your clothes that night we
spent together." It was something of an exaggeration...but she
had a point to prove. "My dress got twisted amongst the bed-
sheets and your suit was perfectly placed over the chair."

"I don't remember it that way."

"Hah," she scoffed. "You have a selective memory."

"I remember everything about that night," he said and drove
down the street. "Left, you said?"

"Left," she repeated. "We'll drive past my sister's bed-and-
breakfast."

"I know where that is already."

Her brows came up. "You do?"

He nodded. "Of course. I stayed there last night."

* * *

Daniel knew it would make her nuts. But he'd thought it was a good idea at the time and Evie Jones seemed to agree. After Mary-Jayne had kicked him out of her house the evening before, he'd driven around the small town for a while and come across Dunn Inn by chance. The big A-framed house stood silhouetted amongst a nest of Norfolk pines and the shingle out front had told him exactly who the place belonged to. So he'd tapped on the door and was met by Evie's much younger husband, Scott, and within minutes Evie herself was insisting he stay at the bed-and-breakfast while he was in Crystal Point.

"You stayed at my sister's place?"

She was all outraged, and it made him grin a little. "Sure. Something wrong with that?"

"Something? Everything! Of all the manipulative and conniving things I could imagine you—"

"I needed somewhere to stay," he said quickly. "You told me to leave, remember?"

"Ever heard of a thing called a hotel?" she shot back. "There are many of them in Bellandale."

"I wanted to stay in Crystal Point."

"Why?"

He glanced at her belly. "You have to ask?"

She glared at him. "Don't use the twins as a way of getting around this. How long do you intend on staying?"

"As long as I need to."

"You could stay for a lifetime and nothing would change. I will not marry you. Not now and not ever."

"We'll see," he said, with way more confidence than he felt.

The truth was, he was tired of arguing with her about it. She was as stubborn as a mule. Last night he could have stayed with her. He'd wanted to. A part of him had needed to. He'd wanted to spend the night making love to her. And her rejection had stung like a bucket of ice water over his skin.

"What about your job?" she asked. "You can't just pack that in for an indeterminable length of time."

"Sure I can," he said, and flipped a lazy smile and drove toward the beach. "I'm the boss, remember? I can do what I want."

She was clearly fuming. "Solana told me you never take vacations."

"This isn't a vacation," he said, and pulled the car into the parking area.

"No," she said, opening the door. "It's a hunting expedition… and I'm the prey."

Daniel got out of the car, ignoring the niggling pain in his temple. "Such drama. Let's just forget my marriage proposal for the moment, shall we?"

"It's all I can think about," she muttered.

"Well, that's something, at least." He locked the car. "So this beach?"

She crossed her arms and stormed off down the pathway. Daniel had to admit the beach was spectacular. The white sand spanned for several hundred meters until it met the pristine river mouth. No wonder she loved this place so much. It was early winter and a weekday, so there was no one about other than them and a lone dog walker playing chase with his pet. He watched as Mary-Jayne flipped off her sandals and strode across the sand until she reached the water. Daniel looked down at his shoes. They were Italian leather and not designed for the beach. He perched on a rock and took them off, stuffing the socks into the loafers. She'd called him an uptight neat freak on several occasions. Maybe she was right. When he was young he'd been impulsive and adventurous. Now he rarely did anything without considering the consequences. Taking over the helm of Anderson's from his grandfather had changed him. He felt the weight of responsibility press heavily on his shoulders 24/7. The most impulsive thing he'd done recently was go after Mary-Jayne. And even that he did with a tempered spirit.

What he really wanted to do was haul her in his arms and kiss her senseless.

By the time he stepped onto the sand she was twenty meters in front of him. He quickened his steps and watched her as she walked, mesmerized by the way her hips swayed. She had a sensuality that affected him in a way that blurred the lines between desire and something else. Something more. He couldn't define it. Couldn't articulate in his mind what it was about Mary-Jayne that caused such an intense reaction in him. It wasn't simply attraction. He'd felt that before and it had always waned quickly. No, this was something he'd never experienced before. Not even with Simone. His wife hadn't driven him crazy. Loving her had been easy. She had never challenged him, insulted him or made him accountable for his beliefs. But Mary-Jayne did at every opportunity. She questioned everything and anything.

She made him think.

Feel...

It was a kind of heady mix of torture and pleasure.

Which was why making love with her had been so intense. They had chemistry and more. A connection that went beyond physical attraction. A mental attraction that defied logic.

Yeah, loving Simone had been easy. But loving Mary-Jayne... There would be nothing easy about that. Which was why he wouldn't. Why he'd keep it clear in his head what he wanted. His sons. A family. But where? It could never be here, he thought as he walked along the sand. Sure, it was a nice town. Peaceful and safe... Exactly the kind of place to raise children. The kind of place a person could call home. But not him. For one, Mary-Jayne would never agree to it. And he had his life in San Francisco.

She was walking at a leisurely pace now and stopped to pick something up, perhaps a shell. Daniel caught up with her and matched her slow strides.

"It's a beautiful spot."

She glanced sideways. "It's the prettiest beach along this part of the coastline."

"You're fortunate to have grown up in a place like this. To have made it your home."

She shrugged and tossed the shell in the shallow water. "What about you?" she asked. "Where's home for you?"

Daniel rubbed the back of his neck to ease the tension creeping up his spine. "San Francisco."

"That's where you live," she said quietly. "Where's home?"

He shrugged loosely. "When my grandfather was alive he and Solana had a place in the Napa Valley, and I used to go there for school vacations. Miles and Bernie moved around a lot, so my brothers and I always welcomed the stability of my grandparents' small vineyard. But when Gramps died things changed. Gran wasn't interested in the business end of things and decided to sell the place. Solana likes the warmer weather and divides her time between Port Douglas and San Francisco."

She stopped walking and faced him, her hair flipping around her face from the breeze. "So...nowhere?"

"I guess so," he replied, and started walking again.

She caught up with him quickly. "I don't want that for my babies. I want them to be settled. I want them to have a place they can always call home."

"So do I," he said, and stopped to look out over the water. "What's that called?" he asked, pointing to a land mass separated from the shore by an expanse of water that fed from the mouth of the river.

"Jays Island," she replied. "Years ago they used to bring sugarcane ferries up the river, so this was quite a busy spot. Now they use trains and trucks to transport the sugar so the river doesn't get dredged anymore. The sand banks built up and the island came about. Birds nest over there and at a really low tide you can wade through the shallows to get over there. When I was young I used to swim over there at high tide and come back when the tide went out." She laughed and the sound flittered across the wind. "Much to my parents' despair. But I loved sitting on that patch of rock," she said, and pointed to a ragged rock outcrop on the island. "I used to sit there for ages and just let the wind hit my face. It was the kind of place where a person could dream big and no one was around to make judgment. Where *I* could sit without worrying about other people's opinion."

"You mean your family?"

She shrugged. "My family are the best."

"But?"

Her green eyes glittered. "But everyone has a role, you know... My brother, my sisters. Noah took over the family business, Evie's the successful artist, Grace is the supersmart financial whiz who once worked on Wall Street."

"And you?"

Her shoulders lifted again. "I'm just the youngest. The one who got away with everything as a kid. I guess I have the role of being the one who hasn't amounted to anything."

Surely she didn't believe that. "A college education and a big bank balance don't equate to a person's value, Mary-Jayne. There's greatness in simply being yourself."

She offered a wry smile. "Is that why you've worked so hard to climb the corporate ladder? Because you believe it's enough to live a simple life?"

"An authentic life," he corrected, doing his best to ignore the growing throb in his head. "But I didn't really have a choice when I was drafted into the company. My dad wasn't interested, and my grandfather had a lot of health issues. I either joined or the company folded. Too many people were invested in Anderson's... I couldn't let it go down without a fight. So I made a few changes to the company's structure, sold off most of the mining interests and concentrated on the part that I enjoyed. Ten years later the resorts are now some of the most successful in the world."

"And if you hadn't joined the family business, what would you have done?"

"I'm not sure. Maybe law."

She laughed. "Oh, yes, I can see you as a lawyer. You do pose a good argument."

He reached out and grabbed her left hand, and then gently rubbed her ring finger with his thumb. "Not good enough, obviously. This is still bare."

She went to pull away but he held on. "You know why I won't."

"Because you hate me."

She shook her head. "I don't hate you, Daniel."

"No?" he queried as he turned her hand over and stroked her palm. "But you don't like me."

"I don't *dislike* you," she said quietly. "The truth is, I'm very confused about how I do feel about you. And it's not something I'm used to. Normally I know exactly how I feel about everything. I have an opinion and I usually express it. But around you…" Her words trailed. "Around you all I seem to do is dig myself into this hole and say things I don't mean. And I'm not like that. It's not a reaction I'm particularly proud of."

"So I wind you up," he said, still holding her, even though the pain in his head gained momentum. "We wind one another up. What's wrong with that? It'll keep things interesting."

"What things? A marriage where we're always fighting, always at each other's throats? That's not something I want our children to witness." She pulled away and crossed her arms tightly around her waist. "Because if you do, that's about as selfish and self-destructive as it gets."

Selfish? Selfish because he wanted to give his sons his name and the legacy that went along with it. She was the one being selfish—thinking only of herself. Like a spoiled brat.

"If you had any consideration for their future, for what they deserve, then you would see that I'm right," he said stiffly. "But right now you're acting like a petulant child, Mary-Jayne. Maybe this isn't what either of us planned. And maybe you're right, maybe we would never have seen one another again after that night if you hadn't gotten pregnant. But you did, and we are and I'll be damned if I'm going to let you dictate the kind of father I'm allowed to be. This might be a shock to you, but you're *not* the center of the universe, and right now the only thing that matters is the welfare of our sons."

She glared at him. "You're calling *me* self-absorbed? When you think you can simply snap your fingers and get what you want?"

Annoyance swept over his skin. He tried to keep his cool. Tried to get her to show some sense. But be damned if she wasn't the most infuriating woman on the planet!

In that moment a flashing light appeared out of the corner of his eye. And another. A dreaded and familiar ache clutched the back of his head. He recognized what was coming.

"We have to get back. I'll take you home."

And he knew, as he turned and walked back up the sand, that he was in for one hell of a headache.

CHAPTER NINE

TWO DAYS LATER Mary-Jayne got a call from her sister Evie. She'd had a peaceful two days. No Daniel. No marriage proposals. No insults. It gave her time to seethe and think and work.

"I think you should get over here."

She ground her teeth together. She didn't want to see him. She was still mad at him for calling her a petulant child. And she certainly didn't want her sister interfering or trying to play matchmaker. "What for?"

"He's been holed up in his room for forty-eight hours. No food or coffee or anything. I don't want to pry…but I thought you should know."

Mary-Jayne pushed down the concern battering around in her head. "He's a big boy. I'm sure he's fine."

"Well, I'm not so sure. And I have an obligation to my guests to ensure their welfare while they stay here."

"Good… You go and check on him."

"M.J.," Evie said, sterner this time. "Whatever is going on between the two of you, put it aside for a moment. *I* need your help."

Unable to refuse her sister's plea, Mary-Jayne quickly got dressed and headed over to the B and B. Evie looked genuinely concerned when she met her by the side door.

"So what's the big emergency?" she asked as she walked into the house and dropped her tote on the kitchen counter. "Maybe he's gone out."

"He's here," Evie said. "His rental car is outside."

"Maybe he's asleep."

"For two days?" her sister shot back. "Something's not right, and since you're the soon-to-be mother of his babies, it's your responsibility to find out what's wrong."

"I think you're under the illusion that Daniel and I have some kind of real relationship. We don't," Mary-Jayne informed her. "We barely tolerate one another."

Evie placed a key in her palm, touched her shoulders and gave her a little sisterly shove. "Go and find out. He's in the brown room."

There were four guest rooms at the B and B, each one styled in a particular color. Mary-Jayne left the family residence area and headed into the bigger section of the house. She lingered outside the door for a moment and finally tapped. Nothing. She tapped again.

She was about to bail when she heard a faint sound. Like a moan.

Did he have a woman in there?

The very idea made her sick to the stomach. He wouldn't... surely.

She stared at the key in her hand. What if she opened the door and found him doing who knows what with some random woman? She wouldn't be able to bear it.

Suck it up...

She pushed the key in the lock and slowly opened the door. The room was in darkness. The heavy drapes were shut and she couldn't hear a sound. There was someone on the bed, lying facedown.

"Daniel?"

She said his name so softly she wasn't surprised he didn't respond. She closed the door and stepped closer. He was naked from the waist up and had a pillow draped over his head. She said his name again and the pillow moved.

"What?"

His voice was hoarse. Groggy. Nothing like she'd heard before. She squinted to accustom her eyes to the darkness and spotted an empty bottle of aspirin on the bedside table. She took notice of everything, and a thought popped into her head.

"Are you drunk?"

He groaned softly. "Go away."

"You're hungover?"

He rolled slightly and took the pillow with him, facing away from her. "Leave me alone, Mary-Jayne."

She walked around the bed and looked at him. "Daniel, I was only wondering if—"

"I'm not drunk," he said raggedly, clearly exasperated. "I've got a headache. Now go away."

She glanced around the room. Total darkness. He hadn't eaten for two days. Empty painkiller bottle. She got to the edge of the bed and dropped to her haunches.

"Daniel," she said gently, and tried to move the pillow. "Do you have a migraine headache?"

He moaned and his hold on the pillow tightened. "Yes. Get out of here."

She got to her feet and headed into the bathroom, emerging a minute later with a cold, wet washcloth. He hadn't moved. She sat on the edge of the bed.

"Here," she said, and pried the pillow off him. "This will help." She gently rolled him onto his back and placed the cloth across his forehead.

"Stop fussing," he said croakily.

She pressed the cloth around his temples. "Let me help you."

"You can't."

"I can," she said and touched his hair. "My mother gets migraines. I know what I'm doing." She glanced at the empty medicine bottle. "When did you last take a painkiller?"

He shrugged and then moaned, as though the movement took all his effort. "This morning. Last night. I can't remember."

She stroked his head. "Okay. I'll be back soon. Keep the cloth on your forehead."

Mary-Jayne was back in a matter of minutes. Evie had what she needed, and when she returned to his room she noticed he was still lying on his back and had his hand over his eyes. She fetched a glass of water from the bathroom and sat on the bed again.

"Take these for now," she instructed, and pressed a couple of aspirin into his hand. "And I have some paracetamol you can take in two hours."

"Would you stop—"

"Take the pills, okay?" she said, holding on to her patience. "You'll feel better for it." He grumbled again but finally did as she requested. Mary-Jayne took the glass and placed it on the bedside table. "It's important that you take in plenty of fluids."

"Yes, nurse."

"And drop the attitude for a while."

He didn't respond. Instead he rolled over and buried his face into the pillow. Mary-Jayne got up and pushed the drapes together as close as they would go. She knew many migraine sufferers had sensitivity to light. Countless times she'd watched her mother battle for days on end with the nausea and blinding pain.

She stayed with him for the next few hours. She gave him water and made him take some more medication. When she thought he could handle it, she sat on the bed and gently massaged lavender oil into his temples. There was a strong level of intimacy in what she did, but she couldn't let him suffer.

By late afternoon there was significant improvement in his pain level, and she left for a while to make him a sandwich and peppermint tea.

"How's the patient?" Evie asked when she came into the kitchen.

Mary-Jayne looked up from her task. "A little better. He's hungry, so that's a good sign."

Evie nodded and grinned. "Yeah... You were right—you two don't have a relationship at all. What was I thinking?"

"I'm helping someone who's in pain, that's all."

"That someone is the father of your babies. It's a bond, M.J. A strong bond that will forever keep you and Daniel in each other's life."

"I know it will," she said, heavyhearted. "I just don't know why he keeps insisting that we get married."

Evie raised her brows in dramatic fashion. "He lost a child once... I think it's easy to understand why he doesn't want to lose his sons, too."

"Lose them to what?" she shot back.

"Geography," Evie replied. "An ocean between you is a big incentive. Or the idea you might meet someone else one day and get married."

She wasn't about to admit she'd deliberately avoided considering any of that before.

"Marriage without love could never work."

"Are you sure about that?" Evie queried. "I mean, are you sure there's no love there? Looks to me as if you're behaving exactly like a woman in love would act."

She stilled instantly. Her sister's words rattled around in her head.

No, it wasn't true. She didn't. She couldn't.

"I'm not," she said, defiant.

Evie smiled gently. "I've never known you to be afraid of anything. What is it about loving this man that scares you so much?"

Nothing. Everything. Her sister was way too intuitive. "He's out of my league."

"Why? Because he has short hair and a job?"

The reference to her ex-boyfriend didn't go unmissed. "We're too different. And he'll want to shuffle me off to San Francisco.

I don't want to live there. I want to live here. But he'll do and say whatever he has to in order to get his own way. I know he's handsome and can be charming and ticks all the boxes. But I know him… He's a control freak."

"So are you, in your own way," Evie remarked. "So maybe you're not so different after all."

Was that it? Was it their similarities and not their differences that spooked her? He'd called her a hothead. She'd called him arrogant. Were they both guilty of those traits?

Mary-Jayne ignored the idea for the moment and grabbed the tray. "I have to get back in there."

Evie smiled. "See you a little later."

When she returned to his room the bed was empty. The curtains were still drawn and there was a sliver of light beaming from beneath the closed bathroom door. He came out moments later, naked except for a towel draped around his hips, another towel in his hand that he used to dry his hair.

She pushed down the rush of blood in her veins. But his shoulders were so wide, his chest broad and dusted with a smattering of hair and his stomach as flat as a washboard that the picture was wholly masculine. A deep surge of longing flowed through her.

"You're back."

She swallowed hard and tried to not look at his smooth skin. "I'm back," she said, and placed the tray on the small table by the window. "How are you feeling?"

"Weary," he said, and smiled fractionally as he came toward her. "It takes me a few days to come good after."

Mary-Jayne poured some tea and made a determined effort to stop looking at him as if he was a tasty meal. "Have you always suffered from migraines?" she asked, eyes downcast.

He nodded. "Since I was a kid. They're less frequent now, but when one hits I usually just lock myself in my apartment with some aspirin for a couple of days and try to sleep it off."

"Have you tried stronger medication? Perhaps an injection of—"

"No needles," he said, and moved beside her.

He smelled so good. Like soap and some musky deodorant. She swallowed hard and glanced sideways. The towel hitched around his hips had slipped a little. "I should let you have some privacy and—"

"Shy?" he queried, reading her thoughts effortlessly. "It's nothing you haven't seen before."

Mary-Jayne swallowed hard. He was right. She'd seen every part of him. Touched every part of him. Been with him in the most intimate way possible. And still there was something unknown about him, something inviting and extraordinarily sexy. There was nothing overt about Daniel. He wasn't one of those constantly charming men who flirted and manipulated. He was sexually confident but not obvious. It was one of the reasons why she found him so blindingly attractive. He could have her as putty in his hands if he wanted to, but he didn't try to sway her with sex. For sure, he'd kissed her a couple of times, but even then he'd held back. When they'd been kissing in her kitchen days earlier and she'd told him to go, he hadn't lingered. He hadn't tried to persuade her or coerce. Because he possessed, she realized, bucketloads of integrity.

"You know," she said bluntly as she stirred the tea, "if you kissed me right now you'd probably have me in that bed in less than two seconds."

He chuckled. "I know."

"Except for your migraine, of course."

"I wouldn't let a lousy headache get in the way."

His words made her insides jump. She poured a second mug of tea and sat down. "Shall I open the curtains?" she asked, noticing that the only light in the room was coming from the direction of the open bathroom door. "Or are you still too sensitive?"

"I'm okay now."

She pushed the drapes aside a little. "My mother can't bear

light when she has an attack. My dad usually bundles her in the car and takes her to the doctor for a painkiller injection."

He flinched. "Bernie used to try acupuncture rather than meds when I was young to combat the worst of the pain."

"Did it work?"

He shrugged loosely and sat in the chair opposite. "At times. Thank you for the tea and...everything else today."

"No problem. Glad I could help."

He sniffed the air. "I can smell flowers."

She grinned. "It's lavender oil," she explained. "I massaged some of it into your temples. It's something my dad does for my mother."

He rubbed his forehead. "Oh...well, thanks. It helped."

She sipped her tea and pushed the sandwich toward him. "You really should eat something."

He nodded and picked up the bread. "How are *you* feeling? Any nausea today?"

"No," she replied. "I've been okay for the past couple of days." She rubbed her belly and smiled. "And it's a small price to pay for having these two growing inside me."

He regarded her thoughtfully. "You're really happy about being pregnant, aren't you?"

"Ecstatic," she said and smiled. "I mean, it's not what I'd planned...but then again, I don't ever really plan anything. My work, my travels... It's always been a little ad hoc. But now I can feel them, I know I couldn't be happier."

"Except for the fact that I'm their father?" he queried, one brow raised.

Mary-Jayne met his gaze. "I've never wished for it to be any different. I think you'll be a really great dad." She sighed heavily. "And I get it, you know...about why you want to get married. You didn't get a chance, last time, to be a father. That was taken away from you. But I would never do anything to keep you from your sons, Daniel. They're a part of you, just like they're a part of me."

His gray eyes smoldered. "So you think all that, and you still won't marry me."

"No."

He tossed the untouched sandwich back onto the tray. "Okay. I won't ask you again."

It was what she wanted. No more proposals. No more pursuit. But somehow, in the back of her mind, she felt a strange sensation. Like…like disappointment. But she managed a tight smile. "Thank you."

"And custody?"

"We can share it. Of course, I'm going to live here and you'll be in San Francisco…but you can see them whenever you want."

"Don't you think that will confuse them?" he asked quietly. "Me randomly turning up to play daddy."

"At first," she said, and gritted her back teeth. "But it's going to be impossible to share custody when we live in two different countries."

"They could live here for six months and then in San Francisco for six months."

Fear snaked up her spine. "You wouldn't?"

"I wouldn't what?"

Mary-Jayne perched herself on the edge of the chair. "Try to get fifty percent custody. I couldn't bear to be away from them for six months at a time. I know you've got money enough to get the best lawyers, but I really couldn't—"

"You misunderstand, Mary-Jayne," he said, cutting her off. "I meant you and the twins could live in San Francisco for six months. Look, I know you love this town and don't want to be away from it permanently, but perhaps we could meet in the middle, metaphorically speaking. I'll buy you a house near where I live and you could settle there every six months."

"You'll *buy* me a house? Just like that?"

He shrugged. "Sure."

"And fly me and the twins back and forth every six months?"

"Yes."

Meet in the middle? Perhaps that was the only way to settle the tension between them. And as much as she protested, she knew she'd do whatever she had to do if it meant retaining full custody of her babies. "We'll see what happens. Anyhow," she said and got to her feet, "you should rest for a while. You look like you need it."

"Can I see you later?"

"No," she replied. "You need to get some sleep. And I have some work to do. I'm making some pieces for a friend of Solana's and I need to concentrate."

"My grandmother is very fond of you," he said, and got to his feet. The towel slipped a little more and she averted her gaze. It wasn't good for her self-control to keep staring at his bare chest.

"I'm fond of her, too."

"I know," he said, and then added more soberly, "and I apologize if I might have suggested you were not pure in your motives when you got to know her. She told me you turned down her offer to finance your business. I should trust her judgment... She knows people way better than I do."

Heat crawled up her neck. He was paying her a compliment. It shouldn't have embarrassed her, but it did. "I understand you only wanted to protect her. But I genuinely like Solana and would never take advantage of her in any way."

"I know that, Mary-Jayne. But if you need help getting your business off the ground, then I would be more than—"

"No," she said and raised a hand. "My business is mediocre because I'm not all that ambitious... I never have been. I like designing and crafting the pieces, but that's where my interest ends. I started selling them online almost by mistake. My friends Lauren and Cassie persuaded me to start a website showcasing the things I'd made and then all of a sudden I had orders coming in. I do it because I have to make a living doing something, and why not earn money doing what I enjoy creatively."

He nodded as if he understood. She'd expected him to try to

sway her some more, but to his credit he accepted her explanation. "I'll see you soon, then."

"Okay," she said, and shrugged lightly, even though the idea of spending more time with him tied her insides into knots. She liked him. A lot. And that made it increasingly difficult to keep him at arm's length. "I hope you feel better."

It took another two days for Daniel to get back to his normal self. He conference called his brothers to keep up with business and spoke to his grandmother. Solana was keen to know the details of his visit with Mary-Jayne, but he didn't tell her much. He certainly wasn't going to admit she'd turned him down again and again.

On Friday morning he headed to the kitchen and found Evie elbow-deep in some kind of baking.

"Good morning," she greeted, and smiled. "Coffee?"

He nodded and helped himself to a mug and half filled it with coffee. "Cooking for the masses?" he asked as he looked over the large bowls in front of her before he perched himself on a stool by the counter.

"For the fire station," she said cheerfully. "My husband, Scott, is a fireman. He's on night shift at the moment and I usually bake a few dozen cupcakes to keep him and the rest of the crew going."

It was a nice gesture, he thought. A loving gesture. "He's a lucky guy."

She smiled. "I'm the lucky one. He moved here, you know, from California. He'd come here for his sister's wedding to my older brother and we fell in love, but he left a few weeks after he arrived. When I discovered I was pregnant he came back and stayed. He knew I could never leave here... I had a teenage son and my family. So he changed his life for me. It was a very selfless gesture."

Daniel didn't miss the meaning of her words.

But live in Crystal Point permanently? He couldn't. It wasn't the place for him. He had a business to run. He couldn't do that from a tiny town that was barely a spot on the map. Plus, he had a life in San Francisco. Friends. Routine. A past. He'd known Simone there. Loved her there. Grieved her there. To leave would be like abandoning those feelings. And Mary-Jayne had made her thoughts abundantly clear. He was pretty sure she didn't want him anywhere near her precious town. That was why he'd suggested she come to San Francisco for six months of the year. It was a sensible compromise. The only way around the situation.

"I'm glad it worked out for you," he said, and drank some coffee.

One of her eyebrows came up. "Things have a way of doing that, you know."

"Or they don't."

She smiled. "I like to believe that anything is possible...if you want it enough."

It was a nice idea, but he didn't really agree. He'd wanted his wife and daughter to be safe. But fate had other plans. Things happened. Bad things. Good things. Sometimes it was simply a matter of timing.

"She's always been headstrong," Evie said, and smiled again. "Don't let that bravado fool you though. Underneath she's as vulnerable as the next person."

"I know she is. She's also stubborn."

"Perhaps that's because she thinks you shouldn't always get your own way?" Evie suggested.

He laughed a little. "You might be right. But I'm not out to change her. I only want to be a father to my children."

"Maybe that's where you're going wrong," Evie said. "Maybe you need to concentrate on her first and foremost."

"Nice idea," he said ruefully. "Have you met your sister? She's not exactly giving me an opportunity."

"She's scared of you."

Daniel straightened. "Of me? Why? I'd never harm her or—"

"Of course you wouldn't," Evie said quickly. "I mean she's scared of what you represent. You're...normal... You know... not a—"

"Unemployed musician?" he finished for her. "Yeah, we've already had the ex-boyfriend discussion. She's antiwealth, antisuccess, anti-anything that gives her a reason to keep me out of the little bubble she's wrapped in."

"It's protection, that's all. Her first boyfriend was a deadbeat who stole her money. The one after that was a lazy so-and-so. If she's with you, it's as if she's admitting that she's not who everyone thinks she is. That all the other guys were just a phase... an aberration. That she isn't really a free spirit who does what she wants. It means that she's as vulnerable to a perfectly respectable and nice man as the rest of womankind is."

Daniel laughed. "So you're saying she won't marry me because I'm not a deadbeat?"

"Precisely."

He was still thinking of Evie's words when he was in town later that morning. Bellandale was a big regional town and had sufficient offerings to get what he needed done. By the afternoon he was back in Crystal Point and pulled up outside Mary-Jayne's house around five o'clock. She was in the front garden, crouched down and pulling weeds from an overgrown herb garden. She wore bright pink overalls that showed off her lovely curves and the popped-out belly. He watched her for a moment, marveling at her effortless beauty. His insides were jumping all over the place. No one had ever confounded him as much as Mary-Jayne Preston.

She stood up when she realized there was a car by the curb. She dropped the gloves and small garden fork in her hand and came down the driveway. Her crazily beautiful hair whipped around her face.

Daniel got out of the car and closed the door. "Good afternoon."

"You look better," she said as she approached. "Headache all gone?"

"Yes. How are you feeling?"

"I'm good," she said, and came beside the car. "Nice wheels. It doesn't look like a rental."

Daniel glanced at the white BMW and rattled the keys. "It's not."

Her eyes widened. "You bought a car?"

He nodded. "I did. Do you like it?"

She shrugged. "It's nice, I suppose. Very…highbrow."

A smile tugged at his mouth. "It's a sensible family car."

She looked it over and nodded. "I suppose it is. Since you had the rental, I didn't realize you needed a car."

"I don't," he said and grabbed her hand. "I still have the rental." He opened her fingers and rested the key in her palm. "It's yours."

Her eyes instantly bulged and she stepped back. "Mine?"

He nodded. "That's right."

The moment it registered her expression sharpened. "You bought me a car?"

"I did. I thought you—"

"I have a car," she said stiffly. "And it works just fine."

Daniel glanced at the beat-up, rusted yellow Volkswagen in the driveway. "Your car is old and not roadworthy."

Her hands propped onto her hips. "How do you know that? Have you taken it for a spin around the block?"

"I don't need to," he replied. "Take a look at it."

"I like it." She stepped forward and put the key back in his hand. "And I don't need another."

Daniel let out an exasperated breath. "Does everything have to be a battle between us? So I bought you a car. Sue me."

"I can't be bought."

Annoyance surged through his blood. "I'm not trying to buy you. I bought something *for* you. There's a significant difference."

"Not to me," she shot back. "First it's a car and then what…
a house? Maybe one to match the house in San Francisco you
want to buy? What then? A boat? What about a racehorse? Don't
forget the jewels. I'll probably need a private jet, too."

"You're being ridiculous. It's just a car."

"Stop trying to justify this. Take it back. I don't want it."

He kept a lid on his simmering rage. "I want my sons to
be safe, and they won't be in that jalopy," he said, and hooked
a thumb in the direction of her old VW. "Be sensible, Mary-
Jayne."

"I am sensible. And they'll be perfectly safe," she said hotly.
"I would never put them at risk. But I won't let you tell me what
to do. Not now, not ever."

He shook his head. "This isn't a multiple-choice exercise,
Mary-Jayne. And I won't compromise on this issue. The car is
yours." He took a few steps and dropped the key on top of the
letterbox. "I want you to have it."

"I don't care what you want!"

Daniel stilled and looked at her. Her cheeks were ablaze, her
hair framing her face, her chest heaving. A thousand conflicting emotions banged around in his head. And he knew there
was no reasoning with her. No middle road.

"No," he said wearily. "I guess you don't."

Then he turned around and walked down the street.

CHAPTER TEN

BOSSY. ARROGANT. Know-it-all.

Mary-Jayne had a dozen names for him and none of them were flattering.

He'd bought her a car. A car! Without discussing it with her first. Without any kind of consultation. He really did think he could do whatever he liked.

On Saturday afternoon she headed to her parents' place for lunch. The whole family got together once a month for a day of catch-up that included lunch, dinner and plenty of conversation and games with the kids. It was a Preston tradition, and since she'd missed the get-togethers while she'd been away, Mary-Jayne looked forward to spending time with them. Her father was manning the barbecue with her brother, Noah, while her brothers-in-law, Scott and Cameron, played pool in the games room, as Noah's wife, Callie, kept their kids entertained. Evie's toddler and Grace's newborn were the center of attention in the kitchen while her mother fussed around making her famous potato salad. Her best friend Lauren was there, too, with her fiancé and her own parents. Lauren was Cameron's sister and her fiancé, Gabe, was Scott and Callie's cousin. It was a close-knit group. The blood ties alone made it a mammoth exercise to remember who was related to whom. She cared for them all, but as she sat at the kitchen table, one hand draped over her abdomen and the other curled around a glass of diet soda, she experienced an inexplicable empty feeling deep down, almost through to her bones.

She couldn't define it. She should he happy. Elated. She had her babies growing in her belly and her whole family around her. But something was amiss. Something was missing. *Someone was missing.*

She quickly put the idea from her head.

"Where's Daniel today?"

Her mother's cheerful voice interrupted her thoughts. She shrugged. "I have no idea."

Barbara frowned a little. "I thought he might have liked to come and meet everyone."

"I didn't invite him."

The room fell silent, and she looked up to see her mother's frown.

"I did," Evie added quickly. "But he said he wouldn't come unless you asked him to be here."

Shame niggled between her shoulders. "Good. He's finally showing some sense."

Evie sighed. "What's he done now?"

Mary-Jayne couldn't miss the disapproval in her eldest sister's voice. It irritated her down to her teeth. "He bought me a car," she said tartly. "A brand-spanking-new BMW with all the trimmings." She laughed humorlessly. "Imagine me driving around town in that."

The three women stared at her. It was Grace who spoke next.

"That was very thoughtful of him, don't you think? Considering how old and unreliable your current car is."

Mary-Jayne's jaw tightened. "I know it's old. And I know it's unreliable. But it's mine by choice because it's what I can afford. And he wasn't being thoughtful… He was being controlling."

Evie tutted. "Have you considered that perhaps he only wants you and the babies to be safe while you're driving?"

"That's what he said," she replied impatiently. "But I know Daniel and he—"

"Didn't his wife and baby die in a car accident?" Grace again, equally disapproving as Evie and their mother.

"Yes, they did," Evie supplied.

"And wasn't the other car involved an *old and unreliable* vehicle that had a major brake failure?"

"Yes," Evie said, looking directly at Mary-Jayne.

She sat up straight in the chair.

I don't care what you want...

Her careless words banged around in her head. Simone and their baby had died because the car that struck them had a broken brake line. She realized what he must have thought when he saw her old car—that history might repeat itself. That their sons' lives might be at risk.

It wasn't control that had motivated him to buy her a car. It was fear.

She stood up, her hands shaking. "I have to go out for a while." She looked toward Grace. "I'm parked behind you. Can you ask Cameron to move your car?"

Evie pointed to a set of keys on the counter. "Take mine," her sister suggested pointedly. "He's there alone, in case you're wondering, working in the office. My other guests left yesterday."

Mary-Jayne nodded, grabbed the keys and left.

The trip took just minutes, and she pulled the Honda Civic into the driveway. The gardens at Dunn Inn were like something out of a fairy tale, and she walked up the cobbled pathway, past the wishing well and headed up the steps to the porch. A couple of the French-style doors were open, and she slid the insect screen back. Her sister's artwork graced most walls, and the furnishings were well matched and of good quality. Evie had a style all of her own. There was a small office off the living room and when she reached the doorway she came to a halt.

Daniel sat in the chair, earphones on, tapping on the computer keys. She came behind him and touched his shoulder. He flinched and turned, tossing the earphones aside.

"Hi," she said, and dropped her tote.

He wore jeans and a blue shirt that looked as though it had been tailored to fit his gorgeous frame. His gray eyes scanned her face, his expression unreadable.

"I thought you had a family thing to go to?"

"I did," she said. "I do."

"Then, what are you doing here?"

"I left." She shrugged one shoulder. "I wanted to see you."

He swiveled the chair around and sat back. "So you're seeing me. What?"

Mary-Jayne swallowed hard. "You're working. I'm probably interrupting and—"

"What do you want, Mary-Jayne?" he asked impatiently.

She let out a long breath. "To apologize."

He stood up immediately and folded his arms. "Consider it done."

"I was wrong, okay," she said when she noticed his expression was still unmoved. "I shouldn't have reacted the way I did. I shouldn't have *overreacted*. I didn't stop to think about why it was so important to you that I have a new car." She rubbed her belly gently. "But I get it now… I understand that you need to know that our sons are safe because of what happened to your wife and daughter… You know, how the other car was old and had brake failure." Her throat thickened as she said the words. She looked at him and tried to read what he was thinking. But she couldn't. She wished she knew him better. And wished she understood the emotions behind his gray eyes.

The shutters were still up, so she pressed on.

"And I shouldn't have said that I didn't care what you wanted. I didn't mean it," she admitted.

His jaw was achingly tight. "I can't bear the thought of you driving around in that old car."

"I know," she said softly. "And I understand why you feel

that way. I should have been more considerate of your feelings. But sometimes, when I'm with you, I react before I think about the consequences. It's not a conscious thing." She waved her hands. "But between you and me there's all this...tension. And getting mad at you is kind of like a release valve for that."

The mood between them suddenly altered. There *was* tension between them. Built on a blinding, blistering physical attraction that had never been truly sated. One night would never be enough for that kind of pull. Daniel had known it all along. She realized that as she stared up at him, breathing hard, chest heaving. That was why he'd pursued her for a month after Solana's birthday party. And that was why she'd refused him. She was scared of those feelings. Terrified of the way he made her feel. Because she still wanted him.

"Daniel..."

She said his name on a wispy breath. His eyes were dark, burning and filled with desire. It was heady and commanding. It made her shake with longing and fear. Of course she wasn't afraid of him, only the hypnotic power he had over her.

He groaned, as though he knew he was about to do something he probably shouldn't. But Mary-Jayne didn't care. In that moment, with nothing between but barely a foot of space, all she wanted was to be in his arms.

"I'm trying so hard to fight this."

"I know. But it's me you're fighting," he said softly. "Not this."

He was right. She fought him. In her heart she felt she had to. But in that moment all her fight disappeared.

"Make love to me," she whispered and reached out to touch his chest.

He flinched against her touch as though it was poker hot. "Are you sure that's what you want?"

She shrugged lightly. "The only thing I'm sure about is that I'm not sure about anything anymore."

He reached for her shoulders and molded them with his

hands. He fisted a handful of her hair and gently tilted her head back. "You drive me crazy, do you know that?"

She nodded a little. "I don't mean to."

"You can trust me, you know," he said and lowered his head toward her face. "I'm not your enemy. Even if it does feel as though most of the time we're at war with each other."

He kissed her then. Not gently. Not softly. But long and deep and fueled with heated possession. Mary-Jayne kissed him back and wrapped her arms around his waist. "Do you have any idea how sexy you are?" he whispered against her lips.

"No," she said, and smiled as she trailed her lips along his jaw. "We've got the place to ourselves... Let's not waste any time."

He got her to his room in ten seconds flat. He closed the door and locked it.

They stood opposite one another by the bed. Last time there'd been no thinking, nothing but desire and pure instinct. This was different. This was conscious and planned and fueled by more than simple attraction.

"Do you know what I thought the first time I saw you?" he asked quietly.

Mary-Jayne shook her head.

"I thought," he said as he reached for her, "that I had never seen a woman with such beautiful hair in all my life."

He kissed her again, and she shuddered and tossed her head. When he pulled back she was breathing so hard she thought her lungs might explode. He slipped her T-shirt off one shoulder and trailed his mouth along her collarbone. There was such blistering intensity in his touch that it thrilled her to the soles of her feet. He kept kissing her, making her sigh and moan until finally she begged him to take her to the bed.

"What's the hurry?" he muttered against her neck.

Mary-Jayne ran her hands over his chest. His heart beat furiously behind his ribs and her hand hovered there for a moment. Last time they'd made love as if there was no time to waste.

But now he seemed in no rush to get her naked and between the sheets. He was taking his time exploring her mouth with his own and gently smoothing his hands across her back and shoulders. They stood kissing like that for minutes. Or was it hours? She couldn't tell. She was too overwhelmed by the narcotic pleasure thrumming through her body at the seductive tone of his skilled touch. By the time they worked their way to the side of the bed she was a wriggling mass of need.

He stripped the T-shirt over her head and Mary-Jayne watched, fascinated as he slowly undressed her. It was intensely erotic and made her long for him with such urgency she could barely breathe. When she was naked, when her shirt was on the floor and her bra dispensed with, he hooked his thumbs under the band of her briefs and slowly skimmed them down over her bottom and legs. Then he was on his knees in front of her, touching her belly, pressing kisses across the curved, tightened skin. She'd never experienced anything more intimate or soul reaching in her entire life. He reached up to cup her breasts, and they felt heavy in his hands. As he gently toyed with her nipples, every part of her body felt more alive, more sensitive to his touch than ever before.

She whispered his name, and he looked up to meet her gaze. He was still fully dressed and she wanted nothing more than to feel his skin against her, to wrap herself in his embrace and feel his body deep within hers. Mary-Jayne curled her fingers around his shirt collar and found the top button. She flicked it open with eager hands.

"Take this off," she instructed with way more bravado than she felt.

He smiled, urged her to sit, and once she was settled on the bed he shrugged out of his shirt. Shoes and socks and jeans followed, and once he was naked he sat beside her.

"Better?" he asked, reaching for her again, kissing her neck and shoulders.

Mary-Jayne sighed heavily. "Much."

He palmed her rounded belly. "Pregnancy has made you even more beautiful, if that were possible."

It was a lovely thought. She'd never considered herself all that beautiful. Not like her sister Grace. Or Evie, with her dancing eyes and seductive curves. She was pretty at best. Not even particularly sexy. But beneath Daniel's glittering gaze she felt more beautiful than she ever had in her life.

She placed a hand on her belly. "Are we going to be able to do this?" she asked, smiling a little. "My middle is expanding at an alarming rate."

Daniel grasped her hand and spanned his own across her stomach. "I'm sure we'll manage just fine, darling."

Darling...

It was the first endearment he'd said to her. And it sounded so lovely coming from his lips that emotion unexpectedly gathered at the back of her eyes. She wanted that and more. Despite every argument and every rational part of her brain telling her it was madness—she wanted to be the woman he called darling every day of his life.

Because...

Because she loved him.

She'd fallen in love with the father of her babies. Wholly and completely. Even knowing that he didn't love her back and that he was all wrong for her and she for him. None of that mattered. Her heart had decided.

"What are you thinking?" he asked.

Mary-Jayne shook her head. "Nothing... Just...kiss me."

He smiled and found her mouth again. His kiss was long and slow and everything she wanted. She kissed him back with every ounce of feeling in her heart. He lowered her onto the bed and began to make love to her with such excruciating sweetness she could barely stop herself from calling out his name. He touched her, stroked her and worshipped her breasts with his mouth and hands until she was quivering in his arms. By the time he moved his hand between her legs to caress her she was so fueled with passion she rose up and over and found release almost immediately. It was wondrously intense, and when she came back to earth and the stars had stopped exploding behind her eyes she saw that he was staring down into her face.

"What's wrong?" she asked tremulously, pushing air into her lungs.

"Not a thing," he replied, and kissed her again. "So I guess we don't have to be too concerned about birth control?"

She grinned and stretched. "The horse has already bolted on that one."

Daniel laughed and rolled over, positioning himself between her legs. She relaxed her thighs and waited, so consumed with love for him in that moment that if he'd asked her for the moon she would had flown into the sky to catch it for him.

When they were together, when she couldn't tell when she began and he ended, Mary-Jayne let out a contented moan. He moved against her with such acute tenderness her heart literally ached. Nothing had ever felt so good. And she'd never been more connected to anyone than she was with him as he hovered above her, taking most of his weight on his strong arms, ensuring she was comfortable and relaxed. Release came to her again, slow and languorous and fulfilling, and when he shuddered above her she held on, gripping him tighter, longer and with more feeling than she ever had before in her life.

When he moved and rolled over onto his back, they were both breathing madly. Mary-Jayne closed her eyes and sighed. When her breathing returned with some normalcy she shifted onto her side and looked at him. His chest rose and fell, and he had his eyes closed. He reached for her hand and linked their fingers.

"You know," he said, and sighed, "we should do it down on the beach."

"Do what?" she asked, and kissed his shoulder. "This?"

"Get married. What else?"

Mary-Jayne stilled. A little voice at the back of her mind chanted that she should grab his idea with both hands and say a resounding *yes*. But she couldn't. He didn't love her. He never would. Sure, the sex was incredible and she had his babies growing inside her, but not even that was enough to sustain a lifetime relationship. He had to know that. Only a fool would believe otherwise. She loved him. But she wasn't about to become strapped to a one-side marriage.

"You said you wouldn't ask again," she reminded him.

He shrugged. "I can't help it. I want what I want."

"I can't."

"Or won't?" he asked.

"Both," she admitted, and rolled onto her back. "Can't we just get to know one another a little, Daniel? I mean, I hardly know anything about you and—"

"Because you've never asked," he said a little more harshly. "Okay—I'm thirty-four and recently had a birthday. My favorite color is yellow and I loathe brussels sprouts. When I was fifteen I chipped my two front teeth and now I have veneers. I was seventeen the first time I had sex and since my wife died I've slept with just over half a dozen women. I like imported beer but rarely drink. I haven't had a meaningful conversation with my dad in years and I still think it sucks that I never knew my real mom." He pulled himself up and draped the sheet across his hips. "Satisfied?"

Mary-Jayne sat up and covered her bare breasts with her arms. "That's not what I meant. I'm talking about time. We need time to get to know one another."

"We don't have it," he said flatly. "You live here. I live in San Francisco. I need an answer, Mary-Jayne."

She pulled herself across the bed and got to her feet. "Then, it's no."

No. Again.

Was there a bigger sucker than him?

Daniel sprang out of the bed and watched her as she snatched up her clothes. "You're being rash…as usual."

"I'm being honest," she said, and pulled on her underwear. "And sure, I'm impulsive and over the years it has gotten me into trouble every now and then. But in this I'm not being rash. I'm using my head," she said, and looked him over with deliberate emphasis. "And not the part of my anatomy that you are if you think having great sex is enough of a reason to get married."

"They're the reason," he said, and pulled on his jeans as he motioned to her belly. "Our children. The great sex is a bonus."

She tossed a shoe at him. And then another.

The first one hit him in the shoulder and the second sandal he caught midair. There was so much fire and spirit in her, so much passion. Daniel was inexplicably drawn to her like a moth to a flame. He liked that she wasn't a pushover, even though it drove him to distraction. "Stop throwing things at me."

"Well, you stop doing what you're doing and I will."

Daniel dropped the shoe and shrugged, holding out his hands. "What have I done now?"

"You know exactly what," she said on a rush of breath. "You know how I feel, Daniel. I don't want to get married and live somewhere else. I want to live here, in Crystal Point. I want our children to grow up in a home, not a house. And I want my family around me while I raise them."

"While *you* raise them?" he said flatly. "Which is exactly my point. *We* need to raise them, Mary-Jayne, together. And I think today proved that we can. We have a connection that's—"

"We had sex," she corrected. "But it's not enough. The truth is, you confuse me when you kiss me and touch me, and then I can't get any of this straight in my mind. I won't let you use sex as a way of—"

"*You* came here today, remember?" he reminded her, cutting her off. "*You* asked me to make love to *you*, remember? Not the other way around. I've left you alone these past few days… just as you asked."

She stilled. "But…"

Her words trailed and she glared at him, her eyes glittering with a kind of fiery rage. She was brash and argumentative and generally on the attack...but caught out, and she was as meek as a lamb. She was a fascinating contradiction. And he craved her more than he'd ever wanted any woman in his life.

"You came here today looking for me. For this," he said and gestured to the bed. "Because we have an insane attraction for one another that neither of us expected."

She sucked in a long breath. "I came here today because I felt bad for what I said the other day. I felt guilty, okay?"

"So today was about sympathy? Throw a crumb to the lonely widower whose wife and baby died?"

"No," she said quickly. "Of course not. I just thought we could...talk, that's all."

"Talk about what?" he asked. "You and me? There is no you and me, right? Or do you want to know about Simone? Or our daughter? What do you want to know? How long I sat in hospital the night my wife died? Eight hours," he said, feeling the memory of those hours through to the marrow in his bones. "Do you also want to know that I never got to say goodbye to her? I never got a chance to tell her what she meant to me— hell, I never even said it enough when she was alive. And yes, I held my daughter's lifeless body for a few moments before they took her away. Do you want to know if I cried? Once, after the wake when everyone had left and I realized for the rest of my life I'd be living with the fact that my daughter's birthday was the same day she and her mom died."

He stopped speaking and looked at Mary-Jayne. Her eyes brimmed with tears, and he immediately felt bad. He didn't want to upset her. He wanted to do the exact opposite, if she'd only let him.

"I'm so sorry..."

"You can't have it both ways," he said as he retrieved her skirt and T-shirt and passed them to her. "Yes, my wife and baby died. And yes, sometimes I feel alone *and* lonely because of that.

Who the hell doesn't feel alone at times? But if you want to be here, then really be here, Mary-Jayne. Stop making excuses."

"I'm not," she said, wiping her eyes before she quickly slipped into her clothes.

"You are," he said, suddenly impatient. "And the next time you turn up on my door and ask me to make love to you, it'll only happen if my ring is on your finger."

"Then it will never happen again."

He shrugged, pretty sure she didn't believe that any more than he did. "You should get back to your party."

She shoved her feet into her shoes. "Would you like to come with me?"

He cocked one brow. "Are you sure that's what you want?"

"What I want is for us to get along for the sake of our children." She planted her hands on her hips and spoke in a quiet voice. "I'm trying to be rational and realistic. I don't want to be trapped in a loveless and empty marriage. And if you're honest with yourself, if you can think of only that and not about custody of the babies or how challenging it's going to be to raise them together when we live on opposite sides of the world, you'd realize that you don't want that, either. Especially after the way you loved your wife."

A loveless and empty marriage? Was that what she truly thought it would be? Were her feelings for him that hollow? He did his best to ignore the way that idea made him feel.

"I want," he said with deliberate emphasis, "my family."

"So do I," she said quietly. "But *my* family is here, Daniel. In Crystal Point. I like living a few streets away from my parents and having my sisters and brother close by. I don't come from a family where we greet one another with a handshake and live in different parts of the world. I like knowing that 'I love you' is the last thing I hear from my mother when I hang up the phone after I speak to her, and I like knowing that my dad would be there for me in a heartbeat if I needed him. And maybe that sounds like a silly TV movie to you, but it's what I want for my children."

For a second he envied her. It didn't sound silly at all. It sounded real and authentic and exactly what he'd hoped he'd have for his own children one day. Being around Mary-Jayne and her family had only amplified that need. He wanted to tell her that. But he held back.

I don't want to be trapped in a loveless and empty marriage.

That was what she imagined they'd have. Not a marriage like her siblings' or her parents'. But something less, something that would never measure up to the standards she witnessed in her life. It would never be enough. They would never be enough.

"We should get going," he said, and grabbed his shirt. "I would like to see your parents again."

She nodded and made her way across the room.

They drove separate cars to her parents' home. Him in his rental. She in her sister's Honda. He knew the BMW still sat outside her house. She hadn't driven it once, he was sure. Sh was stubborn and infuriating. When they arrived at the P ton house, he got out and met her by her car door, not sa word about the old VW he spotted in the driveway, eve gh he hated the idea of her driving something so un and potentially dangerous.

"I'm sorry about before," he said, and to elbow. "I didn't mean to make you cry."

She sniffed. "Okay...sure."

He rubbed her skin. "I don't enjoy seeing you upset."

She nodded, eyes still glistening. "I know that. I don't mean to upset you, either. I just don't seem to be able to help myself sometimes."

Inside, he was welcomed by her family with the warmth he'd come to expect from them. They were good people, and it made him think about the dig she'd made about handshakes and living on opposite sides of the world. She was right. He was close to his brothers but not in the way she was with her siblings. And his relationship with Miles and Bernadette had been taxing most of his life.

He was by the pool talking to her brother and enduring a moderate kind of grilling about his intentions when his phone rang. He excused himself and picked up the call on the fifth ring.

It was Caleb.

Daniel listened to his brother's concerned voice, and once he ended the call went looking for Mary-Jayne. She was inside, in the kitchen with her mother and sister-in-law.

"I need to talk to you," he said, and ignored the thunder behind his ribs.

She must have picked up on his mood, because she complied immediately and ushered him into the front living room.

"What is it?" she asked once they were alone.

"I have to leave."

"Oh, okay. I'll see you Monday, then. Remember I have an appointment with my OB at ten."

"I'm leaving Crystal Point," he said again, firmer. "Caleb just called me—Bernie's in the hospital in Cairns. She had a massive heart attack a couple of hours ago."

Mary-Jayne gasped and gripped his arm. "Oh, how awful. Is there anything I can do?"

Marry me and stay by my side...

He reached out and touched her belly, felt the movement of his babies beneath his palm and experienced such an acute sensation in his chest he could barely breathe. The connection was mesmerizing. Her green eyes glittered brilliantly, and he got so caught up in her gaze he was rooted to the spot.

"I could... I could..." Her voice trailed off.

"What?" he asked.

She shrugged a little. "I'm not sure... I just thought perhaps I could..."

She could what? Come with him? A part of him wanted that more than anything. But that couldn't be what she meant. She'd have to care one way or another. Daniel swallowed hard. "Take care of yourself, Mary-Jayne."

"You, too," she whispered. "Give your dad and Bernie my love."

But not you...

He got the message loud and clear.

"I'll talk to you soon."

"Please let me know how she is."

Daniel nodded, suddenly numb all over. "Sure." He shrugged off her touch and walked to the door, but something stopped him. Then he turned and looked at her.

"What?" she asked softly.

"I've just realized that you're a fraud, Mary-Jayne," he said. "You walk and talk like some restless free spirit who can take on the world, but underneath all that talk is someone who's afraid to truly be who she is."

She frowned. "That doesn't make sense."

"Doesn't it? You've wrapped yourself up in this image of being a certain kind of person and it's as though you've locked yourself in a cage. Admit it, if I was some unemployed, tattooed and unsuccessful guitarist things would be very different. You'd have nothing to hide behind. You say you don't want to be trapped in a loveless marriage—but that's not it. You just don't want to marry *me*. Because if you did it would mean that everything you've ever stood for is a great big lie. It would mean that you've settled for the safe road, and then everyone around you would know that your boldness and bluster is just an act and that you're as mainstream and sensible as the rest of us. And that's what scares you—being like everyone else. That's why your last boyfriend was a deadbeat and why your business fails to get off the ground. You think that makes you a free spirit? You're wrong... All that makes you is a coward."

Then he turned on his heel and left.

CHAPTER ELEVEN

"ARE YOU STILL feeling unwell?" Evie's voice cut through her thoughts.

Mary-Jayne battened down the nausea she'd been battling for a week. She'd spent the morning babysitting her niece while Evie and Scott attended an art show in Bellandale. She loved looking after Rebecca and considered it good practice for when her babies arrived.

"On and off. The crackers help a little, but yesterday I spent an hour bent over the toilet bowl. I saw my doctor the other day and we discussed some medication I can take to alleviate the nausea if it gets much worse. I just don't want to do anything that might harm my babies. But after yesterday I think I'm going to have to take his advice. I've got another doctor's appointment tomorrow at three."

Evie grimaced. "That's not much fun. Other than that, is everything going okay?"

"With the pregnancy? Yes, no problems. Except I'm getting as big as a house."

"You look lovely as always," Evie assured her. "Heard from Daniel?"

"Nope."

Evie's brows furrowed. "Everything okay on that front?"

"Nope," she said and sighed. "We sort of had a fight before he left."

"Just a fight? Anything else?"

Her sister was way too intuitive. Mary-Jayne shrugged. She wasn't about to admit he'd called her a coward, or that it was exactly how she felt. "Sex isn't enough to sustain a marriage... no matter how good it is."

Evie came around the kitchen counter and rested her hands on the back of a dining chair. "Why didn't you go with him?"

She shrugged, hurting all over. "He didn't ask me."

"Maybe he thought you'd say no."

She shrugged again, still hurting, and more confused than ever. She wasn't about to admit to her sister that she missed him like crazy. "I'm not part of his life in that way."

"But you're lovers?"

Heat crept over her skin. She could never lie to Evie. "I guess. Does one night and one afternoon together make us lovers? I'm not sure what that makes us. All it makes me is confused."

"But you're in love with him, right?"

"It doesn't matter what I am," she insisted. "I can love him until the cows come home and it won't change the fact that he doesn't love me back."

"Are you sure?"

"Positive," she replied, aching deep down. She pressed her hands to her belly and rubbed her babies as they moved inside her. "He's all one-eyed about what he thinks we should do. Which is get married and raise our children in San Francisco."

"He said that?" she asked. "He said he wants you to move there?"

She nodded. "Well, he offered to buy me a house so I can live there for six months of the year."

Evie tilted her head. "I thought he might have decided he liked it here."

Mary-Jayne's eyes popped wide. "Daniel live here? In Crystal Point?" She laughed shrilly. "Not likely. Too hometown for him. He's all business and logic. He'd be bored out of his mind in a place like this."

Her sister smiled. "Really? He looked pretty comfortable here to me. And since when did you get all stuck on Crystal Point as a be-all and end-all? You spent a good part of the past ten years away from here, traveling from one place to the next." Her brows came back up. "I can remember a certain nineteen-year-old telling me in no uncertain terms that it was the most boring, uneventful spot on the map before you hopped on a plane for Morocco. I think the folks thought you'd closed your eyes and pointed to a spot on an atlas and thought, 'Why not go there?' And then there was Thailand, and Cambodia, and after that it was Mexico. And wasn't it you who spent three months backpacking through Greece and working transient jobs and peddling your jewelry to patrons in sidewalk cafés to make ends meet? And didn't you recently leave here to bail out your old school friend in Port Douglas with only a day's notice?" Evie smiled. "What's happened, M.J.? Have you lost your restless spirit? Have you realized that this little town is not such a bad place after all?"

"I never thought it was bad. I love this town. I've just always loved traveling and experiencing new places, that's all."

"New places except San Francisco?"

Mary-Jayne stilled. Evie had a point. "You think I should do it? You think I should marry him and move to another country?"

"I think you should do whatever your heart tells you is right."

"That's what I'm doing," she insisted.

"Your heart," Evie said pointedly. "Not your head."

But my heart will get pummeled, for sure...

"I can't." She stood and grabbed her bag. "I have to get going."

Her sister nodded. "Okay. Thank you for babysitting. Rebecca loves spending time with you."

Mary-Jayne smiled broadly. "It's mutual."

Evie reached out and hugged her tight. "By the way, I see you're driving the Beamer."

Mary-Jayne wondered how long it would take for her sister to remark about the car parked along the front curb. She shrugged. "Seemed silly to let it sit there, that's all."

"Smart move. Is it good to drive?"

"Like a dream," she admitted, and grinned. "And two baby seats arrived for it yesterday."

Evie's smiled widened. "He thought of everything, didn't he?"

"Pretty much," she replied, ignoring the jab of pain in her chest. "Anyway, I have to run."

"Let me know how things go at the doctor's."

"Will do," she said as she left.

By the time she got home it was after four. She fed the dog and parrot and took a shower and then changed into baggy sweats and flaked out on the sofa. She flicked channels on the television and stared absently at the screen for an hour. Later, she ate a grilled-cheese sandwich and attempted to do some work on a new bracelet for one of Solana's friends. But she couldn't concentrate. Her mind was filled with thoughts of Daniel and his parting words.

Four days after Daniel left, Mary-Jayne got a text from Audrey informing her that Bernie was finally off the critical list but still in intensive care. There was no word from Daniel. It had been a long, lonely week. Part of her was glad. Part of her never wanted to see him again. Another part missed him so much she ached inside.

Coward...

The word had resonated in her head for days. No one had ever called her that before. No one would ever dare. But not Daniel. He called it how it was. He made her accountable for her convictions. For the first time in her life Mary-Jayne felt as though she had met her match. Her *perfect* match.

If only he loved her...

But he didn't. He thought that physical attraction was enough to sustain a marriage. But in her heart she knew it wasn't. He was kidding himself. Sure, maybe for the first few years everything would be okay. They'd be busy raising their children and there wouldn't be time to think about how loveless their marriage was. But later, once the children were older and there was only them, their differences would be evident and insurmountable. It was an impossible situation. And she wouldn't do it. She couldn't. She owed her babies more than a life where their parents were together for the wrong reasons.

As much as she appreciated her sister's support, Evie didn't really understand. She'd fallen madly in love with Scott and he'd loved her in return. He'd wooed her and fought for her and laid his heart on the line as if nothing else mattered. But Daniel... There was no heart in his proposal. Only logic and his desire to share custody of their sons.

And that would never be enough.

Five days after arriving back in Port Douglas, Daniel and his brothers were still maintaining a rotating vigil outside Bernie's hospital room. Their father hadn't left his wife's side, and at seven o'clock on Thursday evening, Daniel headed for the small hospital cafeteria and returned with two double-shot espressos. Bernie had finally been taken off the critical list, and Blake and Caleb had gone back to the resort to get some much-needed rest while Daniel stayed with his father, ensuring Miles at least ate and drank something.

"Here," he said, and passed his father a take-out cup as he sat in one of the uncomfortable chairs outside the intensive care ward. "And don't let it get cold like the last one I gave you."

Miles managed a grin and then nodded. "Thanks."

His father's pain was palpable. "She's out of danger, Dad. That's good news."

"I know," Miles said, and sighed. "I don't think I could have taken another night of wondering if she was going to make it."

"You heard what the doctor said a few hours ago," he assured his father. "She's going to pull through and be back to her old self in no time."

His dad sighed again. "Who would have thought this might happen? I mean, she's always been so health conscious... I never would have guessed she had a weak heart."

"No one can predict the future, Dad."

His words felt hollow as they left his mouth. How often had he thought that? When his grandfather passed away? When Simone and their baby died? When Mary-Jayne told him she was pregnant?

"Yeah, I know," his dad said, and tapped him on the shoulder. "Thanks for being here this week. It's meant a lot to me."

"I wouldn't be anywhere else."

Miles shrugged a little. "I know you've got a lot going on."

Daniel drank some coffee and stared at the wall ahead.

"You should go back," Miles said quietly. "You need to sort it out."

"Actually, I think a little time apart might be what we both need."

He wasn't about to admit that he missed Mary-Jayne more than he'd believed possible. But he hadn't called her, even though he craved the sound of her voice. And he was right about thinking they needed some time out.

"Nonsense," his dad said gently. "Time apart serves no purpose. Because one day you might find you have no time left, right?"

Daniel looked at his father. Miles had one of his serious expressions on his face, and as much as Daniel wanted to fob the other man off, he resisted. He'd seen that look once before, right after his grandfather had died and Daniel was preparing to step into the role of CEO. Miles had tried to talk him out of it. At the time, Daniel was convinced his father lacked vision and ambition and simply wanted to sell the company. And it had taken years for that idea to fade. It wasn't until the wake after Simone's death that he'd realized that there was more to life than business. More to life than seventy-hour weeks and meetings and racing to catch flights from one corner of the globe to the other. But still, he hadn't changed. He'd kept on doing the same things. He'd drowned himself in work to avoid thinking about all he'd lost.

"How about we concentrate on Bernie getting better and—"

"I'm very proud of you, you know," Miles said, uncharacteristically cutting him off. "I'm very proud of the man you have become."

Daniel's throat thickened. "Dad, I—"

"And I know I never say it enough." His father shrugged. "I guess I'm not sure if that matters to you."

"It matters," he said quietly. "The talking thing... It goes both ways."

Miles smiled. "Your mom was always telling me I needed to talk more to my own father. When you were born I promised myself I'd be a better father than Mike Anderson...but I'm not sure I have been. When your mom died I fell apart. Thankfully Bernie came along and picked up the pieces, even though she had every reason to run a mile. I was a grieving man with a baby, and I had so much emotional baggage it's a wonder she was able to see through all that and still give me a shot."

"She loved you," Daniel said, and drank some coffee.

"Not at first, she didn't," Miles said. "Some days I think she might have hated me. But we worked it out." His father nodded and grinned a little. "And you will, too."

Daniel didn't share his dad's optimism. Mary-Jayne opposed him at every opportunity. And he couldn't see a way out of it. He wanted her, sure. And sometimes...sometimes it felt as though he needed her like he needed air in his lungs. But it wasn't anything more than that. How could it be? They hardly knew one another. She was dreaming about some silly romantic notion that simply didn't exist. So maybe he did think about her 24/7. And maybe he did long for her in ways he'd never longed for anyone before. But that was just desire and attraction. Add in the fact that he wanted the chance to be a full-time father to his sons…and of course it might seem like something else. Something more.

"I loved your mom," Miles said quietly. "But I love Bernie, too. It's not more, it's not less… It's simply a different kind of same."

A different kind of same…

He was still thinking about his father's words for hours afterward. And still when he tried to sleep later that night. His dreams were plagued by images of Mary-Jayne. He dreamed of holding her, of making love to her, of waking up with her hair fanned out on the pillow beside him. He awoke restless and missing her more than he'd imagined he could. And in the cold light of morning he realized one irrefutable fact.

He was in love with her.

And their relationship had just become a whole lot more complicated.

On Monday, with the nausea and lack of appetite still lingering, she went back to her doctor to discuss some medication and get her blood pressure checked. She was waiting for the doctor to come into the room when Julie, an old school friend and now the receptionist from the front desk, popped her head around the door.

"M.J.," she said and made a face. "There's someone out here who wants to see you. Who *insists* on seeing you."

She perched herself on the edge of the chair. "Who?"

Julie's eyes widened dramatically. "He says he's your fiancé."

The blood left her face. There could only be one possibility. "Oh…okay," she said, trying not to have a reaction that Julie would see through and then question. "Tall, dark hair, handsome, gray eyes?"

Julie nodded. "Oh, yeah, that's him."

She managed a smile. "You should probably send him through."

"Okay, sure."

She disappeared, and barely seconds later the door opened and Daniel strode into the room. Mary-Jayne looked him over. He seemed so familiar and yet like such a stranger. He wore dark chinos and a creaseless pale blue shirt. Her heart skipped a beat. She'd never found any man as attractive as him. And doubted she ever would. And deep down, in that place she'd come to harbor all her feelings for him, she was happy to see him. More than happy. Right then, in that moment, she didn't feel alone.

She took a breath and met his gaze. "Fiancé?"

He shrugged loosely. "Got me in the room, didn't it?"

She didn't flinch. "What are you doing here? How did you—"

"Your sister told me I'd find you here."

She nodded. "So you're back?"

"I'm back." He moved across the room and sat beside her. "How's your mother?"

He rested back in the seat a little. "Out of intensive care. She had major bypass surgery for two blocked arteries. She's doing okay now. She'll be in the hospital for another week, though. So why are you here? Checkup?"

Mary-Jayne tried to ignore how her insides fluttered from being so close to him. "I haven't been feeling well and—"

"You're sick?" he asked and jackknifed up straight. "What's wrong? Is it the babies?" he asked and reached out to touch her abdomen.

She flinched a little from his touch, and he noticed immediately because he snatched his hand away. "Just nausea again. And I've lost my appetite."

He frowned. "Why didn't you call me? I would have come back sooner."

She pressed her shoulders back. "You needed to be with your family. It was important for your parents."

"I need to be here for you," he said with emphasis. "That's important, too."

"I'm fine," she insisted, feeling like a fool for thinking his concern must mean he cared. Well, of course he cared. She was carrying his babies. But caring wasn't love. And love was all she'd accept.

He inspected her face with his smoky gaze. "You look pale."

"Stop fussing," she said and frowned. "I'm fine, like I said. Just tired and not all that hungry because of the nausea. But I'm sure it will pass soon."

The doctor entered then, and she was glad for the reprieve. Until Daniel started barking out questions about her fatigue, her blood pressure and the likelihood of risks associated with the antinausea medication the doctor suggested she take if the symptoms didn't abate soon. She gave Daniel a death stare— which he ignored completely.

The doctor, a mild-mannered man in his fifties, just nodded and answered the questions in a patient voice. When he said he was going to draw some blood, Daniel almost rocketed out of his seat.

"Why? What's wrong?" he asked. "If you think there's a risk to her health then I insist we—"

"It's okay," she assured him and grasped his arm. "It's just a blood test. Remember how I told you that my sisters had gestational diabetes? It's only precautionary."

She thought he might pass out when the nurse came in and took the blood. To his credit he sat in the chair and watched the entire thing, unflinching. When it was over and the doctor passed her a note with some more vitamins he wanted her to take, Daniel got to his feet and wobbled a little. She grabbed his hand and held on. Once they were in the corridor she slowed down and looked up at him, smiling.

"My hero."

He frowned. "It's not funny."

"Sure it is. Big, strong fella like you afraid of a little old needle... Who would have thought it possible?"

"I'm not afraid of them," he said, and grasped her fingers,

entwining them with his own until their palms were flat against each other. "I simply don't like them. And just because you aren't afraid of anything, Mary-Jayne, doesn't mean you should make fun of people who are."

She grinned, despite the fact she was shaking inside. Holding his hand, making jokes and simply *being* with him shouldn't have made her so happy. But it did. Even though in her heart she knew it wasn't real. When they were outside he looked around.

"Where's your car?"

She took a second and then pointed to the BMW parked a few spots from the entrance. "Over there."

He glanced at the car and then to her. "Good to see you're coming to your senses."

She shrugged. "I hate waste, that's all. The car seats arrived, too… That was very thoughtful of you."

He gave her a wry smile. "Oh, you know me, an arrogant, entitled jerk and all that."

Mary-Jayne blew out a flustered breath. "Okay…so you're not all bad."

"Not all bad?" he echoed. "That's quite a compliment."

"All right, I'm an ungrateful coward who has been determined to see the worst in you from the moment we met. Satisfied?"

He smiled. "I shouldn't have called you that. I was frustrated and annoyed and worried about my mom and took it out on you. I missed you, by the way, in case you were wondering."

She nodded as emotion tightened her throat. "I might have missed you a little, too."

"I should have taken you with me."

She ached to tell him that was what she'd hoped for. But she didn't say it. "Well, I'm glad she's going to get well."

"Me, too," he said, and grinned. "So, truce?"

She smiled back at him. "I guess. Where are you staying this time? The B and B?"

He shrugged. "I'm not sure. I didn't get the chance to talk to your sister about it. Once she told me where you were I bailed and headed here."

"Would you like to stay for dinner tonight?" she asked.

He nodded. "I would. But I'll cook."

She gave him a colorful glare. "Are you suggesting that my cooking is below par?"

"I'm saying your cooking is woeful." He grabbed her hand and squeezed her fingers gently. "I'll stop at the supermarket and get what we need, and then I'll see you at home."

Home...

It sounded so nice the way he said it. The fluttering she'd had in her belly since he'd first walked into the doctor's office increased tenfold. "Okay, see you a little later."

And then he kissed her. Softly, sweetly. Like a man kissed a woman he cared about. Mary-Jayne's leaping heart almost came through her chest. And if she'd had any doubts that she'd fallen in love with him, they quickly disappeared.

Daniel pulled up outside Mary-Jayne's house a little over an hour later. He'd been all wound up in knots earlier in the morning at the thought of seeing her again, but the moment he'd opened the door and spotted her in the chair in her doctor's office, hands clasped together and her beautiful hair framing her face, all the anxiety had disappeared. She hadn't looked unhappy to see him. She'd looked...relieved. As if she welcomed him there. As if she wanted him there. Which was more than he deserved after the insensitive words he'd left her with, right before he'd returned to Port Douglas to be with his family.

He'd had a lot of time to think about their relationship in the past week. Sitting in the hospital waiting room with his father had been incredibly humbling and at times fraught with emotion. Memories of his own wife had bombarded him. Of the night they'd brought Simone into emergency and he'd arrived too late. She was already unconscious. Already too far gone for the doctors to try to save her. And then he'd waited while they'd delivered their baby and hoped that a miracle would happen and their daughter would survive. But she hadn't, and he'd lost them both.

And while he'd waited at the hospital after Bernie's surgery he'd really talked to his dad for the first time since forever. About Bernie, about his own mother, about Simone and their baby. And about Mary-Jayne. Miles had been strong, more resilient than he'd imagined. He'd wanted to comfort his dad, and in the end it happened the other way around. He was ashamed to remember how he'd always considered his father as weak. As a kind man, but one driven by his emotions. Daniel had mistaken Miles's lack of ambition as a failing. But he was wrong. His father's ambitions were simply different from his own. And yet, in some ways, very much the same. Because Miles had endeavored to be a worthy, caring dad to his sons, and Daniel was determined to emulate that ambition. He wanted to be around his sons and watch them grow into children and then teens and finally into adulthood. He wanted to share their lives and be the best man he could be for them. And for Mary-Jayne, too. He cared about her too much to simply let her be only the mother of his sons. He wanted more. He *needed* more.

And since he'd screwed up big time in the courtship department, he had to go back to square one and start all over again. Like he should have done in the beginning, on that first time they'd met. Instead of making that stupid, off-the-cuff comment about how they'd end up in his condo at some point, he should have asked her out. He should have wooed her and courted her like she deserved. He should have gone to see her while she was in South Dakota at her friend's wedding and pursued her properly, and not asked her to meet him on his turf as though all he was interested in was getting her into bed. No wonder she'd turned him down flat. And since then they'd been at war— arguing and insulting one another. She'd called him arrogant and she was right. He'd come out fighting on every occasion and hadn't let her really get to know him at all.

She wants romance and all the trimmings…

Well, he could do that if it meant she would eventually agree to marry him.

He walked up the path and saw that her old car had a for-sale sign propped inside the back window. It pleased him, and by the time he reached her door he was grinning like a fool.

"Oh, hi," she said, breathless and beautiful in a white floaty dress that came to her knees and buttoned down the front. Her belly had popped out more and she looked so beautiful he couldn't do anything other than stare at her. "Come inside."

He crossed the threshold and walked down the hall. Her little dog came yapping around his ankles, and he made a point of patting the animal for a moment before he entered the kitchen.

"So what are you making?" she asked when he put the bags on the counter.

He started unpacking the bags. "Vegetarian tagine… Spiced carrots…amongst other things."

Her green eyes widened. "Moroccan?" She laughed and the sound rushed over his skin and through his blood. "My favorite."

"Want to help?"

She nodded and tossed an apron at him. "Only if you wear this."

He opened up the garment and read the words *Kiss The Cook*. "Really?"

She shrugged. "You never know your luck."

He popped it over his head. "I already feel lucky."

She came around the counter and methodically tied it around the back. "You mean because of your mother? You must be so relieved that she's out of danger."

"We all are," he said, thinking how he was imagining he'd get to kiss her again and that was why he felt lucky. "My dad couldn't bear to lose her."

"I can imagine," she said, and pulled a couple of cutting boards from a drawer. "I mean, he already lost your mother, so to lose Bernie, too… I mean, I know your mother was the love of his life because Solana told me…but he loves Bernie dearly, you can tell by the way he looks at her."

Daniel stopped what he was doing and stared at her. Her green eyes shimmered so brilliantly it was impossible to look anywhere else. The awareness between them amplified tenfold, and he fought the urge to reach for her and take her in his arms. Instead he met her gaze and spoke. "Just because he loved my mom didn't mean he had less of himself to give to someone else."

She inhaled sharply. "I… I suppose so… I mean, if he was willing to open his heart."

"He was," Daniel said quietly. "He did."

The meaning was not lost on either of them. "And they've had a good marriage, Mary-Jayne. They got married quickly and didn't really know one another very well. But it worked. It *can* work."

She started to nod and then stopped. "But they love one another."

"They do now. They got married, had children, made a life together. So perhaps it did start out a little unorthodox…but in the end it's how it plays out that's important."

She didn't look completely convinced and as much as he wanted to keep pushing, he backed off and returned his attention to the grocery bags on the counter. They chatted about mundane things, like her new car and the weather. She asked after his grandmother and was clearly delighted when he told her Solana wanted to come to Crystal Point for a visit.

"She'd like it here," he said when the food was cooking. He stood by the stove, stirring the pot. "Once Bernie is assured of a full recovery, I'm sure my grandmother will come."

"I'd like that," she said as she grabbed plates and cutlery and took them to the table. "Um…how long are you staying for this time?"

He kept stirring. "I'm not sure. I have to get back to work at some point. I need to go to Phuket for the reopening once the renovation is complete in a couple of weeks."

She nodded, eyed the salad he'd made and sniffed the air appreciatively. "That smells good. You really do know how to cook."

He grinned. "Told you," he said, and then more seriously, "There's a lot you don't know about me, Mary-Jayne. But I'd like to change that. You said we should take some time and you were right. But I don't want to pressure you. So if you want slow, then we'll go slow."

She stopped what she was doing and looked at him. "Honestly, I don't know what I want."

"How about you take some time to figure it out?"

"You said we didn't have time."

He shrugged loosely. "I was mad at you when I said that. We have time."

She nodded a little and took a couple of sodas out of the fridge. "I don't have any of that imported beer you like," she said, and placed the cans on the counter. "But I can get some."

"This is fine," he said, and cranked both lids. "I don't drink much."

They ate a leisurely dinner and she entertained him with stories of her youth, and when she was laughing hard and out of breath he did the same. It was interesting to learn they had both been rebellious as children and teenagers.

"I guess you had to rein in all that when you took over the company from your grandfather? Can't have a respectable CEO wreaking havoc, right?" she asked and laughed.

Daniel grinned. "I guess not. Although I wasn't quite the wayward teen that you were. No tattoos…so I was nowhere near as hardcore as you."

She laughed again. "That's only because you're scared of needles."

"No need to rub it in. I'm well aware of my weakness."

She rested her elbows on the table and sighed. "You don't have a weak bone in your body."

He met her gaze. "I have a weakness for you."

"That's not weakness," she said. "That's desire. Attraction. Lust."

Daniel pushed his plate aside. "Maybe it's more than that."

"More?"

He reached across the table and grasped her hand. "I care about you."

"Because I'm having your babies," she said, and went to move her hand.

Daniel's grip tightened. "That's only part of it."

She looked at him, her eyes suddenly all suspicious as she pulled her hand free. "What are you saying?"

He met her gaze. "Can't you guess?"

"I don't understand. Are you saying that you're… That you have feelings for me…?"

"Yes," he replied. "That's precisely what I'm saying."

Her gaze widened. "Are you saying that…that you're in love with me?"

Daniel nodded. That was exactly what he was saying. He *did* love her. The empty feeling he had inside when he was away from her was love. That was why he couldn't wait to return to Crystal Point. He wanted her. He craved her and ached thinking about it. She was the mother of his babies. And she was vivacious and fun and as sexy as anything.

He'd loved Simone. It had made sense. Loving Mary-Jayne made no sense at all. And yet, in the past few days it had become a clear and undeniable truth.

"Would it be so hard to believe?"

"Yes. Impossible," she said with a scowl and pushed the chair back. "I think you should leave."

Daniel got to his feet the same time she did. "Why are you angry?"

She glared at him. "Because you're lying to me. Because

you'll say and do anything to get what you want and all of a sudden you seem to think that making some big statement about love will make me change my mind about getting married."

"I haven't mentioned marriage," he reminded her.

"It's on the agenda, though, right?"

"Eventually," he replied. "That's generally the result of a relationship between two people who fall in love."

"But *two* people haven't fallen in love."

Right. So she didn't love him. Didn't care. That was plain enough. His heart sank. Maybe she would...someday? If he tried hard enough to earn that love.

"We could try to make this work."

"Like your parents did?" she asked. "Maybe it worked for them because they actually liked one another to start with. I'll bet they didn't call one another names and look for the worst in each other."

Daniel expelled an impatient breath. "I apologized for what I said the last time I was here."

"You mean when you called me a fraud who had locked herself in a cage?" she enquired, brows up, temper on alert. "Don't be... You were right. I have been in a cage, Daniel. But as of this moment I'm out of it. And do you know what... I'm not going to trade one cage for another. Because being married to you would put me right back inside."

"I don't want to keep you caged, Mary-Jayne. I love your spirit and your—"

"Can you hear yourself? Three weeks ago you were calling me a flake and a gold digger and now you've miraculously fallen in love with me. I'm not stupid. I know when I'm being played. So you can come here with your sexy smile and make dinner and act all interested in my childhood and this town, but it doesn't change one undeniable fact—you want me to marry you because it suits you and your arrogant assumption that you can simply take whatever you want. Well, you can't take me."

He took a step toward her, but she moved backward. "What

do I have to say to convince you that I'm serious about my feelings for you?"

"Say?" she echoed. "Nothing. Words are empty. It's actions that matter."

He waved an arm. "I'm here, aren't I? I came back. I feel as if I've been pursuing you for months."

"You first chased me because you wanted to get me into bed," she said hotly. "And now you're chasing me because you want your sons."

"I'm chasing you because I love you."

There... It was out on the table...for her and her alone.

She laughed, but it sounded hollow. "You're chasing me because you think it's a means to an end. Well, forget it. What I want for my life I can't get from you."

Pain ripped through his chest. "How do you know that? Just tell me what you want."

"I've told you in half a dozen ways. I want a man who carries me here," she said and put her hand against her breast. "In his heart. Over his heart. On his heart. Forever. And it might sound sentimental and foolish to you, but I don't care. I think I really know that for the first time in my life. And I have you to thank for it. You've shown me what I want...and what I don't."

"And what you don't want...that's me?" he asked, aching through to his bones.

"Yes," she said quietly. "Exactly."

He moved closer and grasped her shoulders, gripping her firmly. And then he kissed her. Long and hot and loaded with pain and guilt and resentment. When he was done he lifted his head and stared down into her face. She was breathing hard and her eyes were filled with confusion and rage.

He ran a possessive hand down her shoulder and breast and then down to her belly. "Nothing will change the fact that a part of me is growing inside you. Love me or hate me, we're bound together. And we always will be."

CHAPTER TWELVE

THE FOLLOWING SATURDAY, it was her niece's second birthday and Mary-Jayne didn't have the strength of mind to go, or to excuse herself. She'd exiled herself in her little house for five days, working on new pieces, revamping her website, thinking of her work, her babies and little else. She didn't spare a thought for Daniel. Not one. Not a single, solitary thought.

Big, fat liar...

He was in her dreams. She couldn't keep him out.

He'd said he loved her. It should have made her day. It should have...but didn't. It only made her angry. And achingly sad.

He hadn't contacted her. She knew from Evie that he wasn't staying at the B and B, and could only assume that he was at a hotel somewhere in Bellandale. It suited her just fine. She didn't want to see him. Not yet. She was still reeling from his declaration of love. Still hating him for it. And still loving him more than she had imagined she could ever love anyone.

Jerk...

Plus, her belly was getting bigger every day and now she waddled rather than walked. She went shopping for baby clothes with her sisters and cried all the way home because she felt as though part of her was missing. She considered buying furniture for the nursery and then put the idea on hold. The spare room needed significant work. In fact, she wondered how she was supposed to raise two babies in such a small house. Once she put two cribs, a change table and a cupboard in the spare room there wouldn't be much space for anything else. What she needed was a bigger house. With a large yard. With a swing set that the twins would be able to play on when they were old enough.

She felt a sense of loneliness so acute it physically pained her. And nothing abated it. Not her parents or her sisters. Not talking to her long-distance friends or cuddling with her dog on the lounge. Only her babies growing peacefully in her belly gave her comfort.

On the afternoon of the party she laid her dress on the bed, flicked off her flip-flops and started getting ready. The dress was a maternity smock in bright colored silk that tied in a knot at her nape, and the outrageously red sandals were low heeled and comfortable. Or at least they would have been, had she been able to get them on. Her body simply wouldn't bend like it used to. She twisted and turned herself inside out and still the darn sandals wouldn't clasp.

Frustration crept over her skin as she kept trying. And failing. Fifteen minutes later and she was ready to toss the shoes at the wall. Until the tears came. Great racking sobs that made her chest hurt. After a few minutes she couldn't actually remember why she was crying. Which only made her more emotional. More fraught. More miserable.

She considered calling Evie and then quickly changed her mind. Her sister had enough to do organizing the party. And Grace had a newborn and would be too busy. She thought about calling her brother, but once he saw she'd been crying he'd be all concerned and want to know why she was upset and then act all macho when she told him how much she hated and loved Daniel. He'd probably want to go and punch him in the nose. It would serve Daniel right, too. Although she was pretty sure he'd throw a punch as good as he got.

Not that she wanted to see him hurt. That was the last thing she wanted.

She sat on the edge of the bed and cried some more. And thought about how ridiculously she was behaving. And then cried again. She gave the shoes another try and gave up when her aching back and swollen feet wouldn't do what she wanted.

She flopped back on the bed and grabbed her phone. The battery signal beeped. She'd forgotten to charge it overnight. Typical. She flicked through the numbers and reached the one she wanted. After a few unanswered rings it went straight to message service.

"It's me," she said, and hiccupped. "Can you come over?"

Then she buried her head in the pillow and sobbed.

Daniel had been in the shower when Mary-Jayne called. He tried to call her back several times but it went to message. Unable to reach her back, he was dressed and out the door of his hotel in about two minutes flat. He drove to Crystal Point as speedily as he could without breaking the law. Pulling up outside her house, he jumped out and raced to the front door. No one answered when he knocked. He heard the little dog barking behind the door and panic set in behind his ribs. What if she was hurt? Perhaps she'd fallen over trying to lift something heavy? Or worse. He rattled the door but it was locked, and then saw that the front window was open. He pushed the screen in and climbed through, not caring if the neighbors thought he was an intruder. They could call the cops for all he cared. He just needed to know she was safe.

Once he was in the living room he called her name. Still nothing.

He got to her bedroom door and stilled in his tracks. She was on the bed, curled up.

He'd never moved so fast in his life. He was beside the bed in seconds. He said her name softly and touched her bare shoulder. Her red-rimmed eyes flicked open.

"Hey," he said and stroked her cheek. "What's wrong?"

She shook her head. "Nothing."

"You left a message on my cell."

"I know," she whispered. "I didn't know who else to call. And then you didn't call back and then my phone went dead and…" Her voice trailed off.

Daniel's stomach churned. He grasped her shoulders. "Mary-Jayne, what's wrong? Are you sick? Is it the babies?"

"I'm not sick," she said. "I'm fine. The babies are fine."

She didn't look fine. She looked as if she'd been crying for a week. But she'd called him. She'd reached out when he'd feared she never would. It was enough to give him hope. To make him believe that she did care. "You've been crying?"

She nodded as tears welled in her eyes. She hiccupped. "I couldn't…"

"You couldn't what?" he prompted.

"I couldn't get my shoes on!"

And then she sobbed. Racking, shuddering sobs that reached him deep down. He folded her in his arms and held her gently. "It's okay, darling," he assured her.

"I'm as fat as a house."

"You're beautiful."

"I'm not," she cried, tears running down her face again. "And my ankles are so swollen that my shoes don't fit. I tried to put them on but my belly got in the way."

Daniel relaxed his grip and reached for her chin. He tilted her head back. "Would you like me to put them on for you?"

She nodded, and he moved off the bed and found her shoes by the wall. He crouched by the bed and reached for her legs. He slipped the shoes on and strapped each sandal at the ankle. "See…they fit just fine," he said, and ran a palm down her smooth calf.

She hiccupped and some fire returned to her eyes. "Why are you being nice to me?"

"That's my job," he said, and sat beside her. "Isn't that why you called me?"

She shrugged helplessly. "I just called a number... Any number..."

He grasped her chin again and made her look at him. "You called *me* because you wanted me here."

She sighed. "I don't know why. Probably because I was dreaming about you and—"

"Good," he said, feeling possessive and frustrated. "I want you to dream about me. I ache to be in your dreams, Mary-Jayne," he rasped, and pulled her close. "I won't be kept out of them."

"I couldn't keep you out if I tried," she admitted, and then relaxed against him, despite her better judgment, he suspected. "I don't know what's wrong with me. I feel so—"

"You're pregnant," he said, and gently spread a hand over her stomach. "Your hormones are running riot. Don't beat yourself up about being emotional. It's perfectly normal."

Her eyes flashed. "Aren't you Mr. Sensitive all of a sudden?"

Daniel's mouth curled at the edges. "With you, absolutely."

"Only to get what you want," she said and sniffed. "Now who's the fraud?"

He tilted her chin again and inched his mouth closer to hers. "I really did screw up, didn't I, for you to have such a low opinion of me? I generally think of myself as a good sort of person, Mary-Jayne... Give me half a chance and you might, too."

She harrumphed. "Manipulative jerk," she whispered, but then moved her lips closer.

He kissed her gently. "I'm not manipulating you. I love you."

She moaned. "Don't say things you don't mean."

Daniel swept her hair back from her face. "I mean it. And I'll tell you every day for the rest of my life."

"I won't listen," she retorted, and tried to evade his mouth. "And one day I'll find someone who really does—"

"Don't do that," he said painfully, cutting through her words. "That would just about break me."

"I'll do what I want," she said and pulled back. "You don't own me."

Daniel held her still. "Oh, darling... I do. And you own me. You've owned me since the first time I saw you in that store window. And I'm not going anywhere, Mary-Jayne."

"You'll have to at some point," she remarked, all eyes and fiery beauty in her stare. "You don't live here. You live in San Francisco. Then I'll be free of you."

"We'll never be free of one another. That's why you called me today. Admit it," he said, firmer this time. "You could have called any one of half a dozen people and they all would have been here in a matter of minutes. But you didn't," he reminded her. "You called me."

"It was the first number I pressed. It was random, and then my battery died. Don't read anything into it."

He chuckled, delighted and spurred on by her reticence. "Admit it... You're in love with me."

"I am not!" she denied, and pulled herself from his arms. "I don't love you. I never will. I'd have to be stark raving mad to fall in love with you. And you're only saying all this to get what you want."

"I am? Really?" He stood up and propped his hands on his hips. "Have I asked for anything? I've given you space. I've left you alone. I've holed myself up in a damn hotel room for a week, even though all I want to do is be here with you every day and hold you in my arms every night. I haven't sent you flowers or bought anything for the babies even though I want to because I know you'd accuse me of trying to manipulate you. I haven't gone to see your parents and explain to them what you mean to me and assure them I'll do whatever is in my power to do to make you happy even though my instincts tell me I should. I'm *trying*, Mary-Jayne... I'm trying to do this your way. Just...just try to meet me in the middle somewhere, okay?" He placed a hand over his chest. "Because this is killing me."

"So he's still in town?"

Mary-Jayne looked at Evie. Her sisters had come over to cheer her up and bring her some gifts for the babies. The tiny pair of matching baseball caps Grace gave her was so incredibly cute that she cried a little. Which seemed to have become a habit of hers in the past few weeks.

Crying… Ugh!

She had become a sentimental sap.

"I guess so."

"You've seen him?" Grace asked.

"Not for a week. Why?"

Her sisters both shrugged and smiled. It was Evie who spoke next. "It's only that…well… In the past few days he's come to see all of us and told us…"

"Told you all what?" Mary-Jayne asked, pushing up on her seat.

"That he's in love with you," Grace supplied. "That he wants to marry you."

Mary-Jayne saw red. "That no-good, sneaky—"

"It's kinda romantic," Evie said and grinned.

"It's *not* romantic," Mary-Jayne said hotly. "It's deceitful and underhanded. And do you know what else he did? He bought all this baby stuff and had it delivered. The garage is full of boxes and toys and baby furniture and—"

"Oh, how awful for you," Evie said and grinned. "Such a terrible man."

Mary-Jayne scowled. "You're on his side, then?"

"We're on your side," Grace said and smiled gently. "You seem unhappy, that's all."

"I'll be happier when he's gone."

"I don't think he's going anywhere any time soon," Evie said. "He told Scott he's going to buy a house here."

The color bled from her face. "I don't believe it. He wouldn't. He's got a business to run and he can't do that from here."

"Maybe he's found something more important than business," Grace said pointedly.

"Yeah—his heirs. He wants his children. Don't be blinded by the good looks and money."

"We could say the same thing to you."

Mary-Jayne stilled. Her sister's words resonated loud and clear. Was that how she appeared—as a judgmental and narrow-minded snob—and exactly what she'd accused him of being?

She'd resented his money and success without good reason. On one hand, she recognized his honesty and integrity. And yet, when he'd told her the very thing she wanted to hear, she hadn't believed him. She'd accused him of trying to manipulate and confuse her. But what proof did she have that he'd ever done that? None. He hadn't manipulated her to get her into bed. Their attraction had been hot and intense from the start. Not one-sided. She'd craved him and he'd made it abundantly clear that he wanted her. And then she'd convinced herself he was all bad, all arrogance and self-entitlement.

To protect herself.

Because he was nothing like any man she'd previously dated she regarded him as an aberration…someone to avoid…someone to battle. And she had at every opportunity. She'd fought and insulted and pushed him away time and time again. Because loving Daniel meant she would be redefined. He was rich and successful and all that she had professed to loathe. He'd asked her to marry him. He'd said he loved her. And still she let her prejudice blind her.

His parting words a week earlier still echoed in her mind. *This is killing me.* Real pain. Real anguish. And she'd done that to him. She'd hurt him. She'd hurt the one person she loved most in the world. She felt the shame of it through to her bones. He'd asked her to meet him in the middle.

But she could do better than that.

"You look as though the proverbial penny just dropped," Evie said.

Both her sisters were staring at her. "I think it just did. He asked me to marry him. He said he was in love with me."

"That's what he told us, too."

Tears filled her eyes. "I never imagined that I'd fall in love with someone like him. I thought that one day I'd meet someone like myself... Someone who wasn't so...conventional, if you know what I mean."

Evie came and sat beside her and grabbed her hand. "You know, just because he's not a bohemian poet, it doesn't make him wrong for you. If anyone had told me a few years ago that I would fall in love with a man nearly ten years younger than me I wouldn't have believed them."

"Same here," Grace said, and sat on the other side. "I never intended to fall in love with our brother's best friend. But I did. When you love, you simply love. That's the thing that's important, M.J. Not how successful or wealthy he is."

"He's a good man," Evie said quietly. "Give him a chance to prove it."

"What if he's changed his mind?" she asked, thinking of the terrible way they'd parted and how she'd told him she didn't love him and never would. "I said some pretty awful things to him the last time we were together. What if he doesn't want to see me?"

"You need a plan," Grace suggested.

"Leave that to me," Evie said, and she grabbed her phone from her bag.

Three hours later Mary-Jayne was at the B and B, sitting in the garden on a bench by the wishing well. She smoothed down the skirt on her white dress and then fluffed her hair. She'd always loved this spot. Through the vine-covered hedge she saw a car pull up to the curb. Minutes later he was walking up the path, all purposeful and tight limbed. He wore jeans and a polo shirt and looked so good it stole her breath. When he spotted her he came to a halt midstride.

"Hi," she said, and smiled.

His expression was unreadable. "I didn't expect you to be here."

"I didn't expect me to be here up until a couple of hours ago."

His gaze narrowed. "Are you all right? No problems with the babies?"

She touched her abdomen gently. "No... Everything is fine. I feel good. The nausea is gone for the moment. I haven't seen you for a while... Where have you been?"

"I was under the impression you had no interest in seeing me." He took a step closer. "I had a call from your sister. Is she here?"

"No...just me."

His brows drew together. "Subterfuge?"

"Kind of," she admitted. "I wasn't sure if *you'd* see *me* after the last time."

"If you had called me, I would be here. Always. I've told you that before. What's this about, Mary-Jayne?"

He looked so good. So familiar. And she ached to be in his arms. "I'm sorry about what I said the last time we were together."

"Which part? When you said you didn't love me and never would?" he quizzed.

She nodded. "All of it. You came over to help me and I was thoughtless and ungrateful."

"Yes, you were."

She ignored a hot niggle of impatience that crept up her spine. "I hear you're looking at real estate?"

He shrugged loosely. "Do you disapprove of that, as well?"

God, he was impossible. "Of course not. I understand that you'll want to be close to the babies when they are born."

He nodded. "So anything else?"

Mary-Jayne sighed and grabbed the shopping bag by the

bench. She stood up and extracted the two tiny baseballs caps. "I thought you might like these. They're cute, don't you think?"

He took the caps and examined them. "Cute. Yes. Is that it? You got me here to give me a couple of baseball caps?"

"I wanted to see you."

"Why now? Nothing's changed."

"Everything's changed."

His mouth flattened. "What?"

Her cheeks grew hotter by the second. "Me. This. Us. A week ago you told me you loved me."

"I know what I said," he shot back. "I also know what you said."

She took a breath. "Shall we go inside? I'd like to talk to you."

"So when you want to talk, we talk? Is that how this plays out? I don't seem to be able to get it right with you, do I?"

Mary-Jayne let her impatience rise up. "I'm going inside. You can stay out here in the garden and sulk if you want to."

She turned on her heels and walked up to the house as quickly as she could. He was about four steps behind her. Once she was through the French doors and in the living room she spun around.

He was barely a foot away, chest heaving. "Sulk?"

She shrugged. "Sure. Isn't that what you've been doing this week? So I said something mean and unkind. I'm sorry. But you said yourself that I'm running on hormones because of my pregnancy. I should think it's about time you started making allowances for that."

"Allowances," he echoed incredulously. "Are you serious? I've done nothing *but* make allowances since the moment you told me you were pregnant. Nothing I do is right. Nothing I say makes any difference. You trust me, you don't. You need me, you don't. You want me, you don't. Which is it? I'm so damned confused I can barely think straight. I'm neglecting my business, my family, my friends...everything, because I'm so caught up in this *thing* I have with you."

Mary-Jayne watched him, fascinated by the heat and fire in his words. There was so much passion in him. She'd been so wrong, thinking he was some sort of cold fish who didn't feel deeply. He did. He just didn't show that side of himself to the world.

"I do trust you," she said, and moved toward him. "And I do need you," she said, and touched his chest. When he winced and stepped back she was immediately concerned. "What's wrong? Are you in pain? Have you had another migraine?"

"No. Stop this, Mary-Jayne. Tell me what I'm doing here and—"

"I'm trying," she said frantically. "But I need to know if you meant what you said."

He frowned. "What I said?"

"You...you said you loved me," she said, suddenly breathless. "Did you mean it?"

"Do I strike you as someone who says things I don't mean?"

"No," she replied, and blinked back the tears in her eyes. "It's just that...what you said about me being in a cage and about how things would have been different from the start if you hadn't been...well...*you*. If you'd been a dreadlocked, unemployed musician, I wouldn't have been so determined to keep my distance. Because that's what I thought I wanted. What I knew, if that makes sense. All that stuff you said, you were right." She touched his arm, gripped tightly and felt his muscles hard beneath her palm. "For as long as I can remember I've craved freedom and independence. But now I feel as if I've lived a life that isn't authentic. I left home at seventeen, but only moved three streets away from my parents. Some independence, huh? So you're right, I'm a fraud. I'm tied to this little town. I'm not a free spirit at all." She took a breath, not caring about the tears on her cheeks. "And you...you saw through that and through me. What you said about marriage makes sense. Each one starts out differently, like your dad and Bernie. And if this..." she said, and touched her stomach gently. "If this is what we start with, just these two precious babies bringing us together, then that's okay. Because if you do want me, and if you do love me, even a little bit, that will be enough."

He stared at her, holding her gaze captive. "But it's not enough for me, Mary-Jayne."

She froze. "I don't understand…"

"We both deserve more than some half-baked attempt at a relationship."

"But you said you wanted to get married and be a family," she reminded him, crumbling inside.

"I do," he said, and grabbed her hand. "But I want *all* of you, every beautiful, spirited, intoxicating piece. I had a good marriage once. But I want more than that this time. I don't want to leave at six in the morning and arrive home at eight. I don't want to eat out five nights out of seven because work always comes first. I don't want to miss family gatherings because I'm too busy landing some deal or flying from one country to the next. I've lived that life and I was never truly happy. I want us to raise our children together, like *they* deserve."

Tears wet her cheeks again. "I want that, too. You really… You really do love me?"

He grasped her chin and looked directly into her eyes. "I really do love you, Mary-Jayne. And I know they're only words, but they are what I feel."

"Words are enough," she said, happiness surging through her blood. "I love you, too."

"Words will never be enough," he said, and kissed her gently. "Which is why I did this."

"What?" she muttered against his mouth.

"This," he said, and stepped back a little. He tugged at the collar of his T-shirt and showed her what he meant.

Her name, in small but strikingly dark scrolled script, was now written on the left side of his chest. The ink was new and still healing, but she could see through all that to the beauty of what he had done.

"You got a tattoo?" she asked, crying. "I can't believe you did that. The needles... You hate needles."

He shrugged one shoulder. "I love you more than I hate needles." He grasped her hand and held it against his chest. "In my heart. Over my heart. On my heart. Forever."

They were the most beautiful words she had ever heard.

She reached up and touched his face. "I'm so much in love with you, Daniel. And I'm sorry I kept pushing you away."

He held her in his arms. "You had more sense than me. We needed to get to know one another. You knew that. I just arrogantly thought I knew how to fix things."

"At least you wanted to try," she said, and settled against his shoulder. "I've been fighting this and you since the very beginning."

"I know," he said, and laughter rumbled in his chest. "You took off as if your feet were on fire after Solana's birthday party."

"I was in shock," she admitted. "I'd never had an experience like that before."

"Me, either," he said. "Making love with you is like nothing on earth." He kissed her nape. "But you never have to run from me again, Mary-Jayne."

"I promise I won't."

Seconds later they were settled on one of the sofas and he wrapped her in his arms. "There's something about you that draws me. You have this incredible energy...a life force all your own. I love that about you. And I love that our sons are going to have that, too."

She sighed, happy and content and so in love her head was spinning. "So where are we going to live? Here or San Francisco?"

He reached for her chin and tilted her face toward his own. "Darling, do you think I would ever ask you to leave here? This is your home."

"But San Francisco is *your* home."

"It's where I live," he said and kissed her gently. "I don't think I've ever considered anywhere as really home. Until now. Even when I was married to Simone and we had our apartment, most times it was simply a place to sleep."

She couldn't believe what he was saying. "Do you mean we can stay here permanently? I was imagining we'd do some time here and some over there."

He shook his head. "Your family is here. Your roots are here. And I like this town and I want to raise our sons here. If they turn out half as good as you then I'll be a happy man."

"But your business? How can you—"

"I need to let go a little," he admitted. "I need to trust Blake and Caleb more. They have just as must invested in Anderson's as I do… I think it's about time I lessened the reins. You see," he said, and grinned, "I'm learning to not be so much of a control freak."

"Don't change too much," she said, and pressed against him. "I like you just as you are."

He kissed her, long and sweet, and when he finally lifted his head he stared into her eyes. "You know something… I think it's time I proposed properly."

"What a great idea," she said, and laughed, so happy she thought she might burst.

Daniel grabbed her hand and brought it to his lips. "Mary-Jayne, I'm lost without you… Marry me?"

"Yes," she said, laughing, crying and loving him more than she had believed possible. "Absolutely, positively, yes!"

EPILOGUE

Three and a half months later...

AT SEVEN O'CLOCK at night on a Monday, Mary-Jayne's water broke. Daniel was walking into the bedroom when she hovered in the bathroom doorway.

"What is it?" he asked immediately.

She grimaced. "It's time."

Panic flittered across his face. "You're in labor?"

"Yep," she said, and grinned.

He strode toward her. "But there's still nearly three weeks to go."

"We were told I'd probably go into labor early," she said and touched his arm. "Stop worrying."

"I'm not worried," he assured her. "How do you feel?"

"Better now I know what the niggling backache I had all day is about."

"You were in pain and you didn't tell—"

"Stop worrying," she said again, and ushered him out the doorway. "I'm fine." She rubbed her huge belly. "We're fine. Is my bag still in the car?"

He'd insisted they have her baby bag ready for when she went into labor. He'd also insisted on a trial run in the car and had organized Evie to be the backup driver just in case he wasn't around when the time came. Of course she knew that was never going to happen.

In the past few months so much had changed. Since their wedding two months earlier, he'd taken some much-needed time off from Anderson's. His brother Blake had taken on more global accountability, and general managers had been put in place in some of the resorts to alleviate the workload. Caleb was still recovering from an unexpected and serious boating accident and had been recuperating from his busted leg with Miles and Bernie for the past eight weeks. It had been a fraught time for the entire family, but since Bernie's heart attack, the family had become closer and they all rallied around to ensure Caleb had all the support he needed.

Despite all that, she knew Daniel had never been happier. She still marveled at how well he'd adjusted to not having such tight control over the company anymore. He'd learned to trust his brothers and share the responsibility. Of course, with Caleb out of action for a while, there were times when he was needed to fly back to San Francisco or one of the other locations, but he was never gone for more than a few days. And Mary-Jayne didn't mind.

He'd bought a house in Crystal Point just four doors down from Dunn Inn, and she loved the big low-set brick-and-tile home with its floating timber floors, racked ceilings, wide doorways and sprawling front deck that offered an incredible view of the ocean. She surprised herself by how much fun she had purchasing new furnishings. He was generous to a fault, and they had a wonderful time working on the nursery and getting the room ready for the babies.

Their relationship was amazing. *He* was amazing, and she'd never been happier.

The drive to the hospital took twenty minutes, and another

five to find a vacant car space and get her into the emergency ward. She was quickly transported to maternity, and by the time she was settled in a room her contractions were coming thick and fast.

It was an arduous twelve hours later that her doctor recommended a caesarean birth. Mary-Jayne cried a little, and then agreed to do what best for their babes. William and Flynn Anderson were born a minute apart, both pink and screaming and perfect in every way.

Still groggy from the surgery, it was another few hours before she had a chance to nurse her sons. Daniel remained by her side, strong and resilient and giving her every ounce of support she needed. And when he held their sons for the first time, there were tears in his eyes. And he didn't seem to care one bit. Watching him, seeing the emotion and pure love in his expression made her fall in love with him even more.

"They really are beautiful," she remarked as William settled against her breast to nurse and Daniel sat in the chair by her bed and held Flynn against his chest.

Daniel looked at his son, marveling at the perfect beauty in the little boy's face, and smiled. When he returned his gaze to his wife he saw she was watching him. "You did an amazing job, Mrs. Anderson."

She smiled. "You, too. But then again, you do everything well, and I knew this wouldn't be any different."

Daniel reached for her hand and rubbed her fingers. "You know, we're going to have to start letting the masses in at some point. Your sisters are keen to spend some time with you. And Solana has been circling the waiting area with your parents for the past two hours. She's very excited about meeting her great-grandsons."

"I know," she said, and sighed. "I just selfishly want our babies and you to myself for as long as I can."

Daniel stood and gently placed their sleeping son into his

mother's arm, watching, fascinated, as she held them both. It was the most beautiful thing he had ever seen. His wife. His sons. They were a gift more precious than anything he could have ever imagined. Love, the purest and most intense he'd ever experienced, surged through his blood.

"I love you," he said, and bent down to kiss her sweet mouth. "And, my darling, you have me to yourself for the rest of our lives."

Tears welled in her beautiful green eyes. "I never intended to love anyone this much, you know," she said, and batted her lashes. "I never thought it was possible."

"Neither did I."

"It's actually all Audrey and Caleb's doing," she said, beaming. "If they didn't have such a dysfunctional relationship we would never have met."

"Oh, I don't know about that," he said, and chuckled. "Audrey would have returned to Crystal Point eventually and Caleb would have eventually followed her, and since my brother is a hothead without any sense I would have had to come here and sort things out. So I'm pretty sure our paths would have crossed."

Mary-Jayne glanced at the twins. "Maybe you're right. Now they're here I can't imagine a world without these two in it." She looked up and smiled gently. "Speaking of Caleb and Audrey…any news?"

Daniel shrugged. "You know Caleb. He's refusing to get the marriage annulled."

They had all been shocked to learn that Caleb and Audrey were in fact married, and had been just a month after they'd met.

She sighed. "Well, I'm glad we don't have all that drama in our relationship."

Daniel smiled, remembering their own fraught beginnings. "Nah…we were a piece of cake."

She laughed, and the lovely sound echoed around the room.

"Shall I let them in?" he asked, kissing her again.

"You bet."

And he was, he realized as he opened the door, just about the happiest man on the planet. Because he had Mary-Jayne's love and their beautiful sons. He truly did have it all.

* * * * *

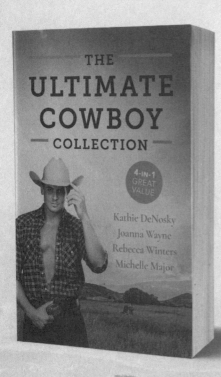

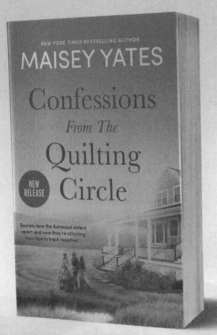

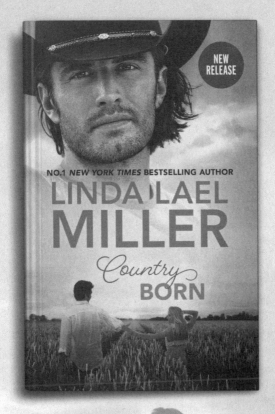

ITALIAN PLAYBOYS

These romantic and passionate Italian bachelors are ready to fall in love.

Two volumes to collect.

Vol 1: *Temptations*
OUT NOW

Vol 2: *Proposals*
AVAILABLE MAY 2022

MILLS & BOON

millsandboon.com.au